THE FORTRESS

CATHERINE GAVIN

THE FORTRESS

HODDER PAPERBACKS

First printed 1964
Hodder Paperback Edition 1969
Second Impression 1970

Printed and bound for Hodder Paperbacks Ltd. by
Hazell Watson & Viney Ltd, Aylesbury, Bucks

SBN 340 10889 4

AUTHOR'S FOREWORD

The Fortress is a novel of the War against Russia generally known as the Crimean War. Its background is the Baltic campaigns of 1854 and 1855, in which the Royal Navy, supported by French naval squadrons and troops, bombarded Russia's northern strongholds and blockaded Russian ports.

With the exception of historical personages and British sea officers, all the characters in the novel are fictitious, but the operations of Her Majesty's Ships and Vessels at sea took place exactly as narrated here.

The documentary research for *The Fortress* was carried out in the National Libraries and Maritime Museums of Finland, Sweden and Great Britain, and at Lewes in the County of Sussex.

In Finland I had the advantage of consulting the National Archives, and of frequenting the Villa Hagasund (now the attractive City Museum of Helsinki) and the fortress, Sveaborg. The fortress is now known to visitors by its Finnish name, Suomenlinna. Since the Baltic campaigns of 1854 and 1855, Finland has fought three wars to gain and preserve her independence, her national integrity and the use of the Finnish language; all of which honours may she long maintain.

To
Dr. Eino Suolahti

CONTENTS

Chapter		Page
1	The Prisoner	1
2	The Molly-O	20
3	Nikita	39
4	Help from a Stranger	64
5	The Golden Peace	82
6	Old Men in Council	100
7	Drift Ice	112
8	Ploughing the Field of Serpents	132
9	"The First Drop of Blood"	158
10	The White Nights	177
11	Lapp Magic I	193
12	Shallow Waters and Granite Walls	212
13	The Red Shawl	233
14	Jack Adrift	258
15	The Tarras Chairman	274
16	The Bonapartes at Home	292
17	The *Duchess of Finland*	314
18	Under a Flag of Truce	341
19	Lapp Magic II	366
20	The Fortress	379
21	Surf Breaking on both Shores	403

Map on page viii

vii

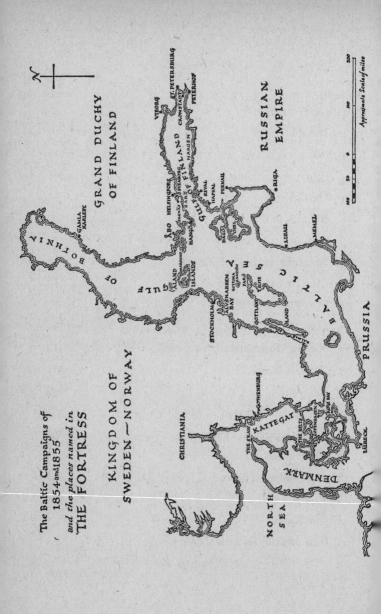

The Baltic Campaigns of
1854 and 1855
and the places named in
THE FORTRESS

KINGDOM OF
SWEDEN—NORWAY

GRAND DUCHY
OF FINLAND

RUSSIAN
EMPIRE

GULF OF BOTHNIA

GAMLA
KARLEBY

ABO HELSINGFORS
SWEABORG
HANGO
GULF OF FINLAND
NARGEN
REVAL
HAPSAL
PERNAU

VIBORG
ST. PETERSBURG
CRONSTADT
PETERHOF

ALAND
ISLANDS

RIGA

STOCKHOLM

ALVSNABBEN
BAY
FARÖ
GOTTLAND

LIBAU
MEMEL

BALTIC SEA

PRUSSIA

CHRISTIANIA

GOTHENBURG

THE SKAW
KATTEGAT
THE BELTS

LÜBECK

DENMARK

NORTH
SEA

N

0   100   200
Approximate Scale of miles

CHAPTER ONE

THE PRISONER

HE came before the magistrate after darkness fell, when a thick wet snow was falling over Gothenburg. In the police court the benches near the potbellied iron stoves were filled with idlers sheltering from the bitter weather, and many curious eyes saw the prisoner dragged up to the bar, handcuffed between two officers of the Watch.

The magistrate considered him; tall, with sandy hair, the long blue coat wet and torn, the knuckles bruised; and scratching his nose with the feather of his quill pen he studied the prisoner's unfocussed eyes shifting round the courtroom, from the official portrait of Oscar I, King of Sweden and Norway, to the clustered candles on the bar before which he stood. The indictment spread between those candles read: "Drunk and disorderly. Assaulted the Watch in the execution of their duty"—it was almost a routine charge in Gothenburg since the great emigration to the United States began to get out of hand. This time, judging from the blood-stained cloth round the prisoner's head and the swelling bruises on his face, he fancied the Watch had given as good as they got.

"Do you understand Swedish?" he began. The prisoner shook his bandaged head.

"German?"

"No."

In careful English: "What is your name?" enquired the magistrate.

"My—name?"

"Yes, your first name and your family name; how are you called?"

"My name is John Brand Endicott."

"Your nationality?"

"American citizen!"

The moving pen halted. The magistrate glanced at a note on the charge sheet: "*Girdleness*, brig, British registry. Owners, Tarras and Company, Aberdeen." He put a further question:

"*Born an American citizen?*"

"Yes."

"Born where?"

"In Portland, Maine."

"What is your civil state?"

"*Master mariner!*"

"If there is any laughter," said the magistrate in the direction of the public benches, "I shall order the court to be cleared. Prisoner at the bar! I will repeat the question in another form. Are you married or single?"

The unfocussed eyes closed. The tall American swayed forward until only his handcuffs held him up. From the back of the court a voice cried suddenly:

"Sir! The prisoner is unfit to plead!"

Brand Endicott came back to consciousness in a narrow room somewhat less squalid than the pen from which he had been dragged before the magistrate. There were bars on the small window high up in the wall, and he could hear a guard's tread in the stone corridor, but he had been given a pallet to lie on and even a rough pillow and a blanket, and candlelight showed a pewter can on the deal table. Close beside his pallet was a three-legged wooden stool, on which a man in a grey cloak was seated.

Brand pulled himself up on one elbow. His whole body was aching and his head throbbed, but his vision was clearer, and he could take in the man beside him from the hem of the fine grey cloak with the astrakhan collar to the greyish-blond locks combed carefully over the bald head. He disliked at sight the long inquisitive nose, and the half smile on the stranger's narrow lips.

"You're coming round, Captain Endicott, I'm glad to see," the man said quietly. "How do you feel now?"

"I'm all right," said Brand. He put his hand instinctively to the back of his head, and looked at fingers wet and red with blood.

"The bandage has slipped," the stranger said. "The police surgeon will visit you again tomorrow morning. Meanwhile, allow me to make you more comfortable, if I can."

He produced an immaculate white linen handkerchief and deftly folded it. His hands, as he bound it round Brand's head,

2

were gentle enough, but he felt the American wince at his touch, and smiled above the blood clots in the sandy hair. Count Erik left his mark on you, my Yankee friend, he thought.

"Like the Good Samaritan, I have brought other bodily comforts," he said aloud. "Will you drink some brännvin?"

"Spirits? Anything," said the prisoner. He held out his hand for the brimming birch bark ladle which his visitor had dipped in the pewter can. The fiery snaps ran over his dry throat gratefully; he coughed, and finished the liquor at a gulp.

"God! that's good," he said, and looked about him. "Am I in prison?"

"Certainly not, Captain Endicott. You collapsed during your preliminary examination, and I took it upon myself to point out to the magistrate that you were obviously unfit to be heard. You were then remanded in custody for the night. You are still at the headquarters of the Gothenburg Watch in the Great Square," said the Good Samaritan precisely. "You'll be brought before the Sheriff in the morning."

The prisoner closed his eyes and drew a painful breath. The other man surveyed him closely. You're a powerful young brute, he thought, but whom do you resemble? That runaway mother of yours? Or the Yankee father, whom we never saw? Or old John Tarras? Yes, about the brow and eyes, I think; but not enough to endear you to Mistress Isabella, fortunately.

He had, unmistakably, a Yankee face before him. The face of a down-Easter, with lean cheeks and a strongly modelled nose and chin, a shaping of the skull which revealed the European heritage and a firm mouth which belonged as clearly to the American past. It was not an unconscious face, as it had been when the prisoner was brought in from the courtroom. Behind the knitted brows recollection and anxiety were struggling with the effects of strong concussion. The watcher saw it and was prepared for the words which came as soon as the prisoner's grey eyes opened:

"What happened to the girl?"

"What girl, Captain Endicott?"

"The girl I took aboard at Marstrand. Did she get away from them?"

"I don't understand you. Get away from whom?"

"You understand me all right," said the American, and his

3

scowl made him look older and more wary. "If you didn't, you wouldn't be here. My own mate didn't get to see me, earlier on, but you did: I figure it's on account of the girl. Who the devil are you?"

"My name is Sven Svensson, Captain Endicott. I am a Gothenburg merchant, and among many other interests I am the Swedish agent of Tarras and Company."

"So you're Mr. Svensson, are you? Then I reckon it's up to you to get me out of here at once. I'm due to sail for Frederikshavn tomorrow."

The agent smiled his thin-lipped smile. "That will depend on the Sheriff," he said. "You have, unfortunately, fallen foul of the law of Sweden, and are not yet free to leave for Denmark."

"I haven't heard what I'm charged with, yet."

"With being drunk and disorderly on the Stone Pier in the early hours of this afternoon. Brawling with liberty-men from the Swedish frigate *Eugénie* and assaulting the Watch when they attempted to restore order. That, so the clerk of the court informs me, is how the charge will run."

"And as soon as I go before the Sheriff," said the American, "I'll blow that charge sky-high."

Mr. Svensson looked at the bruised, determined face, and frowned. "Why in heaven's name didn't you send word to my office as soon as you berthed?" he said. "You were a day late as it was—and Mrs. Tarras, your respected grandmother, expects her ships to adhere to a strict timetable."

"Mrs. Tarras wouldn't want me to pile up the *Girdleness* on the skerries, would she, just to maintain her reputation for punctuality?"

"You must have had ample experience of a rockbound coast when you sailed with your father."

"In Maine we learn to stay in harbour when the fog comes down. It caught me yesterday two hours out of Strömstad, and I decided to put in at Marstrand island for the night. I don't take chances when I'm in command."

"Don't you indeed?" said Mr. Svensson. "I think you took a bigger chance than you realized when you allowed a certain young woman, and the old man with her, to come aboard you at Marstrand. Your mate said he advised you strongly against it."

"You saw West? When?"

4

"When he came to my office, very properly, to report your arrival and tell me you were in trouble with the police."

"Did *he* know what became of the girl?"

"Mr. West only stated"—watching him closely—"that she disappeared as soon as you berthed at Gothenburg. The police have no record of her arrival nor any knowledge of her whereabouts. So far as they are concerned, she never existed."

"And so she was never kidnapped off the Stone Pier," said Brand, "by the gang who gave me this crack on the head and kicked my face in when they had me down? I wasn't drunk, and they weren't liberty-men from the *Eugénie*! They were townsmen, all dressed alike in some sort of grey cloth suits and leather leggings. I'll be damned if there was a sailor in the lot!"

"Could you recognize any of them, do you think?" asked Mr. Svensson softly.

"There's one I'd know anywhere," cried Brand in sudden fury, "the red-haired devil who dragged her into the carriage! And she knew him too, sir. She shrieked out 'Erik!' as soon as she saw him on the pier. She tried to run, and then she slipped in the snow and fell—oh God!" He buried his bruised face in his hands, and Svensson heard him mutter something like "they were too many for me."

Mr. Svensson sighed. "Now let me," he said, "as the agent of Tarras and Company for many years, be quite clear on one point. You took this girl and the old man aboard, although the *Girdleness* has never carried passengers, because they urgently wished to get to Gothenburg. Why did you think it necessary to leave the mate to supervise the discharge of your cargo, and accompany these two persons ashore?"

"Because they'd missed the English packet," said Brand patiently. "The fog was still heavy this morning, and it was nearly noon before I sailed from Marstrand. The *Orlando* left from Gothenburg on time. I thought the least I could do was to see Miss Larsson and her uncle to some respectable—"

"Larsson!" interrupted the Good Samaritan. "Is *that* the name she gave you?"

"Miss Anna Larsson, yes."

"And they meant to cross to Hull on the paddle steamer?"

"They had to," said Brand shortly. "Seeing they meant to emigrate to the United States."

5

"What a little adventuress she is," said Mr. Svensson thinly. "And what a fool she made of you, young man! Now, I don't know what that lady's future plans may be, but I'll be bound they don't include emigration, to America or anywhere else. By this time" (he made to look at his watch) "she is safely back in a comfortable home, and under the protection of her friends."

"That Erik!" said Brand. "Is he her husband?"

"Her husband? No, but he would like to be."

"Will you repeat all this to the Sheriff, sir?"

"I?" said the agent. "Inform the Court of that lady's identity, and those of her relations, when police witnesses can testify to a brawl which took place when I was half a mile away in my own office? I would do a great deal for Mrs. Isabella Tarras, and I was prepared to do my best for her American grandson, but this is asking too much of me—it is indeed."

"Then I'll call witnesses from the *Eugénie*. Let the Watch bring forward the liberty-men I'm supposed to have assaulted—"

"Unfortunately," Mr. Svensson interrupted, "the international situation is so much worse that Admiral Virgen received orders this evening to sail at once for Karlskrona."

"Convenient," said Brand grimly. Then, after an obvious attempt to collect his wits, he added:

"What international situation?"

"Don't you realize that Britain and France are on the verge of war with Russia?"

"I've been at sea for two weeks, and I couldn't read the newspapers in Norway."

"But you arrived in London before Christmas, didn't you, and spent some time with your uncle? You must have known —it must have been obvious to everybody in his office, that the British were spoiling for a fight?"

"I know the Russians smashed the Turkish Navy somewhere in the Black Sea. But that's the hell of a long way from Karlskrona!"

"Very true"—sarcastically. "And the Russian victory at Sinope might well have meant the total defeat of Turkey. But then the British and the French took a hand in the game. They objected to the presence of Russian troops along the

Danube. Surely your uncle Tarras discussed all this with you?"

"I heard him discuss it with his business friends, but I didn't . . . I didn't pay . . ."

"What's that?"

"I didn't think a war with Russia had anything to do with me."

"You will find a good deal of sympathy with that point of view in Gothenburg," said Mr. Svensson drily. He turned to the can of spirits and refilled the birch bark ladle.

"You ought to have food with this, and food will be brought," he said. "But meantime—drink!"

Brand took another gulp of brännvin. Seen in the flickering candlelight, his face was flushed.

"Now try to listen for your own sake," said the persuasive voice. "If I am to help you, we must be agreed on what you are to say to the Sheriff tomorrow morning."

"It only takes two words. Not Guilty!"

Mr. Svensson drew his stool nearer to Brand's side.

"Of course the coming war need have nothing to do with an American citizen," he said. "But if you don't want to get the Tarras Line ships blacklisted in half the ports of the Baltic, you must not become involved with the Russian diplomatic representatives in Sweden. You must not tell, in court or anywhere else, the story of the young lady you were foolish enough to take aboard at Marstrand. She is a Russian subject, and the betrothed wife of a Russian officer."

"She told me she was a Finn," said Brand.

"Surely you know that Finland is a Grand Duchy of Russia? Her father is a high government official at St. Petersburg."

"And her name isn't Anna Larsson?"

"No. I am not empowered to tell you her real name."

"Not empowered, eh?" said Brand slowly. "Whose power are you in, then? Her kidnappers?"

It was a thrust Svensson had not expected from the dazed and injured man. He caught his breath, and hesitated; in that instant Brand's hand shot out and caught him by the front of his furred cloak.

"Her name, God damn you!"

"Her name is Alexandra Gyllenlöve. And I advise you," said the Swede, snatching at his composure, "to forget it as soon as possible."

7

"The old boy along with her—is he a Russian too?"

"No, certainly not. He is an old reprobate called Larsson, and that is his name, who lives out at Kungälv, by the river. He is a dismissed servant of her family, and I hope to see him in the stocks tomorrow."

Brand tried to focus his eyes on the angry face.

"You've got it all mapped out, haven't you?" he said. "What do you want me to do? Plead guilty to drunk and disorderly, and all the rest of that faked charge?"

"Yes, Captain Endicott," the agent said. "That is the quickest way out of your dilemma. Plead guilty, pay the fine, and you'll be set at liberty. Free to sail for Frederikshavn and the North Sea, which, believe me, is the safest cruising ground for British vessels under the threat of war."

"I wish I understood it better," said Brand hoarsely. "All this war talk! . . . I ought to send a message to the American consul."

"As one of his nationals in distress? The American master of a British vessel might provide an interesting problem in international law: but the consul, unfortunately, is on leave in Washington. Come, sir! If you take my advice, the court proceedings will be so short as to make consular aid unnecessary."

"I hope so," said Brand dully. His head was reeling under the hail of words and he had no more protests to make. He scarcely looked up at the rattle of keys in the lock and the gruff words of a jailer:

"Here's the food and water for the prisoner. And Mr. Svensson, sir, it's time for you to be going. We're locking up for the night."

Brand heard the click of tin upon the table. The jailer picked up the can of snaps and the candle and stood waiting while Mr. Svensson fastened the fur collar of his cloak.

"Captain Endicott?"

"Yes?" Brand focussed his eyes, with renewed difficulty, on the tense face of the Swede.

"How old are you, if I may ask? Twenty-three? Twenty-four?"

"Nearly twenty-four."

"Ah," said Mr. Svensson, "the age for chivalry." He looked at the yawning guard and lowered his voice. "Have you thought what that lady's reputation will be worth if it becomes known that she spent a night alone with you in the *Girdleness*? Remember, that is another reason why you should plead Guilty. For Anna Larsson's sake!"

Brand was alone in the remand cell. He sat for a time without moving, until his eyes grew accustomed to darkness brightened only by a ray from Gothenburg's new gas-light shining in at the barred window. The pain in his head was almost intolerable. His mind struggled stupidly with Sven Svensson's cryptic warnings against the Russian war and the Russian girl.

"*Finland is my country!*" He could hear the proud young voice as clearly as it had spoken in the cramped cabin of the *Girdleness*. But now, it seemed, she was a Russian, an adventuress who had lied to him about her name and her purpose, and she was back in a comfortable home tonight while he lay in prison for her sake.

He remembered, whatever Svensson said, that she had not gone willingly to that home. She had tried to run from the man called Erik; she had slipped and fallen in the snow.

Painfully, and using the stool as a crutch, Brand dragged himself up to the table and groped for the tin pan of water. His hand encountered a plate of hard rye bread smeared with some pungent cheese, and that he pushed away in disgust, but there was a full litre measure of water, and when he had rinsed his mouth and spat blood and water on the floor he drank it to the last drop. Then he laid his head down on his folded arms, half conscious, half wandering down the widening corridors of fever, until somewhere in the town a church clock struck the hour.

The sound brought him out of his stupor and back to reality. He felt for the watch he carried in his waistcoat and found it gone. So was the well-filled wallet he had taken from his desk before he left the *Girdleness* with the girl from Marstrand.

The discovery brought him to his feet, ready to shout. He was too dazed to realize that his belongings had been impounded at the time of his arrest, for of that he remembered nothing except the struggle with the police, but he had just enough wits left to reason that he might have put his money, for security ashore, into an inner pocket of his blue frock-

9

coat. With shaking fingers he began to search through the torn lining.

The wallet was not there. What he felt, well below the armpit, was something made of metal.

He had to take his coat off, fighting the pain in his bruised ribs and shoulder, before he could undo the brooch pinned inside it while it hung on the back of his cabin door in the *Girdleness*. When Brand held it into the ray of light from the street lamp he saw that it was made of heavy gold in a triangular design of three leaves on a single stem of gold and diamonds, with a small diamond laid like a dewdrop on each leaf tip. It was possibly antique, certainly of value: such a morning-gift as a Viking might have made to his bride. Brand Endicott knew, as he turned it over in his hands, that it was a parting gift to himself from the girl from Marstrand.

When the dreaming began, wisping through the prisoner's sleep he was beating south in the *Girdleness*, with fog creeping down to hide the dangers of a lee shore. That fog, freezing over the red skerries of Bohuslän, became identified with his own cold stupor, pierced at fitful intervals by flashes which might have been the pain stabbing his head or the glimmer of St. Erik's Light pointing the way to the harbour at Marstrand. Then there was another light, the flame of a log fire; and with it the sound of accordion music and the stamp of sealskin-booted feet as a crew of Norwegian fishermen lurched through a dance with wildly laughing girls who wore yellow caps and crudely flowered aprons. There was also, in the dreaming, the spear of a single candle shining on the face of an old man who was pressing liquor upon him, and in a mixture of Swedish, Low German and a few English words asking questions about his ship and her destination. Then that light blurred out and faded too, and came back as the glow of the oil lamp slung from the roof in the after cabin of the *Girdleness*.

Brand was sitting at his own desk, with a chart of the Kattegat spread out before him. The skylight was tightly closed. The doors leading to the berths of the two officers, each large enough to hold a bunk and a sea chest, were shut: the stove was stoked to capacity and the air was thick with the fumes from the mate's clay pipe. Mr. West himself was installed in a horse-hair elbow chair opposite the captain's desk, with a pot of strong tea and a china mug at his elbow, and an open Bible in his hand.

"Ready to turn in, Mister?" Brand enquired.

The grizzled mate surveyed his young skipper over steel-rimmed spectacles and said reprovingly:

"I'm readin' ma chapter."

It was a scene, and almost word for word a dialogue repeated every night since Captain Endicott took the *Girdleness* out of Aberdeen harbour and entered on his first command in European waters. He said no more, although the mate's presence and the mate's foul pipe were both oppressive, but returned to his study of the approaches to the Göta river and the harbour of Gothenburg. From Aberdeen to Bergen and Stavanger, to Christiania and on to Strömstad, he had been quietly sizing up his Scottish crew. They were not very different from the Maine fishermen among whom he had grown to manhood, and although in the Western Ocean it was the heyday of the bucko mate and the hazing skipper, Brand had learned enough to know that such men were better led than driven. He had no intention of antagonizing his experienced mate, although the man had made it fairly obvious that he was expected to dry nurse the newcomer from America; he now rolled the chart up without comment and turned to the bills of lading. Brand was acting super-cargo as well as skipper of the trading brig, and carried for a Gothenburg importer a consignment of the Aberdeen Lime Company's prime fertilizer. It was not the first time he had gone through the figures, but he rechecked them carefully, being determined to do well on his first voyage to Sweden and Denmark. In the early days of 1854, as the railroads spread across western Europe and the North, there were many opportunities for a young American who had to keep up the reputation of Tarras and Company, which for well over a century had been carrying British goods to every port in the North Sea and the Baltic.

The mate laid down his Bible and stood up with a long stretching yawn.

"It's away to the frost again, I'm thinking," he said. "Hearken to the boots ringin' on the causeway!"

"Somebody's out late," said Brand. It was nearly midnight, and the shouts and laughter from the Marstrand inn had long ago subsided. In the silence of the island night it was possible, even inside the cabin, to hear the sound of footsteps upon stone. A muffled hail came from the quayside.

"Some drunk tryin' to find his ship," said Mr. West with a sniff. He opened the cabin door a crack, and listened.

"*Girdleness* ahoy!"

They heard the clearer shout, and the man on anchor watch reply, and then the mate went hurrying on deck while Brand, with an oath, stooped to collect the papers scattered by the sudden gust of icy wind. As the cold air rushed into the cabin he heard the voice of Mr. West uplifted:

"Ye've come to the wrong place, I'm tellin' ye. We don't carry passengers, to Gothenburg nor nowhere else."

"What's the trouble, Mister?" shouted Brand.

"Two country folk, by the look of them, seeking a passage to Gothenburg. That's queer, though"—the mate checked himself—"the lassie can speak English."

Brand strode to the rail and looked down. On his arrival at the busy herring port, where half the vessels in the Kattegat seemed to have sought shelter for the night, the harbour master had allotted him a berth at the end of the anchorage farthest from the buildings of Marstrand, where the stone quay ended and the rocks and leafless bushes round St. Erik's Bay began. The anchor light in the fore stay flickered over icicles dripping from the boulders and the clusters of snow-berries still clinging to the ragged boughs.

"Lift up your lantern, will you?" he said to the watchman, and as the man obeyed the blur of faces came into view. Brand saw the old man who had pressed drink upon him earlier in the evening, with what looked like a pile of baggage at his feet and a woman, cloaked and hooded, by his side.

"Does somebody down there speak English?" Brand called out.

"I do!" It was the woman who answered. Her face was very pale, and the night wind had blown a strand of fair hair across her brow. "Please will you take us with you as far as Gothenburg? We have money to pay for our passage. We are going to the United States of America."

"There's no accommodation for passengers aboard," said Brand. "You had better go back home and wait for the Strömstad boat to call tomorrow."

12

"We don't live on Marstrand," said the girl, and her voice broke. "Please, sir! Tomorrow, if we can, we must travel on to Hull."

"I would ha' nothing to do with them, skipper," said the mate in an undertone.

"You'd let them freeze to death, would you?" retorted Brand. "Your Bible readings haven't done you much good . . . I don't promise you a passage, but you're welcome to come aboard," he called down to the girl. "Be careful on the ladder."

There were no rails or ropes for a handhold, and the girl's long cloak encumbered her as she climbed up from the quay. Brand caught her in his arms as she stumbled to the slippery deck. There was the freshness of Marstrand in the clean scent of her hair and the cold cheek which for an instant almost touched his own.

"I apologize for the smell of tobacco," he said as he handed her into the cabin, all too aware that the *Girdleness* reeked of the fertilizer cargo from stem to stern. He knew at once that she was not one of the rough girls from the tavern, but used to gentle dealing, when she said courteously, "It is so warm and comfortable here—I am very grateful!" Her teeth were chattering.

Brand caught up the kettle, simmering on top of the flat stove.

"Grog—you can drink a rum grog, I hope? Where have you been to get yourself half-frozen?"

"Are you an Englishman, sir?"

"I'm an American. Captain Brand Endicott at your service."

"But the ship is British?"

"The ship is British, yes. Sit down in this big chair and let me take your cloak."

She obeyed him with a little sigh of relaxation. "I was afraid my—uncle had not understood you, at the inn. He speaks but little English," she said apologetically, for the mate could be heard bawling at the old man over the sound of bundles being dumped upon the deck. "We were very anxious to travel on a British ship."

Brand opened the bottle of rum and began to mix the grog. He had moved as far aside as the tiny cabin permitted to let the light from the ceiling lamp fall full upon the girl. She was quite young, perhaps not yet twenty, and now that the hooded cloak was off he could see that she was lovely, with dark grey eyes and fair hair falling to the little shawl crossed on her shoulders from beneath a yellow cap like those worn by the Marstrand girls. A country-woman's red wool skirt was short enough to reveal her blue worsted stockings; her hand, when she drew off the fingerless harvest glove to take the glass, was the white hand of a lady.

"You will help us, won't you?" she said urgently, and then the mate, obviously indignant, was pushing the old fellow into the cabin, and Brand was spared the need of answering.

"I owe you a drink," he said grimly to the newcomer. "Here, take this, and tell me why you didn't ask me outright for a passage, when you made up to me back there at the inn?"

The man ducked his head and mumbled in Swedish; the girl spoke up.

"Uncle Carl really didn't understand you very well, sir captain. He only went to discover if a British vessel was in port—"

"You could ha' found that out another way," said the mate aggressively. "That's to say, if you're local folk?"

"Oh no!" she said proudly. "Finland is my country! My uncle and I crossed from Arvidsvik today, hoping to go direct to Gothenburg—before the fog came down."

"Ye didna think to go by road to Gothenburg?" said the mate sceptically.

"There are heavy snowdrifts on the river road," she said.

"All right," said Brand, intervening. "You crossed by ferry from the mainland, and then—?"

"I found a place to shelter near the fortress, while my uncle went to look for—you."

"What fortress?"

"It is called Karlsten's Fort, sir captain," she said patiently. "It is a ruin from the old wars."

Brand laughed awkwardly. He found it difficult to take his eyes off her face, tinged now with colour, and the lips which shaped the English words with such precision. "Well, we can't let you go back to a ruined fortress for the night," he said. "The mischief is, that we have no passenger quarters, as you can see for yourself. In daytime, in fair weather, you could have sat on deck from here to Gothenburg, it's not a long trip; but I don't intend to sail until the fog lifts, and

14

that means first light at earliest, and maybe later. You plan to cross to England on the Wilson Line paddle steamer, I suppose?"

"The *Orlando*, yes," she said.

"I can't guarantee to be in Gothenburg before she sails. Noon, isn't it, Mr. West? The Wilson Line keeps to a strict schedule, I'm told."

"Aye, my lass, you've cut the whole thing rather fine," said the mate with sour satisfaction. It was not clear if either of the strangers understood him, for the old man merely took off his sealskin cap and scratched his head, while the girl repeated:

"We can pay for our passage, sir captain—pay you well." She took a little leather purse from the pocket of her skirt and offered it to Brand.

"Put that away," he said roughly. "If I do take you along, it'll cost you nothing, but" (the sight of the purse acting as a reminder) "what about your baggage? I can't very well put your belongings in the hold."

"Better take a look at the stuff first, skipper," said the mate. Brand followed him on deck unwillingly. The fog, he noticed with regret, was coming down thicker since the slight improvement of the evening, and in the penetrating cold he and the Scotsman saw each other as two vague shapes faintly outlined by the anchor light. It revealed a very small pile of luggage: two canvas bags, strapped and bulging, and what looked like a lady's dressing case of morocco leather.

West drew Brand away from the deck housing.

"That's emigrant baggage for ye!" he said contemptuously. "Ye'll not need to shift the fertilizer for that lot, skipper!"

"Is that all they have? Nothing on the quay?" said Brand.

"Not even a basket o' provisions."

"It's not much for a voyage to America."

"America! Oh fie, skipper, you surely don't believe in that rigmarole! They're eager to get out o' Marstrand, that's a fact, but it's the only true word they've spoken since you let them come aboard."

"They want to catch the *Orlando*, don't they?"

"That's their story. They think they can pull the wool over your eyes—Captain."

Brand scowled in the darkness. Though credulous, he was

not a fool, and his midnight visitors had not produced any convincing reasons for their urgency to be taken aboard the *Girdleness*. But he resented the mate's tone, and for the life of him he could not believe that the girl with the delicate features and the steady grey eyes was less honest than she seemed to be.

"You think they're fakes, do you?" he said.

"I think they're fugitives from justice," said the mate portentously. "And ye'll allow me to say, skipper, after thirty-seven years wi' the Tarras Line—thirty-eight come Martinmas—that I don't believe the owners would approve of what you're doing."

The pompous words, dogmatic like all Mr. West's statements, irritated Brand beyond endurance. He felt the pull of the leading-strings of which he had been made acutely aware in Aberdeen. "The owners"—that meant his grandmother, of course; she was the Tarras who mattered. Her amiable son in London was very much "and Company"; her American grandson, long neglected and only recently taken into favour, was expected to behave himself and listen to the wisdom of the tried and trusty mate.

"God damn it, Mister," he said in a sudden explosion of anger, "you're talking like a fool!"

He picked up the leather bag from the icy deck and went back to the cabin.

"All right," he said to the girl, "you can spend the night aboard, and I'll take you on to Gothenburg tomorrow morning. If your uncle doesn't mind sleeping on sails he can be fixed up for'ard, and you can have my berth."

She turned eagerly to the old man and said something in Swedish, at which he nodded, and then, blushing as she looked at Brand, she said, "But you, sir captain? What will you do?"

"I'll do very well in the chair," said Brand. "Don't worry about me! There's just one thing I have to ask you: your names and destination. I have to enter such details, you see, in the ship's log."

Her eyes opened wide, and Brand was aware of the mate at his elbow, drawing a long breath. But she spoke up with hardly any hesitation.

"I am called Anna Larsson. Carl Larsson is my uncle's name."

"Thank you, Miss Larsson. And where are you bound for —Minnesota Territory?"

This time her hesitation was quite perceptible.

"Minnesota? Oh no, I don't think so . . . We have friends in New York," she said.

"Very good," said Captain Endicott. "I'll enter it accordingly. Mr. West, see that Mr. Larsson is accommodated for'ard. Don't worry about your niece, sir; she is quite safe—now."

He hardly knew what made him add the last word: perhaps the anxious look the old fellow gave Anna Larsson as Mr. West shouldered him out of the cabin. The girl herself was still blushing as she took her dressing-bag from Brand with a word of thanks.

"I am ashamed to put you to so much inconvenience, sir."

"I only wish I could offer you more comfortable quarters. But the berth is clean, and you won't have to put up with it for long. By the way, there's a bolt on the door, and the mate sleeps in the berth opposite."

He opened the door as he spoke, and Anna Larsson glanced in at the bunk with its white honeycomb spread, the china ewer and slop pail, the blue frock-coat hanging with Brand's go-ashore suit on a row of wooden pegs. She looked at the skipper of the *Girdleness* in his thick seaman's jersey and pea jacket, a broad-shouldered, even a formidable shape between her and the lantern, and said:

"I thank you from my heart."

"I hope you get some sleep, Miss Larsson. It won't be cold, at any rate. I'll keep the stove going through the night."

"And you will sail at dawn, Captain Endicott?"

"Oh now, I didn't promise that! If the fog lifts before daybreak, yes: but even if you miss the Wilson steamer, there are other sailings to Hull from Gothenburg. The important thing is, when do you intend to sail from Liverpool?"

"From *Liverpool*?"

"That's where the New York steamers leave from," said Brand drily. "Did you think it was from Hull?"

Anna Larsson stared at him without speaking. Brand went on: "It's a very important step, to emigrate, Miss Larsson. Maybe you should stop in Gothenburg for a few days in any case, just to think it over? If you'll forgive my saying so, you don't seem to have made many preparations for a trip to America."

"I want to get out of Gothenburg as fast as possible!"

"The same way as you're getting out of Marstrand?"

The girl had never taken her eyes from his face. As if his square jaw and clear eyes gave her confidence she said:

"I know what you are thinking, Captain Endicott. I want to assure you that Carl—that my uncle and I have done nothing wrong. We have decided to leave the North, and we wish to leave quickly, that is all."

"And you're sorry to leave Finland? Sorry to go so far?"

The tears came to her eyes then, and Brand heard her say "Very sorry!" in a whisper that went to his heart. He moved a step nearer to her. She was tall for a woman, and when he took her chin in his hand and tilted her face up, her mouth was very near his own.

"You didn't want to be seen at the Marstrand inn tonight," he said. "You made sure of going south aboard a foreign ship. Are you in any sort of trouble I could help you to get out of?"

Anna Larsson put his hand gently aside and shook her head.

"But you're running away, aren't you, from somebody or something? . . . You needn't be afraid to tell me. I've got a lot of sympathy with runaways; my mother ran away from boarding school to marry my father, when his ship put in at Bristol, twenty-five years ago!"

The lovely face, with the mark of tears on it, broke into a smile. "I promise you this isn't an elopement," she said mischievously. "You don't think Carl and I are starting on a honeymoon, do you?"

Brand laughed briefly. "No, I don't," he said, "but I want to be sure you both know what you're bound for. Take a night to sleep on it, and remember, when you get to Gothenburg, I won't turn you adrift. I'll do my best to see you safely on your way."

"I know you will." Her hand slipped into his, the fingers tense and gripping. Instinctively, and although it was a foreign gesture, naturally, Brand Endicott lifted it to his lips. Then she was gone into the clean bare sleeping berth, the bolt

18

had shot home, and the absolute stillness of the winter night fell over Marstrand.

When the police surgeon, hasty and indifferent, entered the remand cell in the morning, he found the prisoner feverish but sensible, and ready to go before the Sheriff with a plea of Guilty.

CHAPTER TWO

THE MOLLY-O

"GOODBYE, sir captain," said the warder sarcastically. "Next time you visit Gothenburg we'll have better quarters for you over yonder on the Mill Hill. Separate cells, and a warm welcome from the Watch."

Brand Endicott took the gibe in silence. He had seen enough, through ten days in the open pen of the Central Prison, of what repartee could bring a prisoner, and he was not clear of the foul place yet, although the half dozen scarecrows to be released with him were crowding on his heels. He was given his belongings and signed a receipt. Two of the vagrants had a few coins to claim, but most were penniless, and in a dismal group they reached the prison yard to the tune of tin plates and spoons rattled against the iron bars of the crowded pen.

The gates were opened by two warders, and in a windy daybreak of early March, Brand saw the free world again. The prison was surrounded by other half-derelict buildings, the workhouse, signal station and guard-room erected on the New Wharf of Gothenburg in the course of the past hundred years, and in the lee of one of those a huddle of men and women were waiting, some of the women weeping as the prisoners filed through the gates. Sven Svensson, the Good Samaritan, was not among them. Instead, a small man in a shabby surtout came forward with a familiar nod when the senior warden shouted, "Endicott, Johan! Discharged."

"Good day, Mr. Endicott," said the small man. "A message for you from Tarras and Company, at Aberdeen!"

"Are you from Mr. Svensson's office?" asked Brand.

"I am his confidential clerk, sir. He instructed me to hand you this letter, which reached him yesterday, with his compliments and—regrets. A room has been reserved for you at the Göta Källare, and a passage has been taken according."

"Give me that, damn you!" Brand tore the sheets from the man's hand. It was a letter of the old-fashioned sort, without an envelope, and addressed "To Mr. J. B. Endicott. By favour of Sven Svensson, Esquire." The blob of red sealing wax had been broken.

Brand took in the first searing words. "Disgraceful conduct—Swedish jail—relieved of your command"—he thrust the pages deep into the pocket of his coat. "You can cancel the hotel room and the passage," he said. "I'm going to make my own plans from here on in."

"But Mr. Endicott! I have a vehicle waiting to take you into town. It is too far to walk, I assure you. Sir! What am I to tell Mr. Svensson—?"

"Tell him to go to hell," said Brand. He walked blindly off past the workhouse, with long loping strides which carried him out on the waste land above the New Wharf, where no vehicle could follow him. Only the stares of a few towheaded children, playing near what might have been fishermen's huts, kept him from breaking into a run. He had a humiliating feeling that they knew where he had come from.

When he was clear of the houses and floundering in patches of unmelted snow Brand halted and looked back towards the prison. Along the road that led away from the gates he saw Mr. Svensson's henchman driving slowly back to town in the carriage considered suitable for a discharged prisoner—a broken-down post cart drawn by an aged hack. Satisfied that there was to be no pursuit he looked about him for a flat rock, and with his back to the prison and his face to the Göta river sat down to read the letter from his grandmother.

"John Endicott!" [it began abruptly]

"The return of the *Girdleness* to Aberdeen with Mr. West in command was a great shock to me, and I was still more shocked to read the despatch from Mr. Svensson informing me of your disgraceful conduct and the sentence you are now serving in a Swedish jail. You have brought shame to the name of Tarras, respected in Gothenburg since 1717, and shewn yourself unworthy of the confidence reposed in you. Be advised that you are relieved of the command of the *Girdleness* forthwith, and that no other employment afloat will be offered you until you have served for a long probationary period in our London office. We are instructing Mr. Svensson to reserve a passage for you in the Danish packet *Prinsesse Louise*, calling at Gothenburg on March 5, and you will be met on your arrival at Gravesend. That you will endeavour to redeem your reputation by application and good conduct ashore is the earnest prayer of

> "Your sorrowing grandmother,
> "Isabella Tarras."

It was bitterly cold on the rock above the river. After a while Brand realized that more than half the chill came from the letter of rejection in his hand—that rejection so much more complete than anything he had anticipated. He had known, as soon as he pleaded Guilty to the charge of drunkenness and assault and heard the Sheriff's exemplary sentence of ten days' imprisonment, that his grandmother would be furious, and as the effects of his beating wore off he began to fear that Svensson, and probably the mate as well, would make the worst of the story in Aberdeen. Even so, he had expected more justice from Isabella Tarras. The affection which a young man both of whose parents were dead—his father only recently—might have expected from a grandmother had been conspicuously absent during the week he had spent beneath her roof, but Brand had been greatly impressed by her intelligence, and would never have supposed that she would condemn him without a word spoken in his own defence. On the testimony of two men only, without a full knowledge of the circumstances, she had degraded him from the command of the *Girdleness* to an office stool in London Wall.

His cold hands made clumsy work of folding the stiff pages. As he laid them edge to edge, Brand saw that the autocrat of the Tarras Line had yielded, in a few words on the covering sheet, to the feminine weakness for a postscript.

"If clerical work in London does not appeal to you," he read, "you will find that the Royal Navy needs recruits, and the war with Russia will offer you a path to honour."

The old lady has gone crazy, he thought blankly. I'll ship before the mast in any tub afloat before I jump to a British bo'sun's rope's end ! She must want to see me killed in action, like those sons of hers . . . He remembered what his uncle had said to him one evening when they were alone in the library at Camberwell.

"I hope you'll do well in the Line, young man. If you

prove yourself a good sailor and a good commander it will mean a great deal to your grandmother. You know both my brothers were officers in the Royal Navy. Poor Jack fell at the battle of Navarino, and Harry at the capture of Aden, in 'thirty-nine, and instead of shedding tears for them my mother turned her grief into pride and—I suppose you could call it patriotism. According to her, service in the Royal Navy is the highest calling any man can have. I was twenty-five when Harry was killed, and she'd given up hope of making a blue water sailor out of me—"

"But you went to sea, Uncle Arthur?"

"I was mate in the old *Balgownie*, on the London run, but the business side of the Line was what attracted me, and when my father died the year after Harry, I went ashore for good. So you'll have to be our seafaring man, Brand. Make your grandmother proud of you, and be sure to speak very sympathetically of your Uncle Jack and Uncle Harry whenever she mentions them."

He remembered his uncles now as two anonymous silhouette portraits in black mourning frames, hung on either side of a marble mantelpiece in the gloomy house in Aberdeen. The young sea officers of Navarino and Aden, enshrined as heroes by their mother, were unrecognizable even as men by the next generation. She'd like to turn me into a little black picture too, maybe, thought Brand. Thank you kindly, grandmamma. I'll stay alive.

He wasn't going to war, and he wasn't going to be shipped back to London like a delinquent child before he had his revenge for the beating he had taken in the trampled snow of the Stone Pier, and possibly had a pull at the long nose of that purveyor of good advice, Mr. Sven Svensson. But a search for the red-haired man called Erik and a visit to the agent's office would have to wait; there was something far more important to be done first. He had to give back the brooch with the golden leaves to the girl he still thought of as Anna Larsson.

Although he had forced Svensson to tell him her real name, Brand had forgotten it in his fever; but he had held on to one part of it, *Alexandra*, and to the solitary clue that the old man "lived out at Kungälv, by the river." He had picked up some rudimentary Swedish in prison—all the faster for realizing that

23

the language was not unlike the dialect spoken by the crew of the *Girdleness*—and one of the prisoners had told him that Kungälv was not far away. If he could find old Larsson and make him talk, Brand was sure that a determined man would soon find out where they had taken her—by "they", of course, he meant not only her kidnappers, but Svensson and the Sheriff and Mrs. Tarras and all the sly and powerful ones who thought they could fool an American seaman who wasn't up to their European ways.

The first thing to do was buy food and clothing, and then get started on his journey. Reflecting that he had plenty of cash in hand, Brand scrambled down the rocky ground to the New Wharf, and was half a mile nearer the town before it occurred to him that although Mrs. Tarras, that astute business woman, had cast him off she had forgotten to cancel the ample letter of credit given him before he sailed from Aberdeen. With the funds it made available to him anywhere in Sweden or Norway, he could follow that girl across the country, even into Finland. Or to Russia.

He was still unable to believe in a general war with Russia. When the Russians attacked Turkey, months before, Brand's father was dying after a long and painful illness, and in their little island home the young man had neither time nor inclination to study the Eastern Question, which in any case received scanty space in American newspapers. That a squabble over the guardianship of the Holy Places in Jerusalem should have led to an invasion of "the Principalities" (mysterious Principalities, as remote from a New Englander as the mountains of the moon) and cause the British Mediterranean Fleet to enter the Bosphorus, seemed to have absolutely nothing to do with Young Skipper Endicott, that respected citizen of Portland; and now, six months later, it seemed to have as little to do with the citizens of Gothenburg. On this March morning, with the sun rising and a fresh breeze coming off the river, it seemed impossible that shots fired in the Black Sea should touch off the cannon of the Baltic.

The Göta was full of shipping. Well-fed, sturdy workers were hurrying through yard gates bearing names Brand had already seen on the letters, presumably returned to Aberdeen in his sea chest, which Mrs. Tarras had written to introduce her American grandson to the great Scots merchants of Gothenburg. The port had offered golden opportunities to the exiles of two Jacobite rebellions, and the Scottish nabobs of the Swedish East India Company had been followed by the brewers, engineers and shipbuilders of the nineteenth century. Mrs. Tarras had written to the Carnegie office on South Harbour Street, to the Chalmers family, to the Gibsons from Arbroath who were in jute and linen, and most impressively of all to Alexander Keiller, whose newly opened shipyard at Eriksberg her grandson was now passing on his way from prison. I bet Sven Svensson spread the scandal round, he thought, and his fists clenched in his torn pockets. The sooner I get out of here the better.

Not, of course, that any of the Keillers or the Gibsons would recognize Mrs. Tarras' grandson in the scarecrow climbing the Stigberg hill, wearing the rags of a blue serge coat and hatless in the windy morning. The shallow wound in Brand's scalp had healed by first intention, but his hair required cutting and there was thick stubble on his jaws. He saw one or two of the passing workmen grin as they looked him over, and realized that he must appear to the world like a man emerging from a long debauch.

At the Fish Harbour, where the morning's catch was being sold, the deckhands were crowding into the taverns for bränn-vin and porter, and there were smells of fish frying which made Brand ravenous. He had set his heart on eating his first square meal for ten days in clean garments, off a clean table-cloth, however, and contented himself with stopping at a pushcart where a woman was selling ölust, a hot mixture of milk, sugar and beer which tasted vile but warmed his throat and filled his empty stomach. It also nerved him to try his Swedish on the woman; he attempted first *"Krieg"* and then *"Krig"* to find out about the war, and was reassured by her hearty laugh and the negative headshake that made her gold hoop earrings tremble above her brown neck. He tried *"Bad"* after that, and *"Kladder"*, which she corrected to *"kläder"*, and she had no difficulty in making him understand that a bath and clothing could be had at the far end of the Skeppsbron quay, Brand drained the mug of ölust and walked on.

Two hours later, clean and relaxed after a visit to the Rotun-da steam bath and barber-shop, wearing fresh linen and a respectable dark suit—an easy purchase for an American of his

25

height in a country of tall men—he set down his cup with a satisfied sigh. Freshly caught plaice, a kidney omelette, a basket of assorted breads, spiced cakes and coffee with thick cream had done credit to the dining-room of the Hotel Garni, and he had sent the waiter out for an English paper. As he clipped the end of a good cigar, Brand Endicott felt his anger and humiliation ebbing, and some of his hopefulness in life come back.

"You asked for the *Times* newspaper, sir?"

Brand looked up at the welcomed sound of an American accent. The man reading the foreign papers at the next table smiled pleasantly.

"If you can spare one for a few minutes."

"Take the lot, and welcome," the stranger said. "Join me and look 'em over at your leisure! The latest is a full week old, and there's nothing in it I haven't heard already, or read elsewhere."

"That suits me," said Brand laconically. "I've been at sea,"

He took the chair indicated, picked up one of the papers, and gave a long look at the man opposite. He had a cheerful Irish face, with a snub nose and a long upper lip, and wore a thick reefer jacket buttoned high at the throat. A blue cap, tilted over very crisp black hair, gave him the look of a seafaring man.

"At sea, have you?" he said with a grin. "All the way from New York, maybe?"

"From Portland, State of Maine," said Brand, and grinned himself for the first time in ten days. "I thought I might pass for Swedish in my Gothenburg go-ashores."

"I knew you were a Yankee as soon as you came in," said the other man. "Your walk gave you away! I'm a Boston man myself, name of Ryan." He held out his hand to Brand. "Joe Ryan, owner and master of the *Molly-O*, out of Stockholm. Glad to know you, sir!"

"Glad to meet you, Captain Ryan. My name's Brand Endicott."

Impulsively: "Not the captain of the *Girdleness*?"

"The former captain of the *Girdleness*." Brand got it out, past the sour taste of resentment in his mouth. "I won't interrupt your reading, Captain Ryan."

"Stop a minute." Joe Ryan reached across the table to catch at Brand's arm. The younger man pushed his chair back, ready to fling off the friendly hand and get out of the place, but

Ryan spoke urgently and fast. "Don't think me inquisitive, Captain," he said, "but I came across from Denmark yesterday, and the night before last at Frederikshavn there was a good deal of talk about the Tarras Line skipper who'd had a dirty deal at Gothenburg. When you spoke your name the thing came back to me, that's all."

He saw the smouldering temper in Brand's eyes, and admired his self-control when the young man said quietly:

"A dirty deal? From the Sheriff, you mean? No, I don't think the Sheriff was to blame. He'd made up his mind to make an example of "brawling and riotous Americans"—that's what he said—I reckon it was my bad luck that I was the one he hit on."

"He'll sing another tune in a few weeks' time, or I miss my guess," said Joe Ryan sagely. "The Americans have been in hot water in Gothenburg since the emigration started, what with bad reports coming back from the first parties that went out, and stories of graft and worse among the shipping agents. Not that that deters the country-folk from setting out! There are a thousand emigrants in Gothenburg now, and this will be the biggest emigration year Sweden has ever known."

Brand nodded. "Who did you meet at Frederikshavn?" he said gruffly. "Anybody from the *Girdleness*?"

The Boston man's blue eyes rested sympathetically on Brand's drawn face. "No, from her sister ship. The *Rubislaw*."

"Bound for Aarhus and Kiel," said Brand. "The Baltic ports will soon be ringing with the story."

"I wouldn't gamble on that," said Joe Ryan whimsically. "There's been another topic in the taverns for the past few days. We're expecting fireworks in the Baltic as soon as the ice goes out."

"Oh, God!" said Brand. "Is it true, then? Has Britain declared war on Russia?"

"Not yet, but the Czar has recalled his ambassador from London, so of course the Allies ordered their men at St. Petersburg to come home. That's the usual signal for hostilities."

"What Allies—Britain and Turkey?"

"Britain and France."

"Why the hell are the French mixed up in it?"

Ryan shrugged. "That new Emperor of theirs is crazy for *la gloire*. If the Czar wants Greek priests to guard the Holy

27

Places, then Napoleon III has to insist on Roman Catholics, to show he's as good as Nicholas. Besides which, the papers say he's as uneasy as the British about the arrival of the Russians on the Danube."

"Why don't they fight on the Danube, then? Why start a war on two fronts by attacking through the Baltic?"

"The Allies are sending troops to the Danube, you may be sure. The Guards left London ten days ago, and I reckon that's why the English mail and newspapers are late. The government must be commandeering every transport available, to get troops to the East before the spring. But the public—as far as I could learn in Denmark—is yelling for an attack on the capital. They want to see the Czar captured, alive or dead, in the Winter Palace at St. Petersburg, and an old fire-eater called Napier is to command the squadron they expect to do it. Admiral Napier has pledged his word to anchor in Cronstadt or in heaven, which gives you a good idea of his state of mind—"

"Cronstadt fortress being impregnable?"

"So they say."

"They'll have to attack St. Petersburg by land, then?"

"If they can."

"What damned foolishness." Brand said no more, but sat surveying, in his mind's eye, those charts of the Baltic Sea which he had studied so closely in the cabin of the *Girdleness*. He saw the open water east of Sweden, the winter ice all through the Gulf of Finland and north of latitude 62° in the Gulf of Bothnia, and the shores of Finland and Esthonia through which an invading army might advance on the Russian capital. If he, Brand Endicott, wanted to find a girl in Finland he would have to move quickly unless he wanted to be caught by a British invasion of her country. He had no quarrel with the Russians—as far as he knew he had only seen one Russian in his life. That was a harmless individual called Isidore, who wore corkscrew curls under a greasy black hat, and was given coffee and doughnuts by kind old Miss Betsy Brand whenever he called at the back door of her house in Portland with his tray of needles and pins.

Joe Ryan misunderstood his silence.

"A Russian war need make no difference to the likes of you and me," he said. "We're American citizens. And Sweden - Norway will be the best place to be in the whole Baltic. The

Swedes have had their bellyful of fighting along with the British against Russia. That's what lost them Finland, fifty years ago; this time they'll stay neutral. Which means that for an American shipowner, even a man in a small way of business, like myself, a British blockade of the Baltic could be very profitable."

"Are you in the freighting way of business, then?" asked Brand.

"Yes, but not on the same scale as the Tarras Line," Captain Ryan could not resist saying. "I carry cargoes as and when I pick them up, and buy and sell on my own account from time to time. Would you care to have a look at the *Molly-O*? She's lying at the Packhus quay, not five minutes from here, and we'd be glad to welcome you aboard."

"Much obliged for the invitation, Captain Ryan. I'd like to accept it, but I have to take a trip out of town, I'm not sure how far. Do you happen to know a place called Kungälv?"

"Kungälv? It's not a port of call, but—yes, I seem to know the name—"

"On a river, probably the Göta—" prompted Brand.

"No, I know it now, it's on the Nordre river, not far from the sea. Marstrand's the nearest port to Kungälv."

"That would be right," said Brand on a long breath of recollection.

"And Kungälv is on the high road into Norway," finished Ryan. "I'm going to ask the waiter about the post wagon times."

The waiter serving coffee and liquor came up at a sign and Captain Ryan questioned him fluently in Swedish, while Brand thought of Marstrand harbour and a girl's face caught by lantern light against icicles and snow-berries.

"You're in luck," said Joe Ryan when the elderly waiter bowed and shuffled away. "The wagon leaves for Christiania at midday. Which is a blessing, for the mail only goes north twice a week, and Kungälv is twelve miles away, he says. That's English miles, not Swedish! The only thing is, the wagon leaves from the Hisingen side, so you'll have to allow time to cross on the ferry."

"Fine," said Brand. "I wish I could speak Swedish the way you do."

"I've lived in Sweden going on fifteen years, d'you see? My

poor late wife was Swedish, and we brought our Molly girl back to Stockholm when the baby was only a year old. I've had plenty of time to learn the lingo."

"Did you name your ship after your daughter, Captain?"

"I did an' all—the *Molly-O*, and I call my girl the first mate." Joe settled his blue cap squarely on his curly hair. "Look, Captain—now you know your timetable better, you can well spare an hour at the Packhus quay. Come aboard us, and let my Mary make you a cup of coffee—she'll admire to meet an American, for she's always at me to tell her about Boston—"

"It's out of the question," said Brand hoarsely. "You know, if you heard the story right, you know where I've just come from. You can't want me to meet a young lady of sixteen, your own daughter, the very day that I've—come out of—"

"Steady, lad!" Joe Ryan's voice was as urgent as when Brand had first admitted his identity. "Don't take the thing so much to heart! It's behind you now, however it happened. Get your overcoat on, and that fancy sealskin hat the waiter's hovering around you with, and come see a real coastal trader and the prettiest first mate between Jutland and Hangö Head!"

It took longer than five minutes to reach the Packhus quay, for the streets around the Stone Pier and the Customs House were crowded with emigrants, many listening to the exhortations of a Lutheran pastor who stood on a raised platform between the quays with his white hair streaming in the wind, and others besieging the offices of agents who had promised them a speedy passage to the United States. In vain those agents shouted that the British paddle steamers were arriving late or not at all; the bewildered country-folk, reduced to sleeping underneath the carts they meant to sell at Gothenburg, clamoured for immediate departure. Brand and Joe had to go out of their way to avoid a dispute about a horse, which the purchaser was dragging from the shafts of the cart it had drawn to the city from some remote farm in Bohuslän, while children wept, and a pale woman clutched at her husband's arm crying that if the ship from England never came, they must have the means to go home again!

"Poor devils," said Brand, and Joe shrugged.

"They'll have forgotten it after six months in Minnesota," he said.

The *Molly-O*, which the owner pointed out with pride, was a trading smack of less than a hundred tons, looking small by comparison with the two hundred and thirty five tons of the *Girdleness*. Brand looked her over non-committally. The two Swedish sailors on deck, lounging and spitting into the water, seemed not to have been kept up to their duties, for paint work and bright work were far from brilliant, and the ropes were badly pointed and flemished. The flag of the Stars and Stripes, which made the *Molly-O* conspicuous among all the vessels at the Packhus quay, was sadly faded. Captain Ryan, however, was beaming as he ushered his visitor aboard, and called out "Mary!"

"In a minute, father!" a fresh young voice answered from the galley.

"Hurry up there, pet! We've a visitor!"

"Oh dear!"

The girl who appeared at the galley door had her hands to her hair, shaking black curls like Joe's out of the ribbon which confined them, brushing flour from the front of her calico apron. There was flour on the tip of her nose and her pretty face was as flushed as if Miss Mary Ryan had been baking herself at the galley fire. After the first gasp of dismay at the sight of a stranger she had aplomb enough to forget her appearance, and made her school-girl curtsy to Brand as if they were in a drawing room instead of on the uncaulked deck of a Baltic smack.

"Is this the gentleman about the cargo, father?" she asked when the introductions were over.

"Sure and he never turned up, the villain," said Joe cheerfully. "I wasted an hour of my time waiting on him. Well no, not wasted, since I fell in with a fellow countryman! Captain Endicott is from the State of Maine, my dear."

Sparkling: "An American! That makes you specially welcome, sir. Pray come this way."

Brand followed her into the cabin of the *Molly-O*. It was even more cramped than the cabin of the *Girdleness*, but there was no desk to take up space because Molly, as her father proudly pointed out, had had a drop-leaf table attached to the wall for eating and writing, and the chart cupboard was fitted with extra drawers for correspondence. Instead of a heavy chair there were stools padded with linen cushions in bright colours like those which made sofas out of the cabin lockers. On one of these a cat with ginger fur lay dozing. A guitar with blue and gold ribbons, the Swedish colours, was propped against a small bookcase. There were several novels with gilt spines mixed with nautical manuals, and a pot of yellow crocuses shared the top shelf with a wicker basket full of bright sewing silks.

"Neat, isn't it, Captain Endicott?" said Joe with pride.

"Smartest cabin I ever was in, sir."

"Now Bernadotte, you spoilt idle cat, get up from there!" cried Mary Ryan. "Captain Endicott, do sit down. I've got some cakes just out of the oven, and the coffee is ready—you'll have a cup with us, won't you?"

"I only finished breakfast half an hour ago," Brand protested.

"That's nothing," Joe laughed, as his daughter whisked out of the cabin. "When you've been longer in these waters you'll know the coffee pot is always on the galley fire. Mary is a real little Swede for that, she can drink coffee right round the clock. Now let me fix the table up and get it ready for her tray, because I'll bet she won't be long—"

It was only a few minutes before Mary Ryan carried in the cakes and coffee, but in that time she had brushed the flour from her nose, taken off her cooking apron, and put on a blue silk neckerchief which exactly matched her eyes. She was a small girl, with vivid colouring, and as she perched on one of the stools, intent on pouring the coffee, with the ginger cat purring at her feet, she was as bright as some tropical bird fluttering at the dingy masthead of the *Molly-O*. After her first eagerness of hospitality, however, she was a silent hostess, keeping the heavy cups filled but apparently content to listen to the men discussing freight rates and the prospect of an early spring, until Brand turned to her with the polite question:

"And do you sail with Captain Ryan in all weathers, Miss Mary?"

"Not in the dead of winter, sir. He makes me stay at home in Stockholm then. But this year I've been at sea since the beginning of February, haven't I, father? I went on the Copenhagen run and then to Jutland, and as soon as the ice goes out in the Gulf of Bothnia we're going to Sundsvall. We usually go to Sundsvall twice a year."

She spoke with an air of knowledgeability which Brand thought funny and attractive.

"I can see you've acquired a thorough knowledge of the Baltic, ma'am," he said gravely, and her father, with an affectionate tug at the girl's black curls, put in:

"She knows every harbour and anchorage between Gothenburg and Stockholm, at any rate—more than you'll find marked on most charts; and though she's never learned to swim nor handle a dinghy I've taught her a bit of navigation, and it's astonishing how fast the creature picks it up."

"I could pick it up faster if you didn't always stop and make me sing to you," protested Mary.

"Why not? Don't you want to keep in practice? Molly's ambition is to be the new Jenny Lind," her father explained, and Brand laughed. This kind of affectionate sparring was something new to him.

"I reckon you're pretty good shipmates," he said. "More like a brother and sister than father and daughter, if you don't mind my saying so."

"He loves it," said Mary Ryan. She laid her cheek against her father's, and the two pairs of blue Irish eyes laughed back at Brand. "I'm surprised he hasn't told you already that I was his birthday present on the very day that he was twenty. Poor mamma! She didn't like Boston much."

"Boston's a fine town," Joe insisted, "but to tell you the truth I was a bit of a misfit there myself. When my father left the old sod they told him it was a great place for the Irish, but nobody explained that 'twas hardly the promised land for a black Presbyterian from Londonderry, even if his name chanced to be Ryan. When I was a boy I grew sick of Orange and Green, and getting my nose bloodied fighting the Battle of the Boyne on the banks of the Charles. My brothers took it easier than I did, and learned good trades, but I shipped out before the mast to California as soon as I was turned sixteen."

"So you've doubled Cape Horn?" said Brand with interest.

"I have so, and danced with the señoritas in the plaza at Monterey. Ah, now, if I'd settled there as I half planned to do once I'd been back to Boston and seen my old folks, I might have been a millionaire today. But nobody thought of a gold strike back in 'thirty-five, and anyway I never went on a second voyage to California. Before I was home a week I went to hear an opera performance by a European company, with a girl

33

called Brita Engström singing in the chorus . . . and that was where I met my fate."

There was a friendly silence in the cabin, and Mary asked gently, "Is your family living in America, Captain Endicott?"

So then Brand found himself telling her the story of pretty, delicate Fanny Tarras, the apple of her parents' eyes, who eloped at seventeen with the handsome Yankee sailor, and lived happily with him for ten years before consumption killed her in the fine house on South Street where her husband's kind aunt, Miss Betsy Brand, looked after the invalid and her little boy when Skipper Endicott was at sea. There might have been some boasting in his description of the house in Portland, but it was quite unconscious, for Brand's story was a reassurance to himself, and a reminder that whatever happened to him in Europe he had his roots set deep in Maine. The attention of both the Ryans, and particularly the deep absorption of Mary, drew him out to give more details of his life and background than he would have believed possible in a talk with strangers, chary as he was, after his recent experiences, of believing anything a stranger said. But this girl gave a quick emotional response to his mother's story such as he had not found in his young Tarras cousins—they had seemed more interested, during his stay at Camberwell, in gossiping about the Queen's foreign husband than in hearing about their father's sister and her experiences in America. When Brand spoke of his mother's death, he could have sworn that there were tears in Mary Ryan's eyes.

"I would love to see Portland, and all the wooded islands in the bay," she said at last. "It must be a beautiful town."

"We'll take a trip there when I take you back to Boston," her father promised.

"When!" she said with her gay laugh, and rose to clear the little table. "When the Sea Peddlers have made their fortune?" Brand got to his feet with a glance of enquiry at Joe Ryan.

"That's what we call ourselves aboard the *Molly-O*," said the owner. "The Sea Peddlers. We're in a very small way of business, as I told you, just buying and selling from one port to another. I risked a purchase of sewing-machines at Copenhagen, for instance, but I don't look to get rich from them until midsummer, when Molly here will show the women how to use them, at the country fairs."

"You can do that too, Miss Mary?" said Brand in surprise.

"Oh, I show off lots of our goods at the village fairs," she said. "First I play and sing a little to draw the people"—she indicated the guitar—"like mother used to do. Mother taught me how. But I like it best when we have pretty things to sell, like china plates and silver spoons from Denmark, not sewing-machines! Sometimes I set out the dishes as if we were going to give a dinner party and put bunches of flowers in the vases. Then all the farm people come along to look—"

"I reckon they come to look at you, Miss Mary," said Brand.

She gave him a smiling inviting glance which had nothing of the child in it. In the close quarters of the cabin it struck Brand that neither of the Ryans was quite as youthful as at first appeared. Joe appeared boyish for his thirty-six years, but the first lines of middle age had already been traced on his quizzical Irish face, and Mary, in spite of her loose curls and school-girl manners, showed the aplomb of a woman in the tact which had kept all her questions to his American past without reference to his business in Gothenburg. There was something in her sidelong glance, and in the soft lips, moist and slightly parted, which reminded Brand of the fisher girl who had been his first lover, in the summer when he was sixteen. Mary Ryan had the same sort of skin, with a glow on it, which even in winter kept the gold of summer and the sea wind. Guiltily Brand dragged his mind away from a sudden re-collection of the secret cove on Orr's Island, and the sun-tanned body in his naked arms.

Joe Ryan was still teasing his daughter. "You be thankful," he said, "that I don't ask you to demonstrate the farm imple-ments I've got aboard right now. You'll do better with a sewing machine than a scythe—"

"Farm implements!" said Brand. "Is that your present cargo?"

"Yes, would you like to have a look at it?"

"Very much, and then I ought to be off to the ferry. The post wagon will likely leave on time."

"But aren't you going to stay for dinner, Captain?" Mary cried. Brand smiled and thanked her. "I've trespassed on your kindness too much already," he said.

"Won't you come back some other time?" she persisted.

"We'll be here until tomorrow, and perhaps longer. When are you due to sail?"

Out of the tail of his eye Brand saw Joe Ryan's almost imperceptible headshake. "That depends," he said. "I'm waiting for my sailing orders now. Miss Mary, I can't tell you how much I've enjoyed your hospitality. I hope I may have the honour of meeting you again."

He left her pouting a little, but she took her father's advice not to follow them outside, for the wind of the morning was blowing harder, and snowflakes were beginning to thicken into slush on deck. Brand turned up the collar of his new overcoat and waited with interest while one of the seamen, answering to Joe's shout of "Nils!" helped to raise the hatches. He was curious to see the hold of the *Molly-O*. It had occurred to him that Sea Peddlers might be another name for smugglers, and that a smack putting in at anchorages not marked on any chart had excellent opportunities for trading in spirits and tobacco. Brand was not morally opposed to this, for dodging the Revenuers was an old Maine pastime, and his own father had boasted of running a few illicit cargoes in his youthful days. But the hold, seen by lantern light, showed no traces of contraband, unless it was contained in the crates stencilled with the already well-known name of I. M. Singer & Co. The implements, attached to wall battens, were wrapped in sacking beneath which Brand could distinguish the familiar shapes of scythes, spades and ploughshares.

"Now then," grumbled Joe, when they were back on the windy deck. "If Herr Elmgren had kept his appointment at the Garni with me this morning, I might have been shipping some heavy stuff by now. Four ploughs for a dealer in Halmstad: just what I need for ballast—and for pay."

"I hope you get the job, then," said Brand. "Halmstad. Is that your next port of call?"

"If Elmgren and Company don't want to meet my terms today they will in a few weeks' time," said Joe. "When war breaks out that"—he jerked his thumb at the flag—"will be the most valuable thing aboard the *Molly-O*. An American citizen sailing under the old Gridiron will be run after by all the shippers, as soon as the Swedish Government closes the ports to the belligerents. And that will mean *all* the belligerents, you mark my words!"

"How do you come to fly the Gridiron on a Stockholm vessel, Captain Ryan?"

"The Molly-O—she was the Susan Quimby then—was American-registered when I bought her at Amsterdam, and being an American citizen I had no trouble with the transfer. Now, one question for another, and don't take offence. Is it true what they were saying over in Denmark, that Mrs. Tarras, the head of the Line, is your grandmother?"

"She is."

"Then in your place I would make tracks for Aberdeen as quick as possible."

Grimly: "Not if you were me, you wouldn't."

Joe Ryan looked at him appraisingly. Six feet of manhood, all bone and muscle, a face handsome without the scowl, and a magnetism to which Mary had obviously reacted—he didn't think Brand Endicott had much to worry about! "Lad," he said, "whatever went wrong, it won't take much to mend it. The old lady won't be able to resist you when she sees you walk into her counting-house; no old lady could. And not many young ones, either."

"As it happens, I may be going in the opposite direction," said Brand coolly. "What's the quickest way to Finland?"

"Through the Göta canal to Stockholm and over to Åbo in the mail boat," said Joe automatically. "But—my God, that's quite a trip this time of year!"

"I may not have to go, it all depends. Depends on my visit to Kungälv, I mean."

"Well, if you change your mind, and want a passage to Malmö, I can take you aboard. It won't be luxurious, but it can be done, so don't hesitate if you feel inclined. Daresay the Molly-O could get you south as fast as anything under sail, the way the regular shipping companies have been disrupted."

"Captain Ryan," said Brand, "I'll remember that. And I can't thank you enough for your kindness this morning. It's meant a lot to me." He gave the other man a hard handshake.

"Now if you come to Stockholm," said Joe, following him to the gangplank, "be sure you look us up. Number three, Bollhus Alley! If you can't remember, it's right close to the royal palace, and anyone will show you where the Americans live. Goodbye! Good luck to you!"

"Goodbye, Captain Ryan!"

Mary Ryan had come to the cabin door to wave. Brand waved back to the father and the daughter and started off towards the ferry landing. He felt better and more confident than he had felt for ten days past. It had done him good to meet two Americans, who spoke his own language, and understood his own life. He looked over his shoulder at the *Molly-O*, where the faded Stars and Stripes drooped in the thickening snow. It would be easy to turn back now and accept Joe Ryan's offer of a passage to Malmö. From Malmö he could cross to Hamburg, where any shipping company would offer him a berth, and prove his independence of the Tarras Line. Or he could go to Stockholm with the Ryans, buying and selling in the little ports, and listening to that pretty girl singing to her guitar in the cheerful cabin. He had a notion that she'd be glad if he came back.

Either way he was under no obligation to go on to Finland.

Brand halted in the slush of the Packhus quay. He remembered Joe Ryan's words about the night at the opera in Boston where the Irishman had "met his fate". He recognized that he had come to a similar moment in his own life, when going forward or turning back now would shape his destiny for years to come.

He did not hesitate for long. When the ferryboat came slowly over from Hisingen Brand Endicott was among the waiting passengers, ready for the road to Kungälv, and whatever fate was waiting for him there.

CHAPTER THREE

NIKITA

THAT year spring came early to the Gulf of Finland. By mid-March the currents were moving strongly under the plains of ice that stretched from Cronstadt west to Hangö Head, and the heavy snowfalls had dwindled into occasional snow showers. In some sheltered places along the south coast of Finland the spruces shook off their weight of snow and sap began to run in the alders.

With the earliest signs of spring men appeared on both shores of the Gulf. They tramped across the discoloured snow into Finland, and going south and west from St Petersburg were deployed into Esthonia to reinforce the garrisons at Pernau and Reval. They wore the flat hats and long grey coats of the Russian army, and with them went cavalry remounts, field kitchens, cannon and ammunition wagons. They were the Czar's first line of defence against invasion from the west— the uncurling of the paws of the winter bear.

In Helsingfors, the capital of the Grand Duchy of Finland, the Russian strength was greatly increased in March, 1854. For this there was a special reason : the reason why the Te Deum was sung in the Nicholas Kirk, why flags flew from public buildings and entertainments were ordered by the city fathers. Nicholas I, Emperor of All the Russias and Grand Duke of Finland, had come to visit Helsingfors with his sons, his Ministers and his generals, and a thousand extra troops were needed to secure the safety of the Czar.

On one March morning, when the pale sunlight was obscured and snow clouds again hung over the city, the guard was extended to the South Harbour, where icebreakers always kept the channel open between Helsingfors and the fortress, Sveaborg. The *Kavia*, a little paddle boat which normally carried passengers between the fortress and the Market Square, was ordered to remain at Helsingfors, and no boats were permitted to put out from any of the inhabited islands which ringed the harbour. Instead, patrol boats of the Russian Navy policed the bay. With the sound of their oars muffled by the mist, they moved in and out of the narrow channels dividing the units of the great complex of Sveaborg, listening for any sound on land or sea which might be made by the enemies of Russia.

Sveaborg had been known for a hundred years as the Gibraltar of the North. Where Gibraltar was raised upon one rock, Sveaborg was built on five linked islands, granite in their foundations and stone in their ravelins and bastions, which formed the outer defence of Helsingfors and the grand offensive weapon of the Gulf. Sveaborg was the key which any invader must turn before he could force the lock of Cronstadt and open the gates of Petersburg.

Upon the most southerly and the most heavily fortified of the five islands, Gustafssvärd, there was a heavy concentration of troops and guns for the Czar's visit. The Te Deum was sung in the Greek Orthodox Church on Great East Svartö, and the Russian double eagle flew from the Vargö citadel. Across the narrow straits the regiments stood to arms on Bakholm and Skanslandet, and at one o'clock a royal salute was fired when the King's Gate of Gustafssvärd was opened for the departure of the Emperor. Nicholas went down the shallow granite steps with the barest acknowledgement to the Governor, and drawing his furred cloak round his shoulders took his place in silence in the stern of the Imperial barge. In silence the crew bent to their oars, rounded the point, pulled clear of the fortress and made for Helsingfors.

The city rose out of the broken ice and the grey-green water of the harbour, faintly touched by the pale sunshine breaking through the clouds. The Grand Duke Alexander leaned forward to offer the Czar a compliment on the elegance of his Finnish capital. It was met with a cold nod. The Grand Duke, looking anxiously at his father, wondered if those heavy eyes really beheld the beauty of Helsingfors, or if the Czar's vision was far away with his troops in the Danubian plain. With every stroke of the oars they were coming nearer to the finest waterfront in Europe, nearer to the Swedish Embassy, the Imperial Palace: the harmony of each neo-classical façade varied by the subtle use of pale granite and dark, of terracotta wash and stucco in cream. Carl Ludwig Engel, the architect of the new Helsingfors, had set his masterpiece back from the sea by the breadth of the Market Square and crowned it with the star-adorned blue cupola of the Nicholas Kirk which he had not lived to see completed. The great white cathedral, soaring like a triumph of Christian witness, was soon obscured for the passengers in the Russian barge by the ranks of the Cossacks paraded in close order at the quayside to guard the arrival of the Czar.

The flicker of winter sunlight faded within an hour. By three o'clock iron shutters were closed over the windows of the charming little palace which housed the Russian emperors when they came to Helsingfors as Grand Dukes of Finland, and satin curtains had been drawn in the salon where Nicholas I was holding an afternoon levée. There was now no doubt about the Czar's vision. It was turned outward into actuality, sweeping the guests moving uneasily before his throne.

This throne had some historical significance. Upon it Nicholas' elder brother, Alexander I, had been seated at the Diet of Borgå in 1809, when a Finnish delegation, representing the whole country, took an oath of allegiance to the Czar. At that time Finland ceased to be a part of Sweden, defeated by Russia in the war with Napoleon, and became a Russian Grand Duchy. Forty-five years had changed much in Finland, but the red velvet of the throne was still brilliant, as was the gold of the canopy embroidered with a George and Dragon and with the double-headed black eagle of Russia, holding a sword in one claw, a sceptre in the other. Under the tense hands of Nicholas were again the Russian eagle heads, carved into the arms of the throne and wearing expressions of arrogance which oddly repeated the fixed glare of the Czar.

It was a dull, leaden look, which Nicholas I had cultivated during the thirty years of his reign as a means of subduing any Minister, soldier or woman who ever dared to outface him. It was largely wasted on his Finnish guests, the undistinguished city officials, professional men and their wives, who were normally expected to be elated by an invitation to court, a glass of champagne, and an opportunity to look at the Czar, the Grand Dukes and the dignitaries of the empire grouped around the throne. Today they were unusually restless. Perhaps the spell of the Czar's glare was wearing thin in Helsingfors, or else some flicker of the lights in the golden chandeliers was sending odd shades of expression over the usually stolid Finnish faces, today watchful and ironical as never before. The Finns were guessing, Nicholas realized with fury, at news which was as yet the secret of the Russian few.

Possibly it had been a mistake to postpone the luncheon arranged for that day at the Senate House. Nicholas had known, of course, that there would be vexation and conjecture, but he cared nothing for that. In the morning, after the British envoy had waited upon him, stating his fatal message with cool courtesy, the Czar's one desire had been to get across the bay to the fortress, Sveaborg. To reassure himself by sight and sound that the great sea barrier on the way to Petersburg was, as ever since it passed into Russian hands, impregnable.

Within an hour, now, he would meet the privy council. This was the name given for form's sake to the group of men whose function was to register approval of the Autocrat's decisions. He would tell them, as briefly as possible, the kind of answer he had sent to the government of Queen Victoria and the upstart Emperor of the French. It was powerful. It would have an excellent effect upon the Finns.

Except, of course, that they would know, and soon the whole world would know, that for the first time in fifty years Russia had been challenged by two Powers of the western world, and that the Czar's plans to penetrate still further into Central Europe had been checkmated. Nicholas I bit his bloodless lip and clenched his hands over the carved eagles on the throne.

Under the soft music of the string orchestra he heard a woman laugh.

"Who is the lady who finds amusement in this tedious levée?" he ground out to his entourage, and the Grand Duke Alexander, so often the peacemaker in Finland, said quickly:

"It is Madame Karamsin, Sire."

"Aurora Karlovna? I had no idea she was in Helsingfors." The Czar smiled for the first time that day, and changed his rigid position for a better view of the privileged woman who had laughed at an Imperial reception.

Aurora Karamsin, he saw, was as beautiful as ever. Nearly as beautiful in her forties as when she first appeared in Moscow society, a provincial belle from Helsingfors whose clever sister knew all the right people; certainly more beautiful than in the anxious days of her brief marriage to Paul Demidov, the Croesus of the Ural mines. Married once for fabulous wealth, married a second time for love; with a handsome son, a palace in St. Petersburg and the friendship of all the Imperial family —these were the successes of the girl who had been lovely Aurora Stjernvall, and who for twenty years had been almost a legend to the simple people of Helsingfors.

"I think," said the Czar to his son, "a word with Madame Karamsin would be agreeable !"

He stood up, with a sign to the musicians to continue playing. On his feet, his ruined physique was at once apparent. It was nearly forty years since the time of Waterloo, when Nicholas and his brother Michael were known in Paris as "the Northern Lights", and the slim young Russian colonel of 1815 had become corpulent and slow. Heavily bandaged, with his stomach forced upwards by a corset, his figure bulged hideously below the Orders on his breast as he made his way down the salon to Aurora Karamsin.

The crowd of guests parted respectfully to let him pass. Some of those present, jealous of her enormous wealth and many charities, had said in earlier days that Aurora Karamsin was the Czar's mistress; others, that the Czarevich as well as his father had been her lover. Now they were content to watch her as she stood waiting proudly for the Imperial greeting— Helsingfors' lucky lady, lovely as a full-blown rose.

Aurora Karamsin was the only woman in that gathering of Finlanders to wear the classic Russian court dress. The Czar's dull glance approved the white satin robe embroidered in gold, with a velvet train falling from one shoulder, and the diamond *kokósnik* mounted on a long veil of blond lace, which was set on Madame Karamsin's smooth dark hair. She wore four ropes of matched pearls; and on a fine chain of Ural gold the priceless solitaire called the Sancy diamond, which had been the morning-gift of her first husband, Paul Demidov.

"This is an unexpected pleasure, Aurora Karlovna," said the harsh voice of the Czar. "The Empress told me you intended going to Spa."

"A little later in the season, Sire," Madame Karamsin rose gracefully from her curtsy. "I trust Her Imperial Majesty is well ?"

"Not well enough to come to Helsingfors, I regret to say. And you? Are you in your own house at Träskända or with your stepfather at Hagasund?"

"At Hagasund, Sire, for the happy occasion of your visit. My goddaughter is keeping me company there at present. May I have the honour of bringing her again to your kind attention—Alexandra Gyllenlöve."

The girl whom Brand Endicott had known as Anna Larsson was standing one step behind Aurora Karamsin, dressed also in white satin, but without the older woman's classic magnificence and certainly without Aurora's evident desire to please. Her fair hair was swept up under a pearl *kokósnik*, and her head was held high as she moved forward to curtsy to the Czar. She was aware that the younger Grand Dukes were staring and grinning at the girl who had run away from her wedding to Boris Apraxin; aware too, of the determination beneath Aurora's light touch on her wrist, and of the pretty wistful smile, the jewelled head tilted slightly on one side, which were part of Aurora's studied appeal to the Autocrat. But Nicholas scowled and said angrily:

"Aha! The runaway! So you took Alexandra Ivanovna in charge, did you, madame? The right place for her is with her father. His house in Petersburg is open to her; you had better send her home without delay."

"Is that an order, Sire?" said Alexandra. But the Czar had already turned on his heel; her defiance was covered by Aurora's startled "Alix, hush!" and the opening bars of "Bojé Zara Chrani," the new Russian national anthem. Nicolas I was making for his private apartments, and as the crowd began to move, the two women were swept out into the vestibule where Imperial servants brought them their furred cloaks.

Across the courtyard an officer of the Finnish Life Guards, his grey astrakhan képi worn at a rakish angle, was waiting to hand them into Madame Karamsin's three horse sleigh.

"Aren't we going to wait for grandpapa?" Aurora's only son, the child of her first marriage, had come running down from the balcony of the throne-room, where a few young people had been allowed to watch the levée, and caught up with the ladies at the gate.

"No, Paul; there is a meeting of the privy council," said

Madame Karamsin, and the sixteen-year-old boy remembered his manners, and helped Alexandra to settle her bell-shaped skirt into the fur-lined sleigh.

There were not many such conveyances in the Market Square. Helsingfors was still a small city, only forty years old in its modern form, and most of the Czar's guests were able to return on foot to their homes in the immediate neighbourhood. All had to submit to the inspection of the Cossacks walking their horses up and down the Market Square, and the scrutiny of the officers on duty at a barrier which had been erected to keep the public confined to the gardens of the Esplanade.

"What happened, Alix?" Paul Demidov burst out. "What did His Majesty say to you?"

"Nikita means to send me to Siberia," said Alexandra flippantly. They were just abreast of the barrier, which was being raised to let the troika through, and her clear voice rang out in the cold air to reach the citizens pressed shoulder to shoulder along the North Esplanade.

"Alix, be quiet! Good heavens, have you gone mad?" exclaimed Madame Karamsin. She leaned forward and said urgently to the driver, "Jakob! Cross to Alexander Street and get us out of the crowd!" The man nodded and cracked his whip, the troika swung to the right. Very soon they were in the long main street where lamps were already lit in the small wooden-fronted shops, and making their way out of the city.

Alexandra turned to find Madame Karamsin pressing a lace handkerchief to her eyes.

"Aurora, please don't cry," she said. "Surely nobody ought to cry any more, over anything I say or do!"

"Darling, you're so very indiscreet, and the levée was such a disappointment—"

"You'll feel better as soon as you get home."

The adolescent boy looked from one woman to the other with bright malicious eyes. If Alexandra was going to be in still worse trouble, the better he was pleased. He knew she was in disgrace with their elders and on the strength of it had tried to kiss her two evenings ago, when she had boxed his ears for his pains. Stealthily, under the sable carriage robe, he pressed his knee against hers, and watched her cold pro-

45

file turned towards the street without the slightest sign of feeling. There was more rejection in that indifferent face than in a dozen blows. Sulking, Paul Demidov resigned himself to wait.

The troika had not far to go along the Åbo road before reaching the Villa Hagasund. It had been built twelve years earlier to the order of Madame Karamsin's stepfather, Senator Walleen, in a locality planned as a fashionable new suburb of Helsingfors. The tide of fashion, however, had not flowed in the direction of the Hesperia Park, and Hagasund still stood alone in the craggy ground above one of the many creeks of Helsingfors. The villa, built in the classical style, was approached by a short circular driveway. In the bleak afternoon it looked empty and cold, but as soon as the troika bells were heard lights sprang up in the ground floor rooms and the front door was flung wide open. While Paul handed his mother and Alix from the sleigh, three or four maids in white, wearing bright aprons and kerchiefs, came running to greet the ladies, and a breath of warm air came from the house.

Alix followed Madame Karamsin indoors with a sigh of relief. Hagasund had been like a second home to her since childhood, and for the past two weeks it had been a place of refuge as well, to which she returned all the more thankfully because the bad hour of the Czar's reception was behind her. She could forget the throne room, with its iron etiquette, as soon as she entered the pleasant hall where handwoven rugs in vivid colours lay on the grey stone floor, and tall porcelain jars of forced tulips and narcissus stood on the corner tables. On the walls were carefully chosen paintings by the Finnish artists Ekman and von Wright, and through open doors could be seen book-lined rooms which contained the largest private library in Finland. Carl Johan Walleen had done much in his seventy-three years to encourage art and letters in the Grand Duchy, and the elegant simplicity of the Villa Hagasund was the expression of his cultivated taste.

"Paul dear," said Madame Karamsin to her son. "Your tutor is waiting for you, I feel sure."

"I thought today was meant to be a holiday." But the boy lounged off to his own quarters, and his mother, waving away the maid who started to follow her, went with Alexandra up the polished staircase to the bedroom always kept for her own use. Although Madame Karamsin, in Peterburg, owned a fabulous dwelling on the Morskaia and had a much-loved Finnish home out at Träskända, it pleased her to occupy one of the smallest and simplest rooms at Hagasund, under the roof of the stepfather who had been a kind parent to herself since childhood.

Alix thought it an affectation, although she was fond of her godmother and admired her; even today, when their relationship was strained to breaking-point, she could appreciate the youthful beauty of the matron of forty-five. Aurora made no pretence at being young, unless it was in the gentle refusal to be called "godmamma," or "Aunt Aurora" by the girl less than half her age. She simply was young, supple, vital; the dark hair held not one thread of grey, and the colour in her charming face was natural. Alexandra, now watching her closely, caught the swift glance she threw at her husband's portrait, in the place of honour on a small easel near her bed. Colonel Karamsin was depicted as a typical Russian officer, with his hand thrust inside the breast of his uniform coat in a gesture far more Napoleonic than he had ever adopted outside the artist's studio. He was an amiable, feckless creature whom Alix had never heard express any strong view or positive opinion, but she knew that her godmother adored him, and was perceptive enough to realize that it was Karamsin's love which kept Aurora young and beautiful and kind.

"If you don't want Verna to help you," she said, "you must let me do that," and she set to work unpinning the court train from Aurora Karamsin's shoulder and unhooking the fall of blond lace from the jewelled *kokósnik*. Aurora took the diadem from her own head and sat down gracefully by the low table which held flowers and devotional books.

"Sit down, Alexandra darling," she said gently. "I want to talk to you."

The girl did not at once obey. She had moved to the window, and was staring out across the snow to the dark waters of the Tölö creek, now almost invisible in the dusk. Aurora saw the fingers of one hand clenched in the folds of the white satin skirt, and marked apprehensively the mutinous line of the girl's jaw. Then, in an unexpected gesture, Alix snatched off her own pearl diadem and threw it on the blue silk spread of Madame Karamsin's bed.

"There!" she said, "I don't expect I shall wear that again. I'll ask Uncle Carl to keep it in his safe, and later on I'll give it to Kristina's little girl."

"Oh now, Alix dear, you mustn't talk as if the end of the world had come because the Czar was a little gruff this afternoon!"

"You call that public insult, being 'a little gruff'? Aurora, you know very well I don't care a fig for what Nikita says to *me*. But he was rude to you as well, and that was what I was afraid of when I begged you not to take me to his horrible levée. Oh, I know that won't last! He's much too fond of you, they all are, but surely you see it's impossible I should ever go to court again."

"The Apraxins must have turned the Czar against you," said Aurora. "Really Princess Apraxin has behaved abominably! Her gossip has made a Petersburg scandal out of a silly girlish escapade which could easily have been hushed up. I'm going to write to Katie Karamsin and ask her to get the Czarina to intercede for you with His Majesty."

"Do you think Nikita ever listens to the Czarina? I don't!"

"Alix, please don't call the Czar 'Nikita'!"

The older woman looked at the girl in exasperation. So youthful in her plain white dress, so fragile with her delicate features and pale blond hair, and at the same time so difficult for the most affectionate hands to manage!

"What am I to do with you?" she said. "You talk as if everyone were in the wrong but you. And really, darling, you must take some blame for that foolish affair in Gothenburg."

Gravely: "I'm willing to take all the blame for that."

'You see, when your Aunt Kitty brought you here to me last month, I really thought that *she* had acted foolishly in hurrying you away from Sweden. Poor darling!"

"Don't, Aurora; don't 'poor-darling' her! It isn't fair to make fun of poor Aunt Kitty. She was so horribly shocked when I ran away from Karinlund."

"But now I know what the Apraxin family is making of it," Aurora went on, "I begin to see your Aunt Kitty's point of view. After all, there are other ways of ending an engagement than the one you chose! Boris was a better match than I ever hoped to make for you, but neither your father nor I would have forced you into the marriage if your heart was not

48

in it. Why didn't you confide in us? Why run away to sea under a false name, and get yourself rescued by Erik Kruse, of all men in the world? Erik Kruse, who made sure that everybody would hear of the night you spent alone among all those men on a foreign ship, so that Boris had no alternative but to break off the engagement himself—"

"Don't, Aurora!" She saw the girl blush furiously and bite her lips on a sob.

"Alex, are you grieving over Boris Apraxin? Shall I send for him to come to Helsingfors? I believe he would come willingly, if only his mother—"

"I never want to see Captain Apraxin again."

"Is there some other man? Darling, it isn't possible after all we've heard about him, that you've fallen in love with Erik Kruse?"

"I loathe him, and you know it!"

"But why are you blushing? Did anything happen to you aboard that boat?"

"Nothing happened . . . There was nothing but kindness, and protection—"

"Then why are you behaving like a girl in love?"

"Aurora, please don't go on scolding me!"

"I'm not scolding, I'm trying to find out. Is there really someone you prefer to Boris? Somebody you met in Sweden? Alix, do tell me. You know I'll try to help you if I can."

Silence.

"Is it the Mannerheim boy? He was very attentive to you last summer at Träskända."

"Carl-Robert? He's only a baby."

"Just a year younger than you are, my dear"—and Alexandra remembered too late that her godmother was six years older than Andrei Karamsin.

"He only came to talk about the future of Finland," she said hastily.

"That student nonsense," said Madame Karamsin distastefully. "But Carl-Robert is only your second cousin, after all. It might be a very good thing for both of you."

"The Apraxin fiasco hasn't cured you of matchmaking, I see."

Aurora smiled. Slowly, with expert fingers, she began a ritual which was very familiar to Alexandra. As another

woman might deal patience cards, she began to detach the
separate sprays of precious stones which made up her *kokósnik*
and lay them out on the low table: diamonds on diamonds,
emeralds on emeralds, rubies on rubies, until the surface was
nearly covered with the glittering and all but priceless gems.
Later, she would select certain jewels and rearrange them as
brooches or clips to wear at the reception which her stepfather
intended to give in honour of the official Finnish visitors from
St. Petersburg.

"I wish your father had accompanied the Czar," she said.

"Father is much too clever to court the kind of snub you
and I received this afternoon. Besides, he wouldn't dream
of leaving Madame Ourov to come to Helsingfors."

"What would the Mannerheims think of it, I wonder?"
Aurora disregarded the interruption. "We might stop at
Viborg and visit the young man's father on our way back to
Petersburg."

Alexandra's weakness had been mastered. There was no
trace of tears in her voice as she said:

"Once and for all, I am not going back to Petersburg."

"You heard what the Czar said, did you not?"

"I deny Nikita's right to order me back to Russia."

"Alix, you are *not* to call His Majesty 'Nikita'!"

"That was what your old friend Pushkin called him before
he died. Nikita! Nikita-the-Stick! The man has half a dozen
nicknames in Finland; do you happen to know what they call
him in Siberia?"

"He is your Emperor, Alexander."

"He is not."

"Very well, your Grand Duke, if you prefer it. But please
don't be melodramatic and—Finnish, now of all times!"

"Why *now*, especially?"

"Because the Czar is racked with anxiety about the war
with Turkey. So are we all."

"Why should a few dead Turks, or even dead Russians,
worry Nikita? He has plenty of corpses on his conscience
already."

"Alexandra!"

"Think of the men he slaughtered on his way to power.
Think of the December conspiracy! Nikita waded to the
throne then through the blood of Russians."

"That was nearly thirty years ago, before you were born or thought of."

"What does that matter? Nikita was alive, and he is still the Czar of Russia! Ryléyév died, so did his comrades, so did the regiments massacred in the Isaac Square because they wanted Constantine for Emperor instead of Nicholas. How many others were sent to the mines in Siberia? How many are still confined in the fortress of Peter and Paul because of what happened in December 1825?"

"The Czar was merciful to many of the conspirators. My own sister's husband was among those he pardoned."

"Oh, Aurora! You reduce everything to personal relationships and family ties!"

"Those are all that matter to a woman."

"Have the Romanovs held family ties so sacred?" Alix retorted. "Nikita's grandmother, the great Catherine, knew of the plot to kill her husband. Nikita's elder brother was an accomplice in the plot to murder their own father. Remember the walled-up room in the Michael Palace, which neither the Czar Alexander in his lifetime nor Nicholas now would ever dare to open, because it holds the secret of their father's death?"

"Where did you ever hear of such a horrible thing? Who told you about the Czar Paul's room in the Michael Palace?"

"These things are in the air of Petersburg. The tainted air, that the serfs breathe as they wait for their day of vengeance—"

"You're talking treason; be silent, Alexandra!"

"Are you afraid of spies in the Villa Hagasund?"

It seemed very likely, for Madame Karamsin started when a gentle knock was heard, and even Alix looked nervously over her shoulder as the door opened. But it was only the master of the house who entered, his rosy old face pinched with cold.

"Both together and still talking, my dears?" he said. "I thought you might be resting after the levée."

"We hardly expected you so soon, papa." His stepdaughter rose and laid her hand affectionately on the Senator's arm. "The privy council meeting must have been very short."

"Short and very serious. Will you both come into the parlour, please?"

The adjacent room, to which the old gentleman ushered them ceremoniously, was not one of the grand apartments of

Hagasund, but a pleasant family parlour full of Biedermeier furniture, with oil paintings of departed Stjernvalls and Willebrands and Mannerheims on every wall. There was a harp in one corner, and side tables arranged for tric-trac and dominoes, while in the centre of the room a round table holding an epergne filled with white narcissus was spread with albums of crayon and watercolour drawings. Without asking the ladies to be seated, Senator Walleen took his stand by this table and said gravely that he had very bad news to tell them.

"From the privy council? Oh, what is it, papa darling?" begged Aurora.

"Last night," said the old man, "an English officer named Captain Blackwood arrived in Helsingfors. A courier from the British government, carrying a message of great importance for the Czar. He had travelled overland from Königsberg to St Petersburg, and came here from the capital under escort; so it is quite inexplicable that he was not taken immediately to His Majesty, but allowed to proceed to the Society-house Hotel, as tranquilly as if he were at home in London."

"But what was in the message, Uncle Carl?" Alix said.

"I'm coming to the message," he said querulously. The girl realized that some point of protocol was involved, some grievance that the Finnish Senate had not been told of the courier's audience with the Czar, either before or after it took place at eight o'clock in the morning.

"The only information we received was that the Senate luncheon must be postponed until tomorrow. Much later, after the levée, we were told that the British government had issued an ultimatum to the Czar. The letter Captain Blackwood carried was nothing less than an order to Russia to withdraw all troops from the Danubian Principalities by the thirteenth of April. Exactly six weeks from now.'

"He will never consent!" cried Aurora Karamsin.

"His Majesty refused even to reply to such an ultimatum. The British envoy's instructions were to wait for six days, to give the Czar time to reflect upon his answer. He was told at once that the Czar of all the Russias disdained to parley with the British under a threat of war."

"Then Britain will fight Russia, then?" whispered Alexandra

"Britain is bound to declare war as soon as Captain Blackwood reaches London."

"And France?"

"The Emperor Napoleon III has issued a similar ultimatum."

"But what can the Western Powers *do*? Will this mean danger for André, papa?" asked Colonel Karamsin's wife.

"I hope not, my dear. In any case, it will be months before Britain and France can land troops at the Danube mouth by sea. And they must use the sea route by the Mediterranean; it is quite inconceivable that the Emperor of Austria should allow them to pass through Hungary."

"Not if he has any sense of gratitude," said Alix with a shrug. "After all, it's only a few years since Nikita helped the Emperor Franz Josef to put down the rising in Budapest, using cannon and bayonets against students armed with sticks—"

"Be quiet, child." The old Senator knew better than either woman what the declaration of war would bring. The Russian press censorship was strict in Helsingfors, but Walleen had access to commercial information, and the news of British preparations had been circulating freely along the Baltic shores. He was too old-fashioned to share such information with the ladies, even when Alix was scanning the newspapers and complaining that *Helsingfors Tidningar* contained nothing but the serial of Mr Topelius' latest historical romance. Now he knew the time had come to speak.

"The Danube front will be of less importance," he said. "The principal theatre of war will be the Baltic. Yes, Aurora, my poor girl, there is no help for it! A huge British squadron is ready and waiting to sail into the North Sea; the French will follow, and as soon as the ice breaks we can expect the enemies of Russia to appear off Hangö Head."

"And Finland will be free!" cried Alix Gyllenlöve.

The Senator looked at her incredulously.

"Free from whom?" he asked. "Free from what?"

"From Nikita and the tyranny of Russia."

"Alix, you're talking like a fool," said Walleen, more roughly than he had ever spoken to her. "Finland will be a battlefield. We shall be caught and crushed between two enemies, as we were fifty years ago. I went through the last war, like thousands of other Finlanders, and believe me, *we* were the ones who suffered most! It was *our* land that was ravaged—not Russia, not Sweden—and if the British invade the Grand

Duchy and attack the Russians on our soil, I tell you Finland will be destroyed again!"

"Suppose the Finnish regiments refuse to fight?" said Alexandra. "Suppose they think this is the time to rise for independence?"

"Independence? Spare me that nationalist folly! This is war, Alix! War, not literature; nothing to do with the poetry you and the Mannerheim boy were mooning over all last summer at Träskända—"

"As you encouraged us to do," she retorted. "You were the one who made us read the *Kalevala*, and study the Finnish language—"

"And a pretty sight it was to see you reading aloud to one another, and talking about Vainamöinen, and how Lemminkäinen ploughed the field of serpents. But it was only poetry, child, nothing to do with Finland today. Or with Finland tomorrow, when the British come—"

"It will be the British, then, who'll plough the field of serpents."

"Alix, think what you're saying," Aurora interrupted. "It's wrong and silly, and it's not very kind of you to argue with papa."

"But Finland is my country too," flashed Alix. "Uncle Carl, please don't be angry! Remember, you are one of those who used to tell us that young people must learn to think for themselves. Don't blame us now if you don't like what we think."

The shocked silence which followed was broken by the apologetic entrance of a maid.

"If you please, madame—"

"Verna, we are not to be disturbed—"

"Madame, a foreign gentleman has asked to see Mamsell Alix. He is waiting in the salon now."

"The French jeweller from Alexander Street, come about packing up the wedding presents," said Aurora. "I forgot we arranged for him to call today. You had better have a word with him, darling, but don't decide anything in a hurry, there is no need to send back the Apraxin jewels yet. And do get rid of him quickly! Our guests will be arriving in half an hour."

"Very well," said Alexandra.

She was glad to get out of the room before worse things were said, and Aurora could always be counted on to change the subject. As she shut the door Alix could hear the sweet plaintive voice begin, "You don't think we ought to cancel the reception, papa darling?" and her lips twisted in a smile. Neither the dread of war, nor danger, was likely to come between Aurora Karamsin and any social occasion, even a gathering of elderly men like the quiet soirée planned at the Villa Hagasund. Aurora would rest for half an hour, and rearrange her jewels and her beautiful dark hair, and then sail in ready to charm them all.

Alix, at twenty, felt no need of rest. The expression of her hatred of the Czar and his country, and the news of the British ultimatum, had sent a tide of energy flowing through her body. She would have liked to get her cloak and fur-lined boots and creep out of the house now, hurrying down the Åbo road in the deep ruts the sleighs made in the snow, back to the city. She would have liked to prowl along the Market Square, round the railings of the Imperial Palace, thinking of the Autocrat within, and the ukases falling from his pen as he signed the orders which would make the whole ponderous machine of empire aware that Britain had flung down the gauntlet to the Czar. With impatience, she saw a crack of light beneath the salon door. In her excited state she loathed the very idea of discussing the return of her wedding gifts with the jeweller from Alexander Street.

Yet the man had walked some distance through the snow, and must be seen. She braced herself to get the task over and done with quickly. Everything was to go back, and at once, whatever Aurora said! Alix touched the pearls at her throat. They at least were her own, part of her very few valuable possessions. She opened the door—and saw Brand Endicott.

The house servants, who had not grasped Brand's foreign name, had hesitated to show a gentleman so tall and self-assured to the small room usually reserved for tradesmen and messengers. Brand had been taken straight to the salon, large enough to be known as the banqueting hall of the Villa Hagasund, where a long table had already been draped with white damask and adorned with hot-house flowers for the expected guests. Silk curtains drawn across the three long windows shut out a desolate view over the creek, but the lamps were not yet lit on the gold-inlaid console tables between the windows, and the corners of the big room were in shadow. Through the pool of light under the chandelier Alix came to Brand like some clouded spirit of the snow.

Then her hand was in his, was flesh and blood, and he bowed over it with the foolish words:

"Your servant, Miss Larsson! I hope I see you well?"

"Captain Endicott!" He saw that she was shocked, and taken completely unaware. But she had the dignity to say, almost without hesitation:

"I am very glad to see you again. I have thought about you, many times. Since you have found your way here, you must know that my name is not Anna Larsson. I am Alix Gyllen-löve."

"I do know it, and I ask your pardon for a clumsy joke. You may call yourself by any name you please, for me. I came to Finland only to enquire for you and assure myself that you were safe and among friends."

"I don't understand," she said. "How did you know where to find me? Is the *Girdleness* at Åbo?"

"The *Girdleness* may be at the bottom of the sea for all I know," Brand said roughly. It was how he had meant to talk to her, putting her in the wrong, making her realize what his championship of her had cost him, but already he was weakening under the spell of her presence and her remembered charm. She looked so different with her hair dressed high, and her bare neck, on which the necklace Brand thought of as a string of beads was hardly visible against so white a skin, but she was still the girl of Marstrand and the Stone Pier, and Brand Endicott could no more blame her for his misfortunes than he could have left her, that February night to pass the hours till daylight in the shadow of the island fortress. He said in a quieter tone:

"I found your friend Carl Larsson out at Kungälv, and we had a talk. Well—talk—it wasn't quite that, we just did our best with the few words we had in common, but he told me you were with Madame Karamsin at Helsingfors. When I arrived from Åbo in the post cart today it was quite easy to learn that she was at the Villa Hagasund."

"Yes, of course, everybody knows . . . How is Carl?"

One of the replies he had prepared for such a question was: "None the better for his day in the stocks at Gothenburg!"

But he couldn't look into those pleading grey eyes and get it out. He said:

"Quite well, and he sent you his best respects always, at least that's what I think he said. But our talk, such as it was, was a good deal interrupted. There was a fat trollop in the room with us most of the time who kept telling him to be quiet. Svea, he called her."

"That's Carl's daughter-in-law. He hates her. It was Svea who told Erik Kruse where we had gone, that night."

"I'd like to know more about Erik Kruse."

"It was he who—who took me back to Karinlund from Gothenburg."

"And got me arrested and sent to jail next day."

"You mean you went to *prison*?"

"For ten days."

"But—that's the most horrible thing that could possibly happen to anybody! Oh, Captain Endicott, how can I ask you to forgive me?"

"Forgive *you*! I can't forgive myself for not taking better care of you. I ought to have kept you aboard, taken you across to Denmark or even Scotland rather than let you fall into that man's hands. Did he treat you properly, at least? Take you straight back to the lady at Karinlund?"

"Carl told you about Aunt Kitty?"

"I couldn't understand all he said, you know."

Alix sighed. "You deserve to know the truth about all of us. But please tell me first what you meant about your ship. Is it possible that you are no longer her captain?"

"I was relieved of my command after I was sent to jail," Brand told her grimly, and Alix gasped.

"But how monstrous! You did nothing wrong."

"I was even paid for what I did."

He had the brooch in his pocket. He had meant to return it to her gracefully, but the bitter little speech with the prison taint upon it came out in spite of himself. He saw with remorse that he had shocked her deeply.

"I want to thank you very much for giving me this," he said, and put the heavy golden leaves on their diamond stem into her cold hand. "You surely know I can't keep anything so costly. I ask you, please, to take it back again."

She looked up at him, and her eyes revealed the deep trouble and division of spirit which Brand had begun to realize in Alix Gyllenlöve.

"I knew it was the wrong gift for a man," she said. "But you refused money for the passage, and I had very little else to give away. I thought you might like to have my brooch for a keepsake . . . and give it some day to the girl you love."

"Will you keep it for me till I find her?"

"If you wish." Alix turned the golden brooch in her fingers, and the diamond dewdrops sparkled in the candlelight.

"When you first saw me at Marstrand," she said abruptly, "I was running away from my aunt's house, Countess Kruse's house; the old Gyllenlöve manor, where my ancestors lived two hundred years ago before they left Sweden to settle in Finland."

Brand nodded.

"Aunt Kitty married Count Kruse as his second wife. By his first marriage he had one son, Erik, who was brought up by his mother's family in Prussia. She was a Fraülein Müller, one of a wealthy shipping family in Lübeck."

"But now he lives at Karinlund?"

"Erik? He's an officer in the Swedish Life Guards, seconded to the Third Military District at Gothenburg. His stepmother—Aunt Kitty—is very fond of him. He is at Karinlund as often as he can get leave."

"Hoping to be the lord of the manor some day?"

Bitterly: "If that happened every one of the tenants would emigrate to the United States! They hate him for his overbearing ways; and there was a terrible scandal last year over a country girl who drowned herself in the Nordre river after he seduced her. But the farmers have one consolation—the estate is entailed on my father. And that, of course, is the reason for Erik's pursuit of me."

"Is he a poor man?"

"Oh no! His Prussian relatives are extremely rich. He thinks it stylish to be in the Guards, and pose as the heir to Karinlund, but actually he has an interest in the shipping company, Müllers of Lübeck. He got Aunt Kitty to invest money in some of his schemes, she thinks he's a wonderful business man."

"And was it to escape Captain Kruse's attention that you ran away with an old servant for bodyguard?"

"A servant whom Erik made Aunt Kitty dismiss from the

manor, by the way. No, I didn't run away from Erik Kruse. I wanted to put an end to a marriage engagement I had formed—in Russia."

"You changed your mind about the gentleman?"

"My mind was made up for me by my godmother and my father. But when I went to spend Christmas in Sweden, and could go wherever I pleased—through the woods to Kungälv, and over in the boat to Marstrand with Carl, quite often—and felt the free wind blowing from the west, then I—then I—"

The American looked compassionately at her quivering mouth. To go wherever he pleased had always been his own idea of freedom. But he had been in prison recently; he dimly understood this girl's captivity.

"So then you came back to Madame Karamsin," he said slowly. "Is she going to make up your mind for you again?"

"She would like to make up my engagement with Captain Apraxin. But—look at her portrait—Madame Karamsin is too kind and gentle to force anyone."

The picture she indicated, painted by Perignon of St Petersburg in the previous year, hung on the shadowed wall above the grand piano. Brand was aware of blue eyes and a cloud of dark hair, rows of pearls on a white bosom, and an impression of lace draperies and flowers.

"What a lovely creature!" he said impulsively.

"What a delightful thing to overhear about oneself!"

Aurora Karamsin spoke from the doorway, smiling and gracious as Brand and Alix turned towards her, and Alix quickly presented "Captain Endicott, my rescuer at Marstrand."

"The maids told me a strange gentleman had come," said Aurora, giving Brand her hand. "You are no stranger here, sir! We are all grateful to you for your kindness to Alyssa Ivanovna."

But why did she call me by my Russian name? There was a small core of resentment beneath the excitement in Alexandra's heart as the salon, now brilliantly lighted, filled quickly with Senator Walleen's guests and the reception began. Alyssa Ivanovna—it was the Petersburg form of address, quite out of place in Helsingfors; yet this, of course, was a gathering

59

transplanted from St. Petersburg to the ballroom of the Villa Hagasund. The guests of honour were members of the Finnish Committee, which nominally represented the Grand Duchy in the Russian capital. With this Committee Madame Karamsin had been connected since, as an orphaned child of eight, she had gone to live for the first time in St. Petersburg, when Count Rehbinder was the Finnish Secretary. Now, while disclaiming any political influence ("women have nothing to do with politics, Alix darling") Aurora, with her charm and her colossal wealth, had become one of the great conciliators between Russia and Finland.

Alix, as she moved among the guests, saw how well Aurora was managing the company on this difficult evening of the British ultimatum to Russia. She was mixing the Finns from Petersburg adroitly with the gentlemen from Helsingfors, those members of the Art Union and the Literary Society who were behind the Grand Duchy's dawning nationalism, and somehow steering both sides away from controversial topics, while introducing the American guest to all those who could converse with him in English. Alix thought Brand Endicott was managing very well too.

He was obviously charmed by Aurora. No young man had ever resisted that tilted head, that appealing smile, but Brand was not bowled over by the older woman. Over and over again Alix saw his dark blond head turning towards herself and his eyes searching for her own. She saw to it that his glass was kept filled with champagne. Helsingfors society had moved on in forty years from the card parties, the refreshments of herrings, apples and ölust of its simple beginnings, to champagne and a "cold table" spread with every kind of delicacy; but it was still essentially informal, and young ladies were expected to offer food and drink and be active in the entertainment of their guests. As Alix moved from group to group she heard Brand manfully answering the questions of a Senator who wanted to know America's attitude to the Russian War, and felt proud that the skipper of the jersey and the rough pea jacket should look so well, speak out so well, in the complex world to which he had followed her. She was about to rescue him from the Senator and introduce him to one of the few ladies present, when she heard the butler announce:

"Captain Erik Kruse."

With a gasp, Alix looked at Brand. She saw that he had heard the name, although the servant had not spoken loudly, and few of the guests looked in the direction of the door. Senator Walleen, deaf and worried, was certainly unaware of the new arrival; it was Madame Karamsin alone who swept, before Kruse could enter the ballroom, to intercept him at the door.

"Good evening, Captain Kruse," she said with ice in her tones. "Will you be good enough to come this way?"

Alix was by her side, and Brand a step behind, as Madame Karamsin led Captain Kruse into the parlour where the old Senator had spoken to the two women of the coming war. There, in the lamplight, Brand for the first time studied his adversary of the Stone Pier, while Alexandra's hand lay on his arm restrainingly, and the Swedish officer looked at them all with narrowed eyes.

Kruse was in ordinary evening dress, which he wore well, for the formal black and white suited his red hair and pale complexion, and he carried himself like a soldier. At the moment he was clearly surprised by Madame Karamsin's swift removal of himself from the general company; he was biting his lip as he said,

"I trust my visit is not inconvenient, madame. I wished merely to pay my respects to you and Senator Walleen, and of course to enquire after my charming cousin Alexandra."

"The Senator and I are engaged this evening," said Aurora. "Miss Gyllenlöve thanks you for your solicitude."

"What ill wind blows you to Finland, Erik?" Alix asked.

He turned towards her eagerly. "I'm on leave, Alix," he said. "I'm on my way to Russia for a bear hunt .When do you return to Petersburg?"

"When can I have a word with you alone?" said Brand.

Madame Karamsin turned round sharply. "Captain Endicott!" she said. "I had no idea—I—we have family matters to discuss."

"Forgive me, ma'am," said Brand, "I've been anxious to meet Captain Kruse again. Our last encounter was on the Stone Pier at Gothenburg—"

"Really?" said Kruse with a smile. "Are you the man I saw taken up for brawling with the Watch, when I and my brother officers were escorting Miss Gyllenlöve to her home?"

"Brawling with the *Watch*!" said Brand. "Fighting with *you*, you mean! When will you meet me, sir, and where?"

"I am a guest at the Imperial Palace," said Erik Kruse. "Do you think you are likely to have the entrée there?"

Brand took a step forward. In the mocking face before him he saw personified all his bad luck, all his resentment: it was on the tip of his tongue to cry "Coward!" and follow it up with a blow. But Madame Karamsin stepped between them, with the ease of one accustomed to Russian after-dinner quarrels, and said tranquilly:

"You have made enough trouble for Alix, Captain Kruse; there shall be no more scandal while she is in my care. Captain Endicott, I know you are a man of honour; prove it by returning to the salon with Miss Gyllenlöve and waiting for me there. No guest is ever allowed to leave this house without refreshment, so my son Paul shall play host to Captain Kruse."

. . . "Isn't she clever?" breathed Alix when they were back in the crowded salon. "Taking Erik to the school room—the most snubbing thing she could possibly do—"

"Too clever for me by half," said Brand grimly. "It means that Kruse has got away again, that's all."

"From you?"

"Yes, from me. But I'll find him in Helsingfors—"

"Oh, please, please don't go after him and make more trouble for me!"

Brand looked at her, and the red mist of rage cleared from his eyes. They were right, of course, he couldn't make a row in the Villa Hagasund, and she had been in trouble enough already. He said:

"I've got to talk to you about all this."

"Tomorrow—there will be another soirée, and I know the Senator will invite you to come back—"

"Not in a crowd like this! Can't I see you here, or anywhere, alone?"

They were alone now, as if they were back in the cabin of the *Girdleness*, though the Senator's guests were moving round them, coming up to the buffet table and going away with filled plates, and the servants were bringing fresh bottles of champagne. Alix said, beneath the sound of the party:

"Tomorrow there's the Senate luncheon for the Czar. I could go out while they're getting ready for it and meet you in the town. Do you know the Stone of the Empress in the Market Square?"

"I'll find it."

"There about eleven o'clock. Here comes Aurora!"

Madame Karamsin entered alone. She spoke to a number of guests before taking any notice of Brand and Alix.

"Did you leave Erik in the school room?" said the girl with a nervous laugh.

"Captain Kruse left almost at once, Alix darling," said Aurora tranquilly. "He recollected a previous engagement."

Brand, too, was prepared to leave almost at once. But his formal adieux took time, his farewell to Alix was lingering, and the servants were strangely slow in finding his coat and overboots. When at last he left the house the snow was falling. He looked up and down the road which led from Åbo into Helsingfors. All marks made by sleigh runners had been obliterated; there was no trace, between the Villa Hagasund and the city, of the passage of Erik Kruse.

CHAPTER FOUR

HELP FROM A STRANGER

WHEN the light fell across Brand's face he thought he was back in the remand cell at Gothenburg, with Sven Svensson bending over him, and the candle flickering on the table. He sighed, and pressed his fists into his eyes, but a rough hand shook him by the shoulder, a voice spoke his name, and he became aware that he was lying in his hotel bed at Helsingfors.

"What's the matter? Who the hell are you?" he said.

His eyes were dazzled by a powerful lantern. He seized the hand that held it and swung the light aside. There were three men in the room, two by his bedside, one at the door; and when the third man spoke he recognized the voice of the night clerk.

"Mr. Endicott, it is the Russian security officers. They wish to question you."

"In the middle of the night?"

"It is morning, sir; you have been sleeping well."

"I locked my door," said Brand, "You must have used a pass key."

"It is the regulation, sir," said the hotel man nervously. "Please do not make any difficulties."

"It's only ten to five," said Brand, who had found his watch beneath the pillow. "Why the devil can't they ask their questions at a rational hour?"

"Mr. Endicott—" began the Russian holding the lamp.

"Let me get some clothes on, will you?" said Brand, pushing him aside. He got out of bed; the room was icy cold. He put on his trousers, pulled his belt tight, and closed the open window. As the clerk slipped thankfully into the corridor, Brand drew the curtains and lit the candles on the dressing table. The added light reduced the shock effect of the lantern and allowed him to see the Russians better.

They were tall men in heavy greatcoats, which seemed to be of civilian cut and yet had the appearance of uniform, with flat anonymous faces beneath fur hats without insignia. The man who held the lantern was apparently the leader. He now set it down, unfolded some papers he carried in his free hand, and drew up a chair to Brand's writing table as coolly as if he were in the office of some government building.

"Now sir!" he began in slow but correct English, "are you ready to give me your attention?"

Brand sprawled in the room's one easy-chair and said casually, "Go ahead."

Reading from the papers: "You registered at this hotel as Mr. Brand Endicott. When did you arrive in Helsingfors?"

"Yesterday afternoon."

"Why did you fail to surrender your passport to the hotel keeper?"

"I have no passport."

The Russians conferred in a whisper, the second man bending over the other's chair.

"Where did you enter the Grand Duchy of Finland?"

"At Åbo, I suppose."

"You *suppose*! From what port did you travel to Åbo?"

"Stockholm."

"Direct?"

"By the mail boat via the Åland Islands."

"Which boat?"

"The *Eckerö*."

"Ah. Then you made a call at Degerby?"

"Yes."

"You went ashore?"

"Certainly. I spent the night at the village inn."

"Are you aware that the islands are in the Czar's dominions?"

"I hadn't thought about it."

"The Åland Islands are an integral part of the Grand Duchy of Finland. Did you produce your passport at the inn at Degerby?"

"I have no passport," Brand said patiently.

"You realize it is a serious offence for an Englishman to enter Russian territory without a permit?"

"It may well be," said Brand. "But I happen to be an American citizen."

Another whispered conference. Then: "When did you arrive at Åbo?"

"Two days ago. I mean three now."

"Did you produce your passport to the hotel keeper at Åbo?"

"I wasn't asked for it."

"So! Now you admit to possession of a passport!"

"Just wait a minute," said Brand. He had been more tired the night before than he would admit to himself; and was heavily asleep when the security officers entered, but he was wide awake now, and alert to all the repetitious questioning and the deliberate attempt to confuse him. "I didn't admit to having a passport," he said. "I wasn't asked for one because I didn't go to any hotel when I got to Åbo. I left for Helsingfors at once in the post wagon. I signed my name in the day-book at every post house, as I was told the law requires, but I can't produce a passport because I'm an American citizen and nobody told me I had to have a bit of paper to prove my right to go anywhere I liked in Europe."

"You say you are not an Englishman?"

"I tell you I'm an American."

"Can you produce any proof of citizenship?"

Brand had anticipated the question. He got up and took his wallet from beneath his pillow. In it was the letter of credit from Tarras and Company, which implied that he was still in the pay of a British shipping company, and also the master mariner's certificate he had obtained in the United States. He abstracted it quickly, thrust the wallet with the letter of credit into his hip pocket, and handed the certificate to the Russians.

He saw that they were impressed.

"You see," he said, "I *am* an American. My country is not at war with yours, nor ever likely to be. And if my citizen rights are called in question, I'm prepared to take the matter up with our Minister at St. Petersburg."

The interrogator, after a word with his colleague, was more conciliatory.

"We accept your statement that you are an American, Mr. Endicott. But you will appreciate that all foreigners in Helsingfors are under special surveillance during the visit of His Imperial Majesty. In your case, we require to know what brought you into Finland at this time?"

"Private business."

"Be more explicit, if you please."

"It concerns Senator Walleen," Brand was inspired to say, "I shall attend his reception at the Villa Hagasund tonight."

After this there was a longer confabulation, in which

Brand heard the word *Czarevich* whispered more than once. Finally the interrogator took a fresh sheet of paper from his documents, and dipped a pen in the hotel inkwell.

"Very good," he said. "I am prepared to issue an exit permit, allowing you to remain in Helsingfors until tomorrow. For renewal you will apply to police headquarters. This permit must be stamped by every postmaster along your way and surrendered at the Customs House at Åbo before you sail. Is that quite clear?"

"I guess so," said Brand. He made no effort to take the paper, and gave only a bored nod to the two Russians as they bowed curtly and went out. Then, in one bound, he was at the window, the candles extinguished before he drew aside the heavy rep curtain to look down at the street. It was half past five now and still completely dark, but lamps were being lighted round the harbour buildings, and the Imperial Palace, seen diagonally across the square, was ablaze with light. In the illumination from the open door of his hotel he saw a file of soldiers waiting, at ease, blowing on their hands and stamping in the snow. The two security officers emerged from the hotel. The men came to attention, fell in behind them, and marched off towards the town. It occurred to Brand, as he let the fold of curtain fall, that it was exactly the size of escort suited to conducting a refractory prisoner to the guard-house. He wondered if he owed the visit of the security officers to Erik Kruse.

*   *   *

He was in the Market Square long before the time appointed by Alexandra Gyllenlöve. It was extremely cold and no day for loitering, but he was uneasy in the hotel now, where he had the feeling of being under surveillance, and eager to lose himself among the ordinary people of the town. They were in the Market Square by the hundred, far outnumbering the Russian hucksters in their gaudy blouses and dirty white trousers, whose pushcarts were lined up on the outskirts of the market. The solid market stalls were set up in rows in front of the Stone of the Empress, which was conspicuous in the middle of the Square: a tall obelisk of granite surmounted by the Russian eagle, and commemorating, an inscription ran, the present Czarina's first visit to Finland some twenty years before. On either side of the Stone, from the harbour steps where wildfowl were clamouring for food to the very gates of the palace, the country-folk were selling root vegetables, eggs and butter, wooden boxes and osier baskets, and the thrifty housewives of the town were thronging in to buy.

Brand walked along the avenues between the stalls. He studied the South Harbour, which was reopened to local traffic, and the low irregular line of islands visible at about two miles' distance, which a waterman told him was the fortress, Sveaborg. Then he retraced his steps, and explored the streets on each side of the Esplanade garden up to Engel's beautiful neo-classical theatre, walking on as far as the handsome houses on Bulevarden. It was an easy city for a stranger to learn, the streets being laid out in parallels and clearly named in Russian and Swedish on heavy wooden squares affixed to every corner. It was also beautiful and strange, and Brand, who knew nothing about architecture, instinctively felt pleasure in those perfect harmonies which Ehrenström had planned and Engel executed in so a short a space of time. He walked back in rising excitement towards the Stone of the Empress. The Esplanade neighbourhood was very crowded now, and Cossack patrols had begun to make their appearance. Brand remembered the Senate luncheon for the Czar and wondered if Alix would have trouble in getting in from the Villa Hagasund.

There was a little flower market at the foot of the Esplanade where all the colour of Helsingfors seemed to be concentrated. Here the stalls took the form of small boxes on high legs, with glass fronts, behind which the flowers were protected from the cold by lighted candles. Under the grey skies and the leafless trees of the Esplanade the tiny points of light, dimmed by the frost skeins on the glass, gave a separate and touching charm to the poor pots of crocuses and snowdrops and the more costly tulips and daffodils which were sold in bunches of two or three blooms. Brand looked on with interest and growing sympathy. The Finnish women going home with a few winter vegetables and some coarse fish in their plaited baskets were obviously poor, and clumsily dressed in their thick wadmal clothes and printed kerchiefs. Yet the instinct for beauty was so strong in them that if only half a kopeck was left in their purses they were willing to spend it on one flower—only one —to carry Spring into a winter room.

One Finlander had freesias for sale. These were the most

expensive flowers on display, and few persons bought; Brand particularly noticed the man's good-tempered, broad face, and the pleasant word he gave even to those who shook their heads and bought nothing. He was tall and very fair, of a type more common in Western Finland than here in Helsingfors— Alexandra's type of looks, in a rough, masculine variety— and just as Brand made that comparison, he saw Alix Gyllen- löve herself.

She was walking rapidly towards the Empress Stone, so that he had to hurry to catch up with her, and her quick look of pleasure when she saw him, so different from the stunned face of her greeting at the Villa, was so exciting that Brand nearly kissed her there in the unromantic setting of the potato stalls. Alexandra was wearing a long cloak, and a large hood of fox fur shading from cream to russet, so close-fitting that not one lock of fair hair could be seen: it made a barbaric setting for so delicate a face. She slipped her hand confidently through the arm Brand offered and let him pilot her through the crowd to the foot of the Esplanade garden.

"Where shall we go?" he said. "People seem to be having coffee and cakes in that little restaurant. Would it be per- missible for me to take you there?"

"Oh—I don't think so." Alix considered the little Kappelli café at the foot of the Esplanade. "So many people will gather there to see the Czar go by. Do you think we might go for a short drive instead, perhaps on the road round the bay?"

"As long a drive as you like," said Brand. He looked about him eagerly for a sleigh.

"My maid will go with us, of course. Come here, Anna!"

A squat, small person, whom Brand had scarcely noticed, moved forward to curtsy to the American. He looked down at a tanned, high-cheekboned face, with irregular teeth and deepset eyes, which might have belonged to a woman of any age. Anna wore a short-skirted garment of black cloth and a small scarlet cloth bonnet. Several neck shawls fastened with a brass brooch added to her unusual appearance.

"Anna comes from Lapland," Alix said, "but she has learned to speak Swedish quite well."

"Goddag, Anna," said Brand. The woman grinned and bobbed her head.

"Your Swedish is quite fluent now," Alix said demurely,

and Brand laughed and pressed her hand against his side. It was wonderful to see mischief and laughter in her face, as he remembered it at the moment in the *Girdleness* when she asked if he thought she was eloping with old Carl. Exhilarated, he helped her into the sleigh which drew up beside the kerb and then gave a hand to the Lapp woman, who sat down opposite them with her back to the horses.

"I know now what you did when you ran away to Marstrand," said Brand as they left the Market Square behind. "You borrowed Anna's name and Carl's."

Alix smiled and did not deny it. "Poor Anna Larsson," she said, "she wasn't fated to live long."

"Don't say that, for heaven's sake"

"Why not? Are you superstitious?"

"I've known a good many sailors who were."

"And scared of having Lapps and Finns aboard?"

"We're not at sea now. Look, there's my hotel."

"I know it, of course; that's where balls and luncheons are held now that everybody in Helsingfors is so rich and important. Do you find it comfortable?"

"I thought it was, until about five o'clock this morning, when I had two unexpected visitors."

He saw the brightness drain from Alexandra's face. She said, only shaping the words with her lips, "Russians? Interrogation?" and at his nod indicated the driver, hunched up on his box like a bundle of rags topped by a moth-eaten caracul hat.

"Do look back and admire the view of Helsingfors," she said aloud. "The waterfront is said to look especially fine from here."

"It's a beautiful city," Brand agreed. "Is it your birthplace, by any chance?"

"I was born at Ekenäs, when my father was in the government of Nyland province. But I was a parlour-boarder at Miss Harring's school here, and we had a rented house on the North Esplanade for several winters . . . This is the Ulrikasborg hill and that's the Observatory on top of it."

"Why is the fellow stopping?" Brand exclaimed, as the driver brought the sleigh to a halt.

"We can't go further than the Brunnspark bathhouse. The Russian Army is constructing a new gun emplacement just beyond the point."

It was then that Brand Endicott, all unaware, took his first step towards a war in which he had never quite believed as a reality. It had been predicted for so long, and by now he had discussed it with so many chance-met strangers, that a war between Russia and the West had begun to belong to the realm of fantasy. But "the gun emplacement just beyond the point"—that was reality. He said to Alix, in tones as matter of fact as her own:

"Will it be too cold for you to walk in the park?"

"Of course not." She spoke to her maid and the driver, and allowed Brand to help her down. The Well Park slopes were covered with snow, but one broad pathway had been swept quite clear, and so had narrower paths leading between spruce and birch trees to the gates of handsome new houses, shuttered and silent in their wintry gardens.

"I can remember when all this hill was covered with wild roses, before St. Petersburg people thought of building summer villas here," said Alix. "'Little Russia' would be a good name for Brunnsparken now! . . . Tell me about your early morning visitors."

He told her as they slowly climbed the path. There was no one to overhear them, and they heard no sound except faint echoes from the Russian construction work, where sites were being burned out of the frozen ground for the new artillery emplacement. At the end of Brand's story Alix said positively:

"These men were from the *Tretié Otdelenié*—the Third Bureau in Count Orlov's Secret Department of Police. They didn't ask to see your baggage?"

"No."

"They're probably ransacking it at the hotel just now."

"There isn't much to ransack."

"No books? . . . Good," said Alix as the American shook his head. "The T.O. take their orders from Nikita, and Nikita hates and fears books and ideas . . . It was clever of you to tell the T.O. men you were visiting Senator Walleen."

"I've been worried about that," said Brand. "But the Senator was very pleasant to me yesterday, and he did invite me to come back tonight ... I took a chance it would be all right."

"It was very clever," she repeated. "Uncle Carl is a close friend of the Grand Duke Alexander, and everyone in the Third Bureau wants to stand well with the future Czar."

"Will the Grand Duke be at Senator Walleen's tonight?"

Smiling: "Heaven forbid! The Villa isn't big enough to hold his bodyguard. But the secret police will watch for you to be there, and if you're not—"

"You make it all sound very dangerous."

"It *is* dangerous. Much more so than the dear old Senator realizes. That's what I want to explain to you, why I thought we ought to meet this morning. You've been in trouble once because of me, and you may be in worse trouble still unless you understand Uncle Carl's point of view, and that of the men you meet in his house. They are *good* men, all of them— please be sure of that! But they, the Senator and his friends, they're old men. When they were young, after the last war, they honestly thought they were doing the best thing for Finland by taking service under the Russians. And it's true that in the days of the Czar Alexander, there was some hope that Russia would honour the treaty and give us a Diet—a Congress—of our own. But now they're afraid of the future, just as Nikita has been afraid since 1848, when there were seven revolutions in Continental Europe. They're afraid of the university students, and of all young folk; they're afraid of a liberal Emperor like Napoleon III; they're terribly afraid of change. They don't want to believe what all of us young people know, that the whole Russian Empire is covered with a network of espionage, and that Nikita rules by imprisonment and torture from the Black Sea to the Bering Straits!"

Alix stopped short in the middle of the path, and her gloved hand was clenched upon Brand's arm. Brand looked down at her. The image she held before him was precisely that which he had already formed of Europe: a cockpit of small nations eternally at each other's throats or torn by revolution, or else kow-towing to some tyrant like the British Lion or the Russian Bear. It was detestable, and yet of this girl's truth and sincerity there was no doubt. Conviction was written on that young face with the stormy grey eyes, and the stern mouth he longed to melt with kisses.

"You really hate the Russians, don't you?" he said slowly.

"Yes."

"Is that because of the man you were engaged to, and changed your mind about?" said Brand.

"Oh! You're as bad as Aurora Karamsin!" said Alix furiously. She withdrew her hand and stepped away from him, so near to the evergreens fringing the path that a light sprinkling of snow was shaken from the boughs behind her head and whitened the creamy fox that framed her face.

"Why do you want to reduce what one feels—feels about one's country, to—just personalities? It is *not* because of Boris Apraxin that I hate Russia! It is because I hate Russia that I couldn't go through with my marriage to him! I spent a year in St. Petersburg before I went to Aunt Kitty at Karinlund. Then I began to realize I couldn't condemn myself to a whole lifetime in Russia. Yes, that's how I thought of it: a condemnation . . . Captain Endicott, I lay awake for hours last night, thinking that you went to prison because of me—"

"Not because of you," said Brand, "because of Erik Kruse. And I'll pay him out for that some day."

Her eyes gleamed. "You can hate too?—I'm glad. Well, when you think of prison, think of me. If I had to go back to Russia I should be going back to a land where my own country counts for nothing, the land which enslaved Poland and destroyed freedom in Hungary as completely as thought and free speech have been destroyed in the Russian Empire. For me it would be prison—that is all."

"Prison to go back to your father's house?" said Brand. "He is an official in the Russian service, I've been told."

"Whoever told you that was telling lies!" she said fiercely. "He represents Finnish interests at Petersburg. He became personal assistant to Count Armfelt, the Minister-Secretary of State for Finland, just over a year ago."

"And since then you've had a home in St. Petersburg?" persisted Brand.

"My father's apartment on the Nevsky Prospekt? Yes, I suppose you could call it a home. In fact I was a great deal with Madame Karamsin. And I'm too fond of Aurora to tell her that I came to feel such a—loathing of Russian life, everyday life that is, while I was living in her house. Because Aurora herself is kind and honest. Her whole life has been built on ties with Russia, but at least she uses her wealth and power to do good to others, while her Petersburg friends think only of clothes and jewels, and ignore the poverty at their very doors. That life would stifle me—I can't go back to it."

"What do you plan to do then?" asked Brand Endicott. "Start out again for the United States?"

"I suppose I deserve that from you," said Alix, pale. "You knew quite well we were no emigrants."

"Yes, I knew that all along," said Brand gently. "But you were planning to cross to England, certainly. Where after that?"

"I thought of going to my older sister, who lives in London. She is married to a man in the Swedish Legation there. But I wasn't sure . . . Kristina has been unwell since her little girl was born, and my brother-in-law is a cold, unsympathetic person . . . Only it seemed worth trying—then."

Alexandra's head came up defiantly.

"Erik Kruse did me a good turn when he stopped me from going abroad," she said. "Now I'll be in my own country when the war begins. I'll be here to share in Finland's struggle!"

"Listen, Alexandra," said Brand, and stopped. It was the first time he had used her Christian name, and under extraordinary circumstances—almost as if he were arguing with a man. "Do you really believe the Finns will join with Britain against Russia? I don't know much about what happened in Poland or in Hungary, but do you honestly think your country is suffering as a Russian Grand Duchy? I've only been in Finland for three days. I've seen the secret police in action and they handled me a good deal better than the Gothenburg Watch. Upon my word I've seen no sign of cruelty or oppression! What I have seen is good roads, fine farms, good shops and houses, a beautiful modern city and a land at peace. If you really cared for Finland you would be praying that the war might never start—"

"Why?"

"Because it's easier to start a war than stop it."

"Now you sound like last night's guests at Hagasund," she said angrily. "They were all lamenting, 'Woe to Finland! Remember the Great Wrath that fell upon us when Sweden challenged Russia! Compromise, conciliate, live at peace!' . . . That's what the old men say. Is it so hard for an American to understand that the youth of a nation can be ready to fight for independence—as you did?"

He could hardly tell her that American independence was something he took for granted, something fought for and won long before his time, and associated in his mind chiefly with a steel engraving of *Washington Crossing the Delaware* in the parlour of the old Brand house in Portland.

"All that was eighty years ago," he said.

"Your yesterday is our today," said Alix Gyllenlöve. "Oh, Captain Endicott, you have no idea how I envy you!"

"Because I'm an American?"

"Because you're a man. You can take part in this war, you can join the British and fight the Russians—not like me."

Brand stared at her.

"You European ladies are a ferocious lot," he said. "My grandmother wanted me to join the British Navy, and now you—"

"The Navy!" she exulted. "Certainly, the Royal Navy—the squadron they say will come into the Baltic. Oh, if I only were a man! Oh, for the day when the British Fleet appears off Sveaborg!"

Brand turned and looked out to sea. Beyond the rocks fringing the shore road the waters of the bay stretched wide and desolate, the ice breaking up into strange shapes, circles within circles like the petals of frozen water lilies fretting against the smaller islands lying near the land. The fortress, at which Alix was pointing, was visible only in part, but the arsenal on West Svartö was clearly seen, and the cupola of the Greek Orthodox church stood out from the barrack complex on the Great East Svartö island.

"Are those the forts?" said Brand. "I saw them earlier from the Market Square."

"That is Sveaborg," Alix answered.

"Can it be taken? They say Cronstadt can never be taken."

"God knows," said Alix bitterly. "The Russians took Sveaborg fifty years ago by treachery."

"They must keep a huge garrison there," said Brand. The fortified islands within his field of vision seemed to waver as the mist came down over the water. In the pewter-coloured light he saw the glint of giant muzzles in the distant casemates.

"Four thousand men, at least. And convicts, dragged from the Lubianka prison to slave labour there, building new bastions and gun sites for the Czar. Cruelty and oppression! If you have never yet seen these in Finland, you will find them in every cell and tunnel of Gustafssvärd."

75

"Gustafssvärd is part of it?"

"The strongest part of it. *Kustaanmiekka*; with the King's Gate where the Czar enters, where the great words are written on either side—the words I learned as a school-girl at Miss Harring's and know by heart—"

"Say them to me." He saw that she was wrought to a pitch of excitement which, against his better judgment, had begun to infect himself. "What does it say at the King's Gate, Alexandra?"

"I don't know if I can put it into English . . . How do you say 'the after-coming'?"

"The next world?"

"No; the next people, the ones who will come after us."

"The next generation. Posterity."

"Yes. I can say it now." Alix folded her hands like a girl in class and began:

"*Here King Fredrik laid the first stone in the year 1748. And King Gustaf laid the last. Sveaborg was built with the sea on one side and the shore on the other, thus—thus owning dominion over both sea and land.*" The next words came more slowly and her voice dropped. "*Out of the wilderness of the Vargarskiar islands was raised up the fortress, Sveaborg . . . Posterity! stand here upon your own foundation . . . and put your trust not in the stranger's help.*"

"That's very fine," said Brand. "'Stand here upon your own foundation'—I like that. But—"

"But what?"

"Who were King Fredrik and King Gustaf? Swedish kings?"

"Yes, they were. When Ehrensvärd built Sveaborg, Finland was a Swedish province—"

"So the fortress was part of Sweden's defences first, and now it defends Russia?"

"One day it will belong to *Suomi*, Finland, and only to Finland. You will see!" said Alix, and her locked hands were at her aching throat.

"Do you think Finland will ask help from a stranger, before that day comes?" said Brand. She looked at him uncomprehendingly.

"Don't you see," he said, "you can't have it both ways? You can't repeat with such pride 'don't trust strangers' and at the same time tell an American to go out and fight in a quarrel that's not his own? If you ask for help you must give trust in return."

"If I didn't trust you, would I be here alone with you?"

"If I didn't love you, would I have followed you to Helsingfors?"

He took one stride towards her. The evergreen branches trembled as he moved and the miniature storm of snow crystals again fell upon them both. Then Alix was in his arms, and her mouth beneath his was colder than the snow.

"My darling, you know that I'm in love with you?"

She sighed, and moved into his embrace, and it seemed to Brand that through his heavy coat she must feel the wild beating of his heart. He kissed her cold lips furiously.

"You never loved Apraxin," he said, shaken. "Never!"

"How can you . . . possibly tell?"

But he was silent, fighting his desire to strip the furred cloak from her shoulders and hold that slim body closer and always closer to his own. Her lips, so unaccustomed to kisses, were coming alive for his, and he had to catch his breath to whisper:

"Come away with me, Alix! Don't go back to St. Petersburg! Marry me and come to London with me now!"

She tore herself out of his arms. Her eyes, wide and fixed, were almost black: the large pupils had dilated until the iris showed only a rim of grey.

"No!" she said violently. "I ran away once and lived to regret it; this time I won't make a rash promise, even for you. You . . . if you really love me, you will join the war against Russia—"

"You make that an absolute condition?" he said hoarsely.

"I *must*, Brand; it's what I most believe in—"

"My God," he said, "if I could see *any* just cause—*any* good reason—"

"Stay in Helsingfors, with *their* kind permission," she said with a queer look. "You may find your just cause sooner than you think."

She moved away down the path, frowning: the shoulders of her cloak were wet with the shaken snow. Brand walked beside her; soon they were at the shuttered bath-house, and the driver was taking off the blanket he had laid on his old horse. The Lapp woman came forward silently, with her slanting eyes moving from the American to the girl.

"What time is it?" asked Alix in an ordinary tone, as soon as the sleigh started on the way back to town.

"Just after twelve, if my watch is right."

"We should be able to get through the Square before the Czar's procession starts. He lunches at the Senate House today, you know."

"You'll allow me to take you right to the Villa Hagasund, I hope?"

"Thank you." Alix had summoned to her aid all her social training, all the experience in polite conversation she had acquired at the simple evening parties of Helsingfors and in the scented overheated salons of St. Petersburg. She felt her lips burning and knew her cheeks were hot, but she forced herself to an exchange of meaningless remarks with the man to whom, so short a time before, she had revealed so much of her inmost heart. That her rebuff had angered and grieved him she knew from his short replies when she pointed out various minor landmarks: the islands of Klippan and Bleckholm, the Russian batteries on Stora Räntan, and so on. And with a dawning awareness of her power over him Alexandra saw Brand's stern face relax as they drove on, his eyes linger again upon her own. At last he said:

"You will still allow me to come to the Villa, this evening?"

"I hope you will."

"Thank you," he said. "I—you must forgive me, Alix. I spoke too soon, and took you unaware. I'm sorry."

For answer she touched his hand. He made no effort to keep her fingers in his own, but after a few minutes he said quietly, "About that other matter. We don't know for a certainty that war will come— ?"

"I should say it was inevitable."

"I don't want you to think that I'm a coward."

Before Alix could reply the sleigh once again came to a halt, the driver clapping on his brake so suddenly that Alix was thrown forward into the arms of the Lapp woman, and Brand kept his seat with an effort. The horse had stopped within yards of a barrier, painted red like the Russian mileposts on the Finnish highways, which had been suddenly lowered across the shore road from the end of the South Esplanade to the harbour steps at the corner of the Market Square.

"We are too late," said Alix, recovering herself as her maid, with a giggle, put her little scarlet *hilkka* straight. "The streets will be closed to traffic until the Czar goes by."

Trading on the Market Square had obviously closed before the statutory hour of noon, for the pushcarts had disappeared and all the stalls had been struck in time to allow for a scrupulous sweeping of the cobbles. The Stone of the Empress now stood alone in a space which allowed the pure line of Engel's buildings to be clearly seen, and only the little flower-market, with the candles burning in the miniature hot-houses, remained as it had been earlier in the day. A detachment of cavalry emerging from the barracks behind the Imperial Palace, came down the Square at a smart trot and swung right into Union Street.

"The Finnish Life Guards," sighed Alexandra. "They will be reviewed by the Czar in the Senate Square. Each man will get a rouble, a pound of fish and a ration of brännvin in honour of the occasion."

"Who are the fellows in the light blue uniforms?" Brand was standing up to see better.

"Russian police. Uncle Carl says General Dubbelt sent five hundred men to Helsingfors for the Czar's visit."

"What about the Czar? Will he be on horseback?"

"It's possible. In Petersburg he would never risk it. Here, he might. We are supposed to be peaceable and well-disposed."

Brand looked from her disdainful face to the throng watching so intently from behind the red barriers and the files of blue-clad police. It was a very silent crowd. The harness could be heard jingling when the Cossacks, in their turn, came round the corner of the Imperial Palace. Alix stood up in the sleigh beside Brand.

"Here comes Nikita," she said.

Although the whole square lay between the palace and the barrier across the shore road, they could see the Czar quite clearly as he came through the gates to the sound of fifes and bugles, and mounted the superb stallion which the grooms led up. The Cossack uniform which he had chosen to wear for the occasion was suited to his great height. The skirts of the long coat fell gracefully over his riding boots, and the crossed bandoliers set off the breadth of his shoulders. In his astrakhan fur hat the glitter of a diamond aigrette answered the flash of the escort's saluting swords. Then an officer rapped out an order, the Cossacks moved off and the Grand Dukes, on horseback, fell into place behind the Czar.

"There goes Alexander Nicolaievich, Uncle Carl's friend," said Alix. "The younger is the Grand Duke Constantine. They say he will be appointed Admiral of the Russian Baltic Fleet."

But Brand's eyes were fixed on the Czar, as the Autocrat trotted down the square between the Empress Stone and the Swedish Embassy.

"I suppose that man holds the fate of Europe in his hands today." He spoke his thought aloud.

"*Brand!*"

Alexandra gripped his arm. To the left of the square, from among the flower stalls, a woman had slipped through the file of police, ducked under the barrier, and was running frantically towards the Czar. Her left hand was flung above her head with the fingers spread wide to show that it was empty. In the right she held a sheet of paper, possibly a petition, which she waved as she ran, with a gasping cry of "*Majestät!*"

She never reached the Czar. The Cossack who intercepted her struck her to the cobbles with the flat of his sword. She was on her knees, with blood dripping from her head, attempting to rise again while the Czar, who had not deigned to look in her direction, turned the corner and rode off towards the Senate Square. It required only two dismounted men to overpower her, without weapons, with only vicious blows to ear and jaw, and prepare to tie her hands to the stirrup of one horse before taking the broken creature into custody.

From the middle of the flower-market a man forced his way through the barriers, as the police struggled to quell the shouting, surging crowd. Brand recognized him at once—the tall Finlander who had been selling freesias earlier in the day. He ran out madly towards the fainting woman, and actually succeeded in tearing her hands free. Then her two captors were upon him, and they went down together in a confusion of barbaric Russian uniforms and plain Finnish dress, while the Cossack officers shouted orders and the rearguard came up in a solid mass round the two Grand Dukes. There was the rapid sound of rifle shot as the police began firing over the heads of the crowd.

Many men and women ran wildly up the two Esplanades and through the gardens as a detachment of troops rode headlong into the flower-market, overturning the stalls in a wreckage of broken glass and trampled daffodils. Others lay on the cobbles, moaning, having been caught by a flying hoof or the end of a Cossack knout. There were also those who had escaped hurt and were still clinging to the barriers to watch, as Brand Endicott watched in horror, the drama coming to its climax in the centre of the square.

The flower seller was being systematically kicked to death. A pistol shot, the slash of a knife, would have been less inhuman than that merciless attack, by the Cossacks he had struck and by four more ordered to their assistance, on the man who had risked all to help a woman. The blows of the booted feet could be heard above the shouting and confusion; the man's cries became feebler, became moans. He was scarcely recognizable when two of the Russians seized his body by one arm and one leg and began dragging it towards the harbour, with his blood-smeared cheek scraping along the ground.

"The bastards! The cruel, murdering bastards!" Brand's voice was thick in his own ears. He measured his distance from the barrier. They were coming closer now, there was only ten or twelve yards between himself and that hideous group, and his hand was on the carriage door as he prepared to jump. Then Alexandra's hand closed about his wrist and he heard her say:

"No, Brand! They will kill you too! Remember this is not your quarrel!"

"*Kill me too*," he repeated stupidly. He saw that what she said was true; the man was dead. When the Russians threw their victim down the harbour steps the head was lolling on a broken neck, and there was no life left in the body which hit the water with a force that sent the wild fowl up off the broken ice with screams of dismay. It sank slowly beneath the day's refuse from the market.

"Now you have seen cruelty and oppression," Alix said, white-lipped. "Now you know how the Czar rules in Finland!"

CHAPTER FIVE

THE GOLDEN PEACE

THE statue of Gustaf III, erected at the spot where the Swedish king landed after his great victory over the Russians at Svensksund in 1790, rose majestically out of the quays of Stockholm as the Finland mail-boat returned to harbour. Behind the statue, on the rising ground, the granite bulk of the royal palace seemed to be welded with the roofs of the Old Town and the spires of the great Lutheran churches into a frozen block of indifference to the coming war.

Brand Endicott, with his light travelling bag in his hand, was the first of the *Eckerö's* few passengers to step ashore. It was an awkward time of day to arrive in Stockholm, getting on to the fashionable afternoon dinner hour, and he stood irresolute on the wharf for a few moments, looking towards the North Bridge and reviewing his very slight knowledge of the city. I hope the Sea Peddlers have come back to port, he thought.

He had not been permitted by the Russian Third Bureau to extend his stay in Helsingfors. Although Nicholas I left the city on the day following the incident in the Market Square, all foreigners were under suspicion after what was officially described as "a dastardly attempt on the life of the Czar", and several persons were summarily deported from the Grand Duchy. Brand was not one of those, but there had been a maddening delay after he reached Åbo, where the Russian port authorities claimed his exit permit was not in order and detained him in the town for several days. The Russians were on edge now, as orders to put the Grand Duchy on a war footing came pouring in from St. Petersburg, and word was received from Russia's western agents that Queen Victoria herself, in the Royal Yacht *Fairy*, had led the British Baltic Fleet out to sea. Admiral Napier's squadron had been cheered by crowds lining the English cliffs from Spithead to Dover, and entered the North Sea under sail and steam while Brand Endicott was waiting to go aboard the mail-boat at Åbo.

Of course he had promised Alix Gyllenlöve to join the fight against Russia. That had been inevitable from the moment he held her in his arms under the snow-laden trees of Brunns-parken, and the hideous scene in the Market Square only intensified the sincerity of the promise he made her that same night at a crowded soirée in the Villa Hagasund. In return Alix promised to let him have news of her own whereabouts through Joe Ryan at Stockholm. These were hasty pledges, made under cover of a conversation between three bearded gentlemen who with sublime disregard of the war news were discussing the Fennoman movement; and also underneath the speculative eye of young Paul Demidov. Then they said good-bye, and the light went out for Brand Endicott; if it was ever to be kindled again depended on his own endeavours—and of course on the Czar of Russia and the Emperor of the French, and others who had taken it upon themselves to trade in human lives and happiness.

Meanwhile he was miserably cold after hours on the open deck of the *Eckerö*, and a tavern across the way suggested the immediate comfort of hot rum grog and the means of finding out how to reach Bollhus Alley. He started towards the Baltica, as its sign described it. There was an unusually large crowd round the door and a considerable noise coming from the interior.

"Anything the matter?" Brand asked a bystander. His Swedish was fairly fluent now, for in Finland it had been a case of learn that language or go without, and more than one voice answered his question excitedly:

"British Navymen! Recruiting!"

"My God!" said Brand. "Is Napier in the Baltic?"

The loafers at the tavern door were divided on this point. Some growled "At Vingäsand," while others were for "Kiel!" but an elderly Dutch skipper, with a square grey-blond beard bristling on a square disapproving face, answered civilly:

"There is a Navy ship at Stockholm, sir. Berthed at the Lock for coaling. Some of her crew are going round the taverns; it may be for their own amusement."

"Let me pass, will you?" Brand shouldered his way into the inn. He saw at once that whatever had brought the two Eng-lishmen into the Baltica it was not amusement. They were standing with their backs to the bar, holding pewter mugs of beer; not exactly in a defensive attitude, but with both pairs of eyes roving warily over what was obviously a hostile crowd. There were many Swedish seamen present, and almost as many Dutchmen and Prussians, and three or four half-drunk on brännvin who were obviously British. One of them was shouting as Brand pushed through the crowd to the bar:

"Press-gang! Press-gang! You got no right to come 'ere and persecute honest seamen— !"

"Nobody's pressing nor persecuting,' said the taller of the two men with their backs to the bar. He wore a low varnished black hat with ribbons and a short blue jacket; Brand caught a glimpse of some insignia on the sleeve. "You only 'eard me say, and I'll repeat, that any man who wants to jine the Navy and 'ave a go at the Rooshians, should be at the Customs 'Ouse down the quay at four bells in the first dog watch for free transportation to 'Er Majesty's Steam Vessel *Lightning*. You'll get pay—"

"Transportation!" The word, with all its associations of brutal sentences and Australian convict ships, came back at him in a howl from the drunken group who had already shouted "Press-gang!" The Prussians jeered. The landlord of the Baltica leaned over the bar to remonstrate.

"Gentlemen! You'll have the Watch down on us!"

"Don't worry, guv'nor, we're clearing out—"

"Just a moment," said Brand Endicott, "you're recruiting for the Navy, are you? To serve in *Lightning*, is that right?"

The Englishman summed him up with a glance from hard blue eyes—gentleman's togs, seen a bit o' wear and tear, down-East Yankee twang, seaman's hands; looked like a useful man in a row.

"*Lightning* or the *Duke*, what's it to you, my lad?" he said. "If you're game to jine the Navy, we'll see you right. My name's Billings, bo'sun's mate; why don't you come along to the Franziskaner Inn with Martin 'ere an me, an then we can all randyvoo at the Customs 'Ouse?"

But Brand shied away from the grasping hand.

"You said four bells, didn't you? I've got letters to write and friends to say goodbye to, first."

"'Ere comes the Watch, Billings!" the other sailor exclaimed.

"All right, we're off. Mind you show up, young feller!"

"Press-gang! Press-gang!" The noise was deafening as the Englishmen went out. Brand heard the tramp of the Watch upon the cobbles—a sound remembered from a snowy February morning in Gothenburg—and hastily bought himself a drink. He carried it to a table near the window and looked over the curtain at the waterfront. There had been no encounter between the police and the *Lightnings*: he could see the two bluejackets walking coolly off towards, presumably, the Franziskaner tavern and another recruiting speech, and the crowd round the Baltica was breaking up. He crooked a finger at the pot-boy and asked for writing materials.

At the reason which might have detached one of Her Majesty's Vessels from Admiral Napier's squadron he could only guess; the fact remained that he had been given, at the earliest possible moment, an opportunity to keep his promise to Alexandra. Six o'clock at the Customs House—that gave him rather more than two hours to see the Ryans and follow up a certain line of enquiry which had suggested itself after Alexandra had told him about Erik Kruse's relations in Prussia. Then, by a voluntary act, he would put it out of his own power to act freely for months ahead, and perhaps years. That clock on the tavern wall between the chromolithographs of King Oscar and Queen Josefina was ticking away the last minutes of Brand Endicott's independence.

What he had to fight was his own attitude to a Navy which within living memory had been a weapon of war against the United States. Like all boys bred on the Maine coast Brand had been brought up on tales of the War of 1812 and the great battle in Portland roads between the U.S. brig *Enterprise* and H.M.S *Boxer*, in which the victorious American commander had died in the same hour as his British foe. Sam Endicott, Brand's father, had been present as a youth of sixteen among the crowds who looked on as the Stars and Stripes fluttered to victory, and years later, in Brand's childhood, he had often taken the boy to see the willow-shaded grave where Lieutenant Burrows and Commander Blyth lay at peace together. Skipper Endicott had never drawn a moral from the tale. The lesson he hammered home to Brand was the American victory, the American defeat of the Royal Navy all the way from Portland to New Orleans. And now his only son was going to join that very Navy and fight the Russians.

With a shake of his sandy head Brand turned to the cheap sheets of writing paper. He had never written a love letter in his life, and the Baltica tavern, reeking of ale and spirits and raucous with the arguments of men fighting the idea of the press-gang, was no place for a first attempt. Brand's message to Alix was a brief one, and when he had signed his name he was faced with the difficulty of writing hers. He had a vague idea that all her connexions were titled. Her aunt was Countess Kruse, he knew, and he had heard her father referred to as Count Gyllenlöve. Madame Karamsin appeared to be a commoner, but her son was Prince Paul Demidov and her sister-in-law was Princess Mathilde Bonaparte, as he had heard her say. It was all confusing to a young man from Maine, all part of the European hypocrisy he despised. Brand settled his problem by writing boldly "Miss Alexandra Gyllenlöve, at Hagasund by Helsingfors," and starting at once on a letter to Mrs. Tarras at Aberdeen.

Mary Ryan kept a mirror angled on the two-foot deep embrasure of her parlour window, to bring a little light and interest into a very dark old living-room. Bollhus Alley was a narrow lane of tall seventeenth century dwellings once the town houses of the Swedish nobility and still keeping an air of distinction, but it was undeniably gloomy, and even at the end of March was hardly ever brightened by the sun. The mansion in which the Ryans lived had been divided into apartments for more than a hundred years, but there was a worn blazon above the door with time-eroded Viking heads supporting a shield with quarterings, and the knocker and hinges were of finely wrought iron. The Ryans' flat was on the ground floor, reached by the first door in a long arched stone entry, and there was nothing to be seen from the parlour window but the dark wall of the house opposite. So Mary had installed a mirror among the green house-plants she trained to grow round the panes, and in the few months since her sixteenth birthday this mirror had reflected more than one handsome face as the officers coming and going on palace duty became aware that there was sometimes (tantalizingly, not always) a very pretty girl to be seen in Bollhus Alley. Ever since the Molly-O's return from Gothenburg Mary had lived in hope that some day the mirror would show her the handsome

American who had not come back to sail with them to Malmö. When she looked up that day from her sewing and saw the tall figure pass, her heart gave a leap of pleasure, and she had a moment to slip into her bedroom and put on a new rose-coloured ribbon and a necklace of green glass beads before his knock fell on the door. Brand saw a glowing face of welcome, and a warm little hand drew him down three steps into the living-room as Mary called out joyfully:

"Father, look who's come to see us! Captain Endicott!"

Joe, who had been writing in the back part of the room, jumped up with a shout. "Brand Endicott, by all pieces of good luck! We were talking about you, last night as ever was, and wondering what happened to you. Where have you been since you marched off down the Packhus quay?"

"To Helsingfors and back, Captain, what d'you say to that?" said Brand, returning Joe's handshake warmly.

"I say you're a fool to enter Russian territory if you travelled alone, and by the looks of you, you did," said Joe. "You're thinner, my lad. I'm glad you've come in time to share our herring and potatoes. Mary, put the case-bottle on the table and stop fussing with your curls."

"No, today you're going to be my guests," said Brand. "I want to take you out to the best restaurant in town. Wouldn't you like that, Miss Mary?"

Sparkling: "Oh, I would!" she said.

The Sea Peddlers had been at sea for weeks, and dinner in a Stockholm restaurant sounded delightful to a girl who liked nothing better than to listen to music and collect the admiring looks of men and the appraising glances of other women. She was glad her father did not protest, but repeated his cheerful order to hurry up with the liquor, and she ran into the back kitchen to tell Sofie, their elderly servant, to stop peeling potatoes and wash the best glasses for a guest. Then Mary arranged some thin squares of cheese and smoked eel on black bread, put these with the polished glasses on a tray, and carried it into the living-room in time to hear her father say:

"I *thought* there was something like that in the wind when you asked the quickest way to Finland!" He was putting an envelope into the inner pocket of his coat.

"And here's a short sweet message to my grandmother," said

Brand with a grin. He handed over another letter, and Joe laughed.

"Sensible man to keep in touch with the old lady. Now then, Molly!"

She took the mahogany case holding three bottles from the buffet at the dark end of the room and set it out on the low table between the two men. Joe poured spirits for Brand and himself, and gave the girl a glass of sherry.

"*Skäl*," said Brand, and relaxed in his low chair. "This is mighty comfortable, Miss Mary. You've made this room just as nice as the cabin in the *Molly-O*."

At these words Mary Ryan's heart, so eager for experience, went out to Brand completely. She had worked hard to turn that dark low room, with its irregular steps leading up and leading down, into a bright place, with gay hooked rugs on the polished wood floor, and an oil lamp swung low on its brass stand to make a little pool of light and cheerfulness around the table where they sat. Upon the walls, at eye level, she had tacked strips of linen ornamented with Biblical scenes, the peasant "cock-painting" of an earlier generation. Such things were banned from Stockholm drawing-rooms, but Mary Ryan liked their traditional colours of lemon, terra-cotta and blue, and watched smiling while Brand's amused eyes travelled from the Queen of Sheba, in the dress of the eighteen twenties, driving up to the door of a Swedish manor house owned by Solomon in all his glory and the Marriage at Cana being celebrated by fair-haired country-folk at the long tables of a Dalecarlian farm.

"I see you brought your cat ashore with you," Brand pursued with a smile. The ginger cat, as usual, had found a comfortable chair, against which stood the beribboned musical instrument of the *Molly-O*. "Don't you leave him to take care of the rats aboard the boat?"

"Bernadotte isn't a nightwatchman kind of cat," said his mistress gaily. "He's a palace neighbourhood cat, that's why I called him after King Oscar . . . See, I brought my guitar ashore too. Father did well with the sewing machines, and I'm going to take more singing lessons this spring."

"You can sing for us after dinner, baby," said Joe. "Run and get your cape on now."

She would have liked Brand Endicott's eyes to say, "Don't

be long!" But he merely rose politely when she set down her sherry glass and got up, and before she reached her bedroom door he turned to her father with an urgent question. Mary had no scruple about leaving the door ajar. Her bedroom, up another of the irregular steps, opened directly off the parlour, and she heard every word they said as she sat down before her mirror and took the ribbon from her hair.

". . . *Lightning*, three guns, Captain Bartholomew Sulivan." That was her father. "They say she was the first steam vessel built for the Royal Navy. Not a very warlike contraption—I wouldn't think the Russians had much to fear from her."

"But how comes she to be so far ahead of the Baltic Fleet?" That was Brand, and Mary grimaced at her own pretty reflection. They were talking about the war, of course—always the war!

"Not so far ahead. Napier lay at Vingäsand for a while—you probably don't know that anchorage, it's just outside Gothenburg roads, east of The Skaw in Denmark—and then he took his courage in both hands and passed the Belts."

"So the Fleet is actually in Danish waters?"

Mary took off the glass beads and fitted her best lace collar to the neck of her dress. She was sick of hearing about the British Admiral's daring in passing the Belts. She and her father had crossed that stretch of water between Funen and Zealand in Denmark not once but a hundred times on their lawful occasions, and nobody ever talked as if *they* had shot Niagara Falls in a barrel! She stifled a giggle as she remembered that Birgitta Engström, one of her pretty, heedless girl cousins, thought "passing the Belts" had something to do with dressmaking.

"I had a look at *Lightning*, when she came in to the Lock," said Joe, "and so did half of Stockholm, it seemed like."

"Precious long way to come from Denmark to coal," said Brand.

"Coaling? Don't you believe it! Captain Sulivan came ashore at noon today and was driven off to the British Ministry. You can bet your last dollar he was carrying instructions to the diplomats to get Sweden into the war as Britain's ally. That's my guess at *Lightning's* mission, though they've made a great parade of trying to enlist local pilots for the Baltic Fleet."

"Pilots, hey?"

Mary lost interest in their conversation. She licked one finger and smoothed down the dark curves of her eyebrows. There was no need to pinch her cheeks, for they were just the right colour, and her lips were crimson. She reached out for her glove-box under a doll with tinsel skirts from the amusement park over the water at Gröna Lund, where her father sometimes took her on a summer evening. The doll came from a shooting gallery, for Joe was a good shot, even with an ancient fair-ground musket, and several of his prizes were displayed on the patchwork cushions of Mary's little bed. Two or three other trinkets, also from Gröna Lund, were at the bottom of Mary's glove-box, but Joe had not seen these, nor did he know of the visits when they had come into her possession. She closed the lid hastily and slung on her dark cape. She had a black seal pork-pie hat and a muff to wear with it—far from new, having belonged to one of her rich cousins in Queen Street, but Mary with her flair for colour had sewed a red bird's wing into the jaunty hat, which suited her better than it had ever suited the plump blonde Marta. She saw the admiration she coveted in Brand's eyes when she stepped into the living-room and smiled, "I'm ready!"

It was decided, after Joe had demurred at the expense, that they should dine at one of the Old Town's famous restaurants, the Golden Peace. The place was not far away, and Mary was almost dancing with excitement as she walked downhill, one hand slipped through her father's arm and the other through Brand's with her sealskin muff bobbing on the end of its long cord.

"Shall we have dinner in the cellar?" she asked, as they entered the old inn, where a number of diners were seated in a wood-panelled ground floor room.

"Now that'll do, Miss Molly!" Joe asserted himself. "You just be glad to be here at all, and let the cellar alone . . . It gets pretty rowdy downstairs later in the day," he said in an aside to Brand. "No place for a young lady."

"This is peaceful enough, surely," said Brand as they were shown to a table. "Is that how the inn came by its name?"

"The Golden Peace—that's what King Gustaf III gave to Sweden, after he beat the Russians," said Mary informatively, "and the cellar isn't rowdy, father; its famous, it's where Bellman used to sing!"

"Give Brand a chance to order dinner, honey."

Mary subsided. A stiff damask cloth and fine crystal were being arranged on their table and the waiter was giving his advice on wine: she was content to look at the portrait hung above the fireplace where pine logs were burning, and remember her childish passion for the man in the golden frame.

It was a very good copy of Krafft's famous painting of Carl Michael Bellman, Sweden's national poet, who had sung his own songs and drunk deep in the cellar of the Golden Peace sixty years back in the golden age of Gustaf III. Mary, who had been brought up on his songs, had asked for a cheap reproduction of that picture as her twelfth birthday present, and even now, four years older, she felt the remembered thrill at the sight of Bellman's fair head drooping above the five-stringed mandoline, the white cravat frothing over the red waistcoat, and the full-lipped sensuous mouth parted in a faint smile.

"Ulla, farväl, min sköna!" was what the poet was singing; Mary remembered indulgently that at thirteen she had pestered her father to change her name to Ulrika.

She looked from the painted face of Bellman to Brand Endicott. His dark blond hair was darker than the poet's, the planes of his face harder and more acute, and she couldn't imagine his singing to a mandoline. But she could, and quite accurately, imagine him kissing her, and those brown hands caressing her and she could hear him whisper when he left her, "Mary, farewell, my darling . . ."

Meantime he was eating his dinner calmly, and making sure his guests were well supplied with food and wine. Joe was in great form, telling taller tales of the sea with every glass, and doing justice to fare selected by a hungry man, as thick oxtail soup was followed by a platter of grilled soles, the soles by a brace of roast ducklings, and the ducklings by cheese, which Mary declined. She also refused brandy without any hint from her father, but exclaimed with joy at the spun sugar swan which appeared with the coffee pot, carrying a freight of candied fruits and fondants between its sculptured wings.

"Brand, how lovely!" she exclaimed.

The American appeared not to have heard her. He was frowning at his glass, and her daring little sally of calling him by his first name fell as flat as the wooden floor of the

Golden Peace. When Brand finally spoke it was to her father.

"Joe," he said, "you're a knowledgeable fellow. You see and hear pretty well everything that goes on along the Stockholm waterfront, don't you?"

"When I'm in port, yes."

"Do you happen to know a Prussian firm of importers and exporters called Müller, of Lubeck?"

"Müller and Sons of Lubeck," corrected Joe. "Certainly I do. Their barque *Lorelei* is lying at Slussen right now."

"Have you any idea who their Stockholm agents are?"

"Lindgrens, I think. I could find out."

"Do that," said Brand. "And at the same time, try to find out if Lindgrens are associated in any way with a Gothenburg merchant called Sven Svensson."

Joe Ryan's long Irish upper lip puckered into a whistle of dismay.

"The Tarras agent," he said. "Is this anything to do with—your last visit to Gothenburg?"

Brand grinned. "You can call it Tarras Line business, if you like. I'm anxious to know more about Mr Svensson, and just why he was so eager to keep Mrs Tarras' grandson from getting to know too much about his other activities. And, Joe, these may well go further than an association with the Müller agents here. One of the Müllers themselves has a nephew in the Swedish Life Guards, until quite recently stationed at Gothenburg. Apparently this nephew has an interest in the firm, and I want to find out if he and Svensson are in any enterprise together."

"What's his name?" said Joe.

"Captain Erik Kruse."

"Captain Kruse!" Mary Ryan exclaimed. Bright colour flooded her face as both men looked at her in surprise.

"Do you know Captain Kruse, Miss Mary?"

"I—happened to meet him once."

"Where, Mary?" Joe's voice was sharp. But the girl had herself in hand now. Not for worlds would she have told even so indulgent a father as Joe Ryan how often she had met Erik Kruse, or where she had last seen him. At the Gröna Lund amusement park, where girls as eager for pleasure as herself were willing to skate or dance all afternoon with handsome officers off duty—

"He visits my Aunt's house," she said smoothly. "Cousin Birgitta met him at a reception at the Russian Embassy."

"You didn't tell me about this."

"Father, Birgitta goes to so many parties and invites so many people, I can't remember all their names."

"Parties, yes; but I didn't know the Engström girls were received at the Russian Embassy," said Joe, looking worried.

"I wouldn't see too much of Captain Kruse if I were you, Miss Mary," said Brand. "He's not the right sort of person for a young lady to know."

"You hear that, Mary?" said Joe Ryan. "I don't want you hob-nobbing with army officers at your age, and I'll tell your Aunt Engström and your cousins so. Maybe the sooner we go back to sea the better."

Tears of anger came to Mary's eyes. Brand thought she was just a baby, then, to be fed spun sugar and told how to behave! What made matters worse was that after his warning he was tactfully ignoring her, pretending not to see the tears, but asking the waiter to bring two more brandies and the bill, and then turning to her father.

"Joe, I know this is a lot to ask of you. But I'll pay well for the information about Svensson and Kruse and their affairs, if you'll make up a detailed report and send it on as soon as I can tell you where to find me."

"You're not planning to leave Stockholm already?"

"Right away," said Brand. "In about half an hour . . . You see, the *Lightning* is recruiting seamen as well as pilots for the fleet. And I've made up my mind to join the Royal Navy."

"Brand, are you crazy?"

It was the keynote of all they said to him, repeating all the familiar arguments he had already used on himself, while Brand paid the bill and drained his glass and apologized for leaving them so abruptly, to make their own way home.

"I thought you would be coming home with us," said Mary. She had forgotten her resentment and her lips were quivering as she looked up at him.

"I'm glad I've seen your home on land," said Brand gently. "When the war's over we'll have another dinner at the Golden Peace, the three of us, and then you'll sing that song for me, Miss Mary—if you're not singing in grand opera by then!"

"Well," said her father blankly, "this is a sad ending to a

pleasant afternoon. Look, will I come down to the Customs House with you—"

"Better not, Joe. You've got to take Mary home, and I need to hurry. Remember, I'm relying upon you."

"You can do that all right." Joe's merry Irish face was more purposeful than Brand had ever seen it. He touched his coat. "I'll not forget the letter to your sweetheart."

"Have you a sweetheart, Brand?" Mary's young voice was sharp with jealousy. She watched a slow smile lighten Brand's tired face.

"She's not my sweetheart yet," he said, "I hope she soon will be."

It had been scarcely twilight when they entered the Golden Peace. It was quite dark when Brand left the inn, and turning sharp left hurried down the narrow alley that led back to the harbour. A solitary oil lamp, slung on a chain between two buildings, lit up the dirty lane, but the new gas lighting had been installed along the waterfront, and it was easy to identify the Customs House. At the sight of the crowd strung out along the wharf Brand's first thought was that Billings and Martin must have brought off the most successful recruiting drive since impressment for the Royal Navy ended nearly forty years before. Then he saw the two Englishmen, flanking a slim young officer in white jean trousers, with a frock-coat and a blue visor hat, and in front of them, lined up on the cobbles, exactly three recruits, at whom the crowd of idlers were staring in a shuffling, hard-breathing silence.

"Here's the Yankee, sir!" exclaimed the bo'sun's mate at sight of Brand.

"Is that the lot?" said the officer irritably. "Now then, my men! Are any of you Swedish or Norwegian subjects? *Schweden, Sverige, Norge*? No? And you clearly understand that you have volunteered for active service and go aboard Her Majesty's Steam Vessel *Lightning* of your own free will?"

Brand nodded. Two of the four volunteers apparently failed to understand the question and answered it with grins. The fourth, who had an elderly, wizened Cockney face, knuckled his forehead and said respectfully, "Aye, aye, sir."

The officer seemed satisfied. Whistles shrilled, and a Navy cutter came out of the darkness to the Customs House wharf, with a midshipman in the stern sheets and five seamen in blue-checked shirts at the oars. The volunteers were embarked, the *Lightnings* followed, the oars dipped at the word of command. As the cutter slid out on the black waters of Lake Saltsjön there came a ragged shout from the back of the watchful crowd. Brand had a shrewd suspicion that it was "Press-gang!"

"The Old Man's still ashore," said the Cockney to Brand out of the side of his mouth. The Lieutenant's automatic "Silence there!" checked any reply the American might have made, but Brand was less interested in Captain Sulivan's movements than in the appearance of H.M.S.V. *Lightning* as they approached her under the harbour lamps. She was a diminutive paddle steamer of only 100 h p., dwarfed by many of the Swedish ships then lying at Slussen, the lock opened to Stockholm traffic four years before. Her single smoke stack rose at a curious angle from the deck. She was, as Joe Ryan had said, 'not a warlike contraption', and yet Brand felt a kind of elation, a sense of returning to his proper environment, as he swung himself by the side ropes up the ladder of battens and through the entry port to the deck.

"Touch your 'ats to the quarterdeck." That was the first order to the volunteers, and Brand pulled off his sealskin hat and held it in his hand while their escorting officer reported to the First Lieutenant on the *Lightning*'s tiny poop. One bell struck in the last dog watch as the men in the waist studied the new recruits by lantern light. They were still at work on the preliminary cleaning of the deck after the long day's coaling.

"Pass the word for the bo'sun!" was the order which ended the quiet conference on the poop. The man who obeyed it was older and surlier than his mates, Martin and Billings; he appeared to have a definite sense of injury as he shepherded the recruits down the main hatchway ladder and aft to the gun-room. It was remarkably warm, for although *Lightning* had no ward-room Captain Sulivan prided himself on the comfort of his officers, two of whom, with a look of surprise, went out as the volunteers tramped in. The Cockney's sharp eyes roved round the room, the two younger recruits fidgeted and murmured until the bo'sun called them sharply to attention. The First Lieutenant did not keep them waiting long. He came in briskly, followed by the ship's clerk, and sat down at the large dining table, over which a green baize cloth was spread.

"Now then, you men," said the First Lieutenant, "I understand from Mr Bullock that you all volunteered in Stockholm at your own wish and are not subject to Swedish jurisdiction."

The two youths grinned their uncomprehending grins, and the Cockney said:

"I'm a Londoner, sir."

"All right, we'll begin with you. You understand, in the absence of Captain Sulivan, I am only going to make a note of your names and experience, and your induction into the Navy will follow later. Is that clear?"

"Aye, aye, sir."

"Your name?" asked the First Lieutenant.

"Kedge, sir. David Kedge."

"You've been a Navy man, haven't you?"

"I've sarved me time to the sea, sir. I was a short service man in the old *Imperieuse*. Able seaman, sir, and paid off reg'lar at Pompey, goin' on three years back."

"How old are you, Kedge?"

"Forty, sir."

"Add fifteen years to that, Mr. Cooke. Well, Kedge, they may welcome you back aboard *Imperieuse*, we'll see when we arrive in Køje Bay. You men had better realize that *Lightning* is carrying her full complement, and you will be drafted into other vessels when we rendezvous with the Fleet. Your pay, to December thirty-first of the present year, will be allotted to you by the Pay Clerk of whatever ship you join."

"Begging your parding, sir . . ."

"Well, Kedge?"

"Don't we get no war bounty, sir?"

"We're not at war yet, Kedge.—Your name?" the First Lieutenant shot at Brand.

"John Endicott." It cost him an effort to add the word "sir."

"You're the American, are you?"

"Yes."

"What's your previous experience?"

"Fishing the Banks—sir."

"You're a long way from Marblehead here." They looked at one another across the table: Brand stubborn, determined under his latest interrogation to say as little as possible, Lieutenant Cudlip conscious of his rank and authority, but vexed by a situation not yet covered by the Articles of War. The

British Admiralty, on the eve of war with Russia, had been driven to some odd improvisations, both of ships and crews, and the directive passed down through the chain of command was explicit. Seamen were to be enlisted anywhere in the Baltic, of any nationality, and it was not necessary to make too searching enquiries into their previous experience. This American seaman was in all probability an American deserter, which might well mean complications later, but of that, under the Admiralty order, Mr. Cudlip was compelled to run the risk. Inwardly, he cursed Captain Sulivan's long conference with the Chargé d'Affairs. He, Lieutenant Cudlip, had expected to enlist Baltic pilots, not as ruffianly a bunch of ship-jumpers as he had ever seen in all his years at sea! He decided to waive the request for a certificate of character and competence, and said to Brand:

"Why have you volunteered for the Navy, Endicott?"

"Like Billings said, sir—I want to have a go at the Russians."

The Lieutenant smiled. "Not bad!" he said. "We'll give you plenty of goes before you're through."

The third man, one of the smiling pair, was tall and blond, wearing a thick jersey and heavy sea-boots. He continued to smile pleasantly while the clerk and the bo'sun bawled requests for his name in scraps of several languages; then, in a flash of comprehension, he put his hand to his breast and said with a bow:

"Lauri."

"Try to get his last name, Mr. Cooke," said Lieutenant Cudlip wearily.

"Larry? Larry what?" said the clerk.

"Lauri, Suomi. Suomi—Finland. Gamla Karleby, Finland."

"That gives us a pretty wide choice, my man."

"These are place names, sir," pointed out the clerk. "Gamla Karleby is probably the town he hails from."

"Write him down Laurence Finn then, if that's the name to suit him. How about this man, bo'sun—is he a Finn too?"

The fourth volunteer, tall and gangling, with a rounded head and green cat's eyes narrowed to a slit by his perpetual smile, turned out to be an Esthonian, with an unpronounceable first name and a surname which might conceivably have been Klerck. He was accordingly "written down" as "Nobby" Clark —one of the thousand Nobbies of the Navy. "For if we don't call

97

him that, sir," said the clerk sagaciously, "his shipmates will."

"Pass the word for the surgeon, bo'sun," said Lieutenant Cudlip, getting up. "Then see they get some supper ... All right, my lads! We'll make topmen of you yet."

"Aye, aye, sir." That was Kedge, with a suspicion of irony in the deferential knuckling of his brow. Then, by the light of thick horn battle lanterns, they were on their way down to the after cockpit, where Mr Johnson the ship's surgeon, who was reading *David Copperfield* in his berth, gave them a perfunctory medical examination. He noted that the only one not in good physical condition was the re-enlisted man, Kedge, who had a hernia and symptoms of kidney trouble; but Mr Johnson had also read the Admiralty directive, which succinctly ran 'Do not be too particular', and in record time the four recruits were pulling their trousers up and buttoning their shirts. As Mr Johnson thankfully returned to Dickens they moved on to the purser's store where they were issued, under protest by the purser, with four hammocks for temporary use aboard. It was then the turn of the cook's mate to object, profanely, to the arrival of four men in his galley long after the coppers were scoured and the brick floor scrubbed down for the night. The hands, of course, had had supper at four o'clock, and it was difficult to find mess kids for the newcomers or cans to hold the half gill of rum to which, as Kedge pointed out, they were now legally entitled. This at once drew a disciplinary monologue from the bo'sun.

"Now you 'eard what Lieutenant Bullock said to each and every mother's son of you when you volunteered for service, and you 'eard what the First Lieutenant said, that you joined the Navy of your own free will. No one can't say you was pressed, and no one can't say we shanghaied you orf the dock contrairy to the laws of Sweden. But that don't mean we're goin' to pamper you, nor take none of your sea-lawyerin' jaw— and that means you, Kedge, I know your sort, answering back of the First Lieutenant and arguin' over a narf a gill of rum. Now Gawd knows why we 'ave to be saddled with you in *Lightning* ..."

It went on as long as the silent seamen tore at the slices of cold salt pork and ship's biscuit, which Brand, after an excellent dinner, could only make a pretence of eating. It was all pretty much what he had expected aboard a Royal Navy ship

—the hectoring and the weevilly biscuits and the sound of the second and third bells striking as the last dog watch wore on. Soon a drum beat to quarters for the evening muster. By lantern light, H.M.S.V. *Lightning's* three guns were cast loose, run in and made fast, the ship's company dismissed and eight bells struck. The new recruits, carrying their hammocks, made their way through the lower deck, where the watch below was turning in, to the manger, the only place where they could sleep in a ship already carrying over two hundred men.

Brand removed his boots and part of his clothing and pulled his overcoat across his legs when he crawled into his hammock under the low roof of the manger. It was intolerably hot, for Captain Sulivan kept a stove going at all times on the lower deck, and the dangers of fresh air were averted by keeping the portlids closed even in harbour. It was also very early, and Brand expected to lie awake for hours.

The other recruits were soon asleep. Kedge snored heavily, and the Esthonian laughed and ground his teeth through his dreams while Brand lay still and reviewed the events of the day. He was sure that he had made the right decision, and he felt better than at any time since he walked down the Stone Pier at Gothenburg. Now he had a job to do, and friends who cared what became of him—Joe and Mary. Mary's face when they spoke about his sweetheart! She was rather sweet on him herself, Brand thought, and how very easy it might have been to grow fond of her! She was very gay and pretty, and it was a marvel how she had fixed up that apartment—no wonder Joe was proud of her. But Joe was too young and easy-going to keep her in order—keep her away from a rat like Erik Kruse.

It was odd to think that he might have been sitting in that cheerful parlour now, listening to the promised song, watching Mary playing her guitar, with her rich dark curls falling round her white neck as she bent above the instrument. And then that picture faded from his vision, and in the darkness of the manger Brand saw only Alexandra's haunted, haunting face.

He was asleep, with her image in his heart, long before Captain Sulivan came aboard after a lengthy and profitless discussion at the British Ministry, on one of the last nights before the shattering of the golden peace that had lain over Europe since the cannon ceased to thunder on the field of Waterloo.

CHAPTER SIX

OLD MEN IN COUNCIL

Brand Endicott spent four days in H.M.S.V. *Lightning*, 3, before Captain Sulivan's command rendezvoused with the Baltic Fleet in Køge Bay.

During those four days he was an outsider, looking in at a world with its own tribal customs and its own rigid rules. This Navy world had its own language, and the clipped speech of the officers was as difficult for an American to understand as the Cockney slang of the lower deck. Brand carried out several tasks badly because the orders, as far as he was concerned might as well have been given in Greek, and was thankful to be employed as a leadsman, stationed in the main chains and calling the depths as *Lightning* slid through the rocky channels and shoal waters of Sweden's east coast with an ease which kindled his admiration for her captain's seamanship. To a sailor who knew the rock-bound coast of Maine it sometimes seemed as if Captain Sulivan was going south by instinct, and with this Brand's new shipmates heartily agreed.

"The Old Man, 'e's like a water diviner with an 'azel twig," averred Billings, the bo'sun's mate. "The old *Lightning*, she just fair twitches in 'is 'ands."

H.M.S.V. *Lightning* was the chief, and at that time the only, surveying ship of Admiral Napier's command. Though the frigates were by tradition the eyes of the Fleet, it was *Lightning*'s mission to act as the eyes of the frigates in Baltic waters, and in the badly charted Gulfs which lay beyond. On the way to his Danish rendezvous Captain Sulivan spent some time in surveying Älvsnabben Bay to the south of Stockholm, and then took the inner passage down the Kalmar Sound. On several occasions he hove to and invited the masters of various Baltic craft to come aboard him, particularly when these came from Finland or the Åland Islands, and once, with all hands on deck for the proper courtesies, he saluted the flag of Admiral Crusenstjerna as the Swedish Admiral led a large squadron eastward from the naval base as Karlskrona. The sight of such a convoy, led by three ships of the line and heading for the Swedish island of Gotland in mid-Baltic, caused every man aboard the survey ship to believe war was at last declared. But the message signalled in reply to the British query was *No news yet*.

It was only on such occasions, when Captain Sulivan appeared on the poop, or when he made the rounds of the ship at morning inspection, that Brand had a chance to look at his new Captain, for the senior surveyor of the Fleet had voluminous reports to prepare, not only for the Commander-in-Chief but for the Admiralty Hydrographer. When he did appear on deck the American was constantly struck by the Olympian detachment of a British sea officer, and the aloofness so completely different from anything in his own experience. Yet Sulivan was not cold by nature. He was a Cornishman, warmhearted and impulsive to the point of tactlessness, and the Service mask could hardly hide the emotionalism latent in his handsome face and deep-set dark eyes. Although he had been in command for a matter of weeks only, his concern for the hands' welfare had already made *Lightning* a happy ship.

On Sunday, April 2, Captain Sulivan held divine service at half past ten, after the bell had summoned the ship's company aft, and added, as was his custom, some simple words of his own to the Church rubric. Like many sea officers Bartholomew Sulivan had a deep fund of evangelical piety, and to his extempore prayers for victory in war, if war should come, he added entreaties for their souls' salvation which greatly affected the sentimental congregation seated before him on match buckets and mess kids. When the hands were dismissed to dinner one hardened ruffian who had served a term in Newgate shouted out to Brand and Lauri that 'the old man 'ad a boxful of Bibles brought aboard special to convert them 'eathen Finns with, and convert them 'e flaming well will, if 'e 'as to break their bleedin' necks to do it !'

Lauri's reaction, as usual, was a smile. He was a gentle creature and a good seaman, wrapped in the silence of his own speech as a rule, although he liked to exchange a few Swedish words with Brand, and seemed able to communicate with Nobby, the Esthonian. He owned a mouth-organ, and soon picked up the tunes of "Nancy Dawson" and "Wapping Old

Stairs" which he played by request on this free Sunday afternoon, interspersed with a few strange little airs of his own country, while the watch on deck drowsed with its rolled-up coats for pillows, and the watch below played draughts or swapped yarns.

"We are near the rendezvous now, Mr. Cudlip," said Captain Sulivan to the First Lieutenant, whom he had invited to dine with him in his private cabin. They were sitting over a glass of port, and the time was two o'clock, with a clear sky, a favouring wind, and *Lightning*'s paddles rotating steadily. "This may be the last peaceful Sunday we shall know for many a long day."

"I hope so, sir," said Lieutenant Cudlip with a grin.

Sulivan raised his bushy eyebrows. "Eager for action, are you?"

"Eager for prize-money, sir."

"I may be wrong," said Sulivan, "but I believe the days of the big prizes are over. You heard what the natives have been saying in the past few days. If the Russians bottle themselves up under the protection of their fortresses, we've precious little hope of capturing any of their ships of the line."

"We'll have to cut them out from under their own guns, sir, as Nelson did at Copenhagen," said Cudlip cheerfully.

"What Lord Nelson attacked at Copenhagen was a line of blockships and rafts, Mr. Cudlip," Captain Sulivan rapped out. "A very different matter from Cronstadt and Sveaborg! Nelson *never* attacked a land battery with ships, except on the first day at Tenerife. And even then . . . Come in!" he said, as a knock fell on the door.

Both men were on their feet when the midshipman of the watch entered and saluted. "Lieutenant Bullock's compliments, sir, and he believes the Fleet's in sight!" he blurted out.

By the time the Captain and the First Lieutenant reached the quarterdeck the hail from the look-out man had changed to "Land ho!" and from that moment there was a continuous exchange between the masthead and the deck. The coast of Denmark, at first a line on the horizon, became clearly visible; the topmasts of the British Fleet at anchor in Køge Bay steadied into a full spread of canvas, an expanse of chequered sides, as the look-out man identified ship after ship of the British line.

"Dressed overall, sir," said the First Lieutenant, with his glass at his eye.

"Turn up all hands," said Captain Sulivan.

"Turn up all hands!" Lieutenant Cudlip had no need of a speaking tube to make his voice heard from the taffrail to the flying jib boom ends. Sulivan was watching closely. Under a full head of steam, he calculated, he would be able to swing *Lightning* into her place at the tip of the crescent in which the Baltic Fleet had formed in Køge Bay. He could see the roofs of Køge town, and crowds of Danes out on the hilly shore to see the Fleet just as English folk had gathered on the Channel cliffs less than a month before. Between the two horns of the crescent moved innumerable Danish craft—bumboats, rowing boats and pleasure yachts, even paddle-wheelers come down from Copenhagen with Sunday afternoon trippers, from which the sound of music floated across the bay. But over and above the music came the cheering of ten thousand British sailors, in a roar that told Captain Sulivan and his First Lieutenant what news they should hear, even before the midshipman of signals presented himself at the Captain's elbow.

"*Dragon* to *Lightning*, sir!" he choked. "The signal reads: "BRITAIN HAS DECLARED WAR ON RUSSIA."

"Handsomely, my lad," said Captain Sulivan. "*Dragon* is still signalling." H.M.S.V. *Dragon*, 3, was their next neighbour as they came up to the crescent's tip.

"PREPARE TO FIRE SALUTE IN HONOUR OF HER MAJESTY'S MINISTER TO THE COURT OF DENMARK."

"Acknowledge," said Sulivan. There was just time, as *Lightning* came to her station next to *Dragon*, to hoist ensigns at all masts and a string of flags from the bow to the masthead, between masts and down to the stern so that the survey ship would be dressed overall in conformity with the rest of the Fleet, and to run out her three guns and load before the salute began. It came with a sustained roar which filled Køge Bay and rolled among the budding beechwoods on the shore. Then, when the salute was over, came the beautiful manoeuvre as the tall ships, in unison, lowered their topgallant sails in honour of the Queen's representative. Through his powerful glass Captain Sulivan could see the Minister, Mr. Andrew Buchanan, on the quarterdeck of the flagship with Admiral Napier by his side. He was in full diplomatic uniform and kept his hand stiffly to his cocked hat in acknowledgement of the salute. It was a moment of high pageantry, recognized as such by the Danish sightseers, whose thin cheering came back across the water like an antistrophe to the loud British hurrahs. Under a sky of cirrus cloud, faintly coral tinted in the westering sun, and on a calm sea in which the colours of the Blue Ensign were twenty times reflected, lay the mightiest steam navy which had yet left the shores of England, each unit eloquent of power, from the three-decker flagship, H.M.S. *Duke of Wellington*, 131, displacing 3,700 tremendous tons, H.M.S. *Royal George*, 120, the newly built *St Jean d'Acre*, 101, down to the frigates with the evocative names of *Blenheim*, *Imperieuse* and *Arrogant*. All were painted in the 'Nelson chequer'—black sides and portlids, with white ribands to mark each deck of guns, and the portlids being open, the scarlet paint of their inner sides was seen as vivid streaks of contrasting colour. More than eleven hundred guns, averaging 32 pounds in ball weight, were housed on the gun decks of Admiral Napier's command.

Few of the spectators, on that day when the Baltic Fleet learned that its mission was war, realized that what they saw was not a pageant but the end of an era, and that these were the wooden walls of Old England in their last appearance on the battlefields of ocean. There were ships in that superb crescent which had won their first honours exactly sixty years ago. H.M.S. *Caesar*, 91, and H.M.S. *Royal George* had shared in Lord Howe's victory on the Glorious First of June in 1794. H.M.S. *Ajax*, 60, had fought under Nelson at Trafalgar; H.M.S. *Imperieuse*, 51, captured from the Spaniards in 1804, had fought under British command in the Battle of the Basque Roads in 1809. For romantics these great old full-rigged ships, with their new auxiliary steam power, were witnesses to the most glorious period of England's naval history. For realists like Captain Sulivan they were ghost ships, almost completely unfit to fight a modern war with Russia.

This was Sulivan's thought when much later in the day he was rowed along the lighted line of ships at anchor to go aboard the *Duke of Wellington*. It was a pitch-black evening, with a rising wind whipping across the bay, and Sulivan in the stern of the *Lightning's* cutter kept his boat cloak closely wrapped around him to protect his dress uniform from flying spray. He had been on half-pay for eight years now, as the bottleneck of the Active List remained choked with the surviving veterans of the Napoleonic Wars who still barred the way to promotion, and the price of gold lace was a serious consideration to a man with sons who hoped to follow him in the Navy. The war with Russia, and the patronage of the Hydrographer, had represented the only chance for Sulivan, still a post-captain at forty-three, ever again to hold command at sea, and he was desperately anxious to deserve Sir Francis Beaufort's recommendation, which had given him the survey ship. What exercised his mind, as the cutter came up to *Duke*, and the pipes shrilled and the sideboys took their places, was how far he dared speak the truth to Admiral Napier. Although he was the son and grandson of distinguished sailors, Sulivan was not at ease in the blustering presence of the Commander-in-Chief. At their last meeting, Napier had as good as turned his back on him, in the presence of his own flag captain, and had growled out in a Scots accent that he didna ken what use a surveyor was like to be in Baltic waters. "Pilots, man; give me plenty of pilots that ken the channels thoroughly, and I'll do the rest," he said, and of course subservient George Biddlecombe, the Master of the Fleet, had "respectfully begged to endorse Sir Charles Napier's opinion". The battle of pilots versus surveyors had begun at Spithead; and now he, Sulivan, had returned from Stockholm without pilots, but carrying despatches and a report which, when delivered to the *Duke* that afternoon, could hardly have given satisfaction to the Admiral. Captain Sulivan, as he followed a polite flag lieutenant to Napier's quarters, hoped that on this occasion he would be spared a public snub.

Sir Charles Napier, Vice-Admiral of the Blue, sat smoking at the head of the long mahogany table in the stern cabin of the *Duke*, with Rear-Admiral Chads on one hand, Rear-Admiral Plumridge on the other, and a glass dish which already held the stub of one cigar in front of him. Among the distinguished company of naval officers around the table there was not one civilian: from the vacant chairs Sulivan deduced, as he made his bow, that Mr. Buchanan and his staff had left after the cloth was drawn. With the tactful withdrawal of the Minister who had brought the communiqué from London, the Admiral's dinner party had turned into a council of war.

"Come away in, Captain Sulivan, and sit ye down," said Napier expansively. "I don't believe I need to present you to any of the officers here."

"Your servant, gentleman," said Sulivan. He took his place at the bottom of the table, on which silver dishes of fruit and nuts were arranged between the decanters, and an epergne of silver and crystal even held a few spring flowers. Silver coffee pots, Crown Derby cups and liqueur glasses were disposed on a handsome mahogany buffet. To Sulivan, who had dressed in a berth where there was room for nothing but a shaving mirror and his foul-weather clothes on a peg behind the door, the Admiral's day cabin in H.M.S. *Duke of Wellington* represented luxury.

"What are you for, Captain Sulivan?" pursued the Admiral. "Will you take a glass of port? A cup of coffee and a cognac to hold out the cold? Or a drop of the Auld Kirk to drink confusion to our Russian enemies?"

Napier was in his Scotch mood, the Cornishman observed. Sometimes it amused the Admiral, one of a distinguished Service family of Scottish gentlefolk, to speak with the accent of a countryman: it usually meant that he had been dining well. There was a good deal of the actor in Sir Charles Napier, who had a bouncing, outgoing sense of showmanship which had carried him through many triumphs and disasters in his younger days in the Navy and more recently in the House of Commons. He had the name of being a good leader but a poor second-in-command; indeed, his general reputation for indiscipline had almost cost him the command of the Baltic Fleet. He had got it, Sulivan knew, because Their Lordships of the Admiralty had literally no one of his rank available—no one except Lord Dundonald, energetic as ever at seventy-nine, who had proposed if given the Baltic command to destroy Cronstadt fortress by a chemical process of his own invention. There at the head of the table, employed to defeat the Czar Nicholas and the Russian Empire, sat the man who had defied the Admiralty as the champion of steam power and the prophet of the iron ship—but that was thirty years ago. The same Napier had taken command of the Portuguese Navy and placed Maria da Gloria on the throne of Portugal—but that was twenty years ago. Even fourteen years back, the dashing Charles Napier had captured St. Jean d'Acre, taken the surrender of the Egyptian Army and—to the rage of the diplomats—personally concluded a peace with Egypt. Could this stout, white-haired gentleman, his rosy face becoming ruddier as he lifted his glass to Commodore Seymour, give another bravura performance at the age of sixty-eight?

Looking round the company of elderly and distinguished men, Sulivan wished fervently to see some of his own generation there. He thought of his good friend Captain Cooper Key, now with the Baltic Fleet in command of H.M.S. *Amphion*, 34; and of Captain Hope and Captain Keppel, with whom he had served on the Parana river against the dictator Rosas. To fight a war with Russia the Navy should have commanders in early middle life, experienced but vigorous, instead of these bemedalled greybeards who had been eager lads before the death of Nelson. To the vivid imagination of the Cornishman the dusky lamplit cabin was oppressive with memories of Trafalgar.

"Well, gentlemen!" Napier's voice gathered them all together. "Time's getting on, and there seems to be dirty weather blowing up. I know you're anxious to get back to your ships, but I would like you all to hear, and maybe to question, some points raised in a report Captain Sulivan submitted to me this afternoon."

He flicked the ash off his cigar.

"While Mr. Buchanan was our guest at dinner, we all considered the despatch brought here by *Lightning*—I mean the despatch from Mr. Grey, Her Majesty's Chargé d'Affaires at Stockholm. It informed us of Sweden's determination to remain neutral throughout the war, and to close her ports to all the belligerents. As you already know, I intend to pay a formal visit to His Majesty King Oscar as soon as occasion offers, but I can't flatter myself that my powers of persuasion will be any more successful at Stockholm than they were on my recent visit to the King of Denmark. In other words, we cannot count on Swedish or Danish help."

Admiral Chads said, "The fact that war has actually been declared may make some difference to the northern sovereigns, Sir Charles. Particularly when they hear of the stand taken by the King of Prussia."

"Aye," said Napier, "that's the crux of the matter. Now that Prussia has placed the port of Memel at the service of the Czar, a blockade of the Baltic becomes ten times more difficult. Every port in Prussia is active in the Russian interest, and the devil of it is, it may not end there. An out-and-out military alliance between Prussia and Russia could very well be the next step, and if that comes, we're—" He turned his thumb down, and shook his head.

"In that case we should expect our ally the Emperor of the French to take the Prussians in the rear," drawled Admiral Plumridge. "Let us hope, Sir Charles, it won't come to that!"

"Let us hope indeed," said Napier. Then, in his most brutal and contemptuous manner, he added, "Our ally! Louis Napoleon Bonaparte! After a bloody *coup d'état* the Emperor Napoleon III! I wouldna trust him to come to our assistance in any corner of the globe. He's out for Number One, yon fella! I'll believe in the value of *him* as an ally when he sends me a bigger supporting force in the Baltic than one rotten, half-derelict ship of the line like *Austerlitz*, which has been conspicuous by her absence ever since we passed the Belts!"

A constrained laugh went round the table. Then Commodore Seymour, the Captain of the Fleet, said smoothly:

"If I take your point, Sir Charles, you are telling us that Britain goes into the Baltic campaign without adequate support from her only Western ally, and aware that Prussia may at any time conclude a treaty of alliance with the Czar. Is that so unusual a situation? Lord Nelson and Lord Saumarez, in two different campaigns, waged war in the Baltic under very similar conditions."

"No!" said Napier, his ruddy face suffused with anger. "No, by God they didn't! Admiral Saumarez met the Russian fleet in open water, and chased them from Hangö to Port Baltic before he engaged them and captured the *Sevolod*! This is going to be a campaign against the great forts, when the Fleet will be faced with shallow waters and granite walls, and with the Russia of Nicholas I, not of his dear departed brother!—Sulivan, tell them about the pilots."

Captain Sulivan replied at once to the abrupt command.

"Acting upon information received in Stockholm harbour," he said, "and on the direct advice of our Chargé d'Affaires, I engaged no pilots for the Fleet in Sweden. Some of the men available proved to have Russian relatives, well supplied with funds from official sources. Others had been seen in the company of Russian agents. There is no doubt in my mind that such pilots would do their best to pile up the ships in their charge on the first convenient rock or shoal."

"Which tallies exactly with Mr. Buchanan's accounts of Russian agents presently at work in Denmark," said Admiral Plumridge.

"Aye, that's all very fine," grumbled Napier. "So instead of pilots—whom the Master of the Fleet regards as indispensable— our friend Sulivan brings me in no fewer than four volunteers for the lower deck. Four! That'll not get us far on our way, eh, Captain Gordon?"

The Captain of the flagship laughed dutifully. "Able Seamen all of them, I trust, Captain?"

"No, sir, a scratch lot at present; three foreigners and a time-expired short-service man. And even they were not recruited without difficulty. My First Lieutenant, Mr. Cudlip, was most exercised over the propriety of taking them aboard at all. He had had Swedish neutrality rammed—so well explained to him at Mr. Grey's hospitable table, that he went to great lengths with the men to make sure they knew what they were doing, and were free agents."

"We had a very similar experience in Kiel," said Captain Gordon. "And in Copenhagen they were shouting 'Pressgang!' as lustily as they cheered us in the bay this afternoon."

"Aye, well, there was a great deal to be said for the Impressment Service," growled the Admiral, "and I doubt if the war bounty will make much difference to recruiting. Four volunteers from Stockholm, one hundred and two from Kiel and Copenhagen! A hundred and six men where I need two thousand more, to man a Fleet scraped together in two weeks out of the riff-raff of the ports and the runaway London 'prentices and a handful of ruptured ploughmen from the Shires! Twenty ships and vessels today, and perhaps fifteen more when Admiral Corry's squadron comes up with me, to face —what's the total Russian force against us, Commodore Seymour?"

The Captain of the Fleet read tonelessly from a page of notes beside his place:

"Twenty-seven sail of the line. Ten frigates. Seven corvettes and brigs. Nine paddle steamers. Fifteen schooners and luggers. And," his voice became slightly more emphatic, "one hundred and eighty gunboats. Total armament, three thousand one hundred and sixty guns. Total complement, twenty-seven thousand men."

"The gunboats being their most important weapon," said Sir Henry Chads. "They have the mobility, and the fire power — everything our present squadron lacks."

"Meantime they're bottled up in Cronstadt and Helsingfors," Admiral Plumridge said, "leaving us free to turn our attention to Bomarsund. These were your orders, Sir Charles, I believe?"

"These were the sealed orders I opened at Vingäsand, yes. Captain Sulivan, again, has some information to give us about Fort Bomarsund."

The white heads, the heads plentifully sprinkled with grey, swung slowly back towards the surveyor. The glasses stood half emptied on the table, and the grey cigar smoke coiled in slow wreaths beneath the lamps.

"All the native skippers to whom I spoke on my cruise to and from Stockholm are agreed on one point, gentlemen," said Sulivan. "The Russians, who publicly announced last winter that they would abandon the new works at Bomarsund, are back in strength, and work on the Great Fort is proceeding faster than before."

There was a murmur round the table, a growl of "Naturally!" from Admiral Plumridge, and then Napier looked up from a low-toned conference with a flag lieutenant who had requested permission to deliver a message from the quarterdeck.

"I believe this council should adjourn, gentlemen," he said. "It's blowing up to a gale, and some captains are in difficulties. I shall have copies of the surveyor's report on the Alvsnabben anchorage made up and circulated to you all before we weigh anchor."

"May I detain you with one question, Sir Charles?" put in Admiral Henry Chads. He was one of the gunnery experts of the Navy, which he had entered in the year 1800, and it was not easy for even the choleric Napier, already on his feet, to deny his mild request.

"Proceed, Sir Henry."

"Captain Sulivan appears to be an excellent courier, as well as an excellent surveyor," Chads said quietly. "From the information you acquired, Captain, would you agree with Admiral Plumridge that the entire Russian Baltic Fleet is— 'bottled up' I think was his expression—between Cronstadt fort and the town of Helsingfors?"

"Certainly it is," boomed Napier.

Sulivan wet his lips. "I heard a number of conflicting opinions on that point," he said.

"Such as?"

"Several Finnish skippers believe that a detachment of Russian sail of the line—the number is variously given from six to ten—failed to reach the protection of Sveaborg—that is, the fortress covering Helsingfors—before the Gulf of Finland was iced in. They are said to be lying in the ice between Viborg and Helsingfors," said Sulivan, into a dead silence.

"Then, my dear Sir Charles," said Admiral Chads, "would it not be advisable to proceed with all speed into the Gulf, where the ice is breaking rapidly, and attack this Russian detachment before it can regain either base? A successful surprise action of that nature might be the key to the whole campaign—"

"You forget," interrupted the Commander-in-Chief, "Their Lordships have ordered me to attack Bomarsund; and in the same instructions, paragraph four, they give me this express admonition: 'Do not undertake any desperate work'!"

Chads smiled. "Is it such desperate work, to reconnoitre a fortress, well out of target range, and proceed to the kind of action the British public has been led to expect from us?"

"By God!" swore Sir Charles Napier, and his fat hand smote the table. "I resent that imputation from you, Admiral Chads. I'll undertake any work, however dangerous, if Their Lordships so command! I'll reduce Sveaborg to ashes, and Helsingfors too, if it's thought proper by the Admiralty! What's today? Aye, the second of April, we'll not forget the day, and Her Majesty, God bless her, will be five and thirty years old on the twenty-fourth of May. Fill up your glasses, gentlemen, and I'll give you one more toast. Here's a pledge that we'll celebrate Queen Victoria's birthday in the Winter Palace at St. Petersburg!"

CHAPTER SEVEN

DRIFT ICE

BRAND'S letter to Alix Gyllenlöve reached Helsingfors with the least possible delay, and surprisingly enough without any appearance of having been opened by a Russian postal censor. There was in fact, as Brand had noted when he was detained in Åbo, some hesitation and confusion among the Russian civil authorities as the Grand Duchy was placed on a war footing, and there was also a desire not to antagonize Finlanders of position and influence like Senator Walleen and his household. So the letter to Alix was neither delayed in transit nor lost in the post, but brought to her by a smiling Anna one April morning when the Baltic Fleet, having left Danish waters, was steaming in to its new anchorage at Älvsnabben.

It was not an elegant little three-cornered missive, like the notes Boris Apraxin and her other Russian admirers had slipped into the bouquets they sent Alexandra on ball nights. The cheap paper had been in contact with the ale-stained top of the table in the Baltica tavern, and then with the tobacco pouch carried by Joe Ryan; and Brand's penmanship had apparently not been improved by his one student year at Bowdoin, where—as he told Alix before leaving Helsingfors —his Aunt Betsy had sent him in the vain hope that he might experience a call to the ministry. The force with which he had written "*I love you and I will come back to you*" had almost driven his pen through the thin paper, and a shower of blots followed the bold signature, but it was none the less a man's letter, vigorous and masculine, and Alexandra's face was radiant as she read.

Madame Karamsin was spending the morning in her bedroom with a Swedish woman whose system of rubbing and oiling helped to keep her creamy shoulders and wonderfully slender arms in their perennial beauty, and the rest of the Villa Hagasund was too small for Alix Gyllenlöve that day. She felt Brand very close to her, and with an awakening but strong physical excitement she wanted to be close to him—

even if it could only be in memory; and for that she would have to retrace, alone, the path he and she had walked above the sea. It was odd how she could visualize Brand there more clearly than in the reception rooms of Hagasund, although he had been in all of them during his short stay in Helsingfors. She remembered how much more dignified his plain dark clothes had seemed than the frilled shirt fronts and pointed patent leather slippers of the Finnish gentlemen who had succumbed to the fashions of St. Petersburg. Aurora Karamsin had been charmed with him. Perhaps that was the very reason —since his image at Hagasund reflected the goodwill of so many other people—why Alix wanted to renew it that spring morning for herself alone.

Within an hour of reading Brand's letter she was walking rapidly along the road into the city. In Helsingfors girls enjoyed a great deal more liberty than the most married of matrons in St. Petersburg, and provided her Lapp maid was with her, Alexandra's movements had never been restricted at the Villa Hagasund. Anna was trotting at her heels now, wearing her scarlet *hilkka*, with her short black skirts swinging below her knees, and her snub-nosed brown face turning from side to side in sheer animal enjoyment of the sunshine and the soft breeze blowing up the Tölö creek. From time to time she exchanged a remark with Alix in the speech they had themselves evolved out of Swedish, Finnish and a few Lapp words. It was ten years since Alix's father had found the Laplander, then a woman of about twenty, with her dead infant in her arms, the dead and dying of her tribe around her and their reindeer herd wiped out, when he went to the Far North with a government mission for the relief of famine. He had bought her back to his little manor at Ekenäs, where she was baptized a Christian in the name of Anna, and where she eventually became a useful maid to Kristina and Alix Gyllenlöve. If she still held to any of her Lapp beliefs and customs, only Alix knew it.

It was not long before they reached the first turf-roofed log cabins of Helsingfors. Alexandra walked in the direction of Ulrikasborg by way of the Observatory, for the shore had been closed to civilians for some days. "Improvement of the road surface", was the reason given in the published notices; all Helsingfors translated this as the further enlargement of the Russian battery beyond the point. It was, however, possible to reach the park from the upper slopes of the hill, where smoke was now coming from the chimneys of most of the new villas, and maids and gardeners could be seen at work. In less than three weeks the park and the bay had lost their wintry aspect. There was no snow left on the evergreens; there were even a few green spears of spring flowers pushing their way up through the fallen needles at the base of every tree. Alix drew a long breath. Here they had stood, here he had taken her in his arms, here for the first time in her life she had felt the impulse to abandon herself to the man whose lips were burning on her own. She closed her eyes and felt in the pocket of her cloak for the letter which told her "I love you and I will come back to you".

"Over yonder lies the place of death and danger," she heard Anna say, and came back from the memory of love to the cold light of day.

"The fortress? Anna, you mean Sveaborg?"

"Yes, lady."

"When the British come?"

"After the British come. Danger, death will be near, for him and for you."

One brown forefinger was laid on the letter in Alexandra's hand. "I have seen it, lady," the Lapland woman whispered.

"Al—ix!" The call came from the slopes above them. Alix whipped round quickly.

"Paul, what are you doing here?"

It was young Paul Demidov, Aurora's son, who came lumbering down the path in a heavy fur coat too warm for the spring morning, with a grin half of triumph and half defiance on his sallow face.

"I might ask *you* that," he retorted. "I'm on my way to luncheon at the Princess Yousopovska's. Why are you wandering about alone with your tame witch?"

"Have the Yousopovsky boys arrived from Petersburg? I didn't know it."

"You don't take any interest in my friends or me, Alyssa Ivanovna." The boy had come close to Alix now. She could smell the sandalwood scent of the soap and toilet water Paul used lavishly. He had shaved that day, she saw; the dark shadow which sometimes flattered his upper lip was gone.

"You are at least three hours too early for a Russian luncheon party," Alix coldly pointed out, "even for a children's luncheon in the school-room. Where is your tutor, Paul?"

"Back at the Villa, of course," said the boy angrily. "Don't talk as if I were still in leading strings."

"I think you ought to be! You followed me here to Brunnsparken, didn't you?"

"What if I did? I never have a chance to see you alone, at home." He laid his hand on her arm, and Alix pulled away from him.

"You see me every day, Paul, don't be stupid. Why have you taken to pestering me and following me about? You used to be such a nice little boy—"

"I'm a man now, you see," said Paul Demidov. "Give me a kiss!"

Alix was aware, with her gloved hand raised to push him away, that Anna had come between them, lurching against the excited youth as a dog jumps to defend its mistress.

"Stop, Anna, leave him alone! Paul, get away from me, you little wretch! What would your mother think—"

"What would Mamma say if she knew you came out here alone to read a letter from your lover?" He made an ineffectual grab at the paper still in Alexandra's hand.

"Oh—h . . . !" This time she knew that she would strike him, that nothing could restrain the primitive impulse; and then to her huge relief she saw Madame Karamsin's coachman coming down the path towards them.

"Prince Paul, the horses will catch cold without a blanket —" the man began obsequiously, and Alix seized her opportunity.

"So you couldn't even *walk* here, you spoiled brat," she said in a contemptuous aside to the boy, and aloud to the coachman:

"Quite right, Gregori, you mustn't keep the horses standing. We shall drop Prince Paul at the Princess Yousopovska's villa and then you can take my maid and me back to Hagasund." There was no point in staying in Brunnsparken, even though the sun was shining and the first birds beginning to sing, for the clumsy boy by her side, scowling and blushing as they walked to the waiting carriage, had destroyed all her delicate recollection of the hour with Brand. She looked across the bay at the fortress, Sveaborg, which seemed by some trick of light and shadow to be much nearer to the shore, and then at Anna's closed face. Not that day, nor perhaps for many days, she knew, would the Lapp woman offer any further explanation of her vision of the fortress as a place of death and danger. They drove back almost in silence to Hagasund.

Madame Karamsin was arranging flowers, fully dressed and "Since the day is so fine and darling Paul lunching with some young friends" ready with a project for driving out to her own house at Träskända, which a small staff kept in readiness for her visits all the year round. There were some valuable things at Träskända, although the whole contents were hardly worth the treasures of one room in Aurora's Russian palace, and the caretakers were increasingly nervous in case the fine carpets and furniture should be looted by the British if an invasion did take place. Eventually it was decided, although not on the first visit, that the heavy furnishings must remain in place while the paintings and silverware were sent back to St. Petersburg, and that the same plan should be followed at Dalsvik, the house Aurora had built across the lake from Träskända to be a summer resort for Andrei Karamsin's family.

It became the custom, as the April days went by and the Finnish spring came in with all its gentle delicacy of wind-flowers beneath the birch trees and lake waters lapping free of their sheath of ice, for Madame Karamsin's carriage to carry Alix and herself every morning to either the Dalsvik villa or Träskända, where the great annual cleaning was going on at the same time as the packing of the valuables. Alix welcomed the occupation. It was something to do when her eager young body and strung nerves were crying out to be used to the full, even though the tasks fell so ludicrously short of her desire to further Finland's independence. There was nothing patriotic in counting table silver and supervising the men-servants roping the great chests addressed to St. Petersburg, and she was not helping Finland to become free by listening, on the long pleasant drives to the country, to Madame Karamsin's anxious praises of her "André". The poor lady's anxiety had become panic at one time, when shortly after the British and French declarations of war it was announced that the Russian Army of the Danube had crossed the river at three points and penetrated further into the Principalities, occupy-

116

ing the Dobrudja after heavy fighting and many casualties, but before long she had good news of her husband. Colonel Karamsin himself wrote to say that, with the General Staff, he was now in Bucharest, where the Russian officers were being lavishly entertained by the wealthy boyars of the Principality of Moldavia. Alix, with private amusement, saw that Madame Karamsin was turning over in her mind the possibility of travelling to Bucharest and joining in the exotic gaieties of the Balkans.

Meantime Aurora had her old friends in Helsingfors to entertain, and luncheons to attend at the Society-house Hotel with the select group for whom life seemed to go on much as before the declaration of war. It was easy for Alix, in those busy if purposeless days, to avoid Paul Demidov's adolescent pursuit and Senator Walleen's elderly tirades against what he called "the young barbarians of the age", and with each day that passed the threatened return to Petersburg was spoken of less often. But one morning towards the end of April Madame Karamsin came unceremoniously into Alexandra's room as she was dressing and said:

"Alix, your father has come. He arrived here late last night."

There was something in the girl's blank look which touched Aurora's heart. Something, too, about her youth which touched the older woman's jealousy, sublimely confident of her own beauty though she was. Alix wore a short petticoat and jacket, like a Finnish country girl, but the petticoat was made of white silk and the dressing jacket of white embroidered muslin, over which her fair hair fell straight and shining, turning up slightly at the ends. She had been brushing it vigorously, and the brush fell noiselessly to the thick carpet as Alix whispered:

"Here at Hagasund?"

"No, darling. I mean here in Helsingfors. In fact," said Aurora in some confusion, "he is at Sveaborg. He arrived last night, and is to stay with General Sorokin for some days."

"The guest of the Governor of Sveaborg . . . good heavens!" said Alix. "Papa is rising in the world."

She stooped to pick up the tortoiseshell-backed brush, and Aurora watched the supple movement of the slender back and arm, the straight line of the long bare legs beneath the frilled silk petticoat. "Darling, aren't you cold?" she said with a glance at the open window.

"Cold—no, of course not. Aurora, tell me about papa. When is he coming to see me here?"

"Dearest, he especially asks that we shall go to him. He is here on business, and his time is not his own, but of course he wants to see you and—and talk over future plans. The Sorokins have invited us both for luncheon today, and your father will come to meet us at the harbour at half past twelve."

"Luncheon at the fortress? I thought it was positively closed to Finlanders, unless of course an exalted civil servant like my papa."

"Alix, you're not to be sarcastic. This invitation to you is a compliment to your father, and I do ask you—I implore you not to say or do anything in General Sorokin's presence which might prejudice Johan's career."

"Did I say or do anything to prejudice his career when I was living with him in Petersburg, and *he* was . . . I suppose you could call it living with his mistress, every time that Madame Ourov could get away from Moscow?"

"Now Alix," Aurora, with an elaborate shiver, drew her satin negligée more closely round her and took a chair well out of the draught of air from the window. "Do sit down and let us talk reasonably. Your father, I admit, has been rather imprudent, and Nadine Ourov has made herself and him conspicuous on one or two occasions, but you are much too dogmatic and too harsh in your judgement of them."

"*My mother* taught me the difference between right and wrong, you see."

Aurora sighed as she looked at the girl's reflection in the glass. Alix had sat down at her dressing-table, and the sunshine reflected in the long mirror turned her pale hair to spun gold. It was certainly one of her beautiful days, Aurora thought, when her extraordinary eyes were dark with feeling and her skin—again that tiny pang of envy—was as fresh as the petals of a rose.

"Darling, how well you look," she said gently. "Your father will be so proud of you . . . Don't bother him too much with your mamma's ideas of right and wrong. There are times, you know, when one has to compromise with life . . . and

Eleonora, poor darling, was really never the right wife for Johan."

Startled: "Don't you think she made my father happy?"

"Not as happy as Nadine Ourov makes him."

"But Madame Ourov already has a husband."

"Old enough to be her father. Alix, don't think I condone wrongdoing! I only want you to realize that a brilliant active man like your father *did* find a government post in a Finnish province boring and unexacting, and poor Eleonora *did* make the most of all her little ailments ... it was inevitable when Johan became a widower he would make himself another kind of life. After all, he's still only forty-five! Do try to understand him better, Alix. You two quarrel because you are so like each other! If you had been the son he hoped for so much before you were born, you would be making a name for yourself in public affairs now, just like Johan. I've often thought, when I've heard you and the Mannerheim boy talking so earnestly about Finland, that all your interest and eagerness come to you from your father—"

"And he *does* work for Finland," Alexandra said. The stern lines of her mouth softened. "I'm glad he's here," she said.

Madame Karamsin rose with a smile. "Wear your green dress," she said, "and I shall send Verna in to curl your hair."

"Oh not those horrid Blenheim Spaniel ringlets!"

But Alix's fair hair was arranged in shining curls beneath her pale green bonnet when she took her place in the carriage at noon, and Madame Karamsin had the pleasure of delivering her, a picture of sophisticated elegance, to the handsome man awaiting them at the harbour steps.

"You look charming, my dear. Helsingfors agrees with you." said Johan Gyllenlöve, kissing Alix on both cheeks before pressing his lips to Aurora Karamsin's hand. "You are both magnificent, but dare I entrust such fine feathers to a Navy cutter?"

"Of course you can," laughed Aurora, manœuvring her lilac skirts and huge ermine muff aboard the waiting boat with his assistance.

"*You* look very well, papa," said Alix timidly, as the picked Russian sailors pulled away from the Market Square. It was not quite true, for her father's fresh colour was paler than when she left him in St. Petersburg before Christmas, and there was a finer network of wrinkles at the corners of his dark grey eyes; but it was still an amazingly youthful and at present a good-humoured face. Like Alix, Johan Gyllenlöve was tall, slender when most men of his age were portly, and there was very little grey in his blond hair. He was clean-shaven and wore uniform, like all members of the Imperial civil service, whether they were concerned with public works in Finland or the transportation of state prisoners across Siberia. Alix noticed that he wore his two Orders. She was not particularly observant of Russian uniforms, but as they all three smiled and chatted, and exchanged polite enquiries about the health of relatives and friends it seemed to her that her father wore a different set of buttons and aiguillettes, and carried a new style of dress sword. She supposed it was some vagary of the Czar's, who would willingly have put every educated man in Russia into some form of military uniform.

"But you gave us such very short notice, dear Johan," lamented Madame Karamsin. "Can you not spend one night at the Villa Hagasund?"

"I wish I could, Aurora, but it's most unlikely. General von Berg and I have a huge coastal survey to carry out, from Viborg west to Hangö, and after that to Åbo; we mustn't spend too long at Helsingfors."

He can't intend to take me with him, exulted Alexandra. On an official mission, travelling post, he won't want to be bothered with a woman and her baggage. I shall still be here when the British Fleet reaches Helsingfors—

"Why is General von Berg going to carry out a survey, papa, please?"

"Because the Czar has appointed him commander of all the south coast troops, except the garrison of Sveaborg. Prince Susarov has been given the civil command of Livonia, Esthonia and Courland, and I—"

He paused impressively.

"Yes, papa?"

"His Majesty has put me at the head of the Railway Commission, appointed by imperial ukase seven days ago."

The classical perfection of the Helsingfors waterfront blurred and shook before Alexandra's eyes.

"Is there to be a railway into Finland?" she controlled her

voice to say. "Will the Railway Commission be part of our Ministry?"

"Not exactly, my dear," said Gyllenlöve with the same determined good humour as he had shown since they met. "It has been created to deal with a part of the Empire where the need for a modern transport system is really urgent. The present survey is a matter of technical information, intended to help General von Berg, and as soon as it is completed—say in about two weeks—my Commission and I will start work on a line joining Moscow directly with the Crimea."

"Then you won't be working with Count Armfelt any more?" Alix persisted.

"Not for the duration of the war, at least."

"I can see the harbour on Great East Svartö," Aurora tactfully interrupted. "Dear Johan, how long is it since you and I last came to Sveaborg together?"

He turned to her at once with his pleasant smile. "I don't know, Aurora. Not since before either of us was married. Do you remember the picnics we used to have on Vargön, in the days when Zakrevsky was Governor of Finland?"

"The summer picnics!" said Aurora with a sigh. "Part of our simple pleasures, Alix, when Helsingfors was so small that the arrival of the excursion boat from Reval was a great event!"

"I seem to remember a winter picnic best of all," said Gyllenlöve. "You and Mina Mannerheim, Aurora, and Alex Muhanov and I—we skated on the Vargö lake as long as the light lasted, and then ran all the way back to the Residence for coffee. How old were you then—sixteen? You and Muhanov ran ahead of us, hand in hand—"

"Don't, Johan, please!" There was such raw feeling in Aurora's usually gentle voice that Alix looked at her with surprise. How could they sentimentalize over the picnics of twenty-five years ago when Sveaborg today was one of the greatest armed camps in the world? The cutter was coming in to the landing stage of Great East Svartö now, and she could see the immense crown-work on the first of the fortified islands of Sveaborg. To starboard lay the barracks and dockyards of Little East Svartö, joined to its bigger namesakes by a causeway, while beyond their line of vision a second causeway led to West Svartö, on which were two powder magazines, another barracks and the victualling centre of the whole fortress. Under the budding trees of a lime grove near the little harbour General Sorokin's carriage waited, with a mounted aide de camp in attendance.

"The Sveaborg roads were not made for civilian traffic," said this young man, saluting. "I trust the ladies will not be inconvenienced!"

"We shall be forced to drive at a walking pace," said Gyllenlöve significantly. The island was in fact swarming with troops. Kalmucks, Ukrainians, Georgians, Cossacks—every tribe in the Russian Empire seemed to be represented in the different labour corps tramping past the carriage to work on strengthening the defences of Sveaborg.

"How large is the garrison of the fortress now?" Alix asked abruptly. Her father raised his eyebrows at her tone, but replied quite naturally:

"Six thousand officers and men, I'm told. About the same strength as the garrison of Helsingfors, although that will be increased when General Konakowsky's brigade arrives."

"One Russian to every citizen of Helsingfors, then?"

"Approximately."

Alexandra's heart sank. Against such a force, what possible chance existed for the three hundred and fifty students of Helsingfors University, the only body with the belief and the energy to lead a nationalist uprising? She looked out blankly at the barracks street and saw with her own eyes what she had only known through rumour—long files of Russian convicts, shuffling in chains to the ropeworks, where the shift would be changed at one o'clock. From the barred windows of the tall white garrison buildings, already a century old, glared the faces of soldiers very little more intelligent than the subhuman, dirt-encrusted faces of the convict labourers. Madame Karamsin opened her lilac silk parasol and tilted it between those windows and her eyes.

The carriage rolled downhill and over the trestle bridge which joined Great East Svartö to Vargön, and the aide de camp, riding alongside, pointed out the work going forward to deepen and extend the Russian Navy dockyards which lay under the double protection of the Svartö crown-work and the casements of Vargön.

"This is where the ships of the line will lie, Aurora, as soon as they come through the drift ice from Lovisa," said Gyllen-löve.

"How very interesting !"

Alix said nothing. Her heart was beating fast as they drove up the steep approaches of Vargön, passing under an archway of the great bastion into the quiet but well guarded square which was the heart of Sveaborg. Here, protected by a keep several tiers high, was something like a formal garden, or at least a space of green, well-kept grass which fronted the Governor's residence; and in this garden stood the tomb of Sveaborg's creator, Ehrensvärd.

This had been the scene of the great surrender, forty-six years before, and here, after the fortress fell by treachery to the Russians, a Russian Te Deum had been sung to give thanks for victory at the grave of Ehrensvärd. Alexandra did not trust herself to look at the sarcophagus. She was aware of many eyes upon her as General Sorokin and his lady came out to greet their guests. She gave all her attention to the series of curtsies required as she followed Madame Karamsin's lilac taffeta and ermine furs through the door of the Residence, to which Aurora as a happy girl of sixteen had come running through a snowy twilight more than a quarter of a century before.

"You and I must have a long talk, Alix," Count Gyllenlöve found an opportunity to say quietly after all the introductions had been made and fluted glasses of champagne were offered in the drawing-room of the Residence. "Are you wearing the right kind of shoes for walking, or silly satin slippers like Aurora's?"

"Shoes, Papa." She put one little leather toe-cap beyond the hem of her green dress, and her father smiled.

"Very well, then, I shall arrange it when luncheon is over —after our conference."

It was a small luncheon party by Petersburg standards, consisting of only twenty guests, but it lived up to the Petersburg standards of display, conspicuous waste and frivolous conversation, conducted in not always accurate French. This spared Alix from hearing the sibilants of her Russian name, Alyssa Ivanovna, many times repeated; as "mademoiselle" she was addressed by the two garrison majors between whom she was seated at the lowly end of the table, while Aurora's priceless pearls shone at the right hand of the commanding general. She had ample time, while the majors gave her their uninformed views on ballet, to study the senior member of her father's mission. She had met General von Berg in Petersburg, and knew that he was close to the throne, so close that he had been mentioned as the next Governor-General of Finland. He was of Baltic German stock, with a narrow foxy face and a reputation for cruelty: exactly the sort of instrument the Czar Nikita would use if he had to put down a Finnish uprising.

There were four officers' wives present, all in considerable awe of Madame Sorokin and the legendary Aurora Karamsin, and their talk, after the ladies had withdrawn, fell even below the level of the usual garrison chatter. Their children and their difficulties in getting domestic help from the mainland were their only topics of conversation apart from the Czar's recent visit and its attendant festivities: the spread of the war to Europe seemed to be absolutely taboo on Sveaborg. Alix sat by the closed double windows, replying politely when she was addressed and wondering how long her father's conference with the general would last. It was over an hour before he appeared in Madame Sorokin's boudoir with a pleasant request "for the loan of his daughter for a while".

"Father, may we please look at the monument?" It was her first request as soon as they were out in the fresh air, and almost without waiting for his assent Alix crossed the lawn and stood before the grave of Ehrensvärd.

"Very fine; very beautiful setting," approved the voice of General von Berg, who had come quietly across the turf to join her father. "Is this your first visit to Sveaborg, Alyssa Ivanovna?"

"No, General, I came here once five years ago, when I was in boarding school," she said. "Miss Harring received permission to bring a few pupils to visit the King's Gate, and also the grave of Ehrensvärd."

"Indeed? With what object, may I ask?"

Alix looked at him with smoky eyes. "We had been reading the *Tales of Ensign Stål*, sir. Miss Harring wished us to see the scene which Runeberg describes, of the fall of Sveaborg."

"Charming!" said von Berg, and the smile beneath his red moustache was not pleasant. "Romantic nationalism in a young

124

ladies' school! . . . Pray is your schoolmistress still reading Runeberg with her pupils, Alyssa Ivanovna?"

"Miss Harring has earned her retirement, General," said Johan Gyllenlöve easily. "She was Madame Karamsin's own governess, known to all the family as *Bonne Amie*. A truly refined and talented old lady."

How clever my father is, thought Alix, as General von Berg bowed and with a word of excuse turned back to the Residence. I would have flared up in defence of the poet—our national poet! But father knew that von Berg would never dare to sneer at anyone of whom Aurora chose to approve. I must be silent, and think more, she resolved, as her father led her beneath the great keep and out on the high flat land in the middle of Vargön.

The sea was flowing calmly in from the Gulf of Finland, through the sounds and shoals of Sveaborg into the vast harbourage which surrounded Helsingfors. The sun was in Alexandra's face, and on the fair hair now a little out of curl, and Johan Gyllenlöve was proud of her.

"You really look extraordinary well, my dear," he told her as they strolled past the ornamental lake. "Tell me, when did you last hear from Kristina?"

"About a month ago. Three weeks."

"She and Gunnar Falk were well? The baby well?"

Alix hesitated. "I think so. But Kristina really hasn't got her strength back since little Karen was born."

"Still, she wrote happily? You think she's happy with Gunnar Falk?"

"She's very fond of him, papa. And then she loves London— she likes their kind of life."

"That's good." He looked at her intently. "I want my girls to be happy, Alix—*both* my girls."

Faintly: "Yes, I know, papa."

"That's why I didn't join in all the ranting and raving when you broke off your engagement to Boris Apraxin. Mind! I don't approve of the unorthodox way you chose to do it. I said as much to the young man himself when he called on me, bursting with wounded pride and injury. But after that interview, and another I had with that vicious-tongued old mother of his, I came to the conclusion that you were well rid of Captain Apraxin. And—since the match was of Aurora's

125

making much more than mine—suppose we forget about the whole thing now?"

"Oh, papa, how kind you are! Oh, if you only knew how sick I am of hearing people *talk* about it!"

"I can imagine it," said her father. "But I don't believe you'll have to hear much more. Boris is on the way to the Danube front and Princess Apraxin has gone to their *dacha* in the country; you won't have to see either of them when you come back to Petersburg."

Alix had been prepared for severity. She had to take her courage in both hands before she said:

"But I would rather not go back to Petersburg."

"Indeed! Pray where would you prefer to go?"

"Papa, I want to stay in Finland. If you would allow me to go home to Ekenäs—I would take Anna with me, and you have always kept some servants at the manor, so it must be in good order and quite comfortable—"

"Home to Ekenäs!" said Gyllenlöve. "You must be crazy to think of such a thing. Or I would be crazy, to let you go off with that half-demented Lapp to a lonely manor in Nyland, with a Russian garrison in the neighbourhood, and the whole district unsettled with the war—"

"Then let me go to old Miss Agneta Willebrand at Degerby," Alix interrupted swiftly. "Her house isn't lonely, and she has men-servants and gardeners to take care of us. Just for the summer, papa, please!"

"I see you've come prepared with alternatives," the man said grimly. "You don't seem to realize that Degerby may be as dangerous as Ekenäs, before Admiral Napier has broken his heart against the Baltic forts and taken his antiquated fleet away. Now I intend that you shall spend this summer in safety, and by safety I mean the Demidov palace in St Petersburg, where Aurora has very kindly invited you to be her guest."

"But I've spent nearly *two months* with Aurora, here!"

"And very happily, I'm sure."

"Aurora is very sweet to me," said Alix. "But living with her is like living on chocolate creams—you know, the kind with rose or violet fondant for a filling."

"You'd rather risk your teeth on a piece of nougat?"

"Sometimes I'd like to chew," said Alexandra sharply. ". . . Oh, I'm sorry, papa. I ought not to have said that, I know.

126

Aurora has been an angel to me, not only in the past two months, but all my life ... But I can't help feeling that these long stays with her put me a little on the footing of a poor relation. She gives me so much, and I give her such small services in return, like pouring coffee for her guests and supervising Verna when she does the packing—"

Irritably: "There is no reason to feel yourself a poor relation! I can't match fortunes with the Demidovs—few men in the Russian Empire can—but you girls are very well provided for. Kristina had a handsome dowry when she married Falk, and Ekenäs is secured to you by the terms of your mother's marriage settlement, you know that."

"Then why can't I go and live at Ekenäs?" she persisted.

"Now that will do, young lady! You'll go back to Russia with Aurora whenever she wishes to go, and I expect to see you both settled in the Morskaia before I leave St. Petersburg."

She stared at him. "You're leaving Petersburg?"

"The Railway Commission will have its headquarters in Moscow, Alix. I thought you understood that."

In his evasive look she saw awareness that she had not understood, and as full understanding came Alix, releasing her hold on her father's arm instinctively, saw the reason for his complaisance in the affair of her broken engagement. No more was to be said about Apraxin, and in return nothing was to be said about Nadine Ourov, who at this moment must be preening herself in Moscow, anticipating her lover's establishment in her own city. The temptation was great to answer "Madame Ourov will be delighted!" but even in her jealousy and vexation Alix realized the imperative need to be diplomatic, and only said:

"I thought all the government services were concentrated in St. Petersburg."

"This is a Commission of technicians, because the Czar is fully aware that only technical skills will win a war against France and Britain. It will sit in Moscow because the main railway arteries are to end at Moscow, and because—as I said before—we must transport troops to the Crimea as rapidly as possible."

"But won't the Western Allies attack the Russians in the Principalities?"

Gyllenlöve smiled. "You're not a strategist, my child. The

Principalities have served their turn. The Czar hopes to defeat his enemies by drawing them into the interior of Russia, where they will be defeated as surely as Napoleon after he entered Moscow—"

"Or Charles XII at Poltava," said Alix, and tried to control her trembling hands.

"Exactly. Now the Emperor of the French, having learned nothing from his uncle's errors, is said to have set his heart on the capture of Sevastopol. Therefore sooner or later the Allies will attempt an invasion of the Crimea, to give aid and comfort to their Turkish friends. We shall be ready for them when they arrive, secure in the knowledge that their campaign in the Baltic is as good as lost already."

"What do you mean?" she said, white-lipped.

"Were you listening to what the aide de camp and I were saying as we drove past the Vargön docks? Or were you dreaming about Döbeln at Juutas or some other last-war hero of romance? I pointed out the place where the Russian ships of war will lie tomorrow, or the day after that at latest, when they sail in through the Gustafssund to the safest harbour in the Gulf of Finland. The harbour where Napier will never capture them, or even catch a glimpse of their mastheads, until the war is won!"

"Coming from Cronstadt?" she said stupidly.

"Coming from Lovisa! They were lying in the ice halfway down the Gulf when war broke out. Seven ships of the line, and the Russian Admiralty's greatest anxiety for the past six weeks. You see," he elaborated, "there was a period when the British, *in strength*, could have destroyed them all. Then not only the material loss but the moral loss would have been tremendous. The northern Kings might well have declared for Britain; even Prussia too—who knows? But Admiral Napier, for all his bombast and boasting, has lost his great opportunity. He was afraid to risk Lord Nelson's superannuated three-deckers in the drift ice of the Gulf. He is idling at Älvsnabben now, snug in the lee of the Swedish coast, and if the Russians decide to come out as a combined fleet from Cronstadt and Helsingfors, they should be able to dispose of him quite comfortably before summer is over."

The first clear idea which came to Alexandra was that she had sent Brand Endicott to his death. The invincible British

Navy, failing through inaction to win the key engagement which meant control of all the Gulf of Finland and threatened now with annihilation by the intact Russian fleet—in that horrific picture, presented to her by the father whose intelligence and ability she never doubted, the girl could see only the young American whom her persuasions had forced against his will into the fight. She put his image away from her deliberately. There was something to be resolved first, something which—for all her determination to be diplomatic—had to be plainly stated between her father and herself. She said:

"Papa, I am sorry to hear you say 'we' when you speak of the Russians, as if you felt yourself to be one of them. And I am truly sorry that you have left Count Armfelt's Secretariat. I've always been so proud that you were working with him for the good of Finland."

Gyllenlöve made a gesture of impatience. "What does that amount to? Applause when we install a new horse trough in the market place at Tammerfors? The Railway Commission, in wartime, is more important than the whole administration of the Grand Duchy. After the war it will bring prosperity to Finland—you will see."

He took Alexandra's arm and urged her forward.

"You see the channel between Vargön and Gustafssvärd? It is to be filled in eventually," Count Gyllenlöve explained. "The means of access now is a ravelin and a covered way. As fas as possible we use it only for the conveyance of victuals and ammunition, for otherwise, as you can see, Gustafssvärd is a city in itself."

Alix stared at the great fort. The Russian double eagle flew over the triple line of batteries in a casemated strandwork which defended the open *terre-pleine* in the middle of Gustafssvärd. With newly-sharpened eyes she saw how very difficult it would be for British ships to tackle the continuous lines of sloping earth batteries, which presented nothing for a mark but the muzzles of the guns. Across the narrow Sound of Gustaf a new sloping defence line of turf forts was in the course of construction on Bakholm. She looked over the Sound to the open water of the Gulf.

"Is that one of the warships from Lovisa coming in now?" she asked.

Her father laughed, and told her indulgently that the vessel anchored off Gustafssvärd was an obsolete ship of the line, the *Russia*, built in the previous century—"about the same age as Admiral Napier's scrap-heap fleet," he said contemptuously.

"But I don't understand," said Alix. "What use can an obsolete ship be put to, against the—the enemy?"

"The *Russia* will be put to good use, never fear. As soon as the warships which were held in the ice arrive, the *Russia* will be towed across the entrance to Gustafssund. The enemy ships will find it a formidable obstacle in addition to the fire of one hundred and sixty guns, if they ever attempt to enter the harbour of Helsingfors!"

"But surely Gustaf's Sound isn't the only entrance to Helsingfors?" said Alix.

"What other way can you think of?"

Alix looked across the water to Brunnsparken, where she had walked with Brand. Between the fortress and the mainland lay the island of Långörn, regarded as part of the great defence system and heavily fortified.

"Isn't there a channel between Långörn and West Svartö?" she said. "I'm sure I've seen ships approaching the South Harbour on the Långörn side."

"Very observant of you," approved her father. "Yes, there is a channel, but it's too shallow for ships of the line. A gunboat could go through, but we know Napier has no gunboats, for the present at any rate. If in the future there should be a threat to the Långörn channel, it will be blocked at once by another of our superannuated vessels."

Alexandra halted. The spring wind blew across her hot face as freely as it blew over Marstrand, in a free country; but she was inside the fortress, crushed by the mighty weight of ravelin and bastion, cannon and culverin, and all the witnesses to Russian power. If that power were ever defeated it would only be because people like herself, women as well as men, had the courage to stand up for their convictions. She said boldly:

"Father, you've said it again. 'Our' and 'we', when you mean Russia. 'Our' country is Finland and only Finland—or should be."

"You still have that bee in your bonnet, have you?" said the man. "I begin to think General von Berg was right to give you a good setting-down! 'Romantic nationalism in a young ladies' school', he said. And the right place for it too! Alix, remember this. Whether we like it or not, we are part of an empire at war—a war forced upon us by the West. Your Helsingfors professors and your lady novelists and the *Kalevala* and the *Tales of Ensign Stål* belong to a romantic past which has nothing to do with the world we know."

"Father—"

"In this world, in this war, I believe Russia will emerge victorious. I'm not alone in thinking so. Erik Kruse for one agrees with me, though we all know the Allies are powerful. There may be heavy Russian losses before snow flies again. But Russia will win in the end—if it's only at the peace conference table—and in a few years from now the Czar will make another move into Europe. Because I believe this I accepted the chairmanship of the Railway Commission, and now I stand committed to the Russian side."

"And I am committed to the West," she said.

CHAPTER EIGHT

PLOUGHING THE FIELD OF SERPENTS

JOHAN Gyllenlöve's assessment of the Baltic Fleet was wrong in one important particular. The Commander-in-Chief was not idling in his Swedish anchorage.

Napier and all his officers were furiously busy. They had to make seamen out of a mixed body of old Navy hands, coast-guards, dockyard riggers and incompetent volunteers, got to-gether in a hurry and sent to sea without winter clothing, without oilskins and very nearly without food. They had to fight a war with Russia at the precise moment when the Royal Navy was in a state of transition between the wooden ship and the iron ship, between sail and steam power, be-tween the round shot with which Drake had beaten the Spanish Armada and the shell gun which had allowed the Russians to destroy the Turkish fleet at Sinope in 1853. The old ships converted to screw moved forward into the Baltic in a series of elementary evolutions, in ragged line due to the variations in HPN, without even changing position from divi-sions into line or from line into sailing columns, while their bulging wooden sides and vast sterns struggled clumsily through the new manœuvres of the Chase required by steam. They had to cope with the logistics of coaling, and the social problems posed by the arrival in the ward-room of the Engineer officer—who two years back had been rated lower than the Carpenter. They had solved none of these problems at the beginning of what every officer in the fleet knew would be an arduous campaign, but when Napier hoisted his square blue flag at *Duke's* mizzen topgallant masthead on April 12 he also hoisted a signal which put some heart into the raw and half trained crews.

"Lads," the signal ran, "war is declared. We have a bold and numerous enemy to meet. Should they offer you battle, you know how to dispose of them. Should they remain in port, we must try and get at them. Success depends on the quickness and precision of your fire. Sharpen your cutlasses and the day is your own!"

The rendezvous appointed by Napier on leaving Køge Bay was Landsort island on the east coast of Sweden, twenty miles from the sheltered anchorage at Älvsnabben which had been charted by Captain Sulivan. When Landsort was reached on April 14, Brand Endicott had been rated for ten days as an Ordinary Seaman in H.M.S. *Arrogant*, 46, Captain Hastings Yelverton.

Brand had been entered on the ship's book after the briefest possible induction to the Navy, for Captain Yelverton's sole concern was to have *Arrogant* fully manned and worked up without delay into an efficient fighting unit. He was a typical captain of the Russian War: a man of forty-six who in spite of "interest" (he was a nephew of the Duke of Leinster and the husband of the Dowager Marchioness of Hastings) had been on half-pay for more than ten years, and regarded the Baltic campaign as a heaven-sent opportunity for prizes and promotion. Yelverton was a reasonably humane man, who respected the new punishment Regulations and flogged as seldom as possible, but if the bo'sun's rattan cane was abolished in *Arrogant* a blind eye was turned to the mates' rope's end "starters", and there was no room in the iron discipline of the frigate for the "nice cottage sermons" read by Sulivan to those of his crew who joined him every night for evening prayers. Brand soon realized that where Sulivan had made *Lightning* a happy ship, Yelverton meant to make a taut ship of *Arrogant*.

H.M.S. *Arrogant*, built in 1848, was one of the most modern screw frigates in the Navy, displacing 1872 tons, 360 HPN, and carrying a crew of 450. The hands, of course, were overcrowded, but as *Arrogant's* 46 guns were mounted on the main deck and quarterdeck the men who ate and slept and spent their watches below were at least not compelled to exist between the great red-painted guns and their gun carriages. Brand had fourteen inches of space to sling his hammock between battens, his government issue irons and earthenware in their mess kid, and his place at the eight man mess which included Lauri the Finn, Kedge and Klerck having been sent together to *Imperieuse*. Uniform for the hands was not yet standard in the Royal Navy, but pursers stocked their slop stores with garments uniform in themselves, and Brand was rigged out like every other man aboard in wide blue trousers, a short blue jacket with a broad jean collar and a flat tarpaulin hat with a ribbon.

He adapted quickly to life in the lower deck. Two or three men in his mess had a strong antipathy to Americans, and said so; the others nicknamed him "Yankee Jack" and accepted him as one of themselves. After all, it was not so long since he had sailed before the mast, and it was easy to forget that more recently still he had been a first class passenger on a crack Cunarder and occupied the captain's berth of the *Gridleness*. What galled him was his poor performance in the first seamanship exercises of the crew.

On the strength of their previous experience Mr. Haggard, the First Lieutenant of the *Arrogant*, had placed Brand and Lauri among the topmen, or second to the sheet-anchor men, the best hands in the ship. During their watches on deck the topmen were set to racing up and down the rigging, reefing and unreefing the topsails and sending the topgallant yards down and up, while a thick fog blanketed their movements and their thin clothing was soaked within minutes by rain and spray. At such times Brand was never quite free from vertigo. It was a weakness of his earliest days at sea, which he had thought conquered and daily tried to overcome again, but when mast was raced against mast he lagged behind. while Lauri's acrobatics were spectacular. The boy from Gamla Karleby was invariably the first back on deck, while Brand Endicott was frequently among the last.

"Look alive! Look alive there, you Yankee bastard!"

One of the bo'sun's mates, called Pringle, was always behind Brand, swearing and driving him up to the wet yards, on which his ice-numbed fingers clutched to find a hold, while the deck tilted beneath him, waiting for the crash of a falling body, as the frigate rolled in the heavy Baltic seas. Once, as the gale shrieked in the canvas, he felt the flick of the rope's end, and turned in a rage to drive his fist into Pringle's face, careless of his footing, careless of the terrible punishment such a blow would bring; and he was saved from himself only by a cry of warning from Lauri on the upper topsail yard— more like a seagull's shriek than a human being's in the Baltic

134

fog. That fog might well have hidden the incident from the deck, but Captain Yelverton and the First Lieutenant were standing not far from the foremast when Brand came down.

"Endicott!" That was Yelverton, cold, passionless as usual, raking him with a glance.

"Sir?"

"You were a fisherman in your own country, were you not?"

"Yes, sir."

"You had some experience of reefing, surely? You went aloft, off the Banks?"

"Yes, sir."

"H'm . . . Mr. Haggard, this man is useless as a topman," said Yelverton. "Change his Division to the after-guard. Set him to gunnery practice as soon as we reach Älvsnabben."

"Aye, aye, sir."

The hands were piped to dinner and Brand went sullenly below. The after-guard! His next step down would be to join the waisters, who did the dirty work of the ship! As they started on the salt pork and pease pudding he said moodily to Lauri:

"This is a damned queer way to fight the Czar of Russia."

"Fight? We fight Russkies?" said Lauri hopefully, and Brand laughed in spite of himself. The Finlander had a singleness of purpose which reminded him of Alix, although Brand had discovered during their halting conversations that Lauri's reasons for hating the Russians were not so high-flown as hers, but rooted in his family's sufferings in the last war. Lauri shaved closely every day. so that his cheeks were as smooth as a girl's, and to Brand there was something, painful and yet pleasurable, of Alix Gyllenlöve in the boy's grey eyes and heavy fair hair.

"We'll fight the Russkies some day soon, Larry boy," he said.

"Soon blow 'em out of the water, Larry, now we've got Mister Yankee Jack on guns," said one of the mess with a guffaw. He was a gross, grimy Welshman named Morgan, with two convictions for petty theft at Cardiff on his record, and the day before he had appeared at defaulters' drill, charged with spitting on the deck. Yelverton had sentenced him to wear a bucket round his neck for the rest of the day for the hands to use as a spittoon.

Some of the mess laughed. The day's ration of rum was being served, mixed with lemon acid against scurvy, and sugar and water into the grog which always made laughter easy. Morgan, encouraged, went blustering on:

"Never knew a Yankee any good aloft; never 'eard of a Yankee what could serve a gun. My old father fought 'em forty years back, and that's what he told me. Ivor, he said, the Yankees are a soft lot—"

"Shut your goddamned mouth, Morgan," said Brand loudly, "we beat the hell out of your side, anyway."

"Avast there!" Edgeworthy, the middle-aged Leading Seaman acting as mess cook, spoke up with authority. "Stow it the two of yer! Jack, we don't allow no politics at dinner, it's a time for pleasant sociable talk between messmates. Morgan, you galley-ranger, you'll be changing your mess two Sundays from now if you ain't careful. Give over both of you and let us eat this 'orrible junk in peace."

"'E's right," said the mess in a collective growl, and Morgan subsided. But when the coarse food had been eaten and the grog drunk he started to sing "The Ballad of the Chesapeake and the Shannon," with a wink for his messmates and a meaning look at Brand.

> "The Chesapeake so bold,
> Out of Boston, we've been told,
> Came to take the British frigate
>   Neat and handy, O!
> All the people of the port,
> They came out to see the sport,
> And the bands were playing
> Yankee Doodle Dandy, O!"

It was not unusual for a sing-song to be started on the lower deck after dinner, or even on the main deck during the dog watch. Singing was part of the seafaring life, approved by officers as a wholesome form of skylarking, and in *Arrogant* Ordinary Seaman Morgan, whatever his defects, was admitted to have the finest voice aboard. It was a true Welsh tenor, generally employed on sea-chanteys or the romantic airs warbled by the street-walkers of Cardiff, and now lifted in a famous British ballad of the War of 1812.

> "The British frigate's name,
> Which for the purpose came,
> Of cooling Yankee courage
>   Neat and handy, O!
> Was the SHANNON—Captain Broke—
> All her crew were hearts of oak,
> And at fighting they're allowed to be
> The dandy, O!"

Brand Endicott sat tense and still. He had never heard the song before, but of course he knew the story of the U.S.S. *Chesapeake* and H.M.S. *Shannon*, and their encounter in a battle which even his father had hardly been able to pretend the Americans won. You damned gloating Britishers, he thought, staring at the grinning seamen round the mess-table. It was dark on the lower deck, for the fog was thick outside and the frigate rolling heavily. The portlids were closed as usual, and the rope cables running down the centre of the deck to the hawse-holes in the manger breakwater were creaking and straining. The hawse-holes had been plugged with oakum, but sea water was slowly seeping in; the lower deck had not been completely dry since they sailed from Køge. The Marines were looking out from their after-quarters close to the gun room netting, and from other mess-tables the hands were joining lustily in Morgan's song. Lantern light shone on the Welshman's triumphant face, with the pure clear tenor issuing from between such bloated and scrofulous cheeks:

> "We no sooner had begun
> Than from their guns they run,
> Though before they thought they worked 'em
>   Neat and handy, O!
> Brave Broke he waved his sword
> Crying 'Now, my lads, we'll board,
> And we'll stop their playing
>   Yankee Doodle Dandy, O!'"

Lauri was playing the tune on his mouth-organ. He had no idea what the words meant, but his quick ear had caught the air, and with his constant wish to please his messmates he was happy to provide an accompaniment for a song they seemed to like. Brand knocked his stool back as he rose and took the Finlander by the arm.

"Lay off it, Larry," he said. "You and I had better get to hell out of here."

Morgan stopped singing.

"Don't want to 'ear the rest of it, do you, Jack?" he said. "Rather go on up to the heads and 'ave a good time with your fancy boy, would you?"

Brand kicked over the mess-table and jumped for the Welshman's throat. They went down together in a clatter of earthenware and pewter, kicking and gouging, rolling out into the centre aisle where the hands quickly made a ring round them, ready to bet on Morgan or Endicott as the two men staggered to their feet and began to batter at each other with their bare fists. Into every blow Brand put his resentment: he struck Morgan but he hit at Captain Yelverton, and the "Ballad of the Chesapeake" was only the words and music of what he thought of as the Captain's sneer at the incompetent Yankee reefer. He felt a heavy jolt as Morgan's left hit his jaw. He staggered back for a moment which gave the Welshman time to slip something over his knuckles, saw the flash of steel, and heard a cry of protest from Edgeworth, keeping the ring. There were other shouts from the spectators, but Brand paid no attention: he went into a clinch from which the Welshman wriggled free. There was sweat and blood from Morgan's face on his blue jacket. Brand feinted with his left, waited too long, and felt the bite of the steel spike above his eye as Morgan's knuckleduster found its mark. Then he put everything he had into a right cross, saw Morgan go down with a grunt, slipped in the mess of spilt food and crockery on the planks, and fell upon the prone body of his adversery as the Master-at-Arms came raging in to tear them from each other.

"My dear Grandson, [the letter from Mrs. Tarras began]
"I read your letter from Stockholm with great pleasure, and am rejoiced that you have acted on the advice I gave you to redeem your reputation by volunteering for the Royal Navy.

Your enlistment, and departure for the Baltic, have aroused the liveliest interest in the Tarras Line, and several of our best deckhands have followed you to fight for Queen and Country. The whole nation expects great things of the Baltic Fleet and prays for its triumphal entry to the harbour of St. Petersburg.

"My eldest son, Lieut. John Abernethy Tarras, R.N., was exactly the same age as you are now when he fell gloriously at Navarino. He was in the flagship, H.M.S. *Asia*, 84, from which Captain Edward Curzon wrote to tell me of his gallantry—"

Here followed an account of the battle of Navarino, which Brand was quite prepared to take on trust. He laid down his grandmother's letter with a grin. The old lady had come round immediately, just as Joe Ryan had predicted. He was glad to be back in her good books again and have letters from Britain by the first post delivered to the fleet—even if the one letter he wanted to read was not among them, nor could be until there was an exchange of mail with Stockholm.

He looked around. The watch on deck was idling, extracting the last crumb of interest from the home letters, and near the 68-pr. guns on which Brand and Morgan had been mounted, their hands and feet tied, for a whole watch after their brawl, an English artist was sketching the interesting scene. Brand thought without rancour that "Punishment on the Great Guns" would have made a more realistic study for Mr. Dolby than "Letters from Home" or whatever he was going to call his picture; but of course "Letters from Home", full of sentiment blended with humour, was what the chromolithographers would want for reproduction. His Uncle Tarras had as good as said so, in the second letter Brand held in his hand.

"Your Aunt Adelaide and Cousins Bell and Flora send you many affectionate greetings. They devour the *Illustrated London News* and other pictorial reviews which purport to give us sketches of life with the Baltic Fleet, and live in daily expectation of a great naval victory. Like everyone else in the country from the Queen downwards, my womenfolk are in the grip of war fever, and are convinced that you and Admiral Napier will have taken Cronstadt by midsummer. In London Wall we are more cautious. Lord Aberdeen's government does not appear to me to be acting with any great conviction, and

I greatly fear that before we come to an end of the business, the Russian War will spread over half the world . . ."

Brand put the two letters inside his blue jacket. He knew better than many of his shipmates that Mr. Arthur Tarras, like anyone who had closely studied the Baltic charts, was right to be cautious in predicting a speedy victory at sea. The enemy was safe beneath his fortresses, the British Fleet, unsupported, must patrol and blockade an enormous coastline: the Gulf of Bothnia north to Haparanda, the Gulf of Finland east to Cronstadt, and all the long Russian shore extending through Reval and the Gulf of Riga as far south as Danzig. Nor did the Commander-in-Chief appear to be in any hurry to leave Älvsnabben. He went by land to Stockholm for his diplomatic call on King Oscar I, accompanied by the flag-officers who had to make discreet arrangements for revictualling the fleet from the Swedish islands without attempting to enter port. Meanwhile, the crash of artillery practice echoed from ship to ship around Älvsnabben anchorage.

The gunnery officer of H.M.S. *Arrogant* was Lieutenant William "Paddy" Sulivan, a cousin of the Captain of the *Lightning*. When the beat of drum followed by one ruffle called *Arrogant's* gun crews to exercise in the first afternoon watch after anchoring, he intended to work the men at loading and unloading the guns and in the rapid service of powder from the magazines. Brand was named powderman for one of the sixteen 32-pr. guns on the quarterdeck, served from the after magazine, and took his place with the six men of Number Three gun and the six auxiliaries who assisted in running the gun out and training it with the tackle. Brand's lean face, with the new scar above the left eye from Morgan's knuckle-duster, was grimmer than usual. All his Yankee competitiveness had been roused by his failure to come up to Captain Yelverton's standard of seamanship on the yards: at gunnery exercise he intended to do better than the best.

About twenty years earlier, the Navy had adopted the practice of simultaneous loading, the cartridge, wad and shot being rammed home together for the quicker delivery of the broadside. In the exercise, grummet wads of the right calibre were used instead of powder, and for the service of the 32-pr. guns these were stored in cylindrical tubs covered with a wooden lid and kept in the fore and aft magazines. It was a powderman's duty, on the word of command, to hurry down the hatch to the magazine, answer the challenge of the passagemen or Marine sentries, and receive the ammunition, live or imitation, passed out by the magazinemen through curtains of woollen frieze called fearnought. All this, and the dash back to the deck, took place in the dark, the magazine being feebly lit through a glass window by a lantern placed in the light room; the fearnought was kept damp and the water tank was ready in case of fire or an explosion. A powderman's speed, on which his gun depended, could be hampered by his thick felt slippers, and by the need to carry his jacket wadded round his load of live ammunition.

Brand was at once successful at this exercise. He had excellent nocturnal vision, and was far more sure-footed along the decks than aloft. When Lieutenant Sulivan ordered an end of loading practice, he announced that the service of grummet wads to Number Three gun had been three hundred in an average period of ten minutes, the next best figure being two hundred and forty.

"I want all the gun crews worked up to three hundred, Mr. Sulivan," said Captain Yelverton, who had come to hear the report. "Put Endicott on a gun tomorrow."

"Aye, aye, sir."

So the next day Brand was a dancer in that ballet of death, which began when the tompion was removed from the muzzle of his gun, and the thin lead apron was taken off the vent and the lye-soaked matches flared on their three foot linstocks inside the match tubs half filled with sand. He learned to obey the words of command from *Prime! Point!* through the firing to *Secure the Gun!* and he learned, as Sulivan moved him from the auxiliaries to the gun crew itself, to use the worm and sponge for cleaning the gun, the hand-spikes for shifting its elevation. He was moved from the 32-prs. to one of the two 68-pr. guns mounted on *Arrogant's* quarterdeck. He was given a Colt revolver, a 14·8 mm. Minié rifle, Mark 1853, a bayonet and a cutlass, and taught to use them in manual and platoon exercises as *Arrogant* steamed south-east in foul weather to her new cruising ground off Gotska Sandön island in mid-Baltic. The gunners began to use live ammunition, and the seagulls rose in shrill dismay as the great reverberations echoed among their crags. They worked at quick and horizontal fire; they shot at targets increasingly smaller and more distant in the water, eventually they shot at two hundred, five hundred, seven hundred yards distance at wooden butts and old dismasted boats.

Three days after their arrival, H.M.S. *Edinburgh* came up to starboard, showing the flag of Admiral Sir Henry Ducie Chads, and in due course the Admiral himself was piped aboard H.M.S. *Arrogant*, accompanied by Commodore Seymour. The Admiral and the Captain of the Fleet were working ship after ship at target practice, and both officers watched critically as the drums beat to quarters and the gun crews of *Arrogant* took up action stations and went through the drill.

"Very good, Mr. Sulivan, I congratulate you," said the Admiral formally, when the firing was over and the gun crews stood at ease. "Captain Yelverton has acquainted you with the nature of the experiment we intend to carry out this morning?"

"Yes, sir."

"Have you, yourself, had an opportunity of seeing the Bickford's Improved Water Fuse in operation?"

"Not at sea, sir, I regret to say. I had the advantage of hearing the principle explained by Admiral Douglas, at a recent course in H.M.S. *Excellent*."

"Very well, Mr. Sulivan; then you can supervise the fitting of the fuse. Will you ask for swimming volunteers, Captain Yelverton, if you please?"

The order went down the echelons, ended with the bo'sun's mates bawling "Any swimmers? 'Oo can swim?"

The crew stirred uneasily. "Never volunteer" was a well-established tradition on the lower deck, and in fact very few of the old hands, and certainly none of the town recruits could swim a stroke. Leading Seaman Edgeworthy cleared his throat and stepped forward.

"I can swim a bit, sir."

With one of his rare smiles: "We'll need you in the boat, Edgeworthy," said Captain Yelverton. "Men who can swim underwater are wanted here. You, Endicott! You're an islander, surely you can swim?"

Brand stiffened to attention, much against his will. *Surely you can swim?* in the Captain's cold voice brought back all the resentment of *You had some experience of reefing, surely?*

following his failure on the yards. He would show them! He said:

"I can swim underwater, sir."

"Good. One more!"

"I'm an islander too, sir!" A thin dark Scotsman from the larboard watch was knuckling his forehead.

"Of course you are, Campbell. Fall out the volunteers, Mr. Sulivan, and dismiss the hands."

But even Yelverton the disciplinarian knew that in a ship at anchor it would be impossible to keep his people from watching any experiment that broke the monotony of their days. He withdrew with the senior officers to the starboard side of the quarterdeck, reserved by unwritten law for his own use, and said to Admiral Chads:

"I regret we were unable to provide a larger target, sir. A dismasted skerries ship is hardly an adequate substitute for the walls of Cronstadt."

"Proportionately to the charge of powder used, Captain Yelverton, the experiment is worth carrying out. Moreover, the most recent directive from Their Lordships advises us to waste no more shells on target practice. We must employ the fuses or any other training device we have in hand."

Yelverton pursed his lips. Like all the Captains, he knew that the Baltic Fleet had been sent to sea with a supply of ammunition based on the peace-time establishment. He said tentatively:

"Does that mean that Their Lordships wish the fleet to waste no more time in exercises, sir—but to enter the Gulfs forthwith?"

Chads smiled. "You are eager to engage the enemy, I see. Well, I think I can say that we shall probably weigh anchor tomorrow or the next day at latest. Ah! here come the volunteers."

Brand and Campbell came up to the entry port together while a boat was being lowered, and looked thoughtfully at the water. Both men were stripped to their drawers and had greased the exposed parts of their bodies. There the resemblance ended, for Brand, tall and broad-shouldered, towered over the narrow-chested Highlander.

"It's going to be bloody cold, Jack," said Campbell out of one side of his mouth.

"You bet it is." The Baltic waters stretch away, grey and uninviting, to Gotska Sandön where the gunnery targets had been procured. A cold wind ruffled the surface of the sea.

"Are you sure you can do this, Campbell?" Lieutenant Sulivan asked anxiously. In the soft accents of the Isle of Islay, the Highlander assured him that he could.

"Into the boat with you then."

Mr. Sulivan followed them into *Arrogant's* jolly-boat and they were rowed out to meet a cutter from the *Edinburgh* carrying the fuse and powder they were to use. A Seaman Gunner from the flagship was ready to attach a fuse to a prepared shell.

"Now this here fuse," he said to Brand and Campbell, "has got to be plugged into the shell with a wooden plug, hard enough to take the weight of the shell entirely. Right, sir?" He glanced at Sulivan for confirmation.

"Right it is, my man."

"Then I make the fuse hole watertight with greased canvas plaster—so—and I put the shell in an oilskin. Now *you*" to Brand, "you put the line around your neck."

"What weight of powder are you using, Gunner?" asked Sulivan.

"Ten pounds in each case, sir." He looked at Brand's powerful torso. "'Course, we could 'ave made it heavier, but twenty pounds should do for that target. Enough for the swimmers, too, at a first try."

The tin cases, on thin chains, were hung round the necks of Brand and Campbell, and at a word from Mr. Sulivan they slipped into the water. Brand heard him say "Absolute silence both! Silence in the boat!" as the icy water closed above his head.

. . . He had once thought of water as his natural element, in those State of Maine summers when all the islands of Casco Bay were a boy's playground; but the Atlantic in its autumn chill had never stopped his heart like these Baltic waves where only weeks before the drift ice had begun to melt. The weight of the powder case dragged him down and the added weight of the shell and the long coiled fuse impeded the free overarm movements which should have brought him quickly to the target. Less than twenty yards away, Sulivan had said— hardly a swim at all, and yet the cold and the weight slowed him up so that he had to lift his head out of the water and look for Campbell. The Highlander was in distress too, and was swimming off course, but he righted himself at the end of a long minute and was close at Brand's side as they came up to the wooden hull of the old skerries ship. A chain had been slung there to simulate the forechains of a ship of war. Now Brand and Campbell could tread water, and there was some relief in lifting their chests and shoulders to the upper air. Brand saw that Campbell's hands were blue. His own fingers were stiff as he unslung the box of powder and attached it with Campbell's to the chain. Fixing the shell was a more difficult operation: it required both of them to do the work and start uncoiling, according to Sulivan's instructions, the line of the Bickford fuse in its double covering of gutta percha. It was to be paid out as they swam back to the cutter where it would be set alight.

The return journey was worse than the journey out, even without the weights. Campbell was swimming off course again, his black head bobbing up like one of the seals of his native island; Brand too had to give up the attempt to swim underwater as he let the line unroll. There was a small cork buoy at the end which would allow him to retrieve it if he lost hold, but although his fingers were now quite numb and his lungs bursting he kept up his steady drive towards the cutter until with huge relief he heard Sulivan, breaking his own order for silence, shouting Campbell's name, and saw the Islay man, rolling on the crest of a wave, turn in safety to the boat. Then they were both being hauled aboard, and through the folds of the seaman's jersey he was trying to pull over his head Brand heard "Paddy" Sulivan's enthusiastic "Well done, both men!—Gunner, light the fuse."

Brand became aware of pain, of cuts in his chest and ribs from the powder case and the chafing of the chains. The cutter was moving, away from the target, back to the jolly-boat. Campbell, white-faced but grinning, was drinking brandy from the silver cup of the lieutenant's own flask. "Here you are, Jack!" His throat and lips grew warm.

They came up to the jolly-boat, and without breaking stroke the cutter's crew led the way back to *Arrogant*. Sulivan sat in the sternsheets with his watch in his hand. The fire which had been applied to the end of the Bickford fuse was presumbably travelling, at the estimated rate of three feet per minute, to ignite the shell and powder at the hulk.

"Row, you men!"

Brand saw the line of faces at the frigate's rail and the group of officers with the gold "flash o' lightning" on their hats. The deck of H.M.S. *Edinburgh* was crowded with watchers. *Surely you can swim, my man? Surely I can.*

"Ten minutes, sir?" asked the Seaman Gunner.

"Eleven. I hope to God we haven't had a misfire."

"Twelve. Water got into the shell," said the gunner accusingly to Brand. "You let the plaster slip."

"I swear I—"

The clap of the explosion came deafeningly across the surface of the sea. A column of water, churning with planks and staves, shot up as the old skerries ship disintegrated before their eyes and the travelling wave reached the cutter violently. A cheer was heard from the frigates, and in the boats the sailors were laughing and patting each other on the back.

"We've done it, though! Good for Bickford," exulted Lieutenant Sulivan. "—You two men finish what's left in the flask, and we'll soon have you back aboard for the Admiral's congratulations."

"Thank you, sir," said Campbell. But the American, forgetting the rules for addressing an officer, said as to an equal:

"Well, it worked all right. But d'you think a twenty-pound charge of powder is going to make much impression on a ship of the line?"

Sulivan did not reprimand him. He said—as to an equal— "Endicott, you swim better than you think. Work it out for yourself, man! If you had attached that fuse to a charge *beneath the fore magazine* of a ship of war—well—you and Campbell, and the lot of us, would have stood a very good chance of being blown to Kingdom come!"

The fleet weighed anchor from Gotska Sandön next morning —but only to go back to the anchorage at Älvsnabben. It was the end of April, and the Gulf of Finland was reported clear of ice, but still Napier hesitated to risk more than two or three vessels on a hasty reconnaissance extending hardly farther east than Barö Sound. They came back from a frustrating glimpse, from far out at sea, of the blue dome of the Nicholas

Kirk at Helsingfors, and with the worse than frustrating intelligence that seven Russian warships had come through the drift ice from Lovisa and were safe in the dockyards of Sveaborg. A whisper began to run through the ward-rooms of the Fleet that Napier had remained too long in mid-Baltic and lost his first, best chance to smash the Russians.

The return to Älvsnabben meant that mail from Stockholm was distributed with the fresh beef and vegetables bought in the archipelago, and Brand had the long-awaited letter from Alix Gyllenlöve. It had not been long on the way, for it was dated at Helsingfors only seven days earlier, and it began with such a tender, anxious wish for his safety "in this War in wich I have urget you to figt" that Brand caught his breath with longing for her even while he smiled over the absurd misspellings. But the smile faded as he read that her father wished her to go at once to Petersburg with Madame Karamsin. From a tangle of consonants he made out that Alix herself had wanted to go to "min hous at Ekenäs" or to "(indecipherable) Willebrand at Degerby"—he supposed this was the island Degerby where the mail-boat called. "I *shall* be near you," the letter ended, with vigorous underlining. "*Farväl käre Brand.*—Alix"

I shall be near you. I am determined to be near you—that was what she meant, and those were the words he had longed for weeks to read. But—Alix in Petersburg? From the heart of the enemy's capital, how would she ever make her way to freedom? And from the lower deck of H.M.S. *Arrogant*, how long would it take him to make his own way back to her? Brand turned to Joe's letter with a troubled heart. It was lengthy, and of course he had laid it aside as soon as he saw the small grey envelope which it contained. He skipped over the preliminaries—"good wishes . . . enclose letter which arrived today . . . taking advantage of supply ship's call" . . . Joe Ryan took half a page to arrive at the heart of the matter.

"Mr. Svensson, the Tarras agent at Gothenburg, is certainly involved with Müller and Sons, the Lübeck shippers, and is reported to be a sleeping partner in their concern. Captain Erik Kruse and Mr. Svensson are also the joint owners of the barque *Skylark*, U.S. registered in the name of Thomas Murphy, whoever he may be. The *Skylark* recently delivered five thousand Minié rifles, Mark 1854, at Memel for the use of the Russian Army.

"This is not water-front gossip, but comes from sources I can vouch for, including my own brother-in-law. I read the riot act in Queen Street, I can tell you, when I found the Engströms had been encouraging Kruse to visit there, and I forbade Miss Molly to have anything more to do with him. About the man's commercial activities, of course, I can do nothing. That's up to the British Navy, but I can tell you this, the Lübeck trade is going to play hell with your blockade. The Hamburg merchants are shipping sulphur to Russia— through Lübeck. The Swedes are carrying lead to Riga—from Lübeck. Russian vessels are being transferred to Danish owners at Lübeck, and then they take their cargoes up the Gulf of Bothnia to ports inside the Grand Duchy. I imagine Müller and Sons—and Kruse and Svensson too, of course—are making a fair-sized fortune out of all this.

"Well, it's no business of mine. I'm a neutral, God be praised! At the same time I fairly hate to see Old Glory used as a cover for running rifles to the Russians. Don't know what G. Washington would have had to say to that.

"Mary sends you her love, the forward little minx! She was sorry when you left us in the Golden Peace, especially as I scolded her all the way home about Captain Kruse. She's only a baby, after all! She stood outside the palace for an hour the other day to see Admiral Napier on his visit to the King, and the best she could tell me was that his flag lieutenant was very good-looking! The people cheered him, though—there's more pro-British feeling in Stockholm than you might think.

"Brand, when is Napier going to take real action . . ."

The ageing Commander-in-Chief, tormented by contradictory orders from the Admiralty, had only one more excuse for delaying action. This was that the Governor-General of Finland, acting on the Czar's orders, had ordered all coastal lights extinguished, all pilot stations shut, all seamarks of any sort to be removed from the Gulfs of Finland and Bothnia, and Napier refused to risk his ships in shoal waters until the intrepid Captain Sulivan, in *Lightning*, had marked the north shore of the Gulf of Finland with red buoys and the south with black. Sulivan had already surveyed, and partly buoyed, the southern waters of the Gulf of Bothnia, and to that cruising ground, on May 5, Napier ordered a small squadron of paddle steamers, with the broad pendant of Admiral Plumridge in *Leopard* as their commodore.

The Baltic Fleet was now fully operational and ready to plough the field of serpents, like one of Alexandra's heroes of the *Kalevala*, but the serpents hid in their lairs while the British frigates began hunting in couples up and down the creeks of Finland. The ships of the line lay in blue water, their majestic spread of canvas white against the warmer skies of May, while Captain Cooper Key in H.M.S. *Amphion*, 34, led an expedition to "look in" to the Gulf of Riga, and *Euryalus* and *Imperieuse*, the two great beauties of the fleet, kept watch over the harbour at Reval. The station assigned to *Arrogant* was the gateway to the Gulf of Finland, between Hangö on the Finnish shore to Port Baltic in Esthonia, with a mission to stop and seize all vessels carrying building materials to the new Russian fortifications at Hangö Head. As a hunting mate *Arrogant* had H.M. Steam Sloop *Hecla*, 6, Captain William Hutcheon Hall.

On the first Sunday afternoon after the cruise began Captain Yelverton gave permission for the crew of *Arrogant* to entertain the *Hecla*'s people aboard. "Ship visiting" was usually discouraged as leading to drunkenness and fighting, but Yelverton felt some distraction was due to men who had not set foot ashore for nearly two months, and knew his Master-at-Arms had been keeping smuggled liquor off the ship with great success. The lower deck made preparations for the party: the Sunday "shave and shift" was carried out thoroughly, and shoes were blacked and collar ribbons pressed in honour of the *Heclas*. The cooks produced some extra eatables, and the grog ration was saved for two days to treat the visitors.

At first all went well. One of the *Hecla* hands had brought a kit, or little fiddle, to which Lauri's mouth-organ quickly learned a harmony, so that hornpipes were danced between the mess-tables, and Morgan's tearful ballads were vigorously applauded. Unfortunately the *Heclas* had also brought in under their blue jackets half a dozen bottles of raw potato spirit, bought on a foraging expedition to one of the islands, and this on top of rum was enough to kindle tempers, and start outrageous boasting about the exploits of the *Hecla's* captain, "Old Nemesis" Hall.

There wasn't a fight nowhere—said his men—that Old Nemesis he hadn't managed to be in. Fought in the Channel in the old wars, he had, when he wasn't much more than a kid; then he commanded *Nemesis* for John Company and got services of plate and decorations for all he done fighting the bloody Chinks in China. Then he jumped into the Mersey, gold lace and all, and saved a poor engineer bastard's life, he did, so that even the hands, the *hands* I'm telling you, had subscribed for more silver plate for Old Nemesis—

Licking a split lip, Brand was not quite certain how the fight had started. He thought it was a criticism of Yelverton—"that flaming lah-di-dah Captain of yours"—that had brought him into it, and it was odd, of course, to find himself fighting side by side with Ivor Morgan in defence of Captain Yelverton. But there was no time to consider motives once he was in that heaving mêlée of hosts and guests, bashing at and grappling with one another with all the aimless rage and energy of men whose powerful sex drives had been denied through long weeks of cramped quarters and hard manual labour. It did not last long; the mates soon broke it up with shouts of "Give way there!" and indiscriminate use of their starters. There were enough black eyes and torn jackets, however, to make a poor showing at the evening muster, and at breakfast Leading Seaman Edgeworthy, the philosopher of Brand's mess, declared:

"Them 'Eclas is a rough lot. But if they go for the Rooshians the way they went for us, I don't mind 'aving them alongside in a scrap."

They had their scrap exactly two weeks later, twenty-four hours after a strong force of Russian troops had opened fire on both vessels, as they "looked in" to the creek of Tvärminne, some miles east of Hangö Head.

It was hardly an attack in strength, for one British broadside was enough to dispel the attackers, who fled as soon as H.M.S. *Arrogant's* company of Marines was landed, but a search among the rocks and sandbanks of that barren shore produced several Finnish fishermen who had pulled their boats under cover when they heard the firing start. Most of them were a type already well known to the Marines and seamen, for *Arrogant* in two weeks of steady tacking between Hangö and Port Baltic had stopped no craft more dangerous than a few Finnish fishing smacks, from which square resentful faces stared up at the British frigate much as the Tvärminne fishermen were staring now. One man, however, asked to be taken to the "English *Kapten*", he was a pilot, he said, and could tell the *Kapten* much about the channels—this with many winks, and mysterious signs, which lasted until they took him away from his fellows, and aboard the *Arrogant*.

"Nemesis" Hall was with Yelverton in his cabin, and the sea officers listened expressionlessly to the Finn's description of the "Russky prizes" waiting at Ekenäs for Englanders bold enough to cut them out of the inland harbour.

"Where did you learn to speak English so well, my man?" said Hall.

"In Hull, sir captain. Hull, Newcastle, Leith—I know all ports. English, Scotch, good people, fight bloody Russkies; I help them. You come to Ekenäs, you get big prize."

"Three Russian merchantmen, you say," said Yelverton thoughtfully. "What are they doing there?"

"Loading timber, sir captain. For to build new barracks down at Hangö," the pilot said rapidly, and the captains exchanged glances.

"And those troops that fired on us today are part of the Ekenäs garrison?"

"*Ja.*"

"Are there batteries? Defence works round the town?"

"Four guns by the creek, I know to see, and maybe more."

"Is there a large garrison?"

"One brigade of horse artillery, sir captain. But *no Finland troops!*"

"Very good," said Yelverton. He raised his voice to the Marine sentry at his door: "Pass the word for the bo'sun!"

"We'll keep you aboard tonight," he told the protesting pilot, when the bo'sun came. "No, you won't come to any harm. But it's only eight miles by road to Ekenäs—an active man like you could walk it in two hours!"

"A sensible precaution," approved Captain Hall, when the bo'sun and his charge had gone. ". . . You realize, of course, that this man may have been paid to lead us into an ambush?"

"All the more reason why he should not be free to carry

back information about our strength," said Yelverton shortly. "That reception committee behind the sandbank this afternoon suggests that the Russians will be ready and waiting for us whenever we decide to go up-channel. In any case, Captain Hall, I'm disposed to take the risk and sail for Ekenäs at first light."

"For three Russian merchantmen, loading timber!"

"For *action*, sir! By God, when I think of the luck they've had in the Riga squadron—is it forty prizes or fifty they've taken already?—and the almighty luck of Cooper Key, who received the surrender of the town of Libau and every Russian ship in harbour without firing a shot, while we have cruised for two weeks without sight or sound of the enemy—then I can't hesitate. We'll take Ekenäs and smoke out the Russians; and if *Arrogant* runs aground on a sandbar before we get there, you must stand by to warp me off!"

"I'll do it," said Hall cheerfully. And added, to Yelverton's surprise:

"What day of the month is it?"

"The nineteenth of May."

"Yes. That means we have five days to go until the Queen's birthday, which if you remember we were to celebrate in the Winter Palace at St. Petersburg—"

Yelverton laughed ruefully.

"Ekenäs first, then Sveaborg, then Cronstadt. A tall order for the next five days!"

The frigate and the sloop anchored side by side that night, with a double guard of Marines mounted in case of a surprise attack, and at first light, when food and drink had been quickly taken, the galley fires were extinguished and the fighting decks sprinkled with sand. Then the crew was beat to quarters to the tune of "Hearts of Oak", and carpenters hauled open the great square lids of the gun ports, and in *Arrogant* the Marines and sharpshooters, in *Hecla* a picked number of seamen, took their places on the forecastle with the Minié rifles and side arms. The gun crews fell in, and Brand Endicott, on the big larboard 68-pounder, began to go through the movements he now knew so well. Captain Yelverton, with Mr. Haggard beside him, watched the drip of the five-minute sand-glass with cold approval. It had taken precisely four minutes from the beat of drum to put the frigate into combat order.

Brand, like all the gunners, had stripped to his trousers, with his boots off and his bare feet firm on the sanded deck. Some of the old hands had knotted their kerchiefs loosely round their necks, ready to tie over their ears if the deafening broadsides should be fast and furious, but Lieutenant Sulivan, talking quietly to his men as they passed Tvärminne, explained that there was only a small battery to silence. "A couple of broadsides, starboard and larboard, should do it, lads," he said. "Remember the Commander-in-Chief's signal, and let your firing be quick and precise today."

There had been dense fog overnight, but it was lifting, and the air of the May morning struck pleasantly on Brand's bare chest. The channel leading to Ekenäs was so narrow that he could see meadows running down to the beach on both shores well clear of the tree-line. There were forests beyond the cleared land, not entirely of the firs and spruces characteristic of Finland, but showing the quivering leaves of birch and aspen and the fresh green of the trees from which Ekenäs, Cape of the Oaks, had taken its name. Brand could smell the freshness of grass and wild flowers above the odour of the warm vinegar which had been set in buckets on the deck to overpower, presently, the smell of blood. He had never expected to go into his first action in just this way. An encounter on the high seas was what he had expected and been trained for, not this upriver foray into the heart of Alexandra's own country, the very place where she was born! The fields by the creek were lush and well-cultivated. For all he knew they belonged to her own little manor, "my house at Ekenäs", where if she had had her way she might be barricaded now, with a Russian battery on her land waiting to open fire on the British, whom she called her friends. How were the citizens of Ekenäs going to react, he wondered, when the enemies of Russia appeared suddenly in their midst? The beat of *Arrogant's* screws gave him no answer. The creek narrowed and sandbars began to appear. H.M.S. *Arrogant* shuddered to a stop. There was a moment of confusion, and then that strange new race, the engineers, worked successfully to avert the danger of running aground. H.M.S. *Hecla* led the way triumphantly to Ekenäs.

They came to the cape, when a few turf cabins and wooden one-storey houses began to appear on the banks, where the channel widened out into the broad Pojo vik, here almost an inland lake, with oaks running down to the edge of the calm water. They could see the little town in the distance with smoke rising from the chimneys and the three tall merchantmen lying at the wharf. Houses and ships were reflected in the water as in a mirror, and then all at once the mirror was shattered, the peaceful image was destroyed, by the first shots fired from the Russian battery.

The British guns roared into action. They had the weight and fire power, they were trained by experienced crews, and they silenced the shore battery, as Sulivan had predicted, with exactly two broadsides from the starboard guns. But to larboard the enemy appeared again, as a company of horse artillery led by a Russian major in a green uniform with a spiked helmet, waving his sword, galloped down to the beach and unlimbered two light guns to open fire directly. A ball tore through the *Arrogant's* rigging; one of *Hecla's* masts toppled and fell down, and the mounted Russian marksmen fired heavily on the British sharpshooters at the hammock nettings.

"Prime!"

The 16-lb. charge of powder, the wad, the ball, were rammed home together in the larboard 68-pr. gun. The muzzle, on the word of command, bore to the right. The match flared on its linstock.

"Fire!"

Brand dashed the sweat from his eyes as the gun recoiled. He saw, through the smoke, the Russian major's sword fly skyward like a silver streak of light. It left the man's hand at the last moment, when his hand was still intact: then raw shreds of flesh and green uniform, horribly mixed with the metal of the Russian gun, rose like a fountain of destruction, and the delayed clap of the explosion was followed by the screams of the wounded men now dying on the beach. That terrible sound was soon drowned by another, equally inhuman —the yell of triumph from the British sailors who saw the enemy in full retreat.

"Secure the gun!"

That was Sulivan, who forgot nothing, recalling the captain

of the gun to his duty and Brand from his horror-stricken gazing at the shore. They heard Yelverton calling for full speed from the screws; they were forging up to *Hecla* now, ready to join in cutting out the prizes, and the Marines were forming their company to land and take the town. It was nearly over—the action at Ekenäs, and they had seen what the British broadside could do against a living target: something to be forgotten quickly, to be jeered at with an oath for the defeated, or with profane pride that there were few casualties aboard.

Two killed and four wounded in *Arrogant*. That was what it was customary to call "the butcher's bill", but the damage was proportionately greater aboard *Hecla*, where Captain Hall and his First Lieutenant, Mr. Crew Read, had been struck by metal splinters, like several of the hands. But "Nemesis" wounded was more dangerous than most men intact, and the little sloop steamed in boldly to the shallows to cut out her prize. The Captains had decided against a landing at the town unless there was determined Russian resistance from the shore, and as the enemy had concentrated his strength at the cape, where the Marines were now engaged in spiking his guns, there was nobody to be seen on the Ekenäs waterfront except a few civilians carrying bales and bundles, who appeared to be running for their lives in fear of the invaders.

H.M.S. *Arrogant* lay in the middle of the Pojo *vik*, not daring to risk another grounding by going closer inshore, and the hands were set to clearing away the damage done by the Russian gun. Yelverton, now, was anxious to be out of Ekenäs and steaming safely back to the open Gulf. The orders fell like hail round the ears of his half-stunned crew. Brand worked frantically to clear the tangled rigging. He kept his eyes glued to the ropes and cords and his own fingers, like a horse with blinkers on, shutting out the mental vision of the fountain of torn flesh and green uniforms which had played at the entrance to the channel, back there at the Cape of the Oaks. The voice of his old enemy, Ivor Morgan, although more subdued than usual, came to his ears like an explosion.

"Too bad about Larry, ain't it?" Morgan muttered.

"What about Larry?"

"He got 'it," said Morgan. "Starboard side he was, with 'is

155

rifle at the nettings, and one of the perishing Rooshians must have got 'im right between the sights. Too bloody bad, it is. We're going to miss 'im and the old mouth-organ."

"Is he dead?" asked Brand stupidly.

"Must be," said the Welshman. "Edgeworthy 'elped to carry 'im below. Said the surgeon said Larry didn't have a 'ope in hell."

Brand looked round the busy deck. No doubt it was a crime in the Royal Navy for a hand to go unwounded or unsummoned to the infirmary in the after cockpit, but he was going even if they flogged him for it in the morning. He watched for his chance, and slipped down the forehatch, along those passages now wet with sand and blood which the waisters were already swabbing clean, to the surgeon's quarters. The door of the after cockpit stood open. By lantern light he saw the surgeon of the *Arrogant*, himself stripped to the waist and wearing a tarpaulin apron, bending over a prone form on the table. A surgeon's mate was laying aside an amputated arm. The surgeon was whistling a tune beneath his teeth. The butcher's bill had been very light indeed.

He looked up and saw Brand.

"What do you want, my man?"

"Begging your pardon, sir" (he had the formula pat now, and the knuckling of the forehead) "Ordinary Seaman Endicott, sir. Asking for my messmate, if you please — Larry Finn."

"Yes, that's all very fine, Endicott, but if all the crew came along with kind enquiries we couldn't turn round in the cockpit. All right, come in for a minute. Finn — which one is he?"

"That's him, sir."

There were two forms laid out on stretchers, with sheets drawn over what had been their faces. There was the man on the table, whom the two surgeon's mates were bandaging, there was one delirious, there was Pringle the bo'sun's mate, bandaged and conscious, and lastly there was the boy from Gamla Karleby, who had drifted along the Stockholm wharves to go and fight the Russians. Lauri had been put in a wooden bunk without a pillow and lay there flat and motionless. His chest was covered with lint and a linen bandage, through which the blood had soaked.

"Can't you do anything for him, sir?" said Brand.

"We've done all we could, Endicott. His breastbone was completely shattered."

"I meant give him something to relieve the pain?"

"He doesn't feel any pain now."

Certainly there was no awareness of pain in that calm brow. Lauri's face, with all the healthy colour drained from it and sharpened by the touch of death, held more than ever something of Alix Gyllenlöve, and his long fair hair, straggling over the blood-soaked mattress, might have been her hair, as Brand had never yet felt it beneath his hands. Brand could not speak. The guilt of the gunner, the compassion of the friend, were two hands closing on his throat.

"Better get back on deck, Endicott," said the surgeon, not unkindly. "This poor fellow won't regain consciousness."

"Aye, aye, sir."

But then Lauri's blackened eyelids fluttered in his livid face, and he saw Brand, and recognized him. His lips moved in the imitation of a smile.

"Jack!" he said. "Now—Tuonela!" and he died.

CHAPTER NINE

"THE FIRST DROP OF BLOOD"

SLOWLY, inexorably, the Russian War spread across half the world.

In the Black Sea, by the end of May, eighteen thousand British troops under Lord Raglan and twice as many French under St. Arnaud—already disembarked at Gallipoli—were being ferried up to Varna in preparation for a full-scale invasion of the Crimea. In the White Sea, hundreds of miles to the North, Sweden–Norway manned the ancient fort at Vardö in case of Russian invasion, and three British warships proceeded to blockade Archangel. In the Pacific Ocean the Allied ships outnumbered the Russian by three to one, so that one Russian gunboat fled up the Amur River and two others took refuge in a Kamschatkan harbour. In New York a Russian Purchasing Commission arrived to buy ships and was well received, while readers of the *New York Tribune* read a series of curiously slanted military articles from the paper's esteemed London correspondent, by name Karl Marx.

The Russian War was the principal topic in every city in Europe with the exception of St. Petersburg—supposing St. Petersburg *was* in Europe, as Peter the Great had intended it to be. Alix Gyllenlöve had always had her doubts on that point. For her, Europe ended and Asia began at Bialostrov frontier post on the Russian side, after the traveller had crossed the strip of barren country from Finnish Terijoki and prepared to embark on the twenty miles of desolation leading to the capital upon the Neva. That monotonous plain, with the flat road winding through dirty villages where bearded men in sheepskin jackets lounged against the walls of their hovels and children fraternized with pigs, was for Alix a fit beginning to what she thought of as her Russian prison.

Certainly no captive was ever conducted to prison with more comfort and ceremony. Aurora Karamsin travelled from Finland to Russia in a regular convoy of vehicles, led by her own carriage with Gregori at the reins and Alix wrapped in a fur rug by her side, Paul Demidov in the second vehicle with his tutor and valet, and the maids, Verna and Anna from Lapland travelling with the huge wardrobe trunks. There were grooms, outriders and postilions to make the journey easy. Once or twice on the first day they overhauled a Finnish *bondkärra*, which was a mere box set on an axletree and two wheels, and then the traveller and driver perched on the board nailed across the box looked enviously at the rich lady's equipage as it sped by. Nor did Madame Karamsin condemn herself to wasting time over meals at the post houses, where hours could be spent while dishes of local game like blackcock or capercailzie were stewed to rags for the guests; once the party had gone through the required formality of signing their names in the day book the Karamsin caravan moved on. The houses of friends and often the horses of friends were waiting for Aurora all the way from the Villa Hagasund to the Morskaia.

The fog, which hung so persistently over the Gulf of Finland during these May days, soon burned away in the landward villages, and the winding road led through a beautiful countryside of rivers and waterfalls, with the sea ever present in long arms or sheltered bays where Alix longed to stop and swim. Even Aurora's leisurely progress seemed too swift to a girl who looked back so often at the land they were leaving behind, and who cherished such romantic dreams of the lakes and forests she had never seen.

"Were you ever in the north woods, Aurora?" she asked as they sat at a wayside picnic with Paul and his tutor, under the shade of the birch trees between Högfors and Viborg.

"In the Far North do you mean, Alix darling?" said Aurora. "Oh, no! Your papa has been there, though. He went to Rovaniemi once."

"I didn't mean that," said Alix. "I meant, have you been to Tammerfors, or north of Tammerfors, where the lakes begin, and the forests haven't been cut yet, and the days are longer than they are down here?"

"Listen to her!" said Madame Karamsin to the two young men. "As if the days could ever be longer than they are on the Gulf, in fine May weather, unless it was at midsummer! No, dearest, I have never been to Tammerfors, and I don't intend to go there or anywhere north of Helsingfors until the war is over, and perhaps not even then!"

Her son and his tutor laughed appreciatively. It was time to go. Madame Karamsin was rising gracefully from the slope covered with spring flowers and the pine needles of last winter, and laughingly extended her hand to Alexandra.

"I only meant," said Alix as she rose, "I only meant there's so much of our own country that I've never seen—"

Or perhaps will never see. The thought came back to her unbidden as they went on their way, leaving far behind them the gateway to that strange land of lakes that only the true Finns knew. They were driving on into the border country, "Old Finland", as the earlier settlers liked to call it, coming up to the shores of Lake Ladoga, approaching too close for Alix to the city of the Great Peter. Far behind now were the rocky shores of Nyland, the channel of Ekenäs, Cape of the Oaks, and the tides racing from east to west of Hangö Head! They reached Viborg, where their kinsman Carl-Gustaf Mannerheim was Governor, as Aurora's father had been in the first terrible years after the last war, and they were cordially received at Viborg Castle, although the Governor was ailing and his son Carl-Robert, Alexandra's favourite cousin, had left to bring some relatives out of the danger zone in western Finland. Soon they drove on to the Russian frontier. The guards on duty were ill at ease, and they might have been searched there but for Madame Karamsin's proud reversion to her first husband's title. "I am the Princess Demidova," she said simply; and her son repeated it, getting out of the carriage shared with his tutor, speaking up more boldly than ever in his life before.

"I am Prince Paul Demidov," he said, and threw a handful of roubles on the dusty road. "You there, let us pass without delay!"

The great red barrier was lifted up as noon was striking and Madame Karamsin's horses and carriages passed underneath. "Darling Paul is growing up," she said contentedly. "But imagine such a fuss at Bialostrov! Alix, let us try to sleep a little. We must look our best when we arrive in Petersburg."

Although six high-steppers were now attached in a double troika to Madame Karamsin's carriage it was late in the afternoon before they plodded through the dusty streets of the Great Peter's city to halt before the Demidov palace on the Morskaia. Young Paul, running forward more eagerly than usual, was ready before the step was let down to give his mother his hand and bid her welcome to his father's house. Alix, wearily settling her green skirts for a ceremonial entrance through the splendid doorway, took careful notice of the form of words. Paul means to be master here before long, she thought. I wonder how the Karamsins will relish that?

The palace to which the Russian Croesus had brought home his bride was brilliantly lighted, and a small army of servants stood waiting to greet their mistress in the marble vestibule. There were four footmen always on duty in that hall alone, with a fifth to take the coat of an expected guest and a sixth, in winter, to draw off his galoshes. They were all under the orders of a Swiss major-domo with a gold chain round his neck, who now advanced to offer a welcome to Aurora.

"Is there news from Bucharest, Antoine?" were her first words to him.

"Yes, madame, very good news. His Excellency the Colonel is safe and well, and a letter from him is waiting in madame's apartments."

"Thank God!" breathed Aurora. ". . . Come, children," and she led the way to the velvet-lined lift which carried them to the private apartments on the third floor. The floors below were laid out in reception rooms, including Aurora's ballroom and her famous Golden Salon, both of which on great occasions had to be filled by at least one thousand hot-house plants. There was a scent of forced lilac in Aurora's suite, which was entered by an anteroom where two footmen waited all day to carry out the slightest order of their lady, and included a drawing-room furnished in shades of brown, apricot and gold, a dressing-room for Colonel Karamsin and the vast bedroom, with white polar bearskins covering the floor, which the happy couple shared. Paul Demidov's apartments were also on the third floor, and Aurora with her usual sweetness accompanied Alix to her bedroom before pausing to take off her cloak.

"I've arranged a little surprise for you, darling," she said as the major-domo, who preceded them, prepared to fling open the door. "I had one or two partitions removed, and the old powder closet altered, so now you have a little sitting-room all your own. If this is to be your home for a time I want you to feel quite happy and independent here—"

"You're very, very kind to me, Aurora." There was forced lilac in Alexandra's bedroom too, and some familiar possessions of her own, at which her eyes opened wide. Across the room, through the open door of the new boudoir, both women could see another surprise upon the wall.

"Your mother's portrait, Alix!" exclaimed Aurora. "How in the world did that get here?"

"Count Gyllenlöve's man brought it here earlier in the week, madame, along with the trunks and books belonging to mademoiselle. His Excellency regretted exceedingly that he was obliged to leave for Moscow before the ladies arrived. There is a letter on the desk for mademoiselle."

"Thank you, Antoine; you may leave us," said his mistress. ". . . Alix, he must have closed the apartment on the Nevsky Prospekt!"

"And severed all his links with the past," said Alix flippantly. "Why not? He told me on Sveaborg he meant to do it, as plainly as I'm talking to you now. Anyway, he doesn't need my mother's picture, now he has his railways and his Ourov."

"Let us see what his letter says," Aurora urged.

"There's no hurry. All this is keeping you from *your* mail," Alix reminded her. "Don't you want to read your letter from Andrei?"

"Of course I do!" said Colonel Karamsin's wife. "Shall I tell them to send Anna to you?"

"Not yet."

Left alone in her bedroom, Alix washed her face and hands, tidied her hair and changed her dress. She knew the ways of the Demidov palace well enough; it would not be long before she would be needed, if not in the Golden Salon, then in one of the smaller drawing-rooms on the second floor to help entertain the guests who would start arriving as soon as it was known that Madame Karamsin had returned. Then she went back to the boudoir and opened her father's letter with a flick of the thumb. It contained nothing but an order on Efimov, the leading furrier of the Gostinnoi Dvor, to make Alix a fur cloak from a selected parcel of white Arctic fox pelts. A note attached to the order read "For my good girl who did as she was told."

Alix dropped the papers on the desk. She looked at her

mother's portrait, which Johan Gyllenlöve had never before allowed out of his possession. Eleonora Gyllenlöve was painted in a plain white gown, with a little girl on either side: both children had their mother's delicacy of feature, but only Kristina had inherited her dark hair and large dark eyes. The artist had given the group a pastoral background, with a glimpse of Ekenäs manor in the distance. It was at the Finnish country scene that Alix gazed, while her own eyes filled with tears, and she turned to the wide window impatiently and stared out at the Czar Nikita's capital.

Aurora found her there when she came into the room twenty minutes later.

"Not bad news?" Alix exclaimed, at the sight of that pale and anxious face.

"Not—exactly." Aurora tried to smile. "Just some worries I hadn't quite expected. Alix, that André of mine has left Bucharest! Given up his wonderful Staff appointment to follow Marshal Paskeivich to Silistria! 'I feel it is my duty to volunteer for the front line' he says. Oh dear, and I don't even know where Silistria is!"

"But Paskeivich is on his way back to Petersburg," said Alix, as bewildered as Karamsin's wife. "You know it was announced in Helsingfors that Prince Menshikov was to take over the Danube command."

"Who can believe anything they tell us?" said Aurora crossly. It was the first time Alix had ever heard her criticize the Russian information service, which existed more to mystify the public than to inform, and she wisely made no comment, but fell to coaxing her godmother and assuring her that a post on the staff of an army commander in the field was almost, if not quite, as safe as a post behind the lines at Bucharest. She had petted Aurora back to smiles before the servants came in with a samovar and glasses on a golden tray.

"I told them to bring us tea in your sitting-room, darling, do you mind?" Aurora said. "My apartments are like a post house at present, with everybody coming and going with trunks and clothes." She filled the glasses and put in cut lemon deftly. "And I really must have a cigarette before André's mother and sister get here."

"Are you expecting them so soon?" asked Alix, holding a light for one of the small black Russian cigarettes which

Aurora occasionally smoked while she was alone or with Alix.

"I sent a message asking them to come. I *must* find out about Silistria! They may have a later letter from André. Mine is a whole month old, can you believe it?"

"Perhaps you'll get a whole batch of letters in a day or two," said Alix gently.

"I hope so . . . Oh, I hope so! You know, dear, I've been praying there would be a letter waiting, telling me he was on his way home. After all, André is thirty-nine. Surely a younger officer could take his place at the front? He could serve the Czar as well in Petersburg as at Silistria, I'm sure. And I need him here so badly, so does Paul. If André were at home he would tell me what to do about Anatole Demidov's letter . . ." She looked ruefully at the closely written pages in her hand.

"Have you had a letter from Paul's uncle, Aurora?"

"Yes, a horrible letter. Asserting his right to some say in the boy's upbringing, 'as his father wished' he says, and asking me to send Paul to him at Florence this summer—'To begin his European education' is the way he puts it. Oh, if André were only here to deal with him!"

Alix frowned. She was much too young to have known Prince Anatole Demidov, who had not graced the Russian Empire since the break-up of his marriage with Princess Mathilde Bonaparte, a cousin of the new Emperor of the French—a separation effected very much in the lady's favour, thanks to the intervention of the Czar—but his debaucheries had been legendary even in quiet Helsingfors. The life he now led in Tuscany, where his father had acquired the title of Duke of San Donato, was so continually scandalous that any parent, much less the mother of an only son, might hesitate to confide a boy to his notorious house.

"Do you suppose he has written to Paul directly?" she asked.

"Oh, I hope not! Paul teases me about visiting his uncle. I suppose he imagines Anatole as a great man of the world, and then he complains about the other Demidov house, the one on the English Quay, standing untenanted for so long. He told me the other day that he would like to live there when he married. Did you ever—at sixteen? Really a growing boy is a great problem."

And you've no idea what a problem Master Paul can be, was Alexandra's silent comment. Aloud, she said:

"Why don't you write and tell the Duke that Paul ought not to leave home at present, since he will be entered so soon in the Corps of Pages? And then let him accept the Youso-povsky boys' invitation to their *dacha* for the shooting? I know he wants to do that, and it would take his mind off Florence."

"The very thing, darling, how clever you are," said Aurora, brightening. "The shooting doesn't open until the middle of July, but we can arrange it now, and then he can look forward to it. Who knows, by July, dear André may be home again! And now . . . you are beautifully dressed, I see; let us go downstairs, and be ready to receive his mother."

To be beautifully dressed, and to soothe the Karamsin ladies' anxiety about Andrei, were Alexandra's chief occupa-tions for several days to come. Aurora herself was restored to her usual serenity after a private luncheon with her close friends the Grand Duke Alexander and his wife at the Anitchkov Palace, during which the Czar's heir fully ex-plained the position at Silistria. Marshal Paskeivich, who had indeed handed over the supreme command on the Turkish front to Prince Menshikov, was still unwilling, at the age of seventy-two, to return to St. Petersburg without winning some victory comparable to the slaughter of the students of Poland and Hungary which had already earned him the title of Prince of Warsaw, and had therefore set siege to the Turkish stronghold of Silistria. It was expected to fall to the Russians almost immediately—after which, the Grand Duke gave Aurora his promise, the gallant Colonel Karamsin would be recalled for home leave in St. Petersburg.

In spite of this assurance the colonel's widowed mother and his unmarried sister Lise were in constant need of consolation, preferably in the form of large luncheons and intimate dinners at the Demidov palace. The elder Madame Karamsin was a plaintive creature. Her own husband, Nikolai Karamsin, had been one of the few Russian writers to escape exile to Siberia, possibly because his *History of Russia* had ended unfinished at the year 1613, but the 50,000 roubles with which Nicholas I had endowed his work in progress would hardly have enabled his widow to do well by a large family if Aurora Karamsin had not added her substantial help. Sometimes the old lady spoke pathetically of her summer home in Finland: she was determined to go to Dalsvik with Lise as usual, she said, because the British Fleet, everybody knew, could do nothing in the Baltic. They would leave in two weeks, and then dear Aurora could come on to Träskända with Andrei, as soon as he could get leave . . . The gentle, repetitious planning went on through the seven courses of fish and meat, the three desserts which were always offered to guests at Aurora's luncheons.

It was odd how the topic of summer holidays took precedence over the war with the West, that May in the salons of St. Petersburg. It was only in families where a son or husband was an officer on active service that the progress of the war was ever discussed at any length, and then guardedly, in case an equivocal comment might be interpreted as a criticism of the Czar. The British colony, of course, had packed its boxes and gone home, and one or two persons rash enough to regret their English friends in public found themselves speedily under interrogation by the T.O. branch of the secret police. The serfs, whose sons composed the bulk of the Danube Army, were not supposed to have feelings about the war, any more than the pigs still to be seen roaming round the shacks on the outskirts of the city, and if the shopkeeper class had any opinions they kept those, for the time being, to themselves. Silence, on any topic more controversial than summer holidays, was the golden rule in St. Petersburg in 1854.

Quietly, crushingly, the monotony of the capital's social round once more fell upon Alix Gyllenlöve. The Demidov palace, with its hot air heating system working full blast even while the weather grew warmer, remained hushed and silent until noon each day, while its mistress conferred with dressmakers and jewellers in her private apartments, or consulted her lawyers and accountants on the administration of the vast Demidov estates, for the war had brought increased prosperity to the great ironworks at Nishni Tagilsk in Siberia and to the Ural mines which were the cradle of the Demidov fortunes. At half past twelve Aurora appeared in one of the smaller dining-rooms, and was joined by Alix and Paul for what was known as breakfast unless there were guests, when the meal was luncheon; then the ladies went for a drive or paid calls before tea. There were invariably guests at the early dinner, and then it was fashionable to go out again, for although the war had curtailed the season of balls and dancing parties performances at the various theatres went on as usual. Aurora took her son to a number of parties for young people, which he detested, swearing that the girls all smelt of borax and bread-and-butter. He began to frequent the women of the town, slinking out by night with the complicity of the *dvornik*, or porter, to visit the gipsy singers on Vassily Island with a few rich youths like himself. There were one or two painful scenes between mother and son as a result, but the obvious course of dismissing the *dvornik* never occurred to Aurora. Even the richest woman in Russia could not afford the luxury of turning away a servant who, like all the porters at the great town houses, was certain to be in the pay of the secret police.

Alix was never present at these quarrels. They came to her ears only in the sound of Aurora's sobs and young Paul's voice raised in anger behind the massive mahogany doors of the third floor rooms. That was indeed how the whole of life seemed to her as the month dragged out and June came in, while the streets of Petersburg which she had left deep in winter snow became white with dust, and the long white nights of the north melted through brief darkness into whiter dawns—a play at which she was only a spectator. In Finland it was the wonderful time of midsummer, when in other years she had danced with the young folk of Ekenäs, or with her Mannerheim cousins at Viborg, round the bonfires lighted on St. John's Eve. Now Alix Gyllenlöve was far away from all such gaieties, sitting alone through the empty mornings with no other companion than her Lapland maid.

Sometimes she turned to her bookshelf for relief. But even her favourites, *Rose of Thistle Island* and *The Duchess of Finland*, failed to give her the old sense of pleasure and escape. The tearful, noble heroines with whom she had easily identified herself in the past seemed figures of cardboard, like the Alexandra of last autumn who had listened in this very house to Boris Apraxin's formal courtship, and given him her cheek to kiss, and her hand for the brief adornment of his ring. The books were laid aside, and as the melancholy which was part of Alexandra's Finnish inheritance began to invade her spirit, she thought more and more often of the lakes and forests of Finland which as yet she had never seen, of which the old runes told, and then she would turn to Anna, demanding tales of Lapland, until little by little the superstitions and the myths which were truth to the Lapp woman began to take possession of Alexandra too.

There came a summer morning when with a lighter heart Alix sent Anna to make sure that Madame Karamsin was alone in her apartments, and then to the admiration of the footmen followed the maid through the anteroom to the boudoir where Aurora was reading the *Journal de St. Petersbourg*. She looked up with a cry of pleasure as the girl came in.

"Darling! Efimov sent home your cloak!"

"Do you like it, Aurora?"

"Like it? It's magnificent!"

The furrier had done his work well. What had been merely a parcel of fine skins on their first visit to the Gostinnoi Dvor had been wrought into supple strands of pure white, skilfully mounted on separate panels of white satin and lined with white silk to avoid any danger of weight or bulkiness, and the fox cloak, falling below her knees, swayed gracefully as Alix moved across the room. She looked at her reflection in Aurora's long mirror, hardly needing Aurora's murmurs of approval to tell her she was beautiful, that the long fine hairs of the fox pelts complemented her own fine blonde hair, and that winter white was the perfect foil for her fair complexion. If only Brand could see me now, she thought.

"Darling, you have the most beautiful cloak in St. Petersburg," exulted Aurora. "The Czarina herself has nothing finer!"

"It *is* lovely," said Alix. "I must write at once and thank Papa."

"I should think so! ... and darling," continued Aurora in her persuasive way, "talking of the Czarina! I met Her Majesty at the Grand Duke's luncheon on Wednesday—or did I mention it?"

"No."

"She asked about you. She said very sweetly that it was a long time since you had been present at any of her receptions, and hoped you would attend the midsummer fête at Peterhof."

She saw the angry colour rise in Alexandra's face. "I think you ought to go, my dear."

"What about Nikita? Is *he* at Peterhof—or in the Winter Palace?"

"He has gone to spend a few days at Gatchina."

"Why Gatchina, of all places?"

Everyone in Petersburg society knew that Nicholas I shunned the gloomy palace where he had spent his lonely childhood, burdened with studies and often thrashed by his brutal tutor Lambsdorff through what were to be the formative years of Nikita-the-Stick.

"They are all going to the summer palaces next week," Aurora said. "Alix, have you read the *Journal* this morning?"

"Not yet. Why?"

"There's something in it I think you ought to see."

Alix read the headline which Aurora showed her. Then, with a frown, she slipped out of the fox cloak, laid it across a chair, and taking up the paper read aloud:

"The British Admiral Plumridge has suffered a severe defeat in the Gulf of Bothnia at the hands of the loyal Finnish population of Gamla Karleby. Plumridge, who has already destroyed Finnish property at Brahestad and Uleaborg, attacked Gamla Karleby with his entire squadron, but was beaten off by the fire of the inhabitants. Many prisoners of war were taken by the Finns. Plumridge's squadron retired in disorder with many killed and wounded aboard."

It was not, when poor Alix was able to rationalize it, such devastating news as at first appeared. For one thing, the units of Plumridge's squadron were named, quite correctly, as H.M.S. *Leopard*, *Vulture*, *Odin* and *Valorous*, and there was some comfort in knowing that H.M.S. *Arrogant* had not been at the scene of an action out of which the Russians were making such excellent propaganda. In her dismay and anger, Alix was sure that the Czar's mysterious withdrawal to Gatchina, that desolate palace now given up to the Master of the Hunt and the stud of the Imperial bloodhounds, had something to do with the report of the fight at Gamla Karleby, which she soon convinced herself was a tissue of lies. A British squadron *could not* be beaten off by the citizens of an unimportant little town like Gamla Karleby—not unless they had Russian soldiers at their backs! But she went to a diplomatic reception at the

Austrian Legation that night, and learned enough from a neutral attaché to realize that British sailors had indeed been taken prisoner by Finlanders, and that the first blood reported to be shed in the Baltic campaign was the blood of Finns.

Next day another item of information was given to the Russian press. The Czar had not been idle at Gatchina. He had purchased from a young Swedish scientist named Alfred Nobel a device of his invention for use against enemy ships at sea, and had ordered the mass production in a Petersburg factory of what some papers called "the secret weapon" and others "the infernal machine". Possession of the Infernal Machine, it was stated, gave Russia an immediate and complete advantage over the West.

Read together, as was intended, the two stories had an excellent effect on the morale of the capital. If the British ships were not driven away by courageous Finnish fishermen, they were likely to be blown out of the water by the Infernal Machine, and in the awareness of this St. Petersburg went quietly about its business without caring much that the majestic presence of the British Baltic Fleet was now visible at some point or another on every day and through the long white nights of June. Detaching only the force required to blockade the Gulf of Riga and watch the port of Memel which was the clearing house of all the contraband trade with Russia, Napier had at last appeared in strength in the Gulf of Finland. Rear-Admiral Corry, with nine British sail of the line, had been ordered to Helsingfors to blockade the fortress, Sveaborg. In Barö Sound, due west of Helsingfors, the long-awaited French squadron had at last joined Napier, under the command of a Trafalgar veteran, Vice-Admiral Parseval-Deschênes. From Barö, with British steamers towing the unwieldy French sailing ships, the combined fleets moved steadily towards St. Petersburg, and on Monday, June 26 (June 14 in the Russian calendar) their sails were seen off Tolboukin lighthouse, about eight miles west of the fortress of Cronstadt.

All that afternoon, with the most perfect unconcern, the guests of the Emperor and Empress of Russia drove along the shore road from St. Petersburg to the summer palace. Invitations to the midsummer fête at Peterhof had been issued two weeks back, and neither the Czar nor Petersburg society saw any reason to cancel an occasion which could only be stimulated by the presence of an enemy fleet comfortably out of gunshot range. Petersburg society drove along the flat road, where the marshes of Ingria had been drained to make the pleasure gardens of the Romanovs, with all the enthusiasm of children going to a circus.

Madame Karamsin and Alix were in one of the first carriages to leave the city.

"It was so gracious of the Grand Duke and his wife to invite us to 'Mine Own' before the fête begins," Aurora said, as they came within sight of the first sentry boxes of the Imperial summer homes. "You will enjoy seeing the children, Alix."

"Lean back, Aurora dear, you'll be tired before we get there," said Alix gently. She thought her godmother, for all her appearance of interest in the beautiful gardens they were passing, looked pale and absent-minded, as if the strain of being so long without news of her husband was wearing her down at last. As for Alix herself, she was tired with the deep fatigue of an anxious heart: too tired to take any pleasure in her white embroidered muslin dress, or the green and white silk spray of lilies of the valley tucked under the brim of her wide straw bonnet. It was very warm, and the road was dusty. Both ladies wore fawn-coloured dust capes above their summer dresses.

They passed Sergiefka, the summer home of the Czar's widowed daughter, the Duchess of Leuchtenberg. Next came the residence which the Grand Duke Alexander had named "Mine Own", and then Peterhof itself, all the gardens communicating with each other and with the gardens of Oranienbaum where the Grand Duke Michael lived, as if the Romanovs were one big devoted family, never happy unless they were together. Peterhof, begun like the capital by Peter the Great, had turned with passing generations into a tasteless collection of buildings like a fun fair, with a Greek pavilion, a Swiss chalet, a Chinese pagoda and a Dutch windmill standing in groves ornamented with fountains, waterfalls and statues in bronze and marble. "Mine Own", by contrast, was a modest country house, and the salon where the Grand Duke and his wife received Alix and Aurora was furnished in the English style, with chintz covers on the simple furniture.

There was a table of magazines and newspapers in the window bay and a mahogany stand held pots of ferns.

"How delightfully restful this is," smiled Aurora Karamsin, taking a cup of tea from the hands of the Grand Duchess. "You must be so glad to be in the country at last, Madame."

"It's so important for the children," agreed the Grand Duchess Marie. She was a princess of Hesse, a delicate, complaining creature whose eyes always sought her husband when she spoke, and whose robust little boys were taught to play very quietly in her presence. They were in the room now, standing beside their father as he chatted with the guests. Alix acknowledged, not for the first time, that the man had charm. The Grand Duke had the born diplomat's gift of conversing about what would please his hearers, and he drew Alix out on her visit to Viborg, commenting on the beauty and rising importance of the city in a way that earned conviction. "We are so fortunate in having Governor Mannerheim," he said. "One of the great servants of Finland, like your brilliant father, madamoiselle."

It would have been easy to relax in the company of the Grand Duke Alexander. "The hope of Finland"—Alix had heard him so called often, even by the most patriotic of the nationalists; and in this pleasant family room, alone with his pretty wife and children, it was difficult to realize that he was the heir of Nikita-the-Stick and the future Autocrat of All the Russias. But Alix had thought of herself too long as a castaway in enemy territory to relax now. The reminder of war cut through the moment of peace as the second boy said politely.

"Papa, may we take the lady to look at the British ships at sea?"

"Through the glass, my boy, if they come nearer; not otherwise."

"The British ships!" said Alix faintly. "Are they as near as that?"

"The boys are restless," explained the Grand Duke, smiling, "because we took them for a drive yesterday, to see the enemy come up the Gulf. We drove along the shore road in peasant carts, with a samovar of tea and a basket of cakes, and picnicked among the rocks, and really it was a charming expedition. Also it had the merit of keeping the boys up long past

172

their bedtime, so of course Alexander wants to repeat the experience today."

"Alex is silly," said the elder boy. "I don't want to miss the fireworks at Peterhof!"

"You shall see the fleet and the fireworks too, Nikolai," said a deep voice from the door.

"Papa!" gasped the Grand Duchess, rising hastily. "Mamma Empress! How very kind—we didn't expect the pleasure—"

The Czar of Russia entered the room with a measured step. The Czarina followed him; thin, nervous and smiling with the curious tic and twitching of the head which had afflicted her ever since the December night in 1825 when the Czar put down rebellion with a merciless hand and waded to his throne through the blood of a regiment. She had been a Prussian princess, hating the French since the days of the great Napoleon, rabid against them in the days of Napoleon the Less.

As soon as the ritual bows and curtsies were over she embraced her daughter-in-law.

"Marie dear, are you equal to the fête this evening? We called to enquire as soon as we heard of your long drive yesterday, and your very late picnic . . ."

"I am none the worse, thank you, Madame."

"Most imprudent in your state of health," said the Czar. "Jolting along the shore in a peasant cart, indeed! You should think of your duty to Russia, Marie."

"The boys were very anxious to see the British at close quarters, Sire," said their father. He had buttoned up the jacket of his undress uniform when the Czar came in, and now was standing to attention like a junior officer before his colonel, with his sons stiffly erect by his side.

"Naturally," said the Czar. "That is what I should expect of my grandsons!" He had refused a chair. He now waved away his daughter-in-law's fluttering offer of refreshments. While he remained standing, nobody else could sit, not even the Czarina: they stood in a ring around the Autocrat whose presence turned the pretty living-room into a barrack square.

Nicholas was not in undress uniform, like his son, but in the full regimentals of a Colonel of the Chevalier Gardes. On the rare occasions when he did not appear in uniform it was his custom to say that he "felt as if his skin had been taken away", and even for an afternoon call on his children he had assumed three Orders and a diamond Star. Like a colonel asking privates if the soup was good he put a few questions to each one in turn—short questions, requiring crisp military answers, although Madame Karamsin came in for a special smile and pressure of the hand. Of Alix he took no notice, except to enquire coldly for her father's health ("he does not spare himself in his work for Russia") and then he came back to his grandsons again, and the British Fleet.

"Yes, Nikolai," he said to the elder. "You shall see the enemy fleet from Peterhof tonight—before the fireworks! And if they venture much further east of their present station, you will see fireworks of another sort!"

"The Infernal Machines!" exulted Nikolai, and the Czar overruled his mother's quick "Hush, Niki!"

"Yes, the Infernal Machines," said the Czar gravely, and to his son: "I had your brother's report an hour ago. All the machines were successfully launched at noon."

"And without accident, Sire?"

"Not quite. Two Russian fishing-smacks were sunk during the launching, but we must expect some loss of life in employing a new weapon. It will be a fitting conclusion to our fête tonight," said the Czar with his strange eyes gleaming, "if the guests see a British frigate explode in full view of the palace of Peterhof!"

He is mad, thought Alix Gyllenlöve. He means to destroy the world—or make it Russian, which is the same thing, and who will destroy him? One by one the Romanovs have been murdered. Will murder be Nikita's fate? If I had a knife now, would I have the courage to plunge it into his heart?

"When Napier turns back from Cronstadt," the harsh voice resounded in the listening room, "—as turn back he will, to-morrow or the next day, I shall regard our victory in the Baltic as assured. We have three enemies banded against us, fighting on two fronts, and yet we shall destroy them one by one. I shall have the two great generals, January and February, fighting on my side next winter. As says our great Derzhavin:

" 'And what to thee, O Russia, is an ally?
Advance and the whole universe is thine!' "

174

"How beautiful! How true!" applauded the Czarina. "Marie, the boys ought to learn Derzhavin's poem by heart."

"I will tell their tutor, Mamma Empress."

"Speaking of poetry," said the Czar, dropping his prophetic manner, "that was a remarkable poem by Topelius you showed me yesterday."

"I am glad you thought so, Sire," said the Grand Duke.

"Have you kept the newspaper?"

"I believe so . . . Here it is," A copy of *Helsingfors Tidningar*, carefully folded on the window table, was put into the Czar's hands.

"Our charming visitors from Finland are of course acquainted with the works of Zachary Topelius," said the Czar, with a glance at Alix and Aurora.

"*Heather Bells*—such a delightful collection!" said Madame Karamsin valiantly.

"His present theme, alas, is far from being delightful," said the Czar. "He laments, like all of us, the sufferings which the British have inflicted on the defenceless people of the Grand Duchy . . . *Den första blodsdroppen* is the name of the poem." He looked sideways at the Czarina's palsied head. She was easily made nervous by the mention of blood.

"Alyssa Ivanovna!"

"Sire?" said Alix nervously.

"Swedish is your native language, I believe?"

"Swedish is the language generally spoken by the Finns of Nyland province, where I was born."

"A nice distinction!" said the Czar sarcastically. "Will you translate this poem into Russian for our pleasure?"

Alix took the paper from his hand doubtfully. He cares nothing for the poem, her instinct told her, but he has found a way to give me pain. This is the same Nikita who tortured Ryléyév, who allowed Dostoievsky to be led to the scaffold before the death sentence was commuted, for whom no enemy is too weak to be ignored—

She looked at the close print and read the title aloud: "The First Drop of Blood," And then stopped dead.

"Pray continue," said the Czar inexorably, "I wish the boys to hear this cry from the Grand Duchy—translated by a Finnish loyalist!"

"The springtime now," read Alix, and caught her breath.

"The springtime now is twining her garland fresh and green
And spreading over Finland a carpet fair and sheen
And ye come from the ocean e'er yet has thawed the flood,
In might and pride, ye strangers, to stain the scene with
   blood."

She looked up to see the Czar's smile, and the anxious face
of Aurora.

"Know ye, you Southern warrior—know ye how sweet a
   thing
To every heart in Finland is the return of spring?
When ice and winter vanish we draw new life and breath
And now while Nature smileth . . . you . . .

You come to bring us death," finished Alix, and flung the
crumpled paper to the floor.

"It's hateful—hateful!" she said with a sob, "I won't read
more. I can't!" and she covered her face with her hands to
hide the tears.

"There are faint hearts in Nyland province," said the Czar
Nikita. "We expect courage from our Russian women!"

CHAPTER TEN

THE WHITE NIGHTS

THE Czar's little grandsons scuffed disconsolately at the gravel path which ran under the side windows of "Mine Own". They were in the charge of their father's aide de camp, who stood swinging two pairs of field glasses in one hand and pretending to show no interest at all in the couple walking up and down beneath the rose pergola.

"Lieutenant Bernstorff, *why* can't we go and look for the British ships now?" Nikolai implored.

"You know we must wait for His Imperial Highness, Sir."

Niki and little Alex sighed. They had not been at all disturbed by the scene in the living-room, for in their experience visits from Grandpapa Emperor always ended in disaster. Sooner or later somebody, and usually one of themselves, was reduced to tears, so that they had quite a fellow feeling for the big grown-up girl who made Grandpapa angry . . . though she didn't look grown-up now with her cheeks red with crying and her hair all blown about. She had slung her bonnet by its velvet ribbon on her arm. Papa was speaking to her in the voice he kept for mamma's headaches, and as they came nearer the boys heard Alix say :

"I hope the Grand Duchess will forgive me, Sir. It was very good of you to make excuses for me, and take me out to the garden with the children."

"It was nothing," said the Grand Duke Alexander. "It will all be forgotten long before tonight's fête is over. The Czar, you know, is very much a soldier, and doesn't always understand a lady's sensibilities."

"Papa, mayn't we go on the roof now?" burst out Nikolai, with an agitated sign at the Czarina's little basket carriage, in which the Imperial couple had driven over from Peterhof, standing with a groom by the pony's head at the front door.

"You think we ought to make our escape now, Niki?" said the Grand Duke with a grin. "I think you're right. This way, then, Alyssa Ivanovna."

"This way for the enemy!" shouted little Alexander, as soon as the party had made a quiet return to the house through the side door and climbed three flights of stairs to the attic regions of "Mine Own". The flat roof to which a wide french window gave access had been ornamented with large jars of blue porcelain filled with red geraniums, and a high parapet assured the safety of the children. The Russian double eagle flew from the flagstaff.

"You mustn't spoil your pretty dress," said the Grand Duke to Alexandra.

"It won't spoil." It could have been made of sacking for all she cared, with this unhoped-for opportunity to see the British ships within her grasp. The heat on the flat roof was very great. The sky was cloudless and there was a shimmer on the surface of the Gulf waters. The great fortress of Cronstadt lay directly ahead, like a lean clenched hand with one long forefinger pointing north-west to Sveaborg. Due south of the wrist of the hand the Russian warships, moored head and stern, lay safely in the rear harbour.

"Focus the glasses for Niki and Alex, please," the Grand Duke said to Lieutenant Bernstoff. The aide de camp tactfully drew the little boys away to another part of the roof while his master raised the second pair of glasses to his eyes.

"Yes, the British are in sight," he said. "They obviously intend to try a reconnaissance tonight. One paddle steamer —that must be the survey ship. And two frigates, just as our observers said."

"Can your observers name the different ships, Sir?" said Alexandra.

"Approximately. One of our best men put in at the boat dock at Oranienbaum with a fairly complete report about two hours ago. Admiral Napier has transferred his flag to *Driver*, but I imagine both he and the Frenchman will stay with the three-deckers at Tolboukin. What we see is their flying squadron—*Lightning* with *Bulldog* and *Magicienne*. Would you like to look now?"

"If you please."

At first Alix saw nothing but a blur of water and sky. Then the Grand Duke's fingers closed over hers, adjusting the lens, and the British ships came sharply into her field of vision. They were a brilliant sight, for Napier had ordered every ship going into action to hoist a yellow-blue-yellow pendant over the Blue Ensign at the peak and the Union Jack at the main, and all three were proceeding under a full spread of snowy canvas.

"Papa, shall we see one of the enemy ships blown up by an Infernal Machine?"

Little Alexander, with his big brother monopolizing the glasses, had come up to embrace his father's knees, and the Czarevich, with a laugh, rumpled his golden curls.

"If we're very lucky," he said absently. He took a small but powerful pair of opera glasses from the pocket of his white jacket, and focused them down the Gulf.

"Can you see another frigate coming up to port, Alyssa Ivanovna?"

"Yes, Sir."

"That must be one of the three guard ships of the flying squadron. It might be *Imperieuse*, or *Desperate*. Or *Arrogant* . . . Is anything the matter?"

"The glasses are rather heavy." She dropped her wrists for a moment, and then lifted the powerful German glasses to her eyes again. They nearly hid her face—they *must* hide her expression!

"Is it really likely, Sir, that any of these ships will be destroyed by the secret weapon?"

"If they sail too close to Cronstadt, it's quite possible," said the Grand Duke. He was absorbed in finding the right range for his opera glasses.

"The Infernal Machine floats in the water, then?" persisted Alix.

"At present it is apt to surface. Of course my brother, as Commander of our Baltic Fleet, is quite right to use it, but Mr. Nobel will have to develop the Mark II to remain underwater, and still detonate on contact with a ship's hull. I don't think," said the Czarevich confidentially, "that the Infernal Machine is much more efficient at this stage than the Bickford fuse, which our observers saw the British using in mid-Baltic. However, we shall see."

"Russia seems to have her 'observers' everywhere."

"It's only a question of payment," said Alexander with his pleasant laugh. "You are pale, Alyssa Ivanovna, the heat is too much for you. Shall we go indoors?"

Alix had time for one long look at the British frigate which

179

might be H.M.S. *Arrogant*, coming gamely up for a reconnaissance of impregnable Cronstadt. The perfect cameo of the white ship on the grey-blue sea remained on her sight long after the Czarevich had calmed the little boys' protests, shepherding the whole party back to the staircase, and when she stopped at a hall mirror to tie on her bonnet, it was Brand's ship and not her own reflection which Alix saw in the glass.

The Imperial basket carriage was no longer outside the front door.

The Grand Duke looked at his little sons comically. "Now we're in disgrace," he said. "We should have been here to bid your grandparents goodbye. Mamma is sure to be vexed, when we go in."

"Then do we have to go in right away?" asked the practical Nikolai.

"Shall we take Alyssa Ivanovna on a tour of the garden first?"

The smile the Grand Duke gave Alix was decidedly flirtatious. She remembered the lingering pressure of his fingers on her own when they held the field glasses, and returned his look as boldly as she could. The icy censor in her brain decided that this man, the charmer, was potentially more dangerous than the megalomaniac Czar. The Czar raged and tormented; this man smiled. This man could pet a child and call it lucky to see a great ship rent in two by a silent and invisible enemy. She said with relief:

"Here comes a carriage, Sir. You have other visitors at 'Mine Own'!"

"Not by my invitation," said Alexander with a frown.

"It's one of Madame Karamsin's carriages!" exclaimed Alix. She recognized the second coachman, Igor, and the blazon on the doors. With a ghastly presentiment, she saw Paul Demidov stop the vehicle out of sight of the windows and come hurrying up the gravel drive towards them.

"Sir!" he said, with a quick bow for the Grand Duke. "Alix! Thank God I got here before you went to Peterhof. Where's my mother?"

"Madame Karamsin is indoors with the Grand Duchess," said the Czarevich. "What has happened, Paul?"

"You could have got him home on leave," said the boy. "You promised her! Faith of a Romanov! But you did nothing about it. You let him rot there on the Danube, and now there's this telegram . . ."

"Colonel Karamsin?" whispered Alix.

Desperately: "I don't know how I'm going to tell her, Alexandra. You've got to help me break it to her—"

"Is he killed . . . or wounded?"

"Dead."

The Grand Duchess Marie, that frail and plaintive lady, was the heroine of the terrible hour which followed. While the inexperienced boy and girl were frightened into uselessness, she applied restoratives to bring Aurora out of her first fainting fit, and when that, after an outburst of hysterics, was followed by a second, she sent Lieutenant Bernstorff racing through the gardens to Peterhof to fetch one of the Imperial physicians. When the doctor said it would be dangerous for Madame Karamsin to undertake the long drive back to the city, the Grand Duchess at once ordered guest rooms to be prepared, and after Aurora had been put to bed she even remembered that Paul and Alix, whatever their feelings now, would probably be glad of food and wine at a later hour.

"Do you think I ought to stay at home with them?" she asked her husband, when her French maid came in to remind "Madame la Princesse" that it was time to dress for the evening fête.

"Don't be a fool, Marie! Can you imagine what the Czar would say?"

Alexander spoke more roughly than usual. He had been greatly touched by the grief of Aurora Karamsin, whom he had known since he was a lad of eighteen and she his mother's pretty maid of honour, and touched by guilt whenever he remembered that promise to bring Andrei home from the front. It was almost a relief to get into his dress uniform and escort his wife across the lawns to the marble terraces of Peterhof, where his mother, loaded with the priceless jewels she adored, was waiting to greet the guests.

The little boys were heard laughing and talking on the stairs as they went up to bed, and then all was quiet. Aurora was asleep under heavy sedation, with the youngest child's nurse sitting beside her bed, and Alix and Paul sat down together in the parlour beyond her open door, where supper was laid on a small table.

"When did it happen, Paul?" said Alix in a whisper, and the boy groaned.

"Days and days ago. That's the worst of it! All the time she was going about and enjoying herself he was lying dead, and she didn't know it. They didn't dare make it public, you see, that old Paskeivich had been defeated at Silistria, but your father made it his business to find out about Andrei and then telegraphed to me."

"My *father* telegraphed?"

"Yes."

"And Andrei fell at Silistria?"

"No, at a place called Karakala. I suppose it was in the retreat, but I don't know. He was with a full cavalry troop, the message said, when they ran into a heavy Turkish force at Karakala, and lost one hundred and thirty men and all their guns. Andrei . . . Andrei's body was horribly mutilated. They could only identify it by his ring."

"Don't tell your mother that!"

"I'm not a complete fool . . . She's terribly cut up, isn't she?"

"She loved him very much, you know."

"D'you think she cared for my father like that?"

"She cares for *you*, Paul. Later on, she'll be glad that you were here tonight."

"Oh God," he said, "I've had all I can stand. I'm going to bed. You'd better get some sleep too."

"Don't you want anything more to eat?"

"I'll take a glass of wine upstairs with me."

The servants came in to clear the table. Alix went to look at Aurora, and was reassured by the old nurse's nod and the finger held to her lips. The bedroom prepared for herself was next door, with a little balcony looking across the gardens. It was still broad daylight at ten o'clock, but she could see candlelight in the Peterhof grounds, gleaming on the elaborate supper tables, and hear the sound of violins. The garden fête was well under way; after supper there would be dancing, and fireworks during the two brief hours when, at that midsummer season, it was almost dark on the Gulf of Finland. It was cooler, and Alix shivered in her muslin dress. She found her dust cape in the wardrobe, wrapped it about her shoulders, an sat down in a long cane chair on the balcony.

She was far too tired to sleep. The sight of Aurora's complete collapse, coming on top of the scene with the Czar, had shocked her profoundly, but worst of all was the thought that within five miles at most of where she sat, Brand's ship and many others were running into a secret and imminent danger. Every time she closed her eyes she saw the image of the British frigate, graceful as a swan upon a lake, with the yellow-blue-and-yellow pendant challenging the red white-and-blue of the Union Jack. Subconsciously she was listening for the sound of an explosion out at sea. But the only noise was the crackle and hiss of the Peterhof fireworks when the rockets and golden rains began, and presently the Imperial cyphers and the double eagles and the triumphal arches blazed across the midnight sky Russia's complete defiance of the Baltic Fleet. Alix heard the applause and laughter swell to cheers. She was on her knees then—praying for the comforting of Aurora's sorrow; praying that the Infernal Machine would never find its mark.

Madame Karamsin woke late in the morning, pale and languid from the effects of the drug, but determined to leave for St. Petersburg as soon as the Grand Duchess could be visited in her boudoir and thanked for her great kindness. Then she drove back down the coast road, past the staring peasants who had been lining the roads all night to see the gay company go by, to her own house on Morskaia Street, where the efficient major-domo had already had the great black hatchment placed above the door and ordered crape for the "Suisse" liveries of his staff.

The candles were flickering in front of the ikons of the Greek Orthodox faith, which Aurora's second husband, like her first, had professed; but as soon as his widow reached her own apartments she sat down with a little book of Lutheran devotions and read herself into something like tranquillity. The mood was not to last long, for very soon arrived Karamsin's married sister, Princess Catherine Mestjersky, and the two women wept and clung together until Aurora was flushed and feverish and Alix begged in vain that she would go to bed. In her terrible restlessness she had one fixed idea, to go herself to Finland and break the news to Andrei's mother and sister, and late in the afternoon sent the major-domo to police headquarters for the *podorojna*, or exit permit, without which no one, even of Aurora's rank, was allowed to leave Russia.

Alix herself took it from the man when he returned at six o'clock and laid it on Aurora's escritoire. By that time Aurora had given way to her fatigue and retired to bed, insisting that she would be fit to travel in the morning.

"It's quite absurd and we must all try to prevent it," said Princess Catherine when the rest of the company were at dinner. "Aurora is not equal to such a journey. Besides, she ought to be here when my other brother arrives from Moscow."

"Why don't *he* go on to Dalsvik?" said Paul Demidov impertinently. He had taken his mother's place at the head of the table and was drinking his third glass of champagne.

"Because he must remain in Petersburg until poor Andrei's estate is settled, of course."

"What estate?" Alix was nearly sure that was what Paul muttered, but half a dozen Karamsin cousins were wielding their forks and knives so vigorously that the sarcasm was inaudible, and soon coffee was brought in and the company dispersed. Alix went alone to the Golden Salon, which even on festive nights had never held so many flowers. Bouquets had been arriving all day long, the lovely, expensive tokens of sympathy for a woman much loved in St. Petersburg. The Czar's white lilies were placed beside tributes from all the Grand Dukes, the Minister-Secretary for Finland, and the humble people to whom she had given her charity. Alix sent for paper and a little portable ink well and began to note the names on the various cards. There would be innumerable notes of thanks to be written later.

She was moving round the Golden Salon at this task, and her head was beginning to ache with the mixed scents of the flowers, when she heard raised voices in the hall outside, and Paul Demidov appeared at the open door.

"Alix, listen to this!"

"What is it now, Paul? Oh, *not* another telegram?"

"Your father keeps the wires busy, I must say. Nobody else can get a word through from Moscow today, but he—well, read it for yourself."

The efficient head of the Railway Commission had telegraphed briefly:

"Colonel Karamsin's body has been recovered and will be brought to Moscow. Will advise date arrival Petersburg but suggest you start funeral arrangements. Deepest sympathy, Gyllenlöve."

"Paul, she mustn't be allowed to see the body."

"I'll see to that," said the boy grimly. "I'm going to order it sealed in a lead coffin at Moscow. God, he's been *dead* two weeks already! But that's not the worst of it, Alix. There'll have to be a military funeral now, with the Imperial family present, and the priests—I suppose I'll have to see the Archimandrite, or the Patriarch himself tomorrow—"

"Paul, why don't you let Prince Mestjersky take care of all that?"

"Why don't I? Because I'm my father's son, that's why. I don't want to be run by Katie Karamsin's husband, nor by Andrei's brother, either. I'm sick of the Karamsins, swarming over this place like locusts as soon as mamma's ill. It isn't going to last, I tell you! This will be my house some day, and I mean to be master in it now!"

As he came close to her it struck Alix that the young man had been drinking since he left the dinner table. There was a smell on his breath of marachino, or some other of the sweet, sticky liqueurs he loved, and his eyes were heavy.

"Paul, please don't make things hard for everybody at a time like this. You were so sweet to your mother yesterday, why can't you keep it up just a little while longer? It will be so terrible for her, having Andrei's coffin brought home—"

"I don't want to make things hard for *you*, darling."

She bit her lip at the endearment and Paul muttered:

"You're so beautiful in black, Alix. Your shoulders are so white and smooth—"

He took her in his arms suddenly and masterfully, gripping her waist and pushing his hot face down into the bosom of her dress. He mumbled into the laces at her breast:

"You and I could have a wonderful time, you know, darling. I'm rich, I can give you everything you want. Jewels, furs, your own apartment, everything. Just let me love you—"

"Paul, let me go!"

His answer was to kiss her as Alix had never been kissed in her life before, and even in her frantic revulsion at that moist sucking mouth instinct told her that she would be mad to fight him now. Paul was no longer the loutish boy of Hel-·singfors, but an experienced young libertine who might well

185

take resistance as a challenge to rape, even there in the Golden Salon among the mourning flowers. She risked a moment of yielding, letting her body go limp in his arms and her lips cling to his, and then as he gasped with pleasure she slipped away from him and whispered:

"Not any more, Paul! Not now! Somebody might come!"

He was not too drunk to deny that this was true, and he had left the door wide open. He said:

"When, Alix? When?"

She kept her eyes upon him, smiled brilliantly, made for the nearest bell-rope and pulled it hard.

"Bring champagne for Prince Paul," she said to the footman. "I must go to Aurora Karlovna now."

She ran upstairs. The lift was too slow, too like a velvet prison; she burst into her bedroom, scattering towels and cosmetics to get at a bottle of mouthwash and clean her mouth. She knew exactly what she had to do, and was determined to do it well: there must not be another bungled, amateurish runaway like her flight to Gothenburg. This time she had further to go, and no Brand Endicott to come to the rescue— Brand! She pressed her hands, dripping with cold water, against her cheeks, arranged her hair, and rang for her Lapland maid.

Anna came in, her slant eyes shining, and took her silent place in front of Alexandra's chair.

"Sit down, Anna. With the table between us, so. I want us to think together about the sailor from the West."

"The stranger?"

"He is here, not far from us, tonight."

"On the great ship at sea."

The litany of their questions and answers would have been strange enough if spoken by firelight or by a winter lamp. In the harsh daylight of the Petersburg evening the words had an unearthly ring.

"Tell me," Alexandra's voice fell to a whisper, "is he in danger now? If I stay here, in the house of the Lady Aurora, would I be able to help him, if the need should come?"

"How can I tell? How can I know?"

"You've told such things before—"

"With the drum, yes. But if I brought the drum into Russia the police would have me whipped."

"With the charms, then? Look at me, Anna! With the charms?"

Fascinated, the Laplander took a small skin pouch from her red braid belt and laid the contents on the table. A polished stone, a bear's tooth, a manikin of carved reindeer horn—she fingered them and shook her head.

"I cannot tell the future here," she said. "In Russia there is no *seite*. And in this city of stone, where shall I find a troll stone? We must go back, lady, to the woods we know, and make the drum speak, before we see the future."

"Anna, look at me!"

Alix laid her long fingers over the brown hands that held the charms. The Lapp, with a shiver, looked into the grey eyes, and watched the black pupils dilate in the cold summer light.

"I see nothing," she said in a high voice. "Here there is nothing! At the fortress, Sveaborg, is the danger—not in this place."

In the wide halls of the third floor of the palace, the curtains had been drawn across the harsh white day, and lamplight gleamed in the mirrors placed at intervals above the flower laden marble console tables. Alexandra saw her reflection advancing to Madame Karamsin's suite, with her black silk draperies brushing the Persian carpet, her fair hair pinned into a little knot, and the only glitter about her, the jet beads on the black satin reticule swinging from her wrist.

The footmen in the anteroom were not whispering together, as they so often did on duty, but sitting up straight in their high-backed chairs like mutes at a funeral. They rose and bowed as Alix came in. She motioned them back and herself silently turned the handle of the salon door.

Only two lamps had been lighted there, one near the flower-filled fireplace and one beside the escritoire. Alix saw at a glance that the *podorojna* was still lying where she herself had laid it down. She had taken three quiet steps towards the desk when the door communicating with the bedroom opened and Princess Catherine Mestjersky looked out.

"Who is that?"

"It's only Alix, princess. Is my godmother awake?"

"Yes, and asking for you. Come in, Alexandra."

The older woman, already attired for the night watch in a mob cap and a voluminous taffeta negligée, stood aside to let Alix enter. Aurora was lying in the great bed, with her beautiful dark hair loose and her hands clasped on a cambric handkerchief. A night light and a little tray with a medicine bottle, water and a glass stood on her bedside table.

Alix bent over the bed. Beneath the marks of weeping she saw a little natural colour in Aurora's cheeks.

"Dear, are you feeling better?" she whispered.

"Resting. Hoping to go to sleep again, by and by."

"She has taken her sleeping medicine," the princess said officiously. "Our dear Aurora will have a good night's rest."

Alix glanced at the medicine bottle. "Is there anything I can do for you, Aurora?"

"Only bring me my little Swedish Bible, darling. Katie can't seem to find it . . ."

"Let me make room on your table first."

Alix picked up the tray with the sleeping draught, carried it into the adjoining dressing room, and slipped the bottle quickly inside her reticule. The Swedish Bible was where she expected to find it, in a drawer of the great fitted wardrobe which occupied one wall of the room, and she took it back to the bedroom and put it gently into Aurora's hand.

"You know they're going to bring him back to me?" whispered Aurora. Alix bent her head.

"Only his earthly remains, dear sister," said the princess. "Our precious Andrei's soul is safe in heaven."

"'God's will be done,' said Aurora Karamsin, and fresh tears came to her blue eyes. "God bless you, Alix darling. You must have a long sound sleep tonight."

"Aurora, *please*," Alix took her godmother in her arms. Through the silk nightdress she felt the relaxed flesh of a body no longer young, inhaled the indefinable odour of malaise and medicine which overcame the perfect freshness of the bed linen and the perfume of Aurora's hair. Repressing an instinctive revulsion she said softly:

"Is there anything at all—anything in the world, that I can do to help you?"

Aurora stirred restlessly. "I'm so anxious about Andrei's mother. Tomorrow we must send a courier to Dalsvik . . ."

"Please don't worry her about all that now, Alexandra."

The princess came jealously close to the bedside and Alix stood back at once.

"Dear Katie!" said Aurora drowsily, "you take such care of me!"

She put her hand to her lips and smiled goodnight to Alix. Princess Catherine, with her mouth compressed, escorted the girl to the bedroom door and turned the key in the lock behind her.

So now she was alone in the salon, and it was the work of a moment, with a quick look at both the doors, to take the exit permit from the writing desk and place it folded in her reticule. Out in the anteroom she told one of the footmen to send the major-domo to her, and calmly returned to her boudoir.

"There is a good deal of noise in the vestibule, Antoine," she told the man when he appeared. "Are people coming in to write their names in the book at this late hour?"

The Swiss shrugged. "Mademoiselle knows the custom of St. Petersburg," he said. "The theatres are closing, and many wish to pay their respects to Madame Karamsin at a time so convenient to themselves."

"But not to us," said Alix. "Madame is not to be disturbed any longer by the sound of carriage wheels and callers. Have the front door shut and the lights on the lower floors extinguished, and send the house servants to bed. Tell the *dvornik* to admit no more carriages into the courtyard until noon tomorrow."

They were the first independent orders Alix had ever given in that house, and the man accepted them unquestioningly. When he had bowed and left her she opened her bedroom door and said to Anna:

"It is time for you and me to go back to Finland."

The Lapp woman, with an inarticulate sound, threw herself on her knees and kissed Alexandra's hands.

"Get up," the girl said, "there is no time to waste. You know the people of this house will stop us if they can. We must be quick and quiet."

"We go home *tonight*?"

"As soon as it is dark. Listen carefully. Put in a bag what things you will need for the journey and wait until you hear the clocks strike twelve. Then go out by the servants' door and walk to the post house by the Isaac Square and look for

189

a man with a good face, and two good horses in his *telega*, and hire him to take us to the first post house on the Finland road. No farther! Then have him drive out of the Square and halt beside the Neva, and wait there till I come."

"Lady, the *dvornik*!"

"I remembered the *dvornik*."

Alix took the sleeping mixture from her reticule and took out the cork. It was colourless, odourless, and as the tip of a finger assured her, very nearly tasteless. One dose only had been taken from the bottle.

"Put a spoonful of this liquid in a bowl of coffee and carry it to the *dvornik*. I have ordered the gates closed, and no visitors will come to rouse him. *Destroy the bottle!*"

The narrow eyes gleamed malice and comprehension. The Lapp woman melted from the room, and Alix, with a long sigh, sat down at her dressing-table and drew her little watch towards her. It was not quite half past ten, and the sound of the midsummer evening traffic rolling along the Morskaia rose clearly through her open window. It was forty hours since she had slept.

If the plan worked, and they were clear of the city by one in the morning, then with one change of horses they could be at Terijoki on the Finland side by five. Three good hours before her flight need be discovered in St. Petersburg. Would anyone come after her, as Erik Kruse had followed her from Karinlund to Gothenburg? Certainly not Paul Demidov: he had the lusts, but not the energy, of Captain Kruse. The time to fear Paul was now, in the next half-hour.

It was because of this that Alix was still wearing her evening dress: if by ill fortune Paul, or any servant carrying a message that seemed urgent came to her door she must appear to be sitting up late reading, not dressing for a hasty flight. If she knew the secret of those Lapland spells in which she more than half believed, how willingly she would lay an enchantment of slumber over all the house! And yet the place was certainly quieter. From her window she had seen the gate closed, and the Karamsin cousins had all reluctantly gone home. The long white night was turning at last to dusk.

Eleven o'clock found her walking restlessly up and down the boudoir, reviewing every stage of her wild plan. At Terijoki, of course, the Russian writ still ran, but once in the

Grand Duchy she could claim the protection of Governor Mannerheim, and surely he would put her safely on the way to Helsingfors! And after Hagasund and Dalsvik she would make for Degerby across the water, in the Åland Islands which the British ships must visit, halfway across the Baltic to Stockholm. *Brand, I am on my way to you—* if I can get clear of this house and clear of Russia.

She was not running away from Paul Demidov. His importunity was only the last straw added to the vast structure of her hate for Russia and the man who ruled it. *If I stay I shall try to kill Nikita,* she thought. *And I am not equal to the part of Charlotte Corday.*

It was easier to think of Paul than of his mother. Aurora lying broken in that great bed, with her Swedish Bible and her simple piety, was far harder to leave than Aurora the court favourite, the richest woman in the whole of Russia! Would Aurora ever forgive her for what she was about to do? Would she understand her goddaughter's unscrupulous, compulsive instinct for flight?

At half past eleven, with these questions unresolved, Alix prepared her own travelling bag with necessaries, jewels and money. She took the white fox cloak from her wardrobe and laid it ready on the bed. It might in one way be a risk to wear it, at least for the twenty miles of Russian road, but it would give her the authority she would require at the customs post, and with the frontier guards. She took off the black evening dress and put on her green merino. A white silk scarf to tie over her hair, a dust cape to protect her cloak . . . and she was ready.

Ready for the last, the all-important thing. She opened the leather standish and took out pen and ink. Then she took the *podorojna* from her reticule.

There was an ugly word for what she was going to do. Forgery.

Forgery and false pretences. She pressed her hands over her burning eyes, and saw Brand's ship, white-winged, on the grey-blue sea.

She drew a sheet of writing paper towards her and wrote to Princess Catherine:

"Please give my love to Aurora and tell her I have gone to Dalsvik. I shall ask Senator Walleen to help me break the sad news to Madame Nikolai Karamsin and her daughter and make all arrangements for their return to St. Petersburg. I believe it will make Aurora happier if she knows this is being done."

It was just possible, she thought, grimly considering the sophistry, that bringing Senator Walleen into the business might stop Aurora from ordering a hue and cry after herself. In any case it was time to act, for the city clocks were chiming midnight, and she thought of the *dvornik* drugged and the side door open, and Anna running along Morskaia Street to the post house near the Isaac Square. She unfolded the *podorojna*.

The major-domo had certainly paid more than twice the one and a half roubles required for an exit permit, for the police had left both the date of departure and the destination blank. Only the style and title of the bearer had been entered in Cyrillic characters at the top of the sheet.

Alix reflected. The *telega*, that wretched vehicle in which Anna and she must sit crushed among the straw, was to be hired after midnight. She carefully inserted the new date: June $\frac{28}{16}$ 1854.

Without allowing herself to think, she signed the instrument of freedom in her own handwriting, copying the name already inscribed above:

"Signed: Eva Aurora Charlotta Karamsin, Princess Demidova.

"Destination: HELSINGFÓRS."

CHAPTER ELEVEN

LAPP MAGIC I

THE Finns gave the name of Ahvenanmaa, Country of Perch, to the group of inhabited isles surrounded by a thousand rocky islets which Sweden and the rest of Europe called the Åland Islands. At midsummer, 1854, the Country of Perch became the Country of War, as the first ships from Napier's fleet began to reconnoitre Bomarsund, the nearest and by far the most vulnerable of Russia's three Baltic fortresses.

Early one morning towards the end of July, Anna the Laplander rowed herself from an island pasture to the mainland of Degerby and without effort carried two heavy wooden pails of foaming milk up a steep path half hidden by birch trees. Entering by an empty stable yard she carried the milk to the dairy and set it on the stone slab. Then she went back to the yard to pour cold water over her hands and dash it on her perspiring face.

It was warm and very still. Neither Miss Agneta Willebrand, the venerable owner of the clapboard house, nor her housekeeper Mamsell Josabeth was likely to be about so early, and the only sound was the tuneless singing of a young servant brewing coffee in the kitchen. Anna's nostrils twitched appreciatively. It was some time since she had tasted her favourite dish of smoked reindeer tongue, and a bowl of coffee, drunk with a lump of sugar held between her teeth, was one of the Lapp woman's greatest remaining pleasures in life.

She ran her wet hands over her bare head, plastering the straight black hair against her skull, shook down the skirts she had pinned up for milking, and was ready to enter the front regions of the house. The front door itself was still bolted, by Miss Agneta's recent orders, and the rooms on either side had their blinds drawn, but Anna slipped through the kitchen passage to a small bedroom facing east where the window was wide open and Alix Gyllenlöve lay sleeping in the early sunshine.

Anna stood regarding her young mistress. For three weeks

now she had seen Alix lying in the narrow wooden bed under a home-spun sheet, in the whitewashed room with no ornament but a bouquet of wild flowers on the deal dresser, just as she had seen her lie through her childhood years in such another room at Ekenäs. It never failed to rouse her own frustrated mother love. She sighed deeply, and touched Alexandra's outflung hand. The girl stirred, the dark lashes opened on the brilliant eyes, and Alix smiled.

"Anna? I was dreaming."

"The time for dreams is past," said the Lapp woman. "Today the stranger comes to you again."

"Today?" Bright colour flooded Alexandra's face. "Oh Anna, are you sure?"

"The troll stone has said it, lady."

"You went to the pasture- Without me?"

"It is best to go alone to the *seite*. And for you this is to be a holiday."

"Anna, when will he come?" the girl begged.

"You must rise now, lady, and be ready for your fate. In one hour, and no more, the English ship will come to Degerby."

There was no time to swim that morning. Alix bathed in rain water and put on the plain white bodice and black skirt of the Islanders, with a red braided belt from which swung a key, a fishhook in a woven case, and the Finnish knife, the *puuko*, in its heavy leather sheath. At Degerby Alix had recaptured the simplicity of her country childhood, the best possible antidote to the fevers of St. Petersburg, and the outdoor life, the long calm nights of sleep, had taken away the look of strain which had begun to sharpen the delicate contours of her face. She was glowing with eagerness, fresh as a wild rose, when Brand Endicott found her waiting beneath the birches of Degerby.

Then at the last moment she was nervous, and gave him her hand with a constraint which he broke only with the lightest of kisses on her averted cheek.

"Alix! Darling! My God, I can't believe it!"

"Brand, Brand, are you safe and well?"

He looked superbly well in the summer outfit bought from the purser's store: blue and white checked shirt, white duck trousers and white-lettered "H.M.S. *Arrogant*" on the black riband hanging from his oiled tarpaulin hat. She covered her face with her hands in a little gesture of thankfulness.

"Don't hide your face," he said. "Let me look at you—you wonderful runaway!"

At that, of course, Alix laughed, and Brand took her in his arms and kissed her lightly on the lips.

"Ever since Anna met me I've been picturing what you would look like. I thought you'd be wearing that red skirt and the flowered apron you had on at Marstrand, and the yellow bonnet—"

"Oh Brand, that was my Bohuslän peasant dress!"

"Your runaway dress," he said, and kissed her again. "Darling! As if it wasn't grand enough to set sail for Degerby: but then to see Anna at the quay, ready to tell me you were *waiting for me*, and all I had to do was follow her—"

"Anna knew you'd come today."

"How could she? We only knew it ourselves when the morning watch was called down at Kökar. Captain Sulivan passed the word to the Fleet that there were good springs on Degerby, and—"

"Friendly natives?"

"Oh my darling."

She sighed when he released her from his arms, and said, "How long can you stay with us?"

"Just two hours, Alix. Lieutenant Sulivan, he's our gunnery lieutenant, gave me two hours off duty. But where's Anna? We left Degerby together, and I was in such a hurry to get here I expected to leave her far behind, but she pointed out the way to me and then went off like the wind."

"Yes, Anna came home on the wind," said Alix with a strange look. "She is making coffee for you at the house now. We do our own work here at Degerby—it's not at all like Hagasund."

Brand slipped his arm round her slim waist as they went down the track beneath the birch trees, and the little manor came in sight, with a puff of woodsmoke rising from one chimney.

"It's very homelike."

For a man who had spent nearly four months in the lower deck of H.M.S. *Arrogant*, seeing nothing but the tumbling waters of the Baltic and the rocky coasts of Finland and

Esthonia, the grey clap-board house with its faded yellow shutters, set in a garden full of lilac and roses and late flowering syringa, was a pleasant sight. Brand followed Alix into a cool parlour furnished in the pure Gustavian style of Miss Agneta's childhood, with painted furniture upholstered in faded silk, pictures of the Willebrand ancestors done on glass, and two landscapes in *grisaille* on the walls. Time had stood still in that quiet living-room, where the old clock, in its fat-bellied rococo case, was ticking off the minutes of Brand's precious leave.

He sat down where Alix indicated, on an old red settle with six legs, and looked around.

"It's all exactly as I pictured it," he said, "the very way you described it in your letter."

"Where did you *get* my letter, Brand?"

"After the fleet came down the Gulf of Finland. We lay at Barö Sound for a few days after we left Cronstadt, and did another reconnaissance of Sveaborg. There was mail from Stockholm when we got to Gotska Sandön and that was when I knew you'd got away from Russia."

He looked at Alix. After the first happy greeting she seemed to have withdrawn a little into herself, and instead of coming to sit beside him on the wide settle had taken one of the prim highbacked chairs. It was hard to realize, as he looked at this country girl with her cotton sleeves rolled above her elbows, and her forearms tanned by the July sun, that she had come from the presence of the Czar of All the Russias, and watched the British flying squadron before Cronstadt in the presence of his son and heir.

"When did you leave Cronstadt?" Alix asked.

"Third of July."

"The day I came to Degerby."

"But the *Fleet* hasn't withdrawn from Cronstadt! Napier left a squadron up there under Commodore Martin to keep an eye on the Russian ships of the line. We'd engage the enemy fast enough, if they would ever pluck up courage to come out!"

"But as it was, you could do nothing?"

"Only gunboats could get anywhere near that place. I've an idea they hoped to get swimmers up among the Russian ships with detonating fuses—they worked us hard enough on one called the Bickford fuse—but Napier lost his nerve over the Infernal Machines and swore he wouldn't risk his ships and men on such an invention of the devil. Then there was some sort of fever aboard the flagship. That helped to scare him off."

"And now you're going to attack Bomarsund?"

"You know about that?"

"How could we help it? We've seen the British ships going in to Föglö fjord and steaming north for the past three days. And the British were here early in June, and firing on the fort even then."

"*Hecla* did the firing on Bomarsund," said Brand with a grin. "Trust 'Old Nemesis' (that's what we call Captain Hall) to go in on his own! He came up to us at Cronstadt with all flags flying, and signalled 'Have successfully bombarded Bomarsund' as if the whole thing was over! What a cheer we gave him! But I heard later the Chief was wild because *Hecla* had blazed away all her 10-in. shells without doing any damage but setting the roof of the main fort on fire. But we gave him a good cheer from *Arrogant*, I can tell you that!"

"And now the whole fleet is going up to Bomarsund?"

"With the French infantry in support—if they ever get here. Alix, we've got to win at Bomarsund! The men are desperate for action, and we've got to knock the Russians out somewhere, before the summer's over!"

"But I worry about you so terribly, Brand. When my father said the Russian Fleet would soon dispose of Napier, I was sure I had sent you to your death."

"But the Russians don't dare come out to Napier," said Brand reasonably. "And as for me . . . Well, you sent me into the Navy, there's no denying. But now I'm in it, I mean to see the Russians whipped, that's all."

The young maid, with two long flaxen plaits hanging over her shoulders, came in with a loaded tray, and a long stare for the handsome "Englishman", while Alix arranged a table beside the settle. There was coffee in a fine white china pot, with a service in white and gilt to match, a bowl of raspberries and a jug of thick cream, and a plate of coffee cakes lightly dusted with cinnamon and sugar.

"The raspberries are all for you," said Alix, pouring coffee. "I picked them half an hour ago."

"I haven't tasted berries since I left the State of Maine."

"I haven't picked many since I left Ekenäs."

Brand set down his cup. "You know we went in to Ekenäs, Alix?"

She nodded. "I heard at Helsingfors. You silenced a Russian battery and took out one prize."

"We could have taken three if we'd landed and burned the wharves. Hall might have done it, but not my captain! Yelverton said it would be wrong to destroy Finnish property, and we had done enough when we put the Russians out of action; I guess he was right."

"Where was the battery?"

"On the cape, before the Pojo *vik* widens at Ekenäs town."

"That's where my father taught me to swim. Our house isn't very far from there. You might have seen our landing-stage, green-painted, as you came up the channel from Tvärminne."

"I don't remember seeing a landing-stage. I was standing by my gun."

He thought of the cape at Ekenäs, blood-drenched, and the flying fragments of flesh and metal falling over the beach where a little fair-haired girl had learned to swim. Thank God, that was one picture she would never have printed on her mind!

"I think I hear Cousin Agneta coming," said Alix, jumping up. There was a rustle of stiff skirts on the uncarpeted pine floor of the little hall, and the tap of a stick, and then as Brand rose to his feet a very old lady entered, followed by a tall woman of about fifty, with a housekeeper's keys at her belt.

Miss Agneta Willebrand had once been tall, but lameness and old age had bowed her over her stick, and the bands of hair visible beneath her white lace cap were of purest white. But she acknowledged Brand's low bow with the courtesy of another age as Alix said:

"Cousin Agneta, may I present Captain Endicott, of the Royal Navy?"

"Another of Lord Nelson's gallant captains, sir?"

"No, ma'am." Brand looked appealingly at Alix. She said:

"Brand, this is Mamsell Josabeth, Miss Willebrand's companion." The tall woman bowed repressively.

"Only think," said Alix, carefully and distinctly, "Cousin Agneta knew Lord Nelson when he came into Baltic waters *more than fifty years ago*, and Admiral Saumarez, too, a little later on; she has the most wonderful memory for everything that happened in the last war."

The old lady's blue eyes gleamed intelligently.

"Ah yes," she said, "it *is* fifty years since Nelson's victories; time seems to stand still at Degerby. You are bound for Fort Bomarsund, no doubt, to free the Islands from the Russian yoke?"

"We hope to do so, ma'am."

"There has been fighting already at the fortress, hasn't there, Alexandra?"

"It was before Miss Gyllenlöve came to Degerby," said Mamsell Josabeth.

"So long ago? Then what are the British waiting for, young man?"

"They're waiting for the Emperor of the French," said Brand bluntly. "He wants his share of *la gloire*, as the French say, and he's sending troops to help us take Fort Bomarsund. We have to delay action until they get here."

"The French Emperor? I thought he was in prison at St. Helena."

"Brand means his nephew, Cousin Agneta," Alix said.

"How very confusing. I shall withdraw, and leave you young people to your own good company. You can hardly enjoy the workings of my muddled mind!"

"Thank you for your hospitality, ma'am," said Brand, bowing over her extended hand. The old lady straightened her bent shoulders.

"An officer of the Royal Navy is always a welcome guest in this house," she said. "I shall pray for your victory at Bomarsund, sir. Convey my compliments to Lord Nelson . . . and do arrange, if possible, for my farm-hands to be sent back from the fort before the harvest."

" 'Captain Endicott' !" said Brand with a grin, when the two ladies had left the room. "Thank God my shipmates couldn't hear you. I'm Able Seaman Endicott, that's all—I was promoted after Ekenäs."

"Oh dear," said Alix, "I was thinking of the *Girdleness*, of course. Now I've confused Cousin Agneta more than ever, and

199

she was very muddled today, poor soul. This war has upset her badly, because the man she was going to marry died of wounds after Döbeln's victory at Juutas, and now her mind wanders between that time and the present—you see she was quite alert about Fort Bomarsund. But she does talk as if Admiral Nelson was still alive today!"

"That puts her right in line with half the Baltic Fleet," smiled Brand.

"Captain Sulivan was wonderful with her. She asked *him* if he was one of Nelson's Band of Brothers, and he said no, but his father had been one of Nelson's lieutenants, and he talked to her about Nelson in the Baltic and made her very happy."

"Sulivan of the *Lightning*? Was he here?"

"I was at Degerby village when his ship came in. The British wanted to buy eggs and milk and sheep for slaughtering, so I helped to translate for them, and they gave the people coffee and sugar and some wine. Then Captain Sulivan walked home with me and paid his respects to Cousin Agneta. And before he left he gave me a Bible."

"A Swedish Bible? I knew he carried Testaments and tracts for distribution—"

"He gave some of these to the Degerby folk. But he asked me if I said my prayers every night, and I said yes, the Lord's Prayer, and then he gave me his own Bible with his name in it. Look here!"

She took the well-worn pocket Bible, in which the sailor had underlined many texts over the years, from a hanging bookshelf, and held it out to Brand. On the flyleaf was a flowing signature, "B. J. Sulivan," with a firm line beneath it, and below, in fresher ink:

"For Miss Alexandra Gyllenlöve, July 19th, 1854.

"Ecclesiastes 9, verses 10 and 11."

"Did you look it up?" said Brand.

"Of course. It is very beautiful in English. More than in Swedish, no?"

"I suppose so."

"Will you read it to me? Cousin Agneta wished me to read it to her, but some words I could not pronounce."

Brand turned over the thin india paper in embarrassment. It was years since he had been required to read the Scriptures aloud, or indeed had read them for himself. But the girl who had spoken of her evening prayer with such simplicity was looking at him with her grey eyes burning, and in a lowered voice he began to read:

"*Whatsoever thy hand findeth to do, do it with thy might, for there is no work, nor device, nor knowledge, nor wisdom, in the grave, whither thou goest.*
"*I returned, and saw under the sun, that the race is not to the swift, nor the batle to the strong, neither yet bread to the wise, nor yet riches to men of understanding, nor yet favour to men of skill; but time and chance happeneth to them all.*"

"What does it mean exactly, 'time and chance happeneth to them all'?" said Alix.

"I reckon it means everyone gets some sort of opportunity some time in his life."

"But he doesn't always win, the Scripture says?"

"No, he doesn't always win."

"Oh, how I wish time and chance would come to me!" sighed Alix.

"What about the night you got out of Russia? You didn't let your chance slip then, did you?"

"Oh that! Running away from Aurora was rather like being cruel to a child—"

"She was disappointed when you went away?"

"Disappointed *in me*, was what she said. But Governor Mannerheim wrote to Aurora and to my father both, and advised them to let me stay in Finland now. And at least I'm useful here on Degerby, even if I can only catch fish for the table and hoe potatoes instead of fighting Russians . . ."

"Hoeing potatoes is pretty hard work for a woman. Don't you have a man to do that sort of thing?"

She was silent.

"Alix, is that what Miss Willebrand meant about sending the farm hands back? Have all her men been drafted to Fort Bomarsund?"

"Oh Brand, I didn't mean to tell you. But—yes, it's true. There's hardly a man left on Degerby island, not in the fishing village nor on the farms. The Russians came last week and took them all away."

"To fight against the British?"

Alix flung up her head. "No, *not* to fight against the British! Do you know that although the Russians made our pastors read a proclamation from all the Åland churches that every man and boy must be prepared to fight for Russia or else be sent to the Siberian mines, not one Finlander volunteered? They've been taken to *forced labour* up at Bomarsund! Replacing the roof your Captain Hall set fire to! Completing the stonework of the Half Moon fort! Don't think they were willing to go. They hate the Russians, they want the West to win. But this time they weren't given even the alternative of Siberia. I saw them with my own eyes, Brand, forced out of their cottages, forced into the boats, with a Russian firing squad ready to shoot down every man who attempted to resist!"

At least her agitation allowed Brand to take her in his arms and kiss her, as he had been longing to do ever since they came indoors, and then lead her out of the shadowy parlour where he had begun to feel too big for the spindling Gustavian furniture, into the sunlit garden.

"So you haven't even a gardener's boy left, to pick the raspberries!" he said. "Who keeps the place so tidy? You?"

"Anna and I gather the fruit and vegetables and Mamsell Josabeth keeps the flower beds neat. We must make jam and store as many root vegetables as we can, you see, in case the blockade has to go on. And then we milk the cows over on the pasture island, would you like to see where?"

It seemed as if Anna had anticipated Brand's instant wish to see the pasture. She was waiting for them in the row-boat at the foot of the path, smiling grimly as Alix scrambled aboard, Brand took the oars; after no more than five minutes' steady rowing landing them on a miniature beach among the grey rocks of the little island. It was like so many others of the thousand isles which composed the Åland archipelago, rocky and flat, with about an acre of meadowland in the centre where six biscuit-coloured cows were grazing, with collars of willow plaited with bright braid round their necks, and a rivulet of sweet water flowing between banks of harts-tongue fern to the sea. A small hut of unshaven timber with a stone vent in

202

the roof stood in a clump of birch trees, with willow-herb blooming in profusion round the door.

"What's that?" said Brand. He was looking at a mast of plaited straw, ten or twelve feet tall, which stood at the edge of the meadow. Two straw crossbeams, intersecting below the top of the mast, supported dangling wreaths of withered greenery.

"That?—the *majstång*. I don't know the English name for it. The men put it up for Midsummer Eve, when the bonfires were lit, and of course there's no one now to take it down."

"It looks uncommonly like a gallows to me."

"Don't you like my island?" said Alix, sitting down beside the stream. "Don't you think it's a pretty place?"

"I love it." What he wanted to say was "I love you", but Brand already knew that he must ride his passion on a tight rein, here in this solitary place scented with meadowsweet and wild roses and the sea. His love for Alix had grown deep and strong during the months without her, and now, as he sat down beside her, she was within the reach of his hands, with her fair hair sunbleached to silver gilt at ears and temples and her skin like a fresh apricot. If he touched her now he could stop at nothing until he had made her completely his own. Then to leave her in an hour, to go back to the war again—it was impossible. He said,

"All those Finnish islands—they remind me of Maine, a bit. Where I lived, in Maine, we've the Calendar Islands—supposed to be one for every day of the year."

"You *lived* on an island?"

"Summers, we did. Jewell Island, it was called."

"Pretty name!"

"Better than Junk of Pork, or Pound of Tea, or some of the other places in Casco Bay."

"And did you live in a little wooden house, like our *pörte* back there?"

"Ours was called a 'linter', and it wasn't much bigger. There were spruces around it instead of birches, and scarlet leaves on the sumacs in the autumn, and Virginia creeper spreading all over the rocks instead of heather, like here. And in spring the arbutus flowered, lovely pink blossoms, and I used to take the first bunch over to Portland for my great-aunt Betsy Brand . . ."

He had flung aside his hard hat, with the brave *Arrogant* ribands, when he sat down beside Alix and leaned back on the bank of fern and harebells. Now he felt her cool fingers on his brow, rubbing out the red mark which the hat left, as if she meant to conjure up more of that American boyhood, which memory was recreating for him so strangely on the Baltic beach. Brand was silent, the better to feel those fingers, and the light pressure from each tip, until Alix took away her hand and said:

"Is that how you come to be called Brand?"

"I answer to John, and I'm Yankee Jack to my shipmates, but Brand was my father's mother's family name, and he wanted me to have it. My grandmother Tarras says it's 'A rright rridic'lous name for any Christian body', and she calls me John."

"In Swedish *brand* means 'fire'."

"Good name for a gunner!"

"Oh not fire, for shooting," said Alix. "Just fire, the flame and the burning . . . Brand, did you go swimming when you lived on Jewell Island?"

"I lived in the water, just about."

"I love swimming here. And there's a good diving rock—"

"Oh come now, Alix, is that wise?"

He sat erect and spoke severely, to banish the sudden image of her slim naked body plunging down through the summer air into the water. "You ought to be careful how you come over here with Anna, just to milk the cows, let alone go swimming. In a few days the islands will be swarming with troops and transports—"

"I don't think they'll molest us," said Alix. "The rocks are our best defence, because nothing bigger than a row boat could come up to this beach. Besides, we have our knives." She touched the *puuko* hanging from her belt.

Brand examined the knife in silence, sliding it in and out of its leather sheath.

"A knife isn't much defence against a Russian rifle," he said. "Suppose they land men in some of these remote places, to fire on the British from among the rocks as they did last June? . . . I don't think you're very safe at Degerby, Alix. I wish you would consider going across to Stockholm."

"What in the world should I do at Stockholm?"

"You could visit the Ryans," Brand suggested. "Joe Ryan is an admirer of yours already, and you'd like Mary. She's such a bright amusing little girl."

"How old?"

"Sixteen, going on seventeen, I believe."

"Pretty?"

"Very."

"Oh."

"It worries me to think of you alone with your poor old cousin. By the way, Miss Agneta can't really be your cousin?"

"She was my grandmother's cousin," said Alix with a smile. "We're all related in some degree, you know—the Mannerheims and the Stjernvalls and the Willebrands and us. Brand, no harm can come to us if the Allies only take Fort Bomarsund *quickly*, and break the Russian power in Ahvenanmaa completely . . . and without getting into a fight with the Finns, either."

Brand scanned her face. "I see you've heard about the incident at Gamla Karleby."

Alix remembered the scene in the Grand Duke Alexander's country house, and the hateful reading of "The First Drop of Blood". All she said was:

"Helsingfors was ringing with the story."

"Captain Buckle and Captain Glasse surely managed that operation badly. They sent in their boats twice to Gamla Karleby, calling on the town to surrender, but they let several hours pass in between, and that gave the burgomaster time to send for Russian troops. The second time the British went in the crews were hopelessly outnumbered, and that's why one boat was captured with all hands, and some were killed and wounded."

"But it wasn't only Russians who fired on the British. The Finns fired too, didn't they?"

Reluctantly: "I'm afraid they did, Alix."

"But why did Admiral Plumridge order a raid on Gamla Karleby at all?"

"Because all the warehouses along the shore, whether they were owned by Finns or not, were full of pitch and tar and building materials and other things that Russia needs for making war," he said, as to a child.

"Oh, Brand," said Alix, with her hand to her quivering

mouth, "it's all so different from what I thought it would be!"

He put his arm round her shoulders.

"I know," he said "you thought the Finns would rise for their independence, and fight the Russians—didn't you?"

"Yes."

"I know some who are fighting on our side. One of my messmates was a Finlander, he volunteered along with me at Stockholm just because he wanted to see the Russians beaten. Lauri was killed at Ekenäs, darling, in his very first action, and we buried him at sea; but *he* came from Gamla Karleby, and he could have been killed *there*, by some other Finn's rifle, if he had been sent to *Odin* instead of *Arrogant*."

"That would have been civil war," said Alix. "How . . . horrible."

"Darling, I did try to tell you, in that little park across the bay from Sveaborg, that once a war has started it may go all sorts of unexpected ways. But maybe that's something a man understands better than a woman ever can."

She let that pass. She was gazing out to sea and thinking of her countryman, who had given his life in the struggle against Russia.

"Lauri, you said his name was? Lauri what?"

"He was Larry Finn on the ship's book, but he never told us his last name. Just that he came from Gamla Karleby; and maybe he left a young wife or a sweetheart there, because he said a girl's name just before he died. 'Tuonela!' he said—right at the very end."

Alix pulled away from Brand. Her face was pale.

"Oh, poor Lauri," she said. "Facing that all alone! Tuonela isn't a girl's name, Brand. It is the place of the dead."

"You mean—heaven?"

"Not what we call heaven. It may be hell, the dusky island of the dead, beyond the bridge over the dark river where the Swan of Tuonela sings to the passing soul."

"A legend," said Brand flatly.

"It's a belief—for many Finns like your Lauri. Remember, the Old Gods never really left the north country. How else do you suppose Anna knew you would come to Degerby today?"

"Any fisherman could have seen *Arrogant*'s sails heading in, and told her. There were even fishing boats about when we weighed anchor at Kökar."

"She didn't leave the house this morning until she went to meet you at Degerby, except to come here to the pasture. The troll stone told her you were on your way."

Brand smiled. In spite of that, he felt a little chill. He looked sideways at the withered midsummer wreaths, and the pole which left a gallows' shadow on the grass.

"What do you mean by the troll stone?" he said.

"Her *seite*, the spirit of the place. The Lapps worship trees and stones, and sometimes make sacrifices to them, and offerings of bear's teeth and reindeer horns. I know which is Anna's stone, but I never go near when she makes an offering, because *they* know I cannot . . . quite . . . believe—"

"Believe!" said Brand. He stood up and pulled Alix to her feet. He had never been able to talk freely and simply of his Christian faith, as so many sailors did, whether they sailed from Maine or in the Royal Navy. But the fervent Calvinism which he had inherited both from his American and his Scottish forebears forbade him to be silent now. What she spoke of was heathendom, was pure idolatry, was a breaking of the First Commandment, and he said sternly:

"Alix, you are a Christian. You read your Bible, you say your prayers at night. How can you even half believe in that pitiful savagery? Have the missionaries never carried the Gospel to the Lapps?"

"Yes, and to the Finns and Swedes too, centuries ago," she said defiantly. "But if God exists, does it matter if we call him God or Jubmel?"

He was not theologian enough to argue with the girl he loved. He allowed her to keep the initiative; under the spell, as always, of those eyes in which the grey was now submerged by the black of the dilated pupils, and of the lilting, gentle voice.

"You are a sailor, you know yourself what Lapps can do. They can cloud the sun raise the tempest, and sell the wind in a leather bag to mariners. The Russians were defeated by Lapp magic at Narva field; may not magic help the west to win at Bomarsund?"

Brand had been holding her hands since he raised her from the ground. Now Alix pulled him gently towards her and almost whispered:

"Brand, let Anna read our future on the magic drum!"

"On a *drum*?"

"You see, Anna's father was a *näjd*, a—what is the word? the wise man of his tribe, and though the Russian law forbade it he kept the *trolltrumma* of his ancestors, the magic drum. So, although women are not meant to play the drum, when the whole tribe perished in the famine Anna kept her father's, and this spring she hid it at Hagasund before we went to Russia, for fear of Russian punishment. And now it is here on the island!"

"I thought this had to do with sorcery," said Brand. "Now I see it's only fortune-telling."

"Any old woman tells fortunes with the cards, or the tea leaves. Anna tells the future on the drum."

"Has she ever told *your* future?"

"Once," said Alix with lowered eyes. "Last summer, when we were with Aurora at Träskända, the *arpa* hardly moved that day. But Anna herself was trembling, and her eyes went far back in her head, and she said at the end, 'From one in this room a child will come to save Finland!' . . . and I thought I heard my destiny."

"Was there anybody else in the room?" said the sceptical New Englander.

"Only the Mannerheim boy," said Alix. "Only my cousin Carl-Robert, and Aurora herself. You don't suppose Paul Demidov is the child who will save Finland, do you? He thinks like a true Russian. The Finns are all serfs to him."

"But Alix—"

"The drum is in the *pörte*," Alix said. "Brand, I beseech you, let it speak!"

"All right." It was only something like palmistry after all, not any more occult than the Wheels of Fortune made of cardboard which young ladies sold at Portland church bazaars, with happy predictions written in copperplate upon each spoke. But Alix was unlocking the door of the *pörte* with the key on her waist-belt, and another kind of magic rose up to envelop them with the thick warm air inside the hut.

The place had once been used as a dwelling, probably by a cowman and his family, for two empty wooden beds fixed to the walls now held dried fodder, and there were marks of smoke on the stones of a broken-down fireplace. The airholes in the walls were immovably closed, but through the roof vent fell a shaft of sunlight which turned Alexandra's pale hair into a shower of living gold. The herbal scent of the fodder mingled with the smell of food and smoke and human living clinging to the wooden walls. Brand seized Alexandra in his arms. Fire, the flame and the burning, ran through his loins.

"Alix, say you love me!"

"I love you, Brand."

Then he found words to tell her that her eyes were like the storm clouds over Finland, and her hair scented like the new birch leaves and although she gasped when he kissed her deeply, forcing her lips apart, he felt her mouth become responsive and her slim body moulding itself to his own. He thought of a soft bed on the dried grasses, and of love consummated in the hot half-darkness of the *pörte*, and in the same instant fancied he heard the bo'sun's whistle shrilling, a mile away on the quay at Degerby.

"Alix, I have to go!"

"No! No!" She tore herself out of his arms. "It isn't time yet, Brand! You promised me the drum should speak!"

Alix began pulling at one of the piles of fodder. The drum came out, reindeer hide stretched taut and sewed with sinew thread to a birch frame shaped like a sieve. It was larger than Brand had expected, but he made no attempt to take it from the girl. Suddenly, he was afraid to touch the thing.

Anna was waiting beneath the trees near the hut. She smiled when she saw them emerge, and the American wondered if she had been there, listening, or worshipping her *seite* on the far side of the pasture land. She motioned to them both to sit down on the turf. Then she herself sat back with her knees touching the ground and took the magic drum in her left hand.

"Wait," Alix said to her in Swedish. "I must tell him what the symbols mean."

Brand saw a crude painting of what appeared to be the sun, with rays, and little figures in a ring around it, coloured red with dye made from the alder tree.

"The sun is God," said Alexandra reverently. "God stands above Tiermes and Stuorra Passe, the pagan gods, with the moon and stars still higher, and beneath, the symbols of the earth. Here the Sorcerer's Reindeer, here the Reindeer Pasture, the Meat Trap, the Wind Man, the World's Man, the Man and the Woman—the *arpa* will point to one of the them, when the drum speaks."

Brand nodded. There was something hypnotic in that brown circle with the weird red figures; he found his eyes were fixed upon it as Anna slipped two copper rings from her wedding finger and laid them on the symbol of the sun. She lifted up the drum in a peculiar way, so that her left elbow rested in the artery inside her left thigh, and then from the folds of her black skirt took something which might have been the bone of an animal, or a miniature hammer, and passed it a few times over the surface of the stretched reindeer skin.

"She is warming the drum," whispered Alix. "The rings will move when the drum begins to speak."

The drumming began. Softly, almost caressingly, the hammer started to beat round the sun, which was God, over Tiermes, which was Thor, the god of thunder and war, up and down and round and over the Reindeer, the Wind Man, the Sorcerer with his drum. The two copper rings moved erratically over the surface of the drum. Alexandra's eyes were fixed upon them as the Lapland woman's body swayed to and fro. Anna was holding the drum in such a way that the surface was quite flat, presented to Brand and Alix squarely, like a table, on which to follow the progress of the rings.

"Join hands," said Anna with a groan. "The *arpa* stops."

Alexandra's fingers twined convulsively round Brand's as the two copper rings, quivering to the beat of the banner, sprang apart. One fell squarely across the symbol of the god Thor; the other beside one of the strange red figures which formed the border of the drum.

"War and the World's Man!" Anna said in triumph. "Sir captain, you will be the father of a child!"

Brand felt, rather than heard, that Alix had caught her breath. The drumming began again; the shadow of the midsummer wreaths fell across the drum. The copper rings moved convulsively over the reindeer skin. If every bo'sun's whistle in the Baltic Fleet had sounded in his ear then, Brand would have been powerless to move; he knelt on the springing turf, half aware of the sound of the rivulet and the feel of cold sweat on his frustrated body, incapable of movement while the minutes went endlessly by.

"Anna?" he heard Alix whisper by his side.

The Lapp woman wiped the perspiration from her face. "I can do no more, lady," she muttered. "The drum has spoken its message."

"Tell us the message!"

"*Only so far.*"

CHAPTER TWELVE

SHALLOW WATERS AND
GRANITE WALLS

BRAND Endicott stood two watches aboard H.M.S. *Arrogant*, opposing a massive State of Maine silence to the highly-flavoured questions of his shipmates, before he obtained the privacy of mind, if not of body, required for thinking over the precious hours with Alix. After watering at Degerby, Captain Yelverton took his ship on the short run to Brändö, at the mouth of the Föglö fjord, where colliers newly arrived from England were waiting with supplies of fuel for the fleet, and the afternoon watch toiled in great heat at the grimy work of coaling. *Arrogant* was still steaming south to rendezvous with the flagship in Led Sound, and trailing a heavy pennant of smoke from the new Welsh coal, when eight bells struck in the last dog watch and Brand was free to go below.

He lay in an almost motionless hammock, for there was no wind, the summer sea was calm, and only the vibration of the screws shook *Arrogant* on her southward way. In that hammock, with his broad shoulders cramped into the regulation fourteen inches of sleeping space, Brand had spent many stormy night hours in the Baltic thinking of Alix Gyllenlöve: Alix on the snowy wharf at Marstrand, Alix reciting the Sveaborg inscription; and now he had a new picture of her, Alix of the islands, to add to his gallery. It was not easy to sentimentalize over that picture, much as he would have liked to put it in a golden frame tied with a true lover's knot, for Alix had shown him more of her character, so strangely compound of ice and fire, faith and superstition, in their two hours alone together than he had guessed at before. It troubled him, it kept him from sleeping, to remember that almost the last sight of her before he kissed her goodbye in the garden and ran for Degerby harbour was of her sharpened, avid face hanging above the red symbols of the magic drum.

Brand understood a little—a very little of the belief in the ancient magic of the land which existed side by side in the

Finnish character with a strong and simple piety. Without the intervention of Anna he might have been inclined to treat Alexandra's superstition as something naïve and charming; something which belonged to the quiet house among the birches and the white-haired, memory-clouded old lady leaning on her stick like a benevolent witch. But those red figures on the skin drum had utterly repelled him. The World's Man —was that supposed to be himself? Some kind of fertility symbol, like the town bull, which gave that Lapp witch the right to tell him he would become the father of a child? Alexandra's child? Did Alix herself think of motherhood as the means of bearing a child to save Finland, and nothing else?

He, Brand Endicott, had never given much thought to fatherhood, but if he ever had a son he hoped the boy would have the gumption to aim at becoming President of the United States, no less.

But Alix was adorable. So gentle with that poor old lady, so wild in her response to him, so lovely in that white shirt and black skirt—

With the *puuko* at her belt, ready to strike—

You couldn't imagine Mary Ryan carrying a knife, or believing, half believing, in the Swan of Tuonela and the island of the dead . . .

Brand slept, and in his dreams made love to Alix under the shadow of a gallows rope.

There were many other unquiet sleepers in *Arrogant* that night. It was hot and damp below. The portlids were open, but there was no breeze to stir the windsails which brought fresh air into the lower deck, and as heavy seas had been shipped earlier in the week, after a spell of hot weather had opened the seams on the main deck, there was an ooze of moisture from the planking above the hammocks. Then after three bells in the first watch there was an increasing movement out of the hammocks and up to the heads in the ship's stern. The hands had no conveniences inboard, and a night trip to the heads in wet or stormy weather could be an ordeal; even on this summer night, with no heavy seas running, the heads crowded with men suffering from diarrhoea offered a lively scene of human degradation.

"What the hell have you all been doing?" said the Master-at-Arms, encountering for the third time on his rounds a group of men in scanty underclothing, making for the stern.

"Eatin' too much fruit ashore," said Leading Seaman Edgeworthy, who had been one of the watering party.

"Filling your bellies with rotgut spirits, more like," said the Master-at-Arms. But he noted the disturbed night in his report, and although not one of the hands reported sick next morning, Captain Yelverton held a private conference with the ship's surgeon.

"Severe purging—wasn't that how the cholera started in the flagship?" he wanted to know.

"It was indeed, sir. But there were no more than two cases, if you recollect, before we came down the Gulf, and only five, out of the whole fleet, in *Belleisle* this morning."

"Five's enough for a start in the hospital ship."

"I suggest dosing your entire ship's company with castor oil and turpentine, sir, and letting the hands go ashore with an issue of soap for freshwater bathing next time you water ship."

"Provided the bathing water and the drinking water are kept separate, eh?"

"Oh quite, Captain Yelverton. Troops washing their clothes and their bodies in streams from which the ships drew drinking water was what began the outbreak in the Black Sea."

Yelverton and the surgeon exchanged glances. News from the other theatre of war filtered through to the Baltic slowly, but most officers knew that the great invasion of the Crimea was hanging fire. The spreading cholera epidemic and the rivalry of the French and British high commands kept the Allied armies sweltering through the summer heat at Varna, and on the eastern shore of the Black Sea the Russian fortress of Sevastopol was still unchallenged by the Western powers.

The dissatisfaction among the Allies on the Black Sea front was spreading slowly but surely through the Baltic Fleet. The long patrols, the endless "looking in" at ports like Narva and Windau which offered neither battles nor prizes, the frustrating reconnaissances of Cronstadt and Sveaborg had taken their toll of morale among officers and men. Admiral Napier was responsible for much of the trouble. However discreet his clerks might be, his own indiscreet grumbling revealed that his relations with the Admiralty—and especially with the

First Lord, Sir James Graham—were steadily growing worse. To the great stern cabin of H.M.S. *Duke of Wellington* where the old men sat in council at the beginning of the war, now came younger captains to bombard Napier with plans of action, and models of boats and spars to carry ordnance to the rear of Cronstadt and engage the Neva squadron defending St. Petersburg. Cooper Key of H.M.S. *Amphion*, whose taking of the town of Libau was the most brilliant single action of the spring; Keppel of the great naval name; "Nemesis" Hall of the *Hecla*; Buckle and Glasse, burning to avenge their humiliation at Gamla Karleby—these were not men to be lightly dismissed. It took all the tact of the newly promoted Rear-Admiral Seymour to keep the peace between them and the choleric Commander-in-Chief. It was an immense relief when the attack on Bomarsund was finally announced.

Fort Bomarsund was the personal creation of the Czar Nicholas I, and an integral part of Russia's planned penetration of Europe. With such a military base dominating the open Baltic, at a point normally free of ice, the Czar had taken a giant step towards the North Sea and the eastern shores of Britain.

Bomar Sound itself, from which the new fort took its name was a narrow strait between one of the larger of the Åland Islands, on which were many townships and farms, and the much smaller island of Prästö. The Sound led into the magnificent natural harbour of Lumpar Bay, reached by passages so narrow and shallow that only the most modern Russian gunboats and the island fishermen could approach Fort Bomarsund.

In his calculations, however, Nicholas I had reckoned without Captain Bartholomew Sulivan, of H.M.S.V. *Lightning*, and his uncanny talent for taking ships where no British ships had ever gone before. In June he had taken the survey ship through the islands with a leadsman in the dolphin striker and another in the chains on each side, charting every rock and shoal and buoying out two passages, one entering Lumpar Bay from the south between Ångö island and Lumparland, and the other from the north round the eastern shores of Prästö, on which the Russians had erected a martello tower. When Sulivan came back in July the Russians had removed the buoys. With his infallible memory for any seaway the Cornish captain was able without delay to lead the British ships out of Led Sound into Lumpar Bay.

The great three-deckers, of course, had to be left at anchor in Led Sound, and Admiral Napier transferred his flag to H.M.S. *Bulldog*, 8, to lead the assault on Bomarsund. It was a strange convoy going north, *Lightning* puffing and paddling gamely in advance, the frigates steaming behind with all sails furled. The Finnish women milking cows in the island pastures looked up amazed to see the tall British masts towering over the evergreens, and flaxen-haired children came stealthily to the rocky coves to watch when, in spite of all Captain Sulivan's shepherding, one or other of his flock ran aground. There were four incidents in the four days required to complete the movement north through the Angö passage.

H.M.S. *Arrogant* went up on the first day, and took station in Lumpar Bay about 3000 yards from the red granite Half Moon, as the Great Fort of Bomarsund was sometimes called, without any opposition from the Russian gunners. Outside the half circle, with its double row of embrasures where the guns were mounted and trained on the bay, there was no sign of life except where a few Finnish country folk were seen stolidly working in the fields behind the fort. Reports said that these peasants had been compelled to yoke up their country carts and take the wives of many of the Russian officers to safety in the hamlets of Finby and Kastellholm when the approach of the British ships was signalled.

"Very quiet, sir," commented the First Lieutenant of H.M.S. *Arrogant* to Captain Yelverton.

"If the Russians had the guts of a mouse, Mr. Haggard, their gunboat squadron at Åbo would have been steaming in by Vardö now," grunted Yelverton. He was scanning the fortress through his glass.

"I'd like to see the white of a Russian gunner's eyes again," said Haggard, thinking of Ekenäs. "Pleasant change, after two solid months of intercepting frightened Finns in fishing boats and challenging 'em for contraband !"

"General Bodisco seems in no hurry to gratify you," said Yelverton. "I imagined he would greet us with a salvo, at least, to prove himself a bolder man than his predecessor. Probably waiting for orders from St. Petersburg."

The former governor of Bomarsund had been recalled to

Russia to "explain" the June bombardment so easily carried out by Captain Hall, and it was supposed that he was now explaining in another fortress, the famous prison of Peter and Paul.

"They must have done a good deal of work on the roof since *Hecla* was here," said the First Lieutenant.

"With Finn forced labour, of course. Pass the word for Mr. Sulivan, if you please, Mr. Haggard."

"Aye, aye, sir."

As a result of that order the gunnery lieutenant mustered the gun crews in the next watch and explained the situation to them.

"You see the two martello towers with the double row of casemates, on the rising ground behind the Half Moon," he said. "The tower to the west is marked on our maps as Fort Tzee and the tower to the north-east is Fort Nottich. The rising ground between them is called the Devil's Hill. There's a third martello tower on Prästö island, where the Russians have their hospital and store houses.

"Take a good look at the main fort—the Half Moon. We got here before Nicholas could complete the circle, and the rear defence is nothing more important than a moat. The country folk say only two feet of the walls are solid granite and the other six are rubble. The Half Moon is not impregnable, and with good steady broadsides the walls can be breached. Admiral Chads and General Jones believe the seven-gun battery on the point east of Tranvik—the mud battery—will give us more trouble in the long run than the main fort itself. Let's hope *Arrogant* will have the honour of going in to silence it."

"Right, sir," "Aye, aye, sir." The grinning gunners muttered their approval. They had silenced the Russian battery at Ekenäs in less than five minutes: it seemed logical that if *Arrogant* were ordered to advance over that crucial 3000 yards of water the mud battery at Bomarsund could be speedily knocked out. But the next day dawned, and the next; the bay filled with British shipping, and no order came from Admiral Napier. He was waiting for his French allies.

"Wot the 'ell are we waiting for *now*?" growled the *Arrogants*. "Send 'Old Nemesis' and Yelverton in, and we'll larn 'em Rooshian!"

" 'Ere, Jack, you've 'ad a bit of education," said Leading

Seaman Edgeworthy, on the day when the supply ships *Gorgon* and *Tyre* came up with the newspapers and mail from England. "Jack, I say! Wot do you suppose all this speechifying means?"

"Who's making speeches?"

"The Frogs, o' course, who else?"

The paper Brand took up gave a full account of the departure, on Bastille Day, of ten thousand French troops from Cherbourg "to lead the attack on Bomarsund" and of the speech made by the French Emperor aboard his private yacht *La Reine Hortense*, before graciously offering it for the use of the commanding general. Edgeworthy was a fairly good reader, easily to be excused for stumbling over a bad translation of Napoleon III's eloquence; even Brand wrinkled his brows as he read.

" 'France's civilizing mission' (don't know what he means) 'France's leadership of Europe' (h'm) 'the French alone will bring proud Russia to her knees . . . now let us, all together, sing the national anthem'—what a lot of rot," said Brand without heat.

"To 'ear 'im you'd think the French was running the 'ole show, and us nowhere," said the Englishman. "What day was that again, they was supposed to 'ave left Cherbourg?"

"Their national holiday—fourteenth of July."

Struck: " 'Ere, that's two weeks. *Two weeks*, Jack! What are they doin'—comin' along in row boats?"

But before that day was over the British sailors, and the silent Russians within the fort, heard the French national anthem, "Partant Pour la Syrie", ringing over Lumpar Bay when the French troopships at last arrived. *La Reine Hortense* went regally down the lines of British ships dressed overall, and a salute of fifteen guns was fired in honour of General Baraguay d'Hilliers, another veteran of the Napoleonic Wars. The *vivandières* of the Chasseurs de Vincennes and the 51st of the Line waved pertly to the British sailors as the transports came to anchor in the bay. Waving back at the women, and commenting ribaldly on the red trousers they wore beneath knee-length skirts, and shouting invitations before the inevitable "Silence there!" rang out, helped to keep even the more intelligent seamen from thinking that ten thousand soldiers and nearly as many sailors had assembled to capture one granite fort garrisoned by two thousand Russians, or that fourteen days was too long to have delayed in front of a fortress which was perfectly accessible from the sea.

Brand Endicott thought of it, though not at the time. Then he was waving at the girls and laughing with the rest, but later, just before the August twilight fell on the Sunday night, when there was some activity round the silent fort at last, and a file of Russian troops came down to the bay to bathe. There was something pathetic about those white vulnerable bodies seen across the misty bay. The voices of the Russians had a light and cheerful ring across the water which contrasted oddly with the steady roll of drums from the interior of Fort Bomarsund. There was no bathing for the British, but the men washed more carefully than usual in the heads that night as if they, too, were cleansing their bodies for the morning's sacrifice.

Forty-eight hours later Brand was lying full length in the trampled fern and scrub of the steep ground north of the main fort, under the sandbags of a British battery mounted to shell Fort Nottich. All round him lay sailors in various stages of exhaustion after two days of hauling artillery into position up the rocky ground from the beach-head. Three short 32-pr. guns, four field guns and a rocket tube had been dragged up on two sledges, with one hundred and fifty men harnessed to each sledge. Five thousand sandbags, with fascines, gabions, shot and ammunition had also been carried up five tortured miles by the strongest and ablest men from the ships during the first two days of the bombardment of Fort Bomarsund.

"Gawd, look at that!" said the seaman next to Brand weakly. Prästö island, so close to them across the narrow strait, was now a mass of flames. All day, while the French troops landed south of Fort Tzee and the British north of Fort Nottich, to form a giant pincers movement closing on the two sides of the main fort, the Half Moon itself had been exchanging fire with the Allied ships. But Prästö as yet was not under bombardment : the fires the sailors saw from their heights had been kindled by the Russians. Only the martello tower remained intact on Prästö. The hospital and warehouses were in flames, while on the landward side of Bomarsund the smoke of twenty desolate Finnish homesteads was rising to the sky.

General Andrei Bodisco, the Russian commander, had ordered the earth to be scorched for miles around the fort.

"Why the 'ell don't we have 'orses?" said a familiar voice near the group where Brand was lying prone. "The Frogs 'ave 'orses. They put eight thousand men and I dunno 'ow many guns ashore in double quick time yesterday, all because they 'ad 'orses. Brute beasts, that's what the Navy's made of us: brute beasts, I say."

"Hey there, Morgan," said Brand Endicott.

"Why, if it ain't my dear old messmate, Yankee Jack," said the Welshman, getting up and coming over to where Brand lay. "I thought you went back aboard with Edgeworthy."

"No such luck," said Brand, getting slowly to his feet, "I'm reduced to powderman, got to run the ammunition again tomorrow. How about you?"

"All right except me poor old plates o' meat," said Morgan, who like Brand had picked up Cockney rhyming slang from his shipmates. "Yours look 'orrible too, Jack," he added, looking at the filthy, bloodstained bandages tied round the American's bare feet.

"It's your flaming Navy contractors," said Brand. His feet were cut to ribbons, of course, and had been since the first of the two days hauling, when hardened seamen fell in the ropes and wept with pain; whereupon General Jones ordered a ship's band ashore to cheer them up the painful way to the strains of "Hearts of Oak". The Crimean story was being repeated in the Baltic, where seamen went barefoot because contractors fattening on the war had failed to deliver shoes to the Fleet, or else had sent shoes in all the wrong sizes, made of inferior leather.

"To 'ell with the contractors," said Morgan. " 'Ere, have a pull o' that and you'll be ready for the Rooshians."

"Where did you get it?" said Brand, drinking from the bottle Morgan held out. "That's real French brandy, mate; that's good."

"Got it off a Froggie," grinned Morgan. "Me and some of the 'Eclas sloped off to the French camp last night after we bivouacked. Gawd, Jack, you ought to see the place they've got! Huts built out o' trees for the orficers, and tents in rows and horse lines! Wot about comin' down there with me now, before they make the rounds?"

"Got to get some sleep," said Brand. His head was aching worse than his feet and there was sand inside his shirt and trousers. He felt foul and feverish.

"Come on, old cock," urged Morgan. "Some of them girls in the red pants is ready enough to parleyvoo, and give us a taste of their grub. They got chicken and wine, and I never seen the likes of them to eat greens—they must ha' cleared every farm the Rooshians 'aven't burned. Turnip tops, cabbages, beets—they put some oil mess on the stuff, and swaller it raw."

"Keep them clear of scurvy," said Brand. He took another gulp of brandy and handed the bottle back. He was not tempted by the thought of oily cabbage, not even of fried chicken, but he had a devouring thirst, and all day long had been cramming into his mouth whole handfuls of the blueberries and red currants which grew wild on the northern slopes. After Morgan went away he drank from a spring flowing through the underbrush and lay down again on his tarpaulin. He was dimly aware of the officer on duty shouting something about cholera in the French camp, the French camp was out of bounds, and pictured Morgan at defaulters' drill again, but then he slept. He woke feverish and still exhausted when the whistles shrilled and the heavy boom of the British broadsides rolled again over Lumpar Bay.

After that, for two days and two nights, Brand seemed to be climbing the stairs of an endless treadmill. Running, always running through the sand and over the stones, carrying powder, carrying shot, hearing the words of command, *Prime, Point, Fire*, a thousand times repeated, hearing the yells of French infantry as they stormed the slope and took Fort Tzee. Aware that the mud battery on the point had been silenced not by Yelverton, but by Captain Pelham, R.N.—that Pelham had a British battery in the emplacement, and was inflicting more damage on the Half Moon than any of the ships at sea. Watching the Russian eagles hauled down from Fort Nottich at last, and cheering crack-lipped and dry-throated at the sight; listening all through the moonlit night of the French Imperial day, August 15, to the shrieks of pain, with which were mingled the cries of women ringing from within the Half Moon as the granite walls of Bomarsund began to crumble beneath the Allied fire. At last, in the early afternoon of the next day, General Bodisco raised the white flag, and Bomarsund, a Baltic fortress, was surrendered by the Russians.

In the early afternoon of the next day Alix Gyllenlöve came to Bomarsund.

She came in an ancient skerries ship, not unlike the long-ships of the Vikings and still the best type of boat for navigating in the shallow waters of the archipelago, rowed by a mixed crew of half-grown boys and young women from Degerby village. There had been no breeze on the night of the Allied victory, and everyone aboard had taken his or her turn at the oars as they pulled steadily northward—not through Sulivan's Angö passage, for that was already crowded with war vessels moving back to Led Sound, but on a longer course by Vardö island which brought them to anchor in a little cove just north of the devastated main fort of Bomarsund.

Alix was one of the first to jump ashore, splashing recklessly through the shallows to the rocks.

"Somebody will have to stay with the boat," she reminded them. "We don't want to find it stolen when we're ready to go home!"

After some argument the fisher boys arranged a roster of watchmen, and the first two chosen, Arne and Sten, settled themselves sulkily in the bows of the skerries ship for an hour of sleep. They had been rowing through the night and were tired, but everyone wanted to be first ashore to gloat over the downfall of the Russians. The young people who scrambled over the rocks to the rough track running all the way round the peninsula stood overwhelmed at the sight of so much destruction.

At their back, only the gun-pocked martello tower remained standing on Prästö, surrounded by blackened walls, and the rubble of Fort Nottich could be seen through the trees high on the right. The ruins of Fort Tzee were partly obscured by the Devil's Hill, but straight ahead, as they gazed down the track, the Union Jack and the Tricolore waved side by side over the crumbling red granite of the Half Moon.

"They *are* defeated," said one of the Degerby boys, on a long breath. "The tyrants are crushed for ever."

"Yes," said Alix. "Crushed!"

"And you will help me to find my father, lady?" begged one of the youngest of the girls.

"Your father will be free now, Marie," said Alix confidently. "We shall meet all our friends by and by!"

"Stay with us, lady!" But already they were separated, as the Degerby boys took to their heels and ran towards the Great Fort, pulling the girls behind them, and a score of British sailors, dragging what seemed to Alix like a long iron tube, demanded right of way along the track.

"'Ere, watch out!" "Mind your feet, miss!" The good-natured shouts forced Alix aside, into the sedges of the bay. She was not sorry to be alone for a moment to re-tie the kerchief round her head and shake out the black skirt wrinkled with the night dew. Down in the alder bushes she made herself presentable, with her little pocket comb and a sea-water pool for mirror, and when she emerged she saw an old fisherman sitting in a flat-bottomed boat, placidly baiting his hooks.

"Grandfather!" she hailed him, "Have you seen a British ship called *Arrogant*?"

"Lumparn is full of ships," he told her sullenly. "English, and Frankish, and now the Russians are aboard: how is an honest man to know the one from the other?"

"The *Russians* are aboard?"

"Yes, girl; the great Russian general gave up his sword last night to the fat Englishman, down at the jetty, and there was cheering, and the music played. They call that the honours of war, a man told me, but I don't know. The Russians burned my house down, and I'm hungry."

"Good fishing, grandfather." Alix went on across the rocks. She had not far to go before the whole amazing scene opened before her eyes: the bay full of shipping, surrounded now by bumboats, water hoys and colliers; the land swarming with men in uniform. Among the frigates she saw several British yachts, whose owners had crossed from England to watch the battle in a spirit of gay adventure, and several pleasure steamers from Stockholm. There was even a corvette of the Swedish Navy, flying the Union flag of dark blue carrying the red and blue of Norway, and also flying the Three Crowns, at which Alix opened her eyes; but most of all her attention was caught by the launches, full of men in Russian uniform, which appeared to be putting off from the direction of the Great Fort.

She took a few irresolute steps towards the track. Now she had seen those swarming thousands, among whom civilians as well as men of all the Allied services were freely mixed, the difficulty of finding Brand Endicott came sharply home to her. She had wondered how to reach him aboard *Arrogant*: she realized that it would be at least as difficult to discover him ashore.

There was a constant procession of British seamen on the path by which she stood, some drunk and staggering, but all willing enough to answer the questions fired at them by the people of the yachting parties and the Stockholm trippers. Alix, with an effort, conquered her own timidity. What does it matter what those men think of me, she told herself. Brand came to look for me again and again. I must see him today— I must!

She looked the seamen over carefully. They all seemed much alike in their dusty blue clothes and were heavily bearded. Some were limping horribly on bare feet. At last she saw a man whose hat had an *Arrogant* riband, and started forward.

"Sir—if you please—"

Startled: 'What's that, miss? You English?"

"No, I . . . You sail in *Arrogant*?"

"That's right."

"Do you know—Able Seaman Endicott?"

"Sorry, miss. Not in my watch, he ain't."

"Oh!"

"You sure he's in *Arrogant*? What's his Division?"

"He fires the gun, I think. Also, he swims well."

"Hey, Campbell!" (to a seaman trudging past). "You're a swimmer! Young lady's looking for a fellow called Endicott."

The Highlander's dark face brightened to a smile. "Yankee Jack!" he said. "I know him well, we are paired in some of the exercises. He isn't far away, miss, waiting for the jolly-boat; we're going back aboard."

Alix thanked him and went in the direction he pointed out. It led her closer to the main fort and the jetty where the prisoners of war were being embarked, and there, in a crowd of sailors and civilians, she saw Brand Endicott.

He was blackened by smoke and grime, his shirt torn half

224

off his back, with a Colt revolver in his belt and an empty water bottle dangling at his side. He was talking to a man of middle height, who had a pretty girl hanging on his arm. The girl's face was lifted admiringly to Brand's. The man wore a seaman's jersey and high boots. A cap with a battered visor was set well back on his dark curly hair and beneath blue Irish eyes his mouth was smiling.

Alexandra's heart leapt. She went forward confidently to the little group.

"Brand, I'm here," she said. "And this must be Captain Ryan and his daughter."

"Good heavens, Alix!"

Brand swung round to face her, and Alix saw only amazement in his ravaged face. Then the look of love, which she remembered so well, blotted out the amazement, and he said:

"You came to me!"

"I had to come."

"But I don't understand—"

"I do," said Joe Ryan easily. "The lady came here like all the rest of us to cheer the British victory. You're right, madam; I'm Joe Ryan, this is Mary, and you, of course, are—"

"Miss Gyllenlöve," said Brand stupidly. "Mary, I've told you about Alix—"

"A little," said Mary sweetly. She was prettier than ever, and more aware of it, and she would *not* show her vexation that this Finn girl had come upon them not five minutes after she and her father, after a long search, had found Brand Endicott.

But Alix had no eyes for the Ryans.

"Brand, are you wounded?" she exclaimed.

"Wounded? No, I'm not wounded. We had some rough days, that's all. Alix, however did you get here? Joe, did you call for her at Degerby?"

"I was going to," said Joe, rather sheepishly, "but my first mate here persuaded me to come in by Eckerö and dodge the traffic. She was right, too, we sold our whole cargo—oranges —to the French flagship half an hour after we arrived."

"You look very tired, Brand," said Mary softly. "Won't you come aboard the *Molly-O* and have some food with us?"

"Where's the *Molly-O* lying?" Brand knew she had asked him a question requiring a polite answer, but the right words refused to come, and there was something far more important on the surface of his mind.

"She's lying five hundred yards west of the jetty," said Joe. "We got here early—"

"Good." Brand cut him short. "You stay there, Joe. Don't put in anywhere south of Tranvik, and whatever you do, don't be like those fools from the pleasure boats and go off to visit the French camp."

"Why not?"

"There's sickness there. Alix, I want to talk to you."

Without so much as raising her eyebrows at his tone, she stepped off the path with him at once. There was no privacy anywhere at Bomarsund; even the rough alders above the rocks formed only the thinnest of screens between them and the constantly moving crowd, but at last Brand was able to focus his eyes on Alix, and saw compassion in her lovely face. She seemed to be wearing the same kind of dress as at Degerby, with the addition of something red, and there was a gleam of gold which he identified at last as the brooch he had found pinned to his coat in the remand cell at Gothenburg.

"Alix, remember?" He dared to touch the golden leaves with the tip of one scarred finger, and seizing his hand she clasped it to her breast.

"Oh my darling, you look so tired!"

Brand freed his hand at once.

"Keep away from me!" he said. "I'm not fit to touch you. Do you know what I've been doing all night long?"

"What?"

"Burying Russians."

"I wish I'd been there to help you."

"By God!" he said, and not profanely. "Alix, you don't change, do you? You're the same, all the way through?"

"You should know." She was growing accustomed to the sight of him now: the haggard face with the sandy ten days' beard, the shirt from which both sleeves had been ripped, and the blue trousers torn and grey with the sand of the battery.

"If Joe didn't bring you, how did you get to Bomarsund?" he demanded again.

"I came with some young people from Degerby. I wanted to see the victory, and—and tell you how proud of you I am—

226

and they, the Degerby boys, are here to take their fathers home."

"Their *fathers*?"

"The men the Russians took for forced labour here."

Brand closed his eyes. "Alix," he said, "I want you to go away now. There's sickness here, and other things not fit for you to see. Joe Ryan has sold his cargo; there's nothing to keep him here, and I'll get him to take you out of Bomarsund —to Degerby if you must, to Stockholm if you will."

"And you?"

"I? I'll continue on the path you pointed out to me, you can be sure of that."

"Oh, Brand!" Alix said miserably, and followed him back to where the Ryans waited.

"I've got to go," said Brand abruptly. "The *Arrogant's* boats are due to pick us up in quarter of an hour."

"Then where will you go, Brand?" asked Mary Ryan.

"We'll probably have another 'look in' at Sveaborg," he said indifferently. "Thank God we're not required to ferry prisoners."

"I hear the haul was round about three thousand," said Joe. "What's going to happen to them all?"

"We've been taking them off in launches ever since daylight."

"They're being taken off in launches now," said Alix.

A short walk had brought them abreast of the Great Fort, where a double file of Royal Marines was keeping back the sightseers.

"The French were looting in the fort all night," said Brand. "They didn't get much but gunpowder and tubs of salt fish— and vodka; but it looks as if the Russians kept hold of most of that."

"Why, they're all drunk!" said Mary with a giggle.

It was true that many of the Russian prisoners, with the badges of the 38th Line Regiment on their grey coats, were reeling rather than walking to the jetty which lay west of the main gate of Fort Bomarsund. One group was solemnly dancing the polka, two by two, grappling and clutching at one another like bears, and the British laughed uproariously as two couples fell into the water and had to be dragged aboard the boats. One or two prisoners, those who had stood to their guns for five days, showed fight at the last, and struck out wildly at their guards; they were clubbed over the head with the oars and dragged aboard unconscious.

"But those are Finlanders!"

Brand heard the gasp from Alix, and knew she had seen what he would have given worlds to spare her—the prisoners from the Finnish sharpshooter battalion, some of them with women by their sides, being marched off to an Allied war prison. In spite of his own prohibition, he drew her against his side.

"Don't mind, Alix. Please don't!"

"But these are the men from Degerby!"

He had to hold her with all his remaining strength then, and Joe caught at her hands, as Alix struggled to evade them, and break through the Marine cordon to reach the islanders forced against their will to work for Russia.

"Miss Alexandra, don't! There isn't a thing you can do to help them!"

"I must speak to them! I *must* explain! The British have no right to imprison those men! Their *children* are here now, waiting for them—"

"Alix." It was the shadow of Brand's voice, but it carried such authority that she was silent, though her hands worked convulsively in Joe's firm clasp. "Remember what I've kept trying to tell you? You can't stop the war! It's like a machine now, and we're all caught in it; Alix, don't make things worse for yourself!"

"But what will be done to them?"

"The Degerby men? Sure to be released once they're examined and show their papers, on the transports, aren't they, Joe?"

"Certain to be," said Joe stoutly.

"Miss Gyllenlöve, don't you want to come along to the *Molly-O*?" coaxed Mary.

"That's it!" said Brand. "Look, darling, I'll tell you what I'll do. I'll ask for leave as soon as I'm aboard. They're sure to grant shore leave tonight. Then I'll come back to you and see you started on your way home. Mary, look after her!"

He was gone by the way they had come, with no more farewell than a quick pressure of Alexandra's hand and a wave to Joe. Then the Marines were swarming round them, hurrying them on, as a rattle of drums announced that yet another batch of prisoners was being marshalled to leave the Great Fort.

"Move along there!" "Make way for the prisoners!" "Get those women out o' here!" were the most amiable of the remarks addressed to Joe, and he took the hint and hurried the two girls across the trampled grass and rubble to the far side of the jetty.

"Father, I think Brand's very sick," said Mary, stopping short.

"I think so too," worried Joe.

"Why don't you go after him and see that he's all right?"

"I think I will. Miss Alexandra, don't take it too much to heart, but he may not get leave to come ashore again—you realize that, don't you? And I've some business to discuss with him . . . Look, yonder lies the *Molly-O*. You can get there by yourselves, can't you?"

"Certainly, Captain Ryan," said Alix faintly, and watched him hurry off. She felt a sickening sense of anti-climax.

The two girls turned towards the boat, though Mary watched Alix covertly and knew she was not far from tears. So this is the lady of the letters, she thought disdainfully. With a Finn knife and a leather wallet at her belt and dressed like a peasant, in a red shawl, and those terrible red worsted stockings and short skirts! I thought she was supposed to be a Russian princess, or something very grand. And Mary looked down complacently at the clear-starched white muslin dress into which, like an experienced Sea Peddler, she had changed as soon as they came into Lumpar Bay that morning. She was pleasantly aware that her chip straw bonnet, with the rosy ribbon knotted beneath her pretty chin, had been favourably noticed by every man she passed . . . even if Brand Endicott had hardly given her a civil greeting! She tossed her head.

"It is very kind of you to invite me aboard your boat."

Alix was mistress of herself now, and the formal courtesy took Mary by surprise.

"Not at all," she said, flustered. "We'll have some coffee, and you can rest; you must be tired after your long trip up from Degerby. That's the *Molly-O*, in the next berth."

"Where the Swedish officer is standing?"

Mary's face grew pink with pleasure. "I know who that is," she said demurely.

"So do I," said Alix. For the man in the short blue tunic and white trousers of the Swedish Life Guards had turned round to face them, and was Erik Kruse.

"I had no idea that you knew Miss Gyllenlöve," said Mary Ryan.

"We are cousins by courtesy, my dear Miss Mary," Kruse said jauntily. "We've known each other for the past ten years."

"Ten years too long," said Alix. She studied the narrow face under the *schapska* with the white horsehair plume. "It would be more to the point to ask how long you have known Miss Ryan?"

"Is that any concern of yours?" Mary broke in.

"I think it is," said Alix. "Does Captain Ryan approve of your acquaintance with this man?"

"I haven't the privilege of knowing Captain Ryan," said Erik Kruse.

"Exactly," Alix said. "Miss Ryan, let us go aboard and wait for your father and Brand, and give Captain Kruse leave to return to his military duties, whatever they may be."

"I give the orders aboard the *Molly-O*!" said Mary furiously. "If I wish to receive Captain Kruse, what right have you to stop me?"

"You little fool," said Alix. "You don't know what sort of man he is."

She turned away from the *Molly-O* and the angry girl, back along the stony track, with her head held low.

"Not so fast, please, Alexandra!"

Erik Kruse had come with long strides to her side. They were at a point of the bay shore which was temporarily deserted, for the crowds had gathered to watch the embarkation of the prisoners, and with his gloved hand on her bare arm Kruse had no difficulty in drawing her off the path into one of the thickets of spruce which marked the extreme limit of the French camp.

"So," said Kruse as she stood facing him. "You're playing your favourite masquerade again—the simple peasant girl! I prefer the red Bohuslän costume, though. The present one is very drab."

"Take care, Erik," Alix spoke low. "You haven't your bullies from the Crown Bastion here, remember! If you insult me now, a dozen British sailors will come when I cry out—"

"Try it and see, my dear."

"And the man your heroes set on, six to one, he isn't far away!"

"What, the American?"

"Yes, the American, whom you sent the T.O. men to arrest at Helsingfors! He is free and he is here!"

"Bomarsund is a great meeting-place," said Kruse, trying to speak lightly.

"Did *you* come here to meet that silly girl?"

"What, pretty Molly Ryan, the toast of the Palace Guard?"

"She isn't *that*," said Alix with conviction. "A pretty flirt, perhaps but no more—yet. Not unless you mean to treat her as you've treated others."

"I wouldn't waste my sympathy on Molly, if I were you. Her aunt's home in Stockholm is getting to be well known as a house of assignation—"

"You make everything vile," said Alix. "What are you doing here, if you aren't pursuing her?"

"I'm in attendance on my General, of course. Didn't you see the corvette out in the bay? He is in conference with the Allied commanders, who have made a handsome offer to His Majesty King Oscar—of course in the hope that he'll now enter the war—"

"What offer?"

"Nothing less than what remains of Fort Bomarsund, and all the islands that surround it."

"It is not theirs to offer," Alix said. "This is Finnish soil; now that the Russians are expelled the Åland Islands can be the cradle of a free Finland."

"Still harping on that old string, are you? The Russians have lost one fort and two thousand prisoners to an enemy force ten times as strong. Do you think they are likely to lose Sveaborg?"

There was something in the aquiline face, the cold hazel eyes, which infuriated Alix.

"Are you hoping Russia will win the war?" she cried.

"*Expecting,*" Kruse said.

He had been drawing Alix back among the trees, almost

imperceptibly, while they had talked. Now, without warning, he seized her in his arms.

She lowered her head immediately and stood rigid, not struggling, until he was forced to free one hand to try to raise her face to his.

"You can't take me back to Karinlund by force, as you did last January," she said in a muffled voice.

"No, I can't take you anywhere, but I can tame you—now!"

She drew her knife from its sheath and struck upwards. It was a woman's blow, ill-judged and unskilful, but it caught Kruse on the side of the jaw and ripped up through the flesh of his cheek, narrowly missing his eye, till it met the edge of his helmet and was turned aside. He stared at her incredulous, and then the hard grip of his arm relaxed and the bright blood welled over his face.

Alix fell back with a cry in which dismay and triumph mingled, as he called her a crazy bitch and Finn devil, and tore his tunic open, and ripped at his white shirt for linen to stanch the wound. But the flow of blood weakened him quickly, and he fell to his knees, groping at the tree trunks for support, and changed his cursing to a cry for help. Then Alix threw the Finn knife into the underbrush, and rushed back to the track to lose herself among the crowds.

Mary Ryan stood before her there.

"What became of Erik?" Mary said.

"He followed me. He's—in the wood—somewhere."

"You expect all the men to run after you, don't you? Erik —and Brand?"

It came to Alix then what she must do. She believed in her pain and confusion that she had known it for the past hour.

"Tell Brand I must go back to the men from Degerby," she said, and ran like a hare towards the gates of Bomarsund.

CHAPTER THIRTEEN

THE RED SHAWL

THERE was a light which came and went at the far end of a tunnel, swaying as Alexandra's body swayed, and which at times seemed to be poised upon a tree, or mast, standing high above her head. It was some time before she realized that the light shone only when her eyes were open, because the struggle to lift her lids was so great that she preferred to keep her head down in the pillow, which smelt of smoke and seaweed, and was warm; but at last she turned to ease her cramped position and opened her eyes upon a star.

The star of a summer night in Finland, when the blue melts into grey and the grey into silver, imperceptibly, so that at first the stars are one with the sky and visible only in their separate glory when they seem to be caught in the branches of an evergreen or hung like a lantern on the mast of a ship at sea.

Alexandra was at sea. She knew it by the naked spars and cross-trees above her head, and the beat of the screws, and as she became aware of voices all around her, and the patter of bare feet along the deck, she realized that her pillow was another woman's skirt, and that she had been lying on the planking with her head in a stranger's lap.

"Are you better now, poor thing?" the woman whispered, as Alix sat up and put her hand to her head. Her kerchief was gone and her hair was in disorder, but someone had knotted the red shawl firmly round her shoulders.

"What happened to me?" she said, dazed.

"You fell coming on board the steamer. Don't you remember? There was so much crowding and pushing, and you put your hand out to steady my little boy, and fell . . ."

"I remember now. But surely that was hours ago?"

"We are nearly into Led Sound, so they say."

The stars grew brighter and the moon was up. The old three-deckers lay upon an ocean painted with the colours of the night, each dressed in honour of the victory with the

French Ensign at the main and the Red, Blue and White Ensigns of Britain at the foremast, mizzenmast, and peak. There were lights at all the open ports and cabin windows, and in some ships bands were playing.

"They rejoice," said the woman who sat by Alexandra.

"Where are they taking us?"

"To the English troopships, so my husband says."

"Is your husband aboard?"

"Yes, thank God. I thought we were separated in the crowd, but there he is, sitting on the hatch yonder, taking care of our son. Are you alone?"

"Yes. How long were you inside the fortress?"

"Over three months. And you?"

"Not so long."

There was more movement on the deck now, and orders were shouted to the seamen. The steamer came up slowly to the dark unilluminated shape of a great old sailing ship of the last reign, with the name *Royal William* faintly to be seen.

"My husband will carry the child this time," said the Finland woman to Alix kindly. "You must be careful how you go down the ladder."

But Alix had lost her surefootedness, and clung dizzily to the rope ladders as the prisoners went down the side of the steamer, into the boats, and up to the main deck of the *Royal William*. She stood in the entry port gasping and shaking the loose hair from her eyes, while two British officers, working by lantern light, took the names of every man, woman and child coming aboard.

This, Alix in her confusion had not anticipated. She heard the woman's husband mutter something inaudible, and then "Henry," pointing to the child he carried on his arm. He was urged on, looking back anxiously at his wife, and the Englishman rapped out:

"Your name? *Namn?*"

"Tora Kivi."

"Next there. Your name?"

"My name is Anna Larsson," Alix said.

H.M.S. *Royal William* was the largest of seven British troopships ordered to convey the Bomarsund war prisoners to confinement in the hulks, pending arrangements for their division between Britain and France. It was intended to hold ten Russian officers (although not General Bodisco and his staff) and about seven hundred other ranks, the rest of the captives being sent to H.M.S. *Hannibal*, *Algiers*, *St. Vincent*, *Termagant*, *Sphynx* and *Gladiator*.

No allowance had been made for women and children, but with the Royal Navy's talent for improvisation these were accommodated in what, when the *Royal William* carried her full complement of officers, had been the midshipmen's berth in the after cockpit. It was a den about 12 feet square and 5 feet 6 inches high—one inch too low for Alix—and the only ventilation was through the open door, at which two Marine sentries were posted to guard such desperate prisoners as nine exhausted women and eight crying children. On the first night, at least, the women did not complain of lack of privacy. They piled their shawls and bundles on the huge oak table, covered by the rags of a green baize cloth, which took up half the space in the berth, and lay down in the empty bunks to sleep in snatches and wake in terror every time the Master-at-Arms made his rounds.

Alix slept well enough for the first half of the night. The long sea trip from Degerby to Bomarsund and the emotional shocks of the hours which followed assured a kind of oblivion which even her half stupor on the steamer could not impair. But when the first bell struck in the morning watch, at what she correctly reckoned to be 4 a.m., and the bo'sun's mates began shouting on the lower deck directly overhead, she roused to sudden and complete wakefulness and took stock of her new situation.

She did not allow herself to think of Brand. All that had happened at Bomarsund was so recent and so raw that she deliberately thrust it from her mind, and in the same way she refused to think of where her own rash action in joining the embarking prisoners could lead her. It was of the clapboard house on Degerby that she thought first: of old Miss Agneta's bewilderment when the skerries ship came back without Alix, and the despair of the Lapland maid. Would the real Anna ask the *trolltrumma* to tell her where, and when, she would again see her wilful mistress? Would the drum repeat that cryptic message, *Only so far?*

Alix had run away from silly, fussy Aunt Kitty at Karin-

lund without a moment's compunction, and she had forged
Aurora Karamsin's name on an official document when she
fled from St. Petersburg with no thought of wrongdoing, since
only Russians were to be deceived. But it was not pleasant to
think of poor Miss Agneta, who had given her a refuge, calling
and looking for her in the garden and the fields, and growing
daily more confused between this war and the last. I hope
Mamsell Josabeth has the sense to tell her I've eloped with
one of Nelson's captains, she thought. That'll make everything
all right.

She tried to keep track of the passage of time by the ship's
bell. The midshipmen's berth was partly lit by a dirty scuttle
of thick glass let into the ship's side, and when the cook's
mate came in with biscuits and a communal jug of tea he hung
a lantern on one wall—not without suspicious looks, as if he
thought the "Rooshians" might be tempted to set the ship
on fire. After that nobody came near the women for an hour.
They began to talk a little, fearfully, and Alix learned that
three were Russians from the town of Nijni Novgorod and four
from Old Finland and Karelia. Tora Kivi alone came from
Finland Proper, and spoke Swedish.

"All shipshape here?" cried the brisk voice of the Captain.
He was "looking in" at the berth on his daily round of inspection, accompanied by the First Lieutenant, in much the
same spirit as the frigate captains "looked in" at the fishing
villages along the Gulf of Finland. He hated this part of his
duty, and with freedom to act would have set every woman
and child ashore at once.

"Sir Captain!" Alix spoke up boldly. "This is not a fit place
for little children. We need bedding, and proper food, and
fresh air—"

"Fresh air, hey?"

"And—and sanitary conveniences," said Alix. It was a
great effort to get out the words, but in the feeble light they
could hardly see her blushes . . . and the night, in one particular
respect, had been abominable.

"Upon my Sam," said the Captain. "What sort of Rooshian
Tartar have we shipped aboard? Where do you think you are,
my good girl? In Windsor Castle, visiting the Queen?"

"Well," said Alix, " we *are* Her Majesty's guests in a way,
aren't we?"

The Captain laughed. "All right. We wouldn't like any of you to go back to the Czar and say you weren't well treated aboard a Queen's ship." He called to the Marine on duty. "Pass the word for the surgeon!"

The surgeon had been at work since the middle of the morning watch, examining the Russian prisoners, most of whom were verminous and also half naked, since they had torn off their uniforms and trodden them into the mud in the uproar after Bomarsund fell. After a brief conference with the Captain he appeared in the midshipmen's berth, and rapidly examined the women and children, with Alexandra acting as interpreter.

"Where did you learn to speak English so well?" he asked her at the end.

"At Helsingfors, doctor."

"You're a Finn, then? Not a Russian?"

"I've lived in Russia."

"I see." He looked her over easily, consideringly; noted the long hands and the graceful manner, and suspected a time-honoured, tawdry story behind the rough hair and the peasant dress. A pretty little governess, not clever enough to keep from being seduced by some pampered Russian princeling, finishing up as a camp-follower in Bomarsund—this was how Alix was seen by the ship's surgeon, a fervent reader of novelettes.

"I'll see you get some milk for the children," he said, rising, "and you can have the use of the sick berth roundhouse. Can't have you going up and down to the heads with all those men around! Oh, and any—er—medical supplies you may happen to need—just let me know."

With that the surgeon thankfully escaped back to the Navy world he had known for thirty years, in which the physiology of young women and infants in arms had no place. Soon after that the promised milk arrived, and also some palatable stew, only spoilt for Alix by the smell of rancid butter and mouldy cheese from the adjacent purser's store. The children slept after they were fed, and the nursing mothers also; the rest sat talking quietly until one of the surgeon's mates put his head round the door and said:

"Miss Anna Larsson? Wanted in the sick berth, immediate."

There was a full minute of silence before Alix remembered

to answer to her new name. Then she started up in confusion, and almost ran ahead of the man to the still empty sick berth, where the surgeon was writing at a folding desk.

"Sit down, Miss Larsson," he said courteously, indicating a camp stool. "I have been dining with the Captain, and among many other matters we talked briefly about you."

"Yes?"

"If I may say so, you are obviously an educated woman. Have you had any experience of nursing?"

"None whatever."

"But you could help with general nursing, if you had to?"

"I could try."

"Because of course, coming from Fort Bomarsund, you are aware of the great outbreak of sickness there?"

Cautiously: "I knew there was some sickness in the French camp."

"*Some* sickness! Nearly five hundred Frenchmen died there in the past three days."

"But what *is* it, doctor?"

"Cholera."

"Oh," said Alix faintly. "That's—that's very bad."

"Unfortunately, there is cholera among the prisoners of war. Two cases have already been notified in *Hannibal*, and three in *Termagant*."

"But none in this ship?"

"Not yet. Now, while an outbreak here could be an immediate disaster, we are on the verge of something far more dangerous—taking the disease back to England, where there has been no epidemic for several years."

"We are really going to England, then?"

The surgeon sighed. In the well-lighted sick berth, with his spectacles on his nose, he saw Alexandra more clearly, and realized that she was not the feckless little governess of his first impression. Cold water and a comb had done wonders for her appearance, and he now appreciated the cool beauty of her face, and the odd assumption of authority, of the right to question him, which he had scarcely expected in a prisoner of war. He had met high-bred English ladies with something of that manner, on his rare excursions into London society.

"Yes, we're bound for England. Now tell me: have you, to

your knowledge, been in close contact with any sick person in the immediate past?"

Alix thought of Brand, hoarse and exhausted, and the burning hand which she had held in hers. If only she had known, at Bomarsund, that the fever was upon him then! Followed him back to the beach-head, kept away from Mary Ryan and the ill-fated meeting with Erik Kruse! I went after him, but I didn't go far enough, she thought. *Only so far.*

"Not in close contact," she said. "What can I do to help you?"

"You can keep a sharp look out for any symptoms of fever among the women. The children, too; and especially watch Mrs. Kevi. She's three months pregnant—didn't you know?—and cholera would kill her in a day. If they complain of sore throat or headache, or diarrhoea, let me know without an instant's delay. There's not much to be done for cholera, God knows, but we can always try to do it."

"Yes, doctor."

"How about the last five days inside the fort? When the bombardment began, you women were put in a place of safety, I imagine?"

"Y—yes, of course."

"Where, exactly?"

"In the dungeons," said Alix at a guess.

With lifted eyebrows: "Dungeons, h'm? I didn't hear of dungeons, only the powder magazines . . . At any rate, you didn't drink water from the main well?"

"—I don't think so."

"You know where the main well is, of course?"

"In the centre of the yard."

"You're guessing, aren't you?"

"I'm trying to remember. So much happened at Bomarsund in the last few days . . ."

"But not to you." The surgeon rose. "Perhaps I ought to hand you over to the Captain."

"For what reason?"

"As a suspected Russian spy."

Alix laughed. "Sir doctor, you've no idea how absurd that is. The Czar doesn't send his 'observers' into the midshipmen's berth of a prisoner of war transport when he wants them to enter England. You must look to high society—the women like Princess Lieven and others like her—if you want to discover the secret envoys of the Czar Nicholas. But for reasons of my own, I would be very glad to talk privately with the Captain of this ship."

"You would, hey?" The girl had not risen when he rose. She was sitting on the folding stool as if she were at some grand reception, and only betraying her tension by fidgeting with the fringes of her shawl.

"I will be frank with you, sir doctor. I am here because I wish to find and help some men from the island of Degerby, where I have friends. They never fought the British—never! They were taken by force to do building work for the fortress, and wrongfully captured after it fell. I wish to enlist the Captain's help on their behalf."

"How many were they?"

"Seventeen in all. Sir doctor, their children went to bring them home yesterday—"

"Have you any idea how many prisoners we took on board last night?"

"No."

"Seven hundred. To look for seventeen, even in our own 'tween decks, would be like looking for a needle in a haystack. And the officers of this ship have too many responsibilities to hunt for needles."

"But Brand—but someone I know said they would be sure to be released as soon as they had shown their papers to the British!"

"There will be no examination of papers aboard the *Royal William*. The prisoners we took today are *all* Russians—all the Queen's enemies, whether they fired the cannon or carried the bricks; we can't discriminate. Don't worry too much, my dear!" he said kindly, as Alix got slowly to her feet. "You can help them, you know, by looking after the women. Don't alarm them, don't let them think themselves in danger, and I'll do all I can to make your voyage to England comfortable. God help you all! You'll think the midshipmen's berth an earthly paradise, after you've spent a night in the prison hulks!"

The prison hulks of 1854 were old prize ships of the days before the Napoleonic Wars. Days when Rodney won the

Moonlight Battle, and Horatio Nelson was a midshipman on the Polar expedition—so far back that by Nelson's years of glory the ancient men-of-war were not fit to put to sea, and were used instead by the Impressment Service as Receiving Ships. To them had been dragged, sometimes unconscious and sometimes in manacles, the men seized by the press-gangs to fight against the French. The record of the rage and resentment of such men as knew their letters was knifed in vile words on every beam and deck plank of their floating transit camp.

The great wars ended but the hulks remained. At anchor off the Essex coast, off Sheerness, off Gravesend, they were used for years to imprison criminals sentenced to transportation for life. While hardened offenders found guilty of rape or highway robbery, with others suffering the same punishment for stealing linen or poaching hares, were awaiting transportation to Australia, the old hulks offered them all the vile facilities of Newgate; and the ships which had held so much human misery were rotten through and through when the Russian War began. The British public, which within a few months was to go wild with indignation over conditions at Scutari, could—with eyes to see—have discovered the same degree of degradation and suffering at Sheerness.

It was to the hulk *Devonshire*, at Sheerness, that most of the surviving prisoners were taken, and Alexandra's first sight of Britain was a dreary English waterfront under grey skies with a small crowd of sightseers shivering in the late August rain. It was the first time she had been allowed on deck since the day they left Led Sound. The Baltic anchorage at that time was full of shipping, although the British frigates had already left to reconnoitre Åbo. But beyond the tall masts and chequered sides of the three-deckers Alix could see the granite rocks of the Islands, and the pale sky with the broad band of turquoise where it met the horizon was the sky arched over Finland. She was still at home then; but when the prisoners next emerged on deck—having been kept under hatches all the way across the Baltic and the North Sea—she saw a foreign country, and she wept.

"Get below there! Get below, you Rooshian scum!"

That was the mildest order from their new guards, as the prisoners swarmed over the side of the *Devonshire*, and it was enforced with rope's ends and clubbed muskets as some of the Russians turned and snarled defiance at their guards. Alix and the women, several score in all, were driven down past the cramped between-decks of the old man-of-war to the orlop, well below the water-line, where only two "purser's glims" in cracked horn lanterns lit the foul stowage and the greasy cable tiers.

"You can't keep us here!" cried Alix, when she saw the filthy place. A blow in the face from a man's open hand was the answer—the first blow she had ever received in her life—and even as she staggered under the weight of it the old primitive instinct drove her hand to the *puuko* at her belt. It was perhaps well for Alix that the Finn knife was lying in the underbrush of a spruce wood far away, for the seaman who had struck her pinioned both of her arms immediately, and flung her down among the cable chains.

"That's 'ow we tame wildcats like you aboard the *Devon-shire*," he said. "Any more wanting the same treatment?"

It was the beginning of a reign of terror for the women prisoners. The orlop was immediately above the hold, in which bilge water covered a gravel ballast laid sixty years back, when the mastless hulk was first towed away to rot at its moorings at Sheerness. In that foul sump had accumulated the sewage of the convict days—the rotting cloths, the human excrement, the dreadful fruit of abortions carried out under cover of dark-ness—and from the slime arose a stench unutterable, which hung continually about the women in the orlop. They had arrived from Finland free of cholera; within days, three of them had contracted a low form of jail fever, and were dead.

The naval officers in *Devonshire* were a very different breed of men from the sea officers of the Baltic Fleet. On half-pay, officers by courtesy, they preferred to spend their time in the taverns of Sheerness, leaving the security of the hulk to the Royal Marines, who were on guard duty round the clock. Marines with loaded muskets and fixed bayonets guarded the gangways, and carronades mounted on the forecastle and quarter-deck were trained inboard. When the prisoners exer-cised once a day, the carronades were depressed to sweep the waist, ready to fire round shot into the shifting mass at the slightest sign of insubordination. If the prisoners quarrelled among themselves, that was another matter; the Englishmen regarded the rows that broke out almost daily between Russians and Finns as a form of cock-fighting, and were always ready to place bets on the Finns. Once, when a maddened Finlander choked his Russian opponent to death by strangling him in the skirts of his own great-coat, the Marines did fire over the heads of the frantic throng in the waist, and a half-intoxicated naval officer, brought back at speed from a dockside public-house, threatened to call out the military to quell the riot. There were no police proceedings. The dead man was taken ashore for private burial, for one Russian more or less meant nothing in an England thrilling to the news that the Allied army, 58,000 strong, had at long last embarked at Varna for the Crimea.

In such a forcing-house of evil every form of wrong was bound to flourish from pilfering to prostitution. Alix slept in the cable tiers with her hands clasped on the leather wallet which held the brooch of the golden leaves and the sum of money she had brought away from Degerby, and she held it against her naked breast under the red shawl, whenever a rare issue of laundry water allowed her to wash and dry her blouse and single undergarment. The guards liked to carry food to the women prisoners on laundry days, for then they had the chance to nip and squeeze bare flesh under the thin shawls and summer jackets, and laugh grossly as the women who had virtue to resist them clambered up the tiers and threatened them with iron bars and hoops found in the rubbish of the orlop. Not every woman had that virtue. Most of the Russians, led by the three from Nijni Novgorod, sold themselves willingly for a few coins or a quarter of gin, and that at any hour of the day when the hands or the Marines could sneak away to them. Alix and Tora Kivi and the two Karelian women huddled in a corner, trying to keep the older children from seeing and hearing the brutal rites performed only a few yards off, and praying for their own deliverance.

"Mother, the rats are running over my feet again," lamented Mrs. Kivi's little boy.

Alix gathered him upon her lap. "Don't cry, Henry. This can't last for ever."

"What makes you believe so?" whispered the child's mother.

"Because surely this is the very pit of hell," said Alix. "There can be nowhere lower than this—"

"These Englishmen are beasts and worse than beasts. The Czar, our Little Father, was right to defend us when they went to war—"

"Don't call Nikita 'Little Father'," said Alix doggedly. "The English aren't all like these foul swine."

She remembered Captain Sulivan, courteous and proud, and his tall lieutenants walking with her in the garden at Degerby. She remembered the cool parlour, and Sulivan's gift of his own Bible, and—how vividly!—in the hell of the orlop, she remembered Brand's voice reading the marked passage from Ecclesiastes:

"Whatsoever thy hand findeth to do, do it with thy might . . ."

There was nothing, now, that Alexandra could do but carry water to wash the children of her fellow-prisoners and hush their crying in the darkness, and she did it, during all the forty days and forty nights of their imprisonment in the hulk Devonshire.

The British public cheered by the Bomarsund victory, was incensed to learn that Sir Charles Napier believed it was too late in the year to make a serious attempt on the key fortress, Sveaborg. The French had already returned home, sail, steam and soldiers, except eight hundred of those who had gone ashore so gallantly at Bomarsund, and who had died there of the cholera. Cholera had ravaged the prison transport Hannibal, from which many prisoners of war—including ten Degerby men—were buried at sea, and it was still raging in the Baltic Fleet. The hospital ship Belleisle was left in Lumpar Bay with several other vessels converted to hospital use, and Brand Endicott was one of many sick men whose fever and delirium were increased by the sound of explosions and falling masonry when the Great Fort and the martello towers were finally razed to the ground.

Slowly, as slowly as the war had been got under way, decisions were made at high level on the prisoners in the hulks. General Bodisco and his staff, who had received special treatment, departed in melancholy grandeur to excite interest in France, where the bulk of the Russians were sent to imprisonment in the Ile d'Aix. Napoleon III would willingly have paraded them all through Paris like a Roman victory. He needed parades. Most of his political enemies were in prison or exile since the *coup d'etat* of 1851, and by provoking the Russian War he had got rid of the army officers suspected of plotting his downfall, but every circus that could swell his people's pride and increase their blind faith in him was a good investment for the Emperor of the French. As many prisoners as possible were sent to France, and only one hundred and seventy-five persons who had declared before the British Commissioners that they were Finlanders, and not Russians, were at last removed from the hulk *Devonshire* and transferred to Lewes Prison in the County of Sussex.

"Have you ever ridden in a train, Anna?" asked little Henry Kivi, as they stood waiting on the wharf at Sheerness for the carts to take them up to London.

"Oh yes, quite often. It's very exciting!" she assured him. Henry was excited already. He was the only child left in the *Devonshire*, and some of the decent men among the sailors had given him a few toys and a bo'sun's whistle as parting gifts.

"Where did you go in the train?"

"To a place called Czarskoe Selo."

"Isn't that where the Czar of All the Russias lives?" said Henry. He was a very intelligent little boy of five.

"I believe he does live there sometimes, yes."

"Did you ever see him?"

"I have seen the Czar, Henry."

"Do you wish you were going to Czarskoe Selo now?"

"No, I'd rather be going to Lewes."

"But we'll be put in prison at Lewes, my father says. Where would you ratherest be going?"

Alix hesitated. Then she stooped down and whispered in the little boy's ear:

"Jewell Island."

"Where's that?"

"State o' Maine."

"Why do you make your voice all funny when you say that?"

"Because that's the way people talk in the State o' Maine."

"Is that on the way to London?"

The way to London was long and chilly, and Alix shivered in her red shawl and thin clothing. But the parliamentary train

245

to Lewes was crowded and therefore warm, and the exciting way of travel, so great a change for all of them and so alarming, for the first few miles, to the young Finnish soldiers, was a stimulant to those who had been cooped up in the rat-infested *Devonshire*. The military guards marvelled at the docility of the prisoners, who sat staring silently at the green English fields on each side of the railway line. It was a beautiful October day, and the sun was shining.

"Anna, look at all those people!" Tora Kivi gasped. "Are they—do they mean to hurt us?"

"Oh·surely not." But even Alix shrank back, timid after the weeks in the darkness of the orlop, at the sight of the remarkable group on the platform. The county town of Sussex had been deeply stirred to know that "Russian prisoners" were to be held in the old county jail. It was only a few days since the news of the Battle of the Alma had been received in England— that great Crimean victory for which the public had hungered for so long, and which with the news of the Charge of the Light Brigade seemed to put Sevastopol in the Allied grasp. This alone was enough to make the ownership of "Russian prisoners" highly desirable to the citizens of Lewes. The officials of the borough, wearing their robes of office and accompanied by their wives, were present with the prison governor on the station platform, to watch him take delivery of the ten officers and 154 other ranks committed to his care.

Lieutenant-Colonel Gustaf Grahn, the senior officer present, was fully equal to the occasion. In good English, he stated that "the Finnish officers in the Russian service, and the ladies to whom two of them were married, were happy to arrive in Lewes, where parole had been arranged for them, and where they put their entire trust in their noble and generous enemy." This was applauded, a band struck up, and the "Russian prisoners" were marched out into streets dense with people, through which no traffic could pass until the captives had gone by.

Alix walked with Tora Kivi and little Henry, just ahead of the two Karelian girls who had been with them since the start of their imprisonment. Her fair head was held high. This slow climb from the station to the High Street was an ordeal; she understood most of what the onlookers were saying, and the occasional jeer was less painful to her than the pitying

246

"Poor fellows, they're just boys. Don't they look thin and hungry, though!" She knew too well how pathetic the tall Finlanders looked. They were nearly all under twenty, and so famished that the coarse grey cloth army coats trailing to their heels hung loosely upon them. They wore small four-pointed hats of green cloth, and carried knapsacks with their few possessions on their backs. Their fair complexions and wispy blond hair emphasized their boyish appearance.

"Well, we 'aven't got much to fear if this is a Rooshian sample!" shouted a jovial Sussex farmer, and Alexandra's heart swelled with protective love. They are poor, she longed to cry, and hungry, and defeated, but wait until the Finns are a nation, and we will show you what kind of folk we are! The sad procession turned into the High Street, where the crowd was thickest. The people of Lewes looked at the women and the child. Alexandra's red shawl was a vivid note of colour among the drab greys and blacks. For weeks past, the popular press had been explaining Russia to the English: the auto-cracy of the Czar, the red post-houses, the red customs barriers, the red kilometre marks which marked his rule through All the Russias. Red had become the enemy colour. It was the shawl, snatched up in a joyful moment at Degerby, as much as her stormy face, which made Alix the personification of Red for the crowd, and made it murmur:

"There goes a bold one, her in the red shawl!"

"She hasn't got no stays on, either!"—for the October breeze was moulding Alexandra's thin garments to her limbs, and the curves of breast and thigh were revealed to the greedy eyes of lads and trainers from the stables on the nearby Downs.

"Proper hussy, she is!"

"*Bloody Roo-shian!*"

A boy who sensed the feeling of the mob had thrown a clod. It went sailing over the heads of the stable-boys lining Albion Street, right out into the roadway, and caught Alix hard on the point of the shoulder. It was a soft turf, plucked from the grass verge; the wet earth spattered over the red shawl which had irritated the bovine people, and a great laugh went up.

Alix plodded on. She felt mud on her jaw, but pride forbade

her to wipe it off, and at the sight of her stony face the laughter died. Tora caught at her hand.

"Are you hurt, Anna?" The good woman was in tears.

"Don't—don't let them think we care! Oh, have we far to go?"

Not far. Only along East Street and into North Street and there ahead of them was the War Prison behind its high spiked walls: three storeys of barred windows set in red brick, with two wings between which an exercise yard replaced the treadmill of an earlier time. The jailers were ready and waiting to march them to their cells. The hum of the town, the autumn fields and the clean October air were cut off from the Finland prisoners with the closing of a door. Alix was hustled up a narrow spiral staircase with stone steps and an iron handrail, into a dark corridor with a vaulted roof. She was pushed through a door so low she had to stoop to enter, with Tora and the child at her back. The key was turned and they were alone in their prison cell.

It had a bare stone floor and was nine feet long by seven feet wide. Of the width, four feet was occupied by two plank beds with straw mattresses, one on each side of the cell. That the prisoners were not expected to emerge at all was shown by a hatch in the door for food to be passed through. That hatch could be closed from the inside. but above it was a spy-hole without a shutter, from which the jailers could survey the two women at any time. It was worse than the darkness of the orlop, for here they could be watched asleep, or dressing, or washing at the tap in one corner of the cell, or using the close-stool in the other. In this tiny space three human beings were to live in enforced intimacy for only God knows how many days and nights, taking their pans of food like stalled animals, never certain when a man's eye was watching from the black corridor.

They might have already seen the uttermost pit, but there were other circles of Hell left to explore.

"Once upon a time," Alexandra told little Henry Kivi, "there was a girl who wanted very much to fight a Bear."

"You mean a princess," said Henry, who liked conformity in stories.

"Well, then, a princess, if you like."

248

"And she was beautiful."

"Some people thought she was beautiful. But she didn't allow many people to tell her so; she was too busy thinking about the Bear."

"Had she seen the Bear?"

"Oh yes, she'd seen him. She knew how big and strong he was, and what dreadful staring eyes he had, and how he loved to torture people who were human, and not Bears like himself—"

"So what did she do?"

"Well—she was very foolish—she tried first of all to get a lot of other people, and one special person, to go and fight the Bear in his den."

"And did they?"

"Yes, they did, but the Bear was very strong and sly, and not at all easy to defeat."

"Couldn't she have killed him all by herself?"

"Once she could," Alexandra's arms tightened round the child. "Once she was so close to the Bear and he made her so angry, she might have plunged a hunting knife right into his heart—"

"Why didn't she?"

"Because the trolls had laid a spell on her, so that though she wanted to do everything with all her might, she did well only so far, and then things began to go wrong. She tried to help some people whom the Bear had enticed into one of his horrible lairs, oh, she tried in lots of ways to fight the Bear, and in the end can you guess all she could find to do?"

"What?"

"She took care of one bad little boy."

Henry got off her lap with dignity and retreated to the bed he shared with his mother.

"I suppose that means me."

"It could be you, couldn't it, when you blow that whistle?"

"I think it's a silly story. Tell me again about Otto von Fieandt, instead."

"'Who with seventeen hundred Finlanders held off three thousand Russians at Karstuba'—that Otto?"

"Yes! and then about Lieutenant Sandels at Virta Bridge."

But Alix was not required to tell any stories of the war of

1808 on that foggy November afternoon. The jailer's step echoed in the stone corridor, the jailer's eye appeared at the spy-hole, and his voice said gruffly:

"Rector come to see you."

"Mr. Grignon! What a pleasant surprise!"

"Good-day to you, Miss Larsson. I knew you were alone with our little friend Henry, and I obtained Governor Mann's permission to have a private word with you."

"But I'm delighted! Pray come in."

"Come on, 'Enry," said the jailer. "Come and 'ave a nice game o' dominoes in the guardroom, and a bit o' my old woman's cake."

"Lucky Henry," said Alix, brushing back his flaxen hair. "Just don't you blow your whistle until the cake's all eaten."

"They're kind to him, aren't they?" said the Rector, sitting down on one of the three-legged stools which had been added to the cell.

"Oh, Henry has the run of the prison," said Alix. She smoothed down her thick grey cashmere, a cast-off donated by the Ladies' Benevolent Society of Lewes, and looked expectantly at the Rector. "What news from the Crimea, Mr. Grignon?"

"Nothing good—from the Allied point of view, that is. The casualty lists from the battles at Balaklava and Inkerman grow longer every day, and there are some early reports of a terrible gale in the Black Sea which may well have created havoc among our stores and shipping."

"But the Russian losses in the two battles, sir?"

"Are even heavier than ours.—Miss Larsson, I have come to you straight from the infirmary."

"Oh! how is Erik Kivi?"

"Very ill, I'm sorry to say. And since Mr. Routinfield, the interpreter, is in London today, Dr. Burton thought you ought to be the one to tell Kivi's wife that he'll be operated on tomorrow."

"To remove the splinter of bone?"

"Yes. It should have been done two months ago, of course. The wound is badly infected now, and the prognosis is not good."

"Poor Tora—she'll want to be there!"

"It's not desirable in her present state of health. Besides,

250

three more pneumonia patients were admitted to the infirmary today."

"It's so cruel!' said Alix passionately. "There was not one single case of cholera among us when we came here. And since then, it's been nothing but old wounds festering, and chills turning into pneumonia, and poor Sergeant Grad dying! It was the awful time in the *Devonshire* that began it. And then coming here, to these stone cells, in the rags of their summer uniforms ... Mr. Grignon, we got dresses, I know, and we're very grateful, but the British authorities ought to have done something for the men! When did you last see Colonel Grahn? He is the senior officer—isn't he going to do anything about it?"

Mr. Grignon shrugged. "Colonel Grahn and his party are at the Crystal Palace today," he said.

"The Crystal *Palace*? But that's in London! I thought their parole was only good within a ten-mile limit?"

"So it is. But it was extended today by special dispensation. Some local friends wished to show them the Crystal Palace and other sights of London. That's where Mr. Routinfield went too, by the way."

"Very nice," said Alix flatly.

Mr. Grignon laughed. "Ah, my dear young lady," he said, "Colonel Grahn may have the right to be billeted in a private house, and wear civilian clothing, and visit the Crystal Palace, while you remain behind the bars of Lewes War Prison, but it makes no difference. It is you who are the natural leader of the Finlanders."

"I, Rector?"

"I am judging by achievements only. Who insisted on lanterns in the cells through these long hours of darkness? You did. Who got the prisoners the right to exercise in the yard, and be provided with materials for handicrafts? You, of course. The Ladies' Benevolent Society would be only half as useful here without you—"

"Because I speak English."

"It's more than that."

Diffidently: "Mr. Grignon ... If you mean what you say ... if you think I have done even a little good ... will you give me the privilege of doing a little more?"

"In what way?"

"All those sick soldiers—they need extra comforts. Especially the pneumonia patients—don't they? Warm hospital jackets, and port wine, and calf's foot jelly—"

"I'm afraid there's no government allotment for such luxuries, alas!"

"But I have money," said Alix eagerly.

She slipped off her belt and opened the leather wallet. Very gently, exploring with her fingers, she drew out a roll of roubles, each one wrapped in a thin rag, and put them in the Rector's hands.

"But this is Russian gold!"

"Any bank will change it. That should be worth about £20."

"My child, you must not give away all your money—"

"I have more."

"You're not afraid of being robbed?"

"I was, in the *Devonshire*. Very much afraid! But not here . . . Mr. Grignon! You mustn't tell anybody where the jackets and things come from. Promise!"

"But—what can I say?"

"Say a resident of your parish gave them. I am that, you know!"

She was lovely when she smiled. Mr. Grignon had not often seen Anna Larsson smile, but there was a seduction in it to which the male responded, even while the clergyman acknowledged the truth in the beautiful grey eyes. He said, gravely:

"Yes, you are indeed a resident in the parish of St. John the Baptist sub Castro. But you are not one of my Communicants, Miss Larsson. I have no spiritual authority over you, nor any human right to probe into what I can think of as a strange situation. How is it that a woman like yourself, alone, possessed of means and, I doubt not, of influence, is imprisoned here with poor soldiers and their wives—"

"They are my countrymen," said Alexandra.

The Rector bowed. "And yet—although you attend the services I hold in the prison chapel, you never accompany *your countrymen* to worship when the Lutheran pastor comes here from London— the very devoted minister of the Swedish church?"

Alix smiled. "I prefer your Litany," she said. "How does it go? 'To preserve all that travel by land or by water, all women labouring of child, all sick persons, and young chil-

dren; and to show Thy pity upon all prisoners and captives
. . .' It might have been written for us, don't you think?"

"It was written for everyone, my child."

When the Rector of St. John's had left her, Alix sat without moving on her pallet for a few blessed minutes of utter
solitude. In the better mood, to which his words had aroused
her, and in the absence of the poor peasant woman with whom
all her days and nights were spent, she was able to indulge
herself by thinking of Brand.

She was positive he was alive. It was quite impossible to
believe the massive strength of the American had succumbed
to a fever from which, if many died, so many more recovered.
And as he was alive, he must be somewhere in the Baltic still,
with that great squadron which Mr. Grignon told her was
holding the gate of the Gulf of Finland until the last moment
when the ice came in. It was the thought of Brand Endicott
on duty, and most of all of Brand in prison, which had given
Alix strength to live through the first two weeks at Lewes,
when none of the war prisoners were allowed to leave their
cells for as much as an hour. He went to prison because of me,
was her constant thought. I will prove that I can endure
prison too.

Tora was brought back from the infirmary, pale and tear-
stained, and before Alix had time to translate and soften Dr.
Burton's message, came Henry, redolent of plum cake and
strong sweet tea. Alix decided to let the poor woman talk
on about her Erik and say nothing about the operation until
the following morning. She knew how soon Tora grew drowsy
in the evenings now, and with any luck she would fall asleep
soon after supper and get one good night's rest before she
knew the worst.

"Mother, don't you want to come to the toy-making tonight?" said Henry importantly, as soon as their empty soup
bowls had been passed out through the hatch.

"Mother's head aches, darling. You go with Anna, just for
an hour, and come early to bed, like a good boy." Tora spoke
as calmly as if she were giving orders in her own house, and
Alix was thankful. That phlegmatic calm might save the
child Tora was carrying from some severe shocks in the next
few days. For herself, Alix looked forward to the evening

hour of communal work which her own persistence had won from Governor Mann. She had no skill in handicrafts, but she kept the records of the materials given out, the work performed by each of the men, and the price obtained for the carved boxes and wooden toys which the Ladies' Benevolent Society sold on behalf of the prisoners, in the town.

The toymaking took place in what had been the kitchen of the old County Jail, used after the conversion to a War Prison as a wash house. It was a warm place, for the great copper boilers retained their heat, and the Governor's well-heated living quarters were near by, and over a hundred people were working there together. Alix slipped into a place beside the two Karelian girls, who were embroidering table napkins for a Benevolent Society order, and bowed to any of the men who caught her eye. It nearly broke her heart to see their patience, and even their contentment as the thin curls of white pine wood slid away beneath their knives—intricate patterns upon work-boxes, miniature Midsummer poles, and—in the hands of the most skilful—little wooden figurines of Lapps and fishermen and reindeer. These would be the only records of their nationhood the Finn prisoners would leave in England.

"Anna, you *promised* to tell about Otto von Fieandt!"

Little Henry was not a whining child, but the petting in the guardroom had gone to his head, and he wanted to prove (his friends the jailers were looking on from every corner of the room) that he could make Mamsell Anna leave her accounts and do something to please him.

"Not just now, Henry; be a good boy."

"Ah-h-h! I want to hear you say the *Tales of Ensign Stål*!"

"Not all of them!" said Alix in pretended horror, and the men nearest them began to laugh.

"Well, Sandels at Virta Bridge, then," the child persisted. "That's my favourite."

"Mine too, youngster," said one of the Finnish sergeants. "You give mamsell a kiss from all of us, and ask her to repeat the Tale."

"For shame, Henry!" Alix, laughing, dodged away from the moist lips the little boy dabbed at her cheek. "With all those gentlemen looking on!"

"You might—if you know a song or a poem—just say it for us, Mamsell Anna," said one of the youngest soldiers wistfully.

She knew at once what was in his mind. It would be like a home evening; an evening in his little *pörte* in the forest, by the lake, with the whole family round the fire to listen to some saga of the north. She had already heard some of the men reciting passages from the *Kalevala*, but she knew instinctively that that was not what they wanted now. These were boys of her own generation. They had been children in the Year of Revolutions, 1848; they were living through a war which had sent them into prison and exile, and the mythical heroes of the *Kalevala* were too far removed from the things they knew. *Ensign Stål*—Runeberg's great poetic cycle of the Russian war of 1808, the songs which had made Alix Gyllenlöve a nationalist, like so many others of her generation—*Ensign Stål* should indeed express their urgent mood.

Alix rose to her feet. The Karelian girls looked up in surprise. Some of the men began to clap.

" 'Lieutenant Sandels' !" demanded the little boy excitedly.

"No, wait, Henry." Alix was thinking rapidly. The first poem in the cycle she could not trust herself to say to them. It had been for six years Finland's National Anthem, sung first to Pacius' music at a student's festival at Helsingfors, and since then banned and utterly proscribed by the Russian authorities; she wondered indeed if any of the boys had ever heard it. The same applied to the Lament for Sveaborg—she could not trust her voice to say the poem. But then she had the happy recollection of "Sven Dufva", and began at once on the story of the awkward recruit who

> "Was far more willing, glad and kind, than some
> whose minds were strong,
> And could be made to do all things, but always
> did them wrong!"

It was the right choice for the lads. Everyone had known a Sven Dufva in the regiment, perhaps was one himself; everyone was amused and touched when the climax came, and Sven, when the sergeant called "Retreat !" kept on advancing, and so helped to win the battle for Finland at Virta Bridge.

"More, mamsell, more !"

"It's time to stop, isn't it? Here comes the Governor !" said Alix.

It was the Governor, and Mr. Grignon with him. Both seemed surprised to find the quiet Finns so unusually animated. Lieutenant Mann gave an indulgent sign to the chief warder, granting a few minutes' grace.

"Give us Döbeln at Juutas, mamsell, *please* !"

Alix nodded. It was the greatest of all the Tales, the one on which every Finnish child was nourished. The story of the patriot general who rose from his sickbed and rode to Juutas at the crucial moment of the war of 1808, thereby inspiring his men to victory; the song of the ragged soldiers; the song of faith in Finland—yes, she could do it. Alix looked quickly at Mr. Grignon's watchful face. The poor outbuilding where they were gathered, with its coppers, drying lines and mangles; the double row of deal tables with the toymaking materials; the patient, pinched young faces above the grey uniforms all receded from her view. She saw Helsingfors on a summer morning, with the blue dome soaring above the Senate Square, and Sveaborg lying just across the bay.

> "At Juutas was the cannonading over,
>   And Death his first great harvest there had reaped,
>   The Finnish army, powerless to recover,
>   Prevailed no more, stood broken, ruin-steeped."

The great prelude began. The organ notes of Runeberg brought Döbeln to the scene, cheering the broken men :

> "And shod or unshod is a trifling matter;
>   If you but see we bravely stand, not scatter,
>   The foot will help itself without a shoe!"

With Döbeln at their head the Finns moved forward, the battle of Juutas was won.

> "And e'er the evening shadows had descended
>   The Russian army's might and fire were ended—"

There was a movement in the prison room then, a sigh of satisfaction which shook the prisoners like a breeze shaking a barley field. Alix was scarcely aware of it. Her heart was beating furiously as she hurried on to the great invocation which concludes the Tale. Her one hope was that her voice would neither break nor falter, that she might do justice to the immortal lines. She was there, on the battlefield in the starlight, not in prison, and the young men in grey were there with her, with their hearts on fire for the future of their country—

"O Finland, who shall now thy fate foretoken?
Thy future lot as yet remains unspoken,
   Thy fortune good or ill can none portray;
But howe'er much of joy or grief thou bearest,
Thou ever shall, of all thy days the fairest,
   Remember this—remember Döbeln's day!"

CHAPTER FOURTEEN

JACK ADRIFT

BRAND Endicott got out of the Portsmouth train and stared around him at the bedlam of Waterloo Station. It was about six o'clock on Saturday December 23, the end of the working week and the start of the Christmas holidays. The men pushing through the crowds to the departing trains carried geese and turkeys both feathered and plucked, hampers of fruit and wine, and Christmas packages bulging in their carpet-bags; even the ladies, genteelly holding their bell skirts clear of the dirty platform, wore an air of Christmas festivity in the little sprays of holly or winter violets pinned to their warm pelisses and sable collars. It was a prosperous crowd, a holiday-making crowd : John Bull and his lady off to spend Christmas in some Surrey country-house, bearing gifts, anticipating the kind of celebrations which Dickens and the Prince Consort had recently made popular. Even the police were good-humoured, and turned a tolerant eye on a ragged band of carol singers at the main exit of the new station.

The newsboys were shouting "Napier strikes 'is flag !" and Brand hesitated for a moment, then shook his head at the vendor and walked on. He knew as much about that as the newspaper's correspondent did — or more; he was in no mood for a London rehash of the scene at Portsmouth yesterday, after Old Charley Napier received the Admiralty order which terminated his Baltic command. He was more interested in the bills posted beside the train arrivals and departures; especially in one appealing for subscriptions to the Patriotic Fund "to alleviate the sufferings of our Troops in the Crimea", and a bold "Join the Foreign Legion" ! This informed him that a force of 10,000 foreigners, to be drilled in Britain, was to be raised under the Foreign Enlistment Act "for successful prosecution of the War against Russia".

Brand read this with what might have been taken for a smile. Actually it was a drawing back of the lips, a flash of teeth, which might well have meant anything as he shouldered his dunnage bag and made for York Road. He was aware, from the affectionate letters which had reached him after his recovery from cholera, that a warm welcome awaited him at his uncle's home, and there was ample time to catch a Thomas Tilling bus direct to the pretty house on Camberwell Green. But Brand had no mind for Camberwell, and Tarras Line talk, and the flutterings of Miss Bell and Miss Flora. What he wanted was a night on the town.

The York Arms Hotel, where he took a room, was as new as Waterloo Station, if gas lighting and alarming cracks in the wallpaper above the chimney-breast of the coffee-room were any indication; and yet London soot and London grease had settled upon it so thickly that it might well have been one of the ancient inns in the Borough where coach passengers had been putting up for over two hundred years. Brand ordered hot rum grog by the fire in the coffee-room. The fire was choked by cinders, and the rum was a long way below Navy proof.

"Very quiet here this evening, sir!" said the only other occupant of the room.

"Very," said Brand.

"Most people prefer to stay at home over Christmas."

"I guess so."

"You've just arrived, have you?" pursued the man, who had the appearance of a reasonably successful commercial traveller. "Come a long way today?"

"From Portsmouth."

"Did you indeed? Very interesting! Did you see anything of the Baltic Fleet, returning to harbour? Extraordinary business this of Admiral Napier."

"I saw some units of the Fleet," said Brand, "and I heard the crews cheering the Commander-in-Chief when he went ashore."

"Very generous of them! I doubt if Sir Charles will be cheered in Marylebone, if he attempts to regain his seat in Parliament."

"Why not?"

"Why—my dear sir, consider his gross mismanagement of the Baltic campaign! Nine months at sea, and neither of the great fortresses so much as fired on—"

"What about Dundas in the Crimea?" interrupted Brand. "He had a larger fleet before Sevastopol, with a clear harbour and depth enough to lay his ships alongside the batteries, and he did no better than Napier at Sveaborg. Worse, in fact; at least Napier brought his ships off intact."

"But, my good sir, it was the disastrous gale in November that destroyed our shipping—"

"Blame it on the weather," said Brand, and swallowing down the weak grog he went off to the half empty dining-room, there to consume Brown Windsor soup, the leg of a skinny chicken with boiled potatoes, and Brussels sprouts. It was poor fare, but savoury enough to a man who only a few days before had been rounding The Skaw in a nor'-wester, with all the mess-tables in *Arrogant* liable to be flung sideways between one bite and another, and the pease pudding joining the rum ration on the deck. He saw the commercial traveller come in, scowling, and take a seat with his back to Brand. No doubt there were thousands in England who thought as that fellow did. Brand had been ashore for less than forty-eight hours, but he already knew that all the Navy had done in the Baltic, from the blockade of the Russian ports to the capture of Bomarsund, had passed from the memory of a public which now could think of nothing but the heroism of Miss Florence Nightingale and the sufferings of the troops before Sevastopol. He stolidly addressed himself to cabinet pudding.

There would be Christmas pudding at Camberwell Green, and roast goose and mince pies on Christmas Day, for Mrs. Arthur Tarras kept a good cook and set a bountiful table. Brand supposed he had better show up at his uncle's house next day and do his best to join in the merrymaking. He was luckier than many of his shipmates in having a family home ready to receive him.

But then the only family he really wanted was Alexandra, and he had lost her. When she disappeared from his life she had taken all the eagerness, all the incentive he might have felt to make new plans after the paying off of the Baltic Fleet. His only link with her past at Degerby had been Joe Ryan. After Mary went ashore at the end of the summer season Joe had gone over to Degerby in the *Molly-O* to look for Alix, and he was looking for her still. There was a letter in Brand's pocket addressed care of Poste Restante at Portsmouth, every word of which he knew by heart:

"I called in at Degerby again on the tenth of December. The women are doing their best to carry on with the winter work and I spoke to a good many of them. They all said there had been no news of old Miss Willebrand and her household since they packed up and went to the mainland, probably to Ekenäs, at the end of August. I walked as far as the house, the windows were boarded up and there was no sign of life about the place. If a letter comes, you can be sure I'll send it on directly."

He was sure of it, of course. But in four, nearly five weary months, no letter from Finland had ever come for Brand.

"What do you suggest by way of entertainment for a stranger to this city?" he asked the seedy man behind the reception desk.

"Public entertainment or private entertainment, sir?"

"Let's begin with public."

"Well—many visitors patronize the Haymarket, or the concert rooms along the Strand, sir. Evans' in Covent Garden, or the Coal Hole, are both considered quite the thing. But on this side of the water, sir, we've Astley's, and the Canterbury Music Hall—that's a great attraction, it reopened this week with new decorations. Oh no, you can't do better than take a stroll down the Westminster Bridge Road, sir—whatever you happen to be looking for."

"Right," said Brand, ignoring the man's sly smile.

"But if I may make so bold, sir, I wouldn't carry any loose change in my coat pockets—not so much as a handkerchief—in that locality!"

Back in his chilly bedroom, Brand put two sovereigns in his vest pocket, and the rest in a money belt bought along with his new clothes at Portsmouth. He was carrying more cash than might have been expected, after the twenty-four hour debauch in which the survivors of summer cholera and winter frostbite had celebrated the paying off of Napier's Baltic Fleet. He remembered very little of the lush-cribs of Pompey, except that he had stuck to liquor and said no to lust; but there was no sense in going on like that. He wanted to go to bed with a woman, and why not, since Alix, who ran away from everyone, had also run away from him? He pulled on his overcoat and went out to the frosty street.

It was to be a green Yule, not cold, but damp and foggy; the lamps along the riverside were reflected in the Thames like wavering circles of misty gold. Brand considered crossing Hungerford Bridge to the Middlesex side of the river, but he was not attracted by the Strand cellars or the intimate supper rooms of Covent Garden. He wanted crowds about him, and the brassy gaiety of the new music halls, and prowled away in the direction of Lambeth, where the tide was lapping against the piles, and wooden stairways led down to Stangate Reach. Through the fog Brand saw a few lanterns bobbing along the foreshore, where human derelicts hunted for driftwood and whatever else the Thames might have cast up below the tumbledown wooden warehouses and hovels which had stood on Stangate Bank since the Middle Ages. The Westminster Bridge Road seemed, by contrast, the very pulse of the nineteenth century.

In search of lights and music Brand soon arrived at Astley's New Royal Amphitheatre of Arts. There, gas jets sparkled along a portico extending right out to the kerb, and above the sound of a circus overture a barker in a red uniform was shouting:

"Shakespeare on 'orseback! Walk up, walk up, ladies and gents, and see the grand piebald pony finale of the tragedy of *Macbeth*!"

"I don't want no tragedy," said a pretty girl studying the playbill beside Brand, and the man holding her arm laughed noisily. "Let's go down the Marsh and 'ave a drink, Bill!" Brand followed them at a few yards distance. He didn't want no tragedy either. He'd had enough of tragedy, and so he too went "down the Marsh" into that primeval swamp from which London had emerged, and which now was brilliant with the oil flares of the jellied eel stalls, the ovens and braziers of the baked potato and roast chestnut vendors, and the shop fronts where the last of the Christmas poultry was being sold off. Brand was glad to lose himself in the noisy crowd. Every now and then the noise increased to a roar and a shower of sparks fell over the new railroad embankment, as a train pulled in to the terminal at Waterloo.

In the Upper Marsh, near the railway arch which spanned the highway, he came upon the Canterbury Music Hall. It stood where the old Canterbury Arms had been selling liquor when the wild flowers grew in Lambeth Marsh, in what now was temporarily a waste land, as the ancient tenements came down and the wrecker and the speculative builder moved in. It had been flourishing exceedingly for the past two years.

Brand bought himself a drink in the tavern downstairs and then went up to the hall, paying sixpence for admission. The horseshoe balcony, where a seat cost ninepence, was already filled with the more respectable elements of the huge Saturday night crowd, or at least those who were dressed in the black surtout of the City clerk, and had brought their wives along for an evening's gaiety. In the body of the hall the company was mixed. There were men in the rough clothes of the mechanic or the bricklayer, there were unattached young women with feathered bonnets and rouge on their cheeks; there were decent family parties and a few young men in the blue frock coats of the Navy; all cheerful and joining in the choruses of the popular songs. The new stage of the Canterbury had been decorated, as the playbill said, "regardless of expense", and appropriate backdrops fell behind every number, to great applause from the spectators. There were no footlights, and the chairman and his friends sat at a long table facing the audience with their backs close up against the stage. The other tables seated four persons, or six, and all through the singing the waiters hurried up and down the aisles carrying trays loaded with pint pots and liquor bottles.

"Is it all right if I sit here?" said Brand to a large man with a smudge of grime across his brow, sitting with his arms round two pretty girls.

"Nobody ain't stopping you, mate," said the man amiably, and Brand pulled out the vacant chair with a bow to the two girls. The chairman had just changed his cry from the "Orders, gents, please!" which punctuated every entr'acte, and with a bang of the gavel, and a pull at his own pint pot, declared himself proud to introduce—

"Your own—your very own—*Sam Cowell*!"

The backdrop curtains parted, revealing a view of the Thames and the Houses of Parliament, and to rapturous applause a small man with a square humorous face walked on to the stage. He wore a stovepipe hat and kneebreeches, and twirled a bludgeon in time with the music of his song.

> "In Vestminster not long ago
> There lived a Ratcatcher's Daughter,
> That is, not quite in Vestminster
> Cos she lived t'other side of the water.
> Her father killed Rats and she cried Sprats
> All round about that quarter
> The young gentlemen all touched their hats
> To the pretty little Ratcatcher's Daughter."

"Doodle di," roared the crowd, "Doodle dee! Da dum doodle dee!"

"Do you want a baked potato?" said a demure voice at Brand's side. He looked down at the girl, of whom he had been acutely aware, and saw that the big man had withdrawn his arm from her slender waist. She was very fair, nearly as fair as Alix, with blonde curls and large blue eyes full of laughter, and he liked her smoky voice.

"No, I don't believe so," he said gravely. "I just ate. Could I get you a baked potato?"

"Oh no, thanks, I only asked because you looked like you was a stranger here, and baked spuds is the only eatables Charlie Morton sells. He likes his customers to go for the liquor."

"I guess he does," said Brand. "Will you let me buy you and your friends a drink, then?"

"What, all of us? Coo, you're a toff!"

They all chose gin. Brand paid for four double gins with a sovereign, picked up his change and kept a straight face as the two girls exchanged a knowing look. He gave half his attention to "The Ratcatcher's Daughter". He wanted to make her be the first to speak again.

"You're an American, aren't you?"

"Sure."

"My young lady friend met an American gentleman last week. He came in to the hat shop where she works and after he bought a hat for his wife he bought one for my friend too. Ever so generous, he was."

"Good," said Brand. "Did he go on being generous?"

The girl caught his eye, and giggled. "I believe you."

"'Ere, mate," said the man, "It's my turn to fake the rubber. What'll you 'ave?"

Mr. Cowell took a bow, took an encore, plunged into "Villi-kins and his Dinah". Four more double gins spread a pleasant glow round the table.

"What's your name?" said the girl.

"How about Jack?" said Brand.

She gave him a shrewd look. "You a sailor?"

"I'm a sailor."

"All right, then, what do we call you? Jack Ashore or Jack Adrift?"

"Jack Adrift will do," said Brand. "What's your name?"

"It's Milly, short for Amelia. Amelia Chester, how's that for a name for the halls?"

"Are you on the stage, Miss Chester?"

"Not yet I'm not, but I mean to be. This is my friend Fanny, and this is *her* friend Ben, and now we're all friends round St. Paul's. Ain't it fun?"

"Better fun than the Baltic," said Brand. "Hey waiter, same all round!" He was thawing out at last, thawing from those weeks of 20° below freezing, when every mast and spar of H.M.S. *Arrogant* was sheathed in ice as she ploughed to and fro on her endless patrol between Port Baltic and Hangö Head. He looked round the crowded room. Gobbling baked potatoes, lapping up the beer—not one of them was giving a damn about the war, whether in the Baltic or the Black Sea or Baltimore. "*The Chesapeake so bold*—" He discovered that he was singing.

"Sh, Jack!" Milly nudged him. "Give the artiste a chance!"

He had missed the gavel, and "Your own, your very own" whoever it was, but he couldn't miss the backdrop. It was a distortion, it was an insane caricature, but he recognized what it was meant to be, and so did the midshipmen at the big table on his right. One of them got up and shouted something drowned by the applause.

It was the fortress, Sveaborg.

Brand sat stunned. He heard nothing of the first verse, which the singer, a man in a blue jacket and bell-bottoms, began with a bold

"*What can we luckless sailors do? No fun comes to our share*—"

His eyes were fixed on those grotesque islands, rising as high as Mont Blanc on the backdrop, but still overtopped by the dome of the Nicholas Kirk, as he had seen it so often from far out at sea. "Posterity!" he heard Alexandra's voice, "Posterity! Stand here upon your own foundation . . . and put your trust not in the stranger's help!"

Brand struck his fist upon the table. "They shouldn't do it," he said. "God damn it, it isn't funny—"

"Listen," said Milly, "this is good!"

> "In Helsingfors they lay quite close, 'neath Cronstadt mole
> they crowd,
> They'll not come out and meet the foes whom once they
> dared so loud,
> Like to some worn-out battered hulk each gallant ship so
> stout,
> Behind the batteries does skulk—THE RUSSIANS WON'T
> COME OUT!"

"And bloody lucky for Old Charley Napier they didn't!" shouted a voice from the gallery.

Brand looked quickly at the midshipmen. He had recognized one of them, a mid. from the flagship, who had come aboard Arrogant more than once with orders from the Commander-in-Chief. The boy was half drunk and entirely angry: he was talking furiously to his friends.

> "The Arrogant and Hecla too, gave them a lesson rough,
> Though fighting to our lads was new they proved both
> smart and tough—"

"Precious little fighting they done," said the beery voice from the gallery.

"Hold your tongue, you infernal cad!" shouted the midshipman from the Duke of Wellington, jumping to his feet.

"Order! Order!" The chairman's gavel pounded.

"You stop that song then, do you hear? Don't let them make a mock of the Navy—"

"Nobody wasn't making a mock of the Navy!"

"You 'old your tongue, me young cock-sparrer—"

"Order, gents, please!"

It was an empty beer bottle, thrown down from the balcony, which started the real row on the floor of the Canterbury Music Hall. At one moment all six lads in Navy blue were on their feet, shouting; at the next, they were hitting out in

all directions, and grunting under the blows of the builders'
mates and gas fitters who welcomed any chance for a Saturday
night brawl. The women screamed dutifully, the waiters
charged into the throng. Brand, with a yell, got to the flagship
midshipman in time to prevent manslaughter.

"Not your dirk, sir! Just hit 'em—hard—"

Brand was hitting hard himself. He had an idea that his
new friend Ben was fighting on the Navy side, but a blow that
barely missed his eye made him see double, and after that he
hit out recklessly as the bo'suns' whistles began to shrill. He
had just time to realize that it must be the whistles of the
metropolitan police when a big stevedore hit him a smashing
blow in the stomach which drove him against the wall with
such force that the gas jets shook in the gaselier above his
head.

"Jack! Don't be a fool! Come on!"

He heard Milly Chester's amused voice from a considerable
distance. But her little hand was there, pulling at his own, and
she was somehow edging him away from the mêlée, out of a
side door, and down an iron stair.

"Come on, Jack! You don't want to get your name took,
and be 'ad up for battery!"

"But the midshipmen!"

"They're all right. Trust Charlie Morton to get them out
fast. He doesn't want a turn-up with their Captains."

They reached the stable yard, where an astounded groom
greeted them with "Wot the 'ell—?" and then they were out
into Upper Marsh, with the stables between them and the
mob round the door of the Canterbury, and another island of
light and noise on the corner which was the Bower Saloon.

"You all right, Jack?"

"Yes, fine. Is my face marked?"

"It's swelling something horrid, just there—"

"Don't touch it."

"Poor Jack. If only we had a bit of steak, or a nice cold knife
or something."

"Or a drink," said Brand, pulling her towards the Bower.

"You've 'ad plenty, Jack. See, my place ain't far away, in
Stangate Street. Better let me do something about that face,
hadn't you?"

"What'll your family say?"

267

She laughed ."I'm on my own."

"What about Ben and Fanny?"

"Bless you, they won't worry about us, they'll 'ave gone home. They're polled-up, over Stangate Bank—Ben's a longshoreman."

"Polled-up?"

"Oh—keeping house. Ben looks after her, if you know what I mean."

"Then, you silly Milly," said Brand, pulling her into his arms and kissing her, "I reckon you'd better start looking after me."

At the Bower public-house, where Brand insisted on spending a shilling on a bottle of gin, Stangate Street formed an ancient line of communication between the Upper Marsh and Stangate Reach. In the decay and wreckage of old Lambeth the street had somehow kept a note of elegance, for the little two-storey houses, where grimy curtains covered the small windows, still boasted wrought-iron doorknockers and pediments of Georgian swags and urns in peeling stucco.

"Joseph Grimaldi used to live next door to my place," Milly whispered.

"Who was Grimaldi?"

"Jack! Where was you brought up? One of the most famous clowns who ever lived—well, an actor he was reely."

"Sorry, Milly, I don't know much about the stage."

"Don't make such a row," she admonished him. "These aren't gay rooms, you know!"

She opened an area gate gently, and led Brand down four steps to the basement door. It opened directly into Milly's "place"—a single room, with an eye of fire winking in the hob grate, and two easy-chairs drawn invitingly in front of it. There was a red flock paper on the walls, with several chromolithographs of actresses and dancers. Cut-outs of kittens and puppies and wreaths of flowers had been carefully pasted on the screen which partly hid a large brass bed.

"You sit down," said Milly, taking off her bonnet and shawl, "and I'll see if I can find a bit of steak, and make us a cup of the old River Lea."

"Don't bother about steak, dear," Brand was pretty sure she

had no beef in the house. "My face doesn't look too bad in your mirror."

"Try holding the bread-knife against the bruise then."

Milly plumped down on her knees, and coaxed the fire to life with the bellows. A kettle singing on the hob came quickly to the boil, tea things were brought in from the back scullery, and Milly poured out with the grace of a stage duchess.

"Now," she said, fluffing up her fair curls with her free hand, "tell me why you and the Navy kids kicked up such a proper bull-and-cow up the Canterbury tonight!"

"It was the confounded song," said Brand. "And then that cad in the balcony, taunting us with not fighting. Is it our fault if those Russian bastards *wouldn't* fight?"

"I think you took it all too serious," said Milly.

"Oh, no, we didn't! Making a comic song about the *Arrogant*— look, that was *my* ship, the crack frigate of the Fleet. She was in action at Ekenäs and Bomarsund, and at Köpmansgrund last August, when I was sick—"

"Are those places in the Crimea?"

Brand set down his tea cup. "No, Milly. In the Baltic Sea."

"Oh yes," vaguely, "we was fighting up there, I know. I don't follow the war much. I like a good read though, now and then, when I get hold of a nice love story . . . Well, I'm glad we got clear of the Canterbury, if that was all you was kicking up hell-and-Tommy about. I'm sure I don't want Charlie Morton to tell his coves to keep me out of 'is hall for being mixed up in a breach of the peace! It's taken me weeks, I can tell you, to get him to let me sing in the competition for amateurs he's going to hold on New Year's night!"

"Are you really going to stand up there on that big stage and sing, Milly?"

"You got to make a start some time," she said briefly. "This is my big chance."

"Let's have a song now," suggested Brand.

"Ain't you heard one too many tonight already?" she countered, and the American laughed. He didn't know what sort of sounds that throaty, smoky voice would produce on a platform, but he knew she would be good to look at, with her piquant face—turn-up nose, wide laughing mouth, and all— and she had a tough, capable streak to help her handle an audience like the Canterbury's: she had proved that when she took command of the situation in the hall.

"You'll be a success," he predicted, "and I'd hate to think you'd missed your chance because you and your friends happened to have a quiet drink with me."

"Quiet?" Milly giggled. "You're a real fighter, Jack. You know, at first, when you gave the waiter a yellowboy for the drinks, Fanny and I thought you might be a soft touch, see? And I was going to tell you the tale about how my fancy man went for a soldier and left me with his baby, just to see how you'd take it, like? But I knew you wasn't soft as soon as you started fighting—"

"Did your fancy man go for a soldier?"

"Which one?" she said pertly.

"Yes, which one, Milly?"

The pretty vivid face hardened slightly. "You think I'm on the game, don't you? Well, I'm not. I've a good job, quite independent, at the dressmaker's in the Strand, and some day I'll be a singer on the halls myself—who knows? When I let a bloke come home with me it's only because I like him—it's only a lark to me, like it is to him—"

"Haven't you ever been in love, Milly?"

"Soppy about a boy, you mean? Not likely!"

"But you like to be loved?"

"Sometimes."

"Come over here."

Although her waist was slender, she was solid in his arms, with high round breasts that seemed to disengage a fruity odour of their own, and the hips beneath Brand's hand were round and firm too, wonderful hips. It was enough, for the first few moments, to lie sprawled in the big chair by the fireside, in the warm red room, holding her close and feeling her weight along his limbs, while the candlelight turned Milly's cheek to gold when she raised her lips for his kiss. He buried his face in her hair and inhaled the scent of youth and woman, letting his mind drift away on a tide of sensuality, I don't want no tragedy, I only want forgetfulness and ease. But then his body's claim became imperative, and by her quickened breath and clinging hands he knew she was ready to pay the claim in full, and after that there was nothing in the world but the wide clean bed, and Milly's breast beneath his own.

"There's one thing about a bit of love," said Milly practically, "it very often makes you hungry."

Brand nodded with his mouth full. It was two o'clock in the morning, and they were eating bread and cheese beside the fire.

"I missed me supper last night," the girl went on. "It was gone eight when I came back from work, and I was like a mad thing, hurrying to get off to the Canterbury—"

"Glad you went?"

"Not half I'm not!"

"Good thing I got the gin," said Brand.

"Don't give me any more, dear. I don't want to turn into an old haybag, ready to do the splits for a drop of blue rain."

Brand laughed. Old age and vice seemed far away from that bright face, refreshed by sleep, and the beautiful bosom revealed by Milly's wrap of white ruffled cotton. She had put on her petticoat when they got up, but no bodice, and yet there was nothing slatternly about her tumbled curls and the freely-offered glimpses of her breast. A beautiful, disciplined wanton, a girl who knew where she was going and would get there—Brand in that moment saluted Milly Chester as a future star. He sighed, looking into the red heart of the fire, and they were quiet together.

"You've been thinking about another girl, haven't you, dear?" Milly said at last.

"I've been thinking about you, Milly. You should know."

'Oh, I didn't mean when we was—in bed; I meant *now*. And maybe when you first came into the Canterbury, too."

Brand was silent, admitting her perceptiveness.

"What happened, Jack Adrift? Did she turn you down?"

"She ran away from me," he said from his sore heart.

Milly got up quietly and carried their plates into the back scullery. Then she came back, mixed herself a very small quantity of gin and boiling water, and said:

"You'd better tell me all about it."

It was another spilling, another solace, in its way almost as good as his body's satisfaction, to tell the little London girl the story of his lost love. Milly heard him out to the end before she spoke.

"How long were you ill, Jack?"

"About two or three weeks, I guess."

271

"And it was then you went to this place, Degaby?"

"Degerby. Yes, I got a chance to go ashore on my way to rejoin my ship in Barö Sound."

"You've never been back since?"

"No, but Captain Ryan has called in twice."

"Could you go to this other place, where they're all supposed to have gone off to?"

"Ekenäs? Hardly. It's a Russian strong point now."

"Then is *she* likely to 'ave gone there? After what you've told me how she felt about the Rooshians?"

There it was, of course. Milly had put her small, capable finger on the point which had always seemed wrong about the story of the departure to Ekenäs.

"You take a lot for gospel, don't you, Jack?"

"What do you mean?"

"Well, this girl Mary, who told you Alice said she was going back to Degaby. Did Mary's *father* 'ear her say it?"

"No, he'd come after me. He wasn't there."

"Then 'ow do you know it's true? Maybe Alice never said that at all! Girls can tell some thumping lies, you know, when they're sweet on a man theirselves."

"I guess I don't know much about girls, Milly."

"You know enough to get along with," she retorted. "What you'd ought to do, is think of some other people who'd know where Alice went. *Is* it Alice?"

"No, it's Alix, with an x. There are plenty of people, I suppose, but they're all in St. Petersburg or Helsingfors, and I can't get at them. That's what that damned song was all about?"

"Nobody here in London?" Milly persisted.

Brand stared at her. He had almost forgotten what Alix told him in Helsingfors of her sister's marriage to a Swedish diplomat, attached to the Legation in London. "There just might be somebody," he said slowly. "I've worried so about Alix in Finland, I never gave a thought to her friends right here in London. Thank you, Milly. Thank you more than I can say!"

Milly smiled. "Finished your drink? . . . Well, Jack dear, I think you ought to pad the hoof. It's as late as late—and tomorrow's Christmas."

Brand whispered with his cheek against her breast:

"Won't you let me stay till morning?"

"Better not. Oh, Jack, much better not! Because now I know you will be thinking about her—even when . . ."

She slipped from his arms and went to get his coat from the back room. When she returned to the fireside Brand had laid a little pile of sovereigns on the table.

" 'Ere, what's this?"

"A present for you, Milly."

She faced him with his shabby overcoat, bought months ago in Gothenburg, in her bare round arms.

"You can't afford it, Jack."

"Oh yes, I can."

"Remember what I told you? I'm not on the game. I brought you home because I liked you, see? You paid for the drinks and the bottle; you don't 'ave to leave five jimmy o' goblins for the bread and cheese!"

"That's my contribution to your career," he said, trying to smile. "Get yourself a pretty dress to wear when you sing at the Canterbury!"

"I s'pose you wouldn't come and cheer me on, on New Year's night?"

"Dear, I don't even know where I'll be on New Year's Day."

"Then goodbye, Jack Adrift!"

"Goodbye, sweet little Milly. Bless you."

Milly pulled the basement door open. The fog lifted, and by the light of one street lamp they could see the desolation of the Marsh, the jagged walls of half-demolished houses, and the raw newness of the railway embankment.

"London's changing all the time," said Milly. "What do you bet I'll be singing at the Canterbury myself, come next Christmas Eve?"

"Say," said Brand, with his foot on the area step, "what was that actor's name again, who lived next door?"

"Joe Grimaldi."

"Maybe someday Stangate Street'll be famous because of you."

Milly's chin went up. "Watch out for the top of the bills," she said, "and don't forget the name. Amelia Chester!"

CHAPTER FIFTEEN

THE TARRAS CHAIRMAN

A F E W hours later, when Brand's cab turned in to South Street, Mayfair, the bells of London's churches had finished the Sunday summons to their congregations. South Street was very quiet, as quiet as Stangate Bank when Brand tramped back along the river to the railway hotel : separated by several layers of the class structure from the underworld of the Thames foreshore.

The cab pulled up. Brand, paying the driver, checked the address hastily scribbled on an envelope in his hand with the number of a pleasant eighteenth century house built close to the pavement. It was a tall house, with nursery bars across the top floor windows, and the others discreetly veiled in thick net instead of the fashionable Nottingham lace; there was discretion, too, in the pale face of the footman who opened the front door and took Brand's name. A parlour opening off the vestibule was equally non-committal. Grey satin-striped wallpaper, a grey carpet, four mahogany chairs with plum coloured wool seats, and a water-colour of Drottningholm Castle in a gilt frame above the fireplace where a small coal fire burned, composed a room which gave the least possible indication of its owner's interests and tastes.

"What can I do for you, Mr. Endicott?"

"Mr. Gunnar Falk?"

The man who had entered the little parlour bowed. He was about thirty-five, clean-shaven, with fair hair very slightly tinged with grey, wearing a black frock coat and a well-tied black cravat.

"I'm glad to know you, Mr. Falk. I was afraid you might be out, or gone to church, before I could get here. I had to go to Halkin Street to find out your address."

"To the Swedish Legation? You didn't disturb His Excellency, I hope?"

"I don't think I disturbed anyone," said Brand. "I only asked the porter to tell me which attaché had married a Miss

Gyllenlöve, and he told me your name and address right away."

"Indeed!"

"Look, Mr. Falk, I know this is an awkward time to call, on a Sunday morning, Christmas Eve and all, but I've been serving in the Baltic Fleet, and I only arrived in London yesterday. I came to you as soon as I could, to ask for news of Miss Alexandra Gyllenlöve."

"Of Alix!" Mr. Falk's diplomatic calm was shaken at last. "Are you by any chance the American gentleman involved in a much publicized episode at Gothenburg, nearly a year ago?"

"I am, sir. Since then I've seen Miss Gyllenlöve at Helsingfors, and later on at Degerby, and last of all at Bomarsund, the day after the fort fell. Since that time I've been without news of her. Can you tell me where she is?"

Mr. Falk coughed. "My answer must be given without prejudice, because I have no authority from Miss Gyllenlöve to impart any such information. But as far as I know, she is still with Miss Willebrand at Degerby."

"No, she's not."

Brand's brief explanation of his visits to the island left the two men staring at each other.

"Can she really have gone back to Ekenäs?" said Brand.

"Ekenäs manor has been in Russian hands since September. The Russians moved their district headquarters there after they destroyed their own forts at Hangö Head."

"Then where *are* they? If the house at Degerby is shut up and Ekenäs occupied, where did Miss Agneta and Alexandra go?"

"The Mannerheims may have taken them in at Villnäs," said Mr. Falk without conviction.

"Did Madame Karamsin return to Finland?" asked Brand hopefully. "Perhaps Alix joined her again at the Villa Hagasund."

"Madame Karamsin is not in Finland. She is in Paris with her sister-in-law, Princess Mathilde Bonaparte."

"Mr. Falk, forgive me, but this means a great deal to me. Last spring, before I volunteered for the Navy, I asked Alix to marry me. She refused me then, but since . . . since that time, I've believed . . . she cared for me."

It was very hard to tell his story to this grey man with the long enquiring Swedish nose, but Brand ploughed desperately on !

"When did you *last* hear of Alix at Degerby? When did Madame Falk last have a letter from her?"

Gunnar Falk sighed.

"You touch upon a delicate problem there," he said, and pulled a bell. "Pray forgive me for keeping you standing, your visit was unexpected ! Allow me to offer you some refreshment."

The pale footman brought Madeira and seed-cake on a silver salver. Mr. Falk took advantage of the service to look keenly at his unexpected guest. His diplomatic training had taught him to evaluate men quickly, and he was impressed by the American. He said :

"Mr. Endicott, what I am about to tell you is unconventional but necessary to our understanding. The reason why you found me at home this morning, instead of attending the Swedish church as usual, is because my wife is indisposed. Er —we are expecting a happy event in the near future. Unfortunately Madame Falk has been in poor health since our little girl's birth a year ago, and her physicians now fear that her lungs may be affected. The utmost rest and care is advised for the present, and as soon as she is able to travel I intend to take her to San Remo."

"I'm sorry to hear about Madame Falk, sir, but—"

"But now you understand why I cannot allow her to be disturbed by any questioning or excitement about her sister. We have to avoid feverish attacks for her above all else—and if anyone in this world is calculated to bring on such attacks, it is Alexandra Gyllenlöve."

"Her own sister !"

"Yes, her own sister, Mr. Endicott. The heroine of the Apraxin engagement, the escapade at Gothenburg, the flight from St. Petersburg ! Do you know that Alix forged Madame Karamsin's name to an exit permit from Russia, so that the police spent the next two days at the Demidov palace, putting the whole household under interrogation to know how 'the Princess Demidova' had crossed the frontier while she was at home and in bed in St. Petersburg?"

"I didn't know it," said Brand, "but I'm sure Madame Karamsin came out of it all right. She has powerful friends."

"Powerful, yes; and the police were whipped off by the highest authority in the land; but not before Madame Karamsin was on the verge of a nervous collapse! I don't want that to happen to my wife, and I shall take very good care that it does *not*."

"You mean that if Alix came to your door today, asking for shelter, you would refuse it to her?"

"I should see that she was given shelter, if she required it. But not necessarily here."

"And what are you sheltering behind, Mr. Falk? Your wife's ill-health—or your country's neutrality?"

Gunnar Falk's face grew grim. "You are an American, I think, Mr. Endicott? Very well then. I am not prepared to entertain criticisms of Sweden's neutrality from a citizen of any neutral country."

"I consider myself a belligerent neutral," said Brand. "Put yourself in my place! If you had served on a British frigate for nine months in the Baltic, and had seen the Swedish fleet steaming round and round Gotland doing nothing, with the gunboats which would have enabled us to take Sveaborg *and* Cronstadt this very summer— why, you might take another view of neutrality."

"And Sweden's view of neutrality," retorted Falk, "is that of a country which has waged war with Russia since long before Virginia was a colony. When Napoleon was beaten, we Swedes had been fighting Russia under King after King, in campaign after campaign, for a total of sixty years. That, sir, is a more impressive record than one summer cruise in the Baltic!"

"All right. I'm sorry I brought up the question of neutrality. I reckon I was irritated because you seemed to belittle Alix—"

"I don't belittle Alix—nobody could. She is a beautiful and charming girl who has been hopelessly mismanaged. A delicate mother, a clever and ambitious father, a childhood running wild at Ekenäs and then permission to associate with all the extreme nationalist elements in Finland—the Runebergs and the Snellmans and their so-called literary circles—all that has produced a very wayward and troublesome young lady. I fear you're only the last in a long list of those who have suffered from Alexandra's caprice."

"I love her," said Brand.

Gunnar Falk coughed. "If she—er—still returned your affection, surely she would have found means to communicate with you?"

Brand ignored this. "What about her father? Is he another of the relatives you're protecting your wife from?"

"Since we are speaking confidentially, sir, I'll admit Count Gyllenlöve is one of our family problems. You know, of course, that he is in the Russian civil service, and very highly regarded at St. Petersburg? The latest news of my father-in-law is that he is married."

"Married!"

"Last month. He has been—er—attached for some time to a Madame Ourov, the wife of a banker in Moscow. Well, with more tact than the *mari complaisant* usually shows in such cases, Monsieur Ourov died in August. His widow lost no time in marrying again."

"Good luck to them," said Brand. "Does this make any difference to you?"

"Only in so far as my wife was *most* distressed," said Gunnar Falk solemnly. "The new Countess Gyllenlöve is a woman not thirty years old, so the advent of a second family is highly probable. This is never an agreeable prospect for grown-up children."

"Worse things happen at sea," said Brand. He grinned. "I begin to understand your real problem, Mr. Falk. You're caught in the cross-fire between your wife's father, the Russian official, and her sister, the Finnish patriot. Very difficult! Well, I won't embarrass you further. I'll go back to Halkin Street and see if any other Swedish attaché is courageous enough to help me!"

"To do what?"

"To find out where the Finnish prisoners were taken after Bomarsund."

Gunnar Falk got up. He had flushed. "Surely you don't expect to find Alexandra among *them*?"

Brand rose too. "It's possible," he said hoarsely. "I—she was very much upset . . . I had a message which . . . only last night" (he had been going to say "in the small hours of this

278

morning", and quickly corrected himself) "it was suggested to me that the message I got was wrong. Suppose she didn't go 'back to Degerby' but 'with the Degerby prisoners'? How can I find out where they are?"

"You don't need to go to the Swedish Legation for that," said the diplomat. "All the surviving Finnish prisoners are in Lewes jail."

The harsh words burned in the grey room, where the thick net curtains shut out the pale sunshine of Christmas Eve.

"The—survivors?" Brand got out.

"Thirty of them died before the middle of December from pneumonia or neglected wounds, or both."

"How do you know all this?"

"The Swedish community in London is not so heartless as you appear to believe, Mr. Endicott. The pastor of our Lutheran church—who happens to be a connexion of my own—has visited Lewes, and through one of the local clergymen, distributes comforts and gifts to the prisoners. The members of the Swedish church subscribe to these, and my wife, who was born in Finland, has given generously."

"Naturally," said Brand without sarcasm. "Is there still—illness and suffering among them?"

"At least there is no real hardship apart from close confinement. Governor Mann is a humane person, and the prisoners help each other a great deal. The English clergyman has described one remarkable young woman who helped with the sick, and kept up the spirits of the others at recreation by telling Finnish legends and reciting patriotic poems—you know the sort of thing—"

"I know Alix," said Brand.

Gunnar Falk's hands slowly clenched. "You don't mean—you don't think it could be Alix?"

" 'Posterity, stand here upon your own foundation—' " said Brand. "Can't you hear her?"

"Impossible! In every way, impossible! This is a Finnish girl, a peasant; her name as the Rector gave it doesn't remotely resemble Gyllenlöve. It was a perfectly ordinary name, the kind of name you come across every day in Stockholm, if I could but remember it—"

"I can," said Brand, and his voice broke. "It's Anna Larsson!"

The Scotch express was late at Aberdeen, but even so it was

still dark in that northern city when Brand Endicott arrived there on the last morning but one of the old year. The same changes were going on in Scotland as in Lambeth Marsh; in the twelve months since his previous visit the railway had moved on from its old terminal at Ferryhill to a new covered station at Guild Street, and a new goods line was moving down the quay. Brand gave his portmanteau and his address to a wizened porter in a blue Highland bonnet. He was travelling in decidedly better style on this trip, with solid leather luggage and a handsome overcoat of heavy cheviot cloth, for which Tarras and Company had paid.

"We owe you an apology for the Gothenburg affair, my boy," Mr. Arthur Tarras had said. "I'm putting you through the books as having been on half pay as captain of the *Girdleness* since last February. We must reward the sailors who fight Britain's battle for her—that's my opinion."

"Every sailor hasn't my good luck," said Brand. He thought of the shipmates he had left behind at Portsmouth. Morgan and Campbell were dead, and laid in the mass grave of the cholera victims at Bomarsund, but Edgeworthy and how many other Able Seamen had been paid off just before Christmas, with no prospect of employment until the Finland ice went out in April? He pocketed the Tarras guineas thoughtfully.

Now he was on his way to see the chairman of the Tarras Line, that prejudiced and obstinate old lady who still held the pursestrings of the Company, and he walked off up Market Street, the old Putachie-side, rehearsing what he had to say to her. The sky began to lighten behind the slate roofs and narrow Baltic spires of Aberdeen. This was a northern city like Helsingfors, although without Helsingfors classical harmonies, and there was a look of the Gulf of Finland in the ice-rimmed water of the harbour. Could Alix ever learn to be happy here?

He turned into Union Street, the city's main artery; noted that the new railway tracks to the north were being laid along the bed of the old Denburn, and stopped for a moment to watch the workmen coming on the job, blowing on their hands and slapping their chests in the bitter December morning. This was the thing which had most interested him when he first came to Europe; the railway network which was beginning to form behind the principal seaports. This was where he had expected his own commercial future to lie, when he first took the *Girdleness* out past the North Pier, Norway-bound. And now his life, his love, and his future were bound up in the war with Russia.

Opposite the County Rooms Brand turned left and made his way to a tall dark house at the far end of Dee Street. Aberdeen had expanded westward since John Tarras, a native of Fraserburgh, took his young wife to live there in 1806, the fifth year of their marriage; granite squares and garden terraces attracted the new generation of prosperous shipowners. But Isabella Tarras declined to move, though her mansion was too big for a widowed lady with two maids and a gardener-factotum. "My things will get a scatter soon enough," she liked to say, "but as long as I live I'll keep a grip of them."

Unlike the other houses on Dee Street, Mrs. Tarras' home had a large garden, now frozen over, between the solid granite building and the public path. The entry to the garden was through a heavy iron gate with an arch which supported a coal gas lamp, still lighted, and swinging in the winter wind. It never failed to remind Brand of the entrance to a graveyard.

There was nothing funereal about the vestibule, when an elderly maid opened the front door. A rush of warmth and the scent of good food swept out to envelop the American as the maid dropped her old-fashioned curtsy and said :

"Come away, sir, come away ! We've gotten Maister Arthur's telegraphs, and the mistress has been like a hen on a hot girdle expecting ye, and wantin' her breakfast—"

"The train was late, Betty," said Brand. He squared his shoulders and opened the dining-room door.

In memory, his grandmother had always appeared to him as at least six feet tall. The lady trailing black velvet skirts across the carpet as she came to greet him was not, in fact, above average height, although her white "cockernony bonnet" of fine Malines lace gave her two extra inches, and her extremely erect carriage added at least one more. At seventy-three, Isabella Tarras had only a few threads of grey in her dark hair, and brown eyes as observant as a girl's looked keenly from her plump and wrinkled face. It would never have occurred to the old Scotswoman to kiss her grandson, but she shook hands with him warmly, and exclaimed :

"Come away, John, come into the fire; you'll be perished with the cold!"

Then, as the young man advanced further into the room, and the grey morning light from the bay window fell on his haggard face, Mrs. Tarras faltered in her welcome, and said in a different tone:

"Eh, laddie, you've turned to look very like your grandfather."

"Do you find me changed, then, ma'am?" said Brand, trying to speak lightly.

"You're tired, that's what it is," said Mrs. Tarras, still in that fluttered tone. "Ye'll be none the worse of a dram while Betty makes the tea. That trains is enough to kill a body."

Nine in the morning was early for whisky, but Brand took the dram-glass with pleasure, and with a formal word of good wishes drank the measure off. His grandmother poured less than half a glass for herself and sipped it slowly.

"I trust you've enjoyed good health, ma'am, this past year?" he said politely. The year of the Russian War, the year so momentous to Alexandra and himself, had left no trace upon the hale old woman, nor upon the room where she received him. The mahogany chairs were arranged in their usual order against the walls, the mahogany sideboard held the customary decanters of whisky, port and sherry; his grandfather's flat-topped dask, at which Mrs. Tarras now worked, still occupied most of the window space and—he couldn't help glancing in their direction—the black silhouettes of Lieutenant John Tarras, R.N., and Lieutenant Harry Tarras, R.N., still hung on either side of the marble mantel.

"I've kept very well, John. Now here comes Betty; sit in about and get something to eat."

When the maid had left the room Brand said:

"There's just one thing I'd like to settle before we have breakfast, ma'am."

"What's that?"

"I want to pay back the money I borrowed on your letter of credit. I needed some of it for urgent expenses before I joined the Navy."

"I got the drafts from Stockholm," she said non-committally.

Brand laid money on the desk. "I think that covers it," he said. "Thank you."

"You've given me too much."

"That's interest on ten months' loan at three per cent."

"Very good." Without comment Mrs. Tarras swept the sovereigns into the top drawer of her desk. Brand noticed that the telegrams he had helped his uncle to draft were arranged in a neat pile under a granite paperweight.

He pulled out her chair at the head of the table and asked the question which had been in his mind for months.

"Grandmother—when you didn't cancel my letter of credit last February—you didn't forget it, did you? You really wanted me to be free to make up my mind?"

Mrs. Tarras looked up at him with a hint of youthful mischief in her rosy face.

"Put it down to experience, laddie. I just wanted to see what you would do. And now tell me about your passage from the Gulf to Portsmouth."

Brand told her, from the far side of a breakfast table loaded with good Scottish fare. There was tea at Mrs. Tarras' place and excellent coffee at Brand's, and between, an array of sparkling silver dishes holding eggs and bacon, smoked kippers, a cold ham and a glistening brown mould of potted head. There were oatcakes, bannocks, scones, and a plate of the bakery rolls called baps and butteries without which no Aberdeen breakfast was complete, and there were several kinds of jam and jelly. Brand ate heartily. Mrs. Tarras took tea and toast, and listened; he might have seen, if the room had been lighter, that her hands were trembling. But he was well embarked on the narrative no one had asked him to tell since his return.

"We had some mighty bad days at the end of November, ma'am. When the ships of the line went home, Captain Rundle Watson, in *Imperieuse*, took command of the squadron, and we patrolled from Älvsnabben to Hangö, and Hangö south to Dager Ort, to keep both the Gulfs blockaded. My captain used to run as far east as Nargen, even after the ice began forming—he was the only captain who dared to do it after the snowstorms started. How it snowed off Dager Ort! There were strong easterly gales blowing day and night—"

"When did you get your sailing orders, then?"

"First of December. The rendezvous was Kiel, but we parted company with the squadron east of Bornholm island."

"And you anchored on the 20th. *Arrogant* took her time."

"Our job was to round up the stragglers. Captain Yelverton was determined that *Arrogant* should be the last ship to leave the Gulf, and the last through the Kattegat. And she was!"

It was much easier to talk to Mrs. Tarras than he had expected. Where before there had been coldness and criticism, there was now lively interest, and even softness in her dark eyes. She was asking sympathetically about his illness after Bomarsund.

"What did the doctors say started it?"

"One said it was the raw fruit and vegetables we ate, another said it was contaminated water. I don't believe they know much about it yet."

"But you made a good recovery. You have a strong constitution, just like me . . . Now, if you're not for another cup of coffee, we'll sit round to the fire, and not ring for Betty to clear away till we've had our talk."

Brand looked for a hassock, which he remembered the old lady liked beneath her feet, and sat down in what had been his grandfather's chair.

"Your uncle has been bombarding me with telegrams," said the chairman of the Tarras Line. "The last was about 'a definite proposition of yours, of which he heartily approved'. Arthur and you must have had some busy days in London."

"After the holiday—yes, we did."

"When I got Arthur's first despatch, just saying you were back and had a new plan, d'ye know I some thought ye might be thinking of staying on in the Navy?"

"Oh no, ma'am. We Baltic boys are fair weather sailors, as I've been reminded a score of times since I came back. We're all on the beach now, even my captain, and Captain Sulivan, and all the rest of them—right up to Admiral Napier."

"Napier's finished," Mrs. Tarras spoke abstractedly. Her eyes were on the silhouettes of her dead sons. It might have been another boy, her own John, talking of "my captain". She remembered how he had idolized Captain Curzon, who had written such fine things about him after Navarino . . .

"The Royal Navy keeps the seven seas, John, not just the Baltic. Ye've done so well, it would be quite possible to get you a commission, if you would rather the Navy than the Tarras Line."

"What d'you mean I've done so well? I got promoted to Seaman Gunner, with twopence extra pay a day, but I'm not cut out for a sea officer. And I don't want to spend my life in the British Navy. You keep forgetting I'm an American citizen."

Mrs. Tarras ignored this. "Then I got another message, more mixed-up-like than the first, which gave me an inkling that you wanted to command the *Girdleness* again."

"She's snug at her berth at Regent Quay, isn't she, along with *Devanha, Balgownie* and *Cornhill*?"

"You know fine none of my Baltic ships can put to sea under war conditions. Or rather, you know I wouldn't risk them."

"Like Admiral Napier. No, I don't aim to command the *Girdleness*."

"Well, what *do* you want?"

"I want to go on fighting Russia."

Mrs. Tarras, without taking her eyes from Brand's face, turned back the front of her velvet skirt from the heat of the fire, revealing six inches of black taffeta underskirt, before she spoke.

"What will you do then? Re-enlist in the spring?"

"Hang about till the spring? Worse still, go on hanging about at sea until whoever gets the Baltic command makes up his mind to attack Sveaborg—when the Admiralty gives him the gunboats and the mortars to do it with?"

"Well?"

"I want to command my own ship at sea. Attack the Russians and their Infernal Machines wherever I can, and make a profit for you at the same time."

"How?"

"You know very well that the only ships which can move freely in the Baltic now are American ships. President Pierce has just made it clear in his State of the Union message that such ships and their captains have the whole power of the United States behind them. Your Aberdeen fleet is laid up and the London freighters working the coasts, but my uncle knows of an American-registerd ship for sale at London, and if the registry were transferred to me, an American citizen, I could sail for any Baltic port that's free of ice, with any cargo you like, and come back with hemp and flax for the Aberdeen mills, in spite of the blockade."

His grandmother rubbed her nose. "Ye've something actually in view? What is she?"

"A snow brig—the very thing for the Baltic trade."

"Ye would need six or eight of a crew for that. Of course you would sign on some of the Tarras deckhands?"

"If I can get one or two men used to Navy discipline, who can handle a light gun."

"God preserve me! You surely don't expect to use a gun to get a cargo o' hemp out of Malmö!"

"I told you I wanted to *fight the Russians*, grandmother."

"Do ye expect a snow brig with a light gun to engage a Russian warship, man?"

"I'm not thinking about the warships. 'The Russians won't come out'—I heard a comic song about that in London; but their agents will! Your Mr. Svensson for one, and others like him, who use the Prussian ports for running guns to Russia, and send articles contraband of war north to Haparanda and then into the Grand Duchy—"

"We dismissed Sven Svensson as our agent in Gothenburg after we had your report that he was trading with the enemy."

"That doesn't cancel my account with him, ma'am. I want to come up with him some day when he's running supplies to Russia and send a shot across his bows—"

"And if the contrabanders sail in convoy ye've a very good chance of getting caught yourself."

"My friend Joe Ryan knows every creek and cove in the Baltic. We won't be caught."

"Ye're not going to ship this man Ryan, are you?"

"As mate, if he'll agree."

"It would be a great mistake, in my opinion, to take on some wastrel Irishman—"

"Joe's not a wastrel. He hasn't built up a big business like the Tarras Line, but he makes a decent living, and he knows the Baltic trade from the level of the small stores and the country fairs. He's a man I can rely on, and that's important. You see, I'm not the simpleton I was when I first came here from the United States. A year ago I listened to everybody, took everybody's advice, and where did I end up? In jail at Gothenburg. Joe was the first person, the only person, who showed me any human kindness then. He's the man I want for mate aboard the *Duchess*."

286

"Is that the brig?"

"That's her present name: *Hertiginnan av Finland*."

"Well," said Mrs. Tarras, "that's quite a story you've had to tell."

Brand loked at her hopefully.

"The purchase of a new ship is a real serious matter to a Company with four of its fleet laid up. However, I was never one to put all my eggs in one basket. I've investments in the Aberdeen tea clippers and the Australian wool and passenger trade. I'm not at the back of my hand for money, but whether I ought to finance a privateer is quite another matter."

"My grandfather did a bit of privateering in the old days, didn't he?"

Mrs. Tarras laughed, and the lively young woman who had lived through the Napoleonic Wars looked out from her brown eyes.

"Aye, he did that, when he was a young skipper in the coastal trade. He never went ashore without a pistol in his belt in those days, for fear the press-gang would set upon him in some English port. 'Isabella,' he used to say to me, 'I'll never be pressed alive'."

"Well then, grandmother—"

"I'll think the matter over," said the old lady. "I won't say another ship wouldn't come in quite handy. Arthur is aye at me to convert the Line to steam, but I tell him there's plenty money to be made yet under sail. For one thing, there's bound to be a big demand for tombstones and monuments after the war, and there's our chance to carry freight for the Aberdeen granite works . . . Aye, we could use five vessels instead of four in the local trade, once the orders begin to come in for the monumental masons."

"You're looking far ahead, ma'am."

"Further than you are," Mrs. Tarras said, but not unkindly. "Well, we'll leave it at that for the present. I'll write to Arthur and get full particulars of the brig as soon as the New Year be bye."

"Grandmother, can't you write today?"

"Oh fie, this needs serious consideration. I would like to see you cheat the Russians and run the blockade, for mark my words the blockade has done more harm to British trade than it's done to the Czar of Russia. But if it's a question of

287

American registry, could we not come to some arrangement with this man Ryan to take on the *Molly-O*?"

"She's not heavy enough for armament. And I want to be able to mount a carronade."

"Ye might as well say a cannon! Do you expect to pick up a carronade in the first ship's chandler's shop you come to? And even without armour, there's the transfer of the registration. Ye'll have to see the American Legation about that, and then there's the Letters of Marque to be issued. Na, na, this is not a thing to be done in a hurry."

"Grandmother, for God's sake!"

Brand's self control broke. He buried his face in his hands, and his long painful breath was very like a sob.

"What ails you, laddie?"

Mrs. Tarras shook down her velvet skirt and rose in concern. She stood beside her grandson, one hand hovering undecidedly over his thick sandy hair. He did not move, and she changed the intended caress to a brief pat on his shoulder.

"John, you're fair worn out, and not much wonder. Away upstairs to your bed and get a good sleep, and we'll speak it over again at dinner time."

Then Brand looked up and caught at her fingers, and the hard young face, weather-beaten by the Baltic gales, reminded Isabella Tarras so much of her dead husband that she clenched her free hand in the lace fichu at her old breast, where the rebellious life still burned. He said:

"But there isn't any time to lose!"

The old woman, still with her hand in his, said slowly:

"What way not? Is there something in all this ye havena told me?"

"Grandmother, there's a girl."

In a flash of illumination Mrs. Tarras exclaimed, very loudly: "The girl at Marstrand!"

"No, I didna ring the bell for ye, Betty, and you know it fine," said the mistress composedly to the elderly maid. "But since ye're here, you may as well clear the table. And put some coal on the fire."

The interruption gave Mrs. Tarras time to command herself. She sat down at the big desk, put on her spectacles, and pretended to look through the telegrams from London. When the

288

door finally closed behind the servant she said sharply to Brand, who had followed her:

"Draw in about a chair, man, and sit down. Desks are not for sittin' on."

"I'm sorry, ma'am."

"So it's the lass from Marstrand, is it? I thought we hadna heard the last of her . . . Ye better tell me the whole thing."

Thus for the second time in a week Brand told Alexandra's story to a woman. He told more than he had told Milly Chester, suppressing nothing but the details of her flight from St. Petersburg, but emphasizing Alexandra's hatred of Russia, her belief in a free Finland, and her devoted following of himself to Bomarsund. It was impossible to guess his grandmother's reactions. She heard him out to the end with calm, as if, after proposals of privateering, a girl in prison held no surprise for her, and her first comment was entirely practical.

"But are you sure this girl in Lewes is her?"

"Oh, there's no mistake. Mr. Falk and I drove to the Swedish church together and interviewed the pastor. He'd never seen Alix himself, but the English Rector had described her exactly . . . and— and she'd sent him a brooch to sell, to buy stuff for the prisoners, that I knew as soon as I saw it. Golden leaves— I've seen that brooch before," said Brand, and his voice grew thick.

"But you didna go off post-haste to Lewes yourself?"

"Falk advised against it. He put matters on foot at once, through the Swedish Legation, to get an order of release, and then we'll go down to Lewes and take her away."

Mrs. Tarras shifted the granite paperweight. "What on earth would be her motive in going off with the war prisoners? I never heard tell of sic' a thing!"

"Nor did I; but then that's Alix! Finland means everything to her; she was so certain the Finns would rise against Russia, and now they haven't—" His awkward gesture expressed some of Alix's deep distress of spirit.

"There's no chance at all of a Finnish revolt?"

"Oh—if Napier had gone up to Sveaborg and caught the Russian warships there last April, or if Plumridge's squadron hadn't made that fool attack on Gamla Karleby, there might have been a chance. But those were the two big mistakes, and there was no getting over them, in spite of Bomarsund."

"And this is what Alice is most concerned about?"

"Finland, and what happens to Finland? Yes."

"It's not natural," said Mrs. Tarras.

"I say it is. I remember my mother's stories about William Wallace, and Robert Bruce the liberator, when the Scots won their freedom from the English . . . and the way Alix looks at it, that's just where the Finns stand now."

"I say it's not natural," repeated the old lady. "A young lass needs a man and a twa-three bairns more than she needs politics."

"I aim to be the man," said Brand.

"Are you sure?"

"She's the only one for me, I know."

"But I do *not* like all that running away," said Mrs. Tarras with a sigh. "What are ye going to do with her once she's set at liberty? Could she not stay at her brother-in-law's quietly for a while, till we see how the war turns out? You'll have enough to do, if and supposing you go to sea again, without dancing attendance on a young lady!"

"Falk says a pardon will hardly carry permission to remain in England. Alix is technically a Russian, you see. That's why I want us to get married right away."

"That damned Russians!" said Mrs. Tarras. "They've upset the whole apple-cart."

"That's why we're fighting them, so they don't get a chance to upset it again."

"Aye, but in the meantime—! John, I won't pretend I'm pleased about this. I thought when we got you here to Europe you would take up with some nice lass that we knew all about —one of Arthur's girls, maybe. Bell, now, or even Flora, would make you a fine wife. That would be a good match for the Tarras Line."

"I forgot about the Tarras Line as soon as I saw Alix."

"Aye, ye gave us proof of that at Gothenburg," said the old lady tartly. "Ye still need the Tarras money, I notice, to help you on your way! Where would you be if I told you flatly I wouldna finance your venture? You would have to wait a while for your marriage at that rate."

"Oh, no, I wouldn't," said Brand coolly. "I came to you first, grandmother, because Uncle Arthur thinks the project sound. He's willing to invest in it, and I thought you were interested in beating the blockade. But if you're not, I'll raise money for the *Duchess* in another way."

"How?"

"I'll mortgage my house in Portland."

"The house Miss Brand left to you? That would be a pity. It's a good solid house, you said; you should try to keep your title free."

Brand shrugged. "It'll raise a good solid mortgage."

"Aye, you're very tenacious, John. Verra determined! And what will you do with your wife while you're at sea chasing the Russian agents?"

"She'll sail with me."

"Preserve me! Tak' a lassie to the Baltic in the dead o' winter, with the sea full of dangers, and the enemy God knows where?"

"Didn't you sail with my grandfather when you were first married, and dodge the French down-Channel, in the old lugger that was the first ship in the Line?"

"Ah, my laddie! That was another war and another world than this."

"Only to you," said Brand Endicott. "This is our world and our war. For Alix and me there's only—now."

CHAPTER SIXTEEN

THE BONAPARTES AT HOME

AFTER the green Yule there was a white New Year.

In London the snow started falling late on New Year's Day, continuing all through Tuesday and part of Wednesday, while water pumps froze and householders spread ashes on the slippery streets. Then a strong south-easterly gale blew the storm away over Kent and Sussex, until snow covered the spur of the Downs on which the town of Lewes stood, and by Friday afternoon, when Governor Mann sent for Alix Gyllen-löve, it had softened the harsh red brick of the War Prison and made a fantastic pattern on the spikes above the jail's thirty-foot wall.

If one of the more amiable warders had been sent to fetch her, Alix might have tried to find out the reasons for her summons. But the fellow was surly, and she was dull and half asleep, for as the women prisoners of war grew weaker they slept more, and Tora Kivi since her husband's death had spent hours drowsing with her face buried in her pillow like a sick animal. So Alix trudged along the draughty corridor in silence, was pushed in at the Governor's door, and dropped the bob-curtsy required of the female prisoners before she even raised her heavy eyes.

"Now then, my girl!" said Governor Mann. He was nervous and therefore pompous; the prison doctor, by his side, raised his eyebrows at the staccato voice. "These gentlemen have come down from London on business concerning you. Stand up straight and answer any questions they may put . . . She speaks English, gentlemen."

Alix turned to face a stranger in a black coat—and her sister's husband.

"Is this the woman, sir?" the stranger said, and Alix's hand flew to her trembling mouth. Gunnar Falk gave her no chance to speak. He bowed slightly and coldly in her direction and said at once:

"This is Anna Larsson. I identify her as a native of the

Grand Duchy of Finland, born at Ekenäs in the Government of Nyland in the year 1834. I declare further that her father and sister are alive and are both personally known to me."

"Thank you, Mr. Falk. That appears to be a valid and complete identification."

"Am I to understand that the Home Office is satisfied?" worried Governor Mann.

"That is correct, sir. I now hand you the order of release for Anna Larsson, and formally require you to deliver her from Lewes War Prison to the guardianship of her family and friends."

"Her family being, I presume, in Finland," said the Governor, taking the stiff roll of paper. "I ought to say, on behalf of the Mayor and Councillors of Lewes, that a discharged prisoner must not be permitted to become a burden on the local rates."

"No fear of that, sir," said the Home Office representative with a smile. "Mr. Falk assumes the lady's guardianship."

"Well, Larsson!" The Governor turned to Alix. "My congratulations! Have you nothing to say to such good news? No word of thanks to Mr. Falk for coming here on your behalf?"

"I'm grateful to you all," said Alix faintly. "What—what must I do now?"

"You must wait in the anteroom until the official documents are signed," the Governor told her, and Alix turned blindly, almost stumbling over a chair which the prison doctor, who was to witness the Governor's signature, moved out of her way in time.

"Someone else to see you!" He whispered it, with a meaning look, as he turned the handle of the door to the anteroom. Alix braced herself. She expected to face her sister. She found herself in the arms of Brand.

Then the ice round Alexandra's heart melted, and she sobbed wildly, like a child, with her head on Brand's breast, aware of nothing but his kisses, and his voice whispering, "Alix, darling . . . crazy girl!" and "Safe, I've got you safe!"

"Now then, Alix!" said Gunnar Falk's cold voice behind them. "I imagine you have no desire to linger here?"

She went forward timidly and held out her hand. "Thank you, brother-in-law. It was very good of you to come. How—how did you know where to find me?"

"Ask him," said the Swede, with a nod at Brand. "He'll tell

you the whole story later. Ah, Dr. Burton!" (as the prison doctor entered) "are we free to leave now? Has Miss Larsson any—er— belongings which we ought to send for?"

"I have nothing," Alix declared. "But Tora—I can't go away without saying goodbye to Tora, and poor little Henry!"

"Gently, my dear." Dr. Burton stood foresquare against the door leading back into the prison. "An emotional scene with Mrs. Kivi will do neither one of you any good! She'll be all right; nature takes remarkable care of women at a time like this, and I shouldn't wonder if you were able to do a great deal more for her and all her fellow prisoners, once you are outside these gates. Miss Larsson has been my right hand, sir," he added to Falk. "She well deserves her liberty."

Gunnar Falk bowed. He picked up a cloak of crimson cloth, laid ready on a chair, and put it round Alexandra's shoulders.

"The Governor wishes you to leave by the yard gate," said the doctor. "It will be less public than the main entrance."

They went through a long passage to the open yard where the prisoners took exercise. Alix looked up instinctively and said:

"This is where we were able to see the sky."

The sky was grey with the promise of new snow, and the world beyond the prison walls was revealed, when the turn-keys dragged the great gates open, as nothing more than a muddy highroad, with a few country children trailing home from school and a stable lad leading a horse back from the blacksmith's. Alix drew her first long breath of freedom.

"Doctor," she said, "is that St. John's graveyard, on the far side of the road?"

"Yes, my dear."

"You told me it was very near. I would like—please! to see where the prisoners are buried, before I go."

"Morbid and quite unnecessary!" fumed Gunnar Falk.

"Twenty-eight Finland men are buried there," she told him. "There is to be a little memorial to them, by and by. But none of us has ever seen the grave. Our friends were carried there by strangers."

"If it's what she wants!" said Brand roughly. "Doctor, you lead the way."

The churchyard built round the tower of St. John sub Castro was ancient and not large. It was not far to the grave where the Finnish prisoners had been laid together, in a spot well protected by thickets and thorn hedges from the south-east wind. A thin blanket of snow clung to the newly-levelled turf.

"*Is that* the memorial?" whispered Alexandra.

"That wooden headboard? Most certainly not," Dr. Burton reassured her. "The memorial itself will be of stone. But Colonel Grahn thought, and the Rector quite agreed with him, that such a grave should be marked from the beginning."

"And all their names will be written on the stone?"

"Just as you see them here."

Alexandra read aloud:

> "ERECTED BY THE FINLANDERS,
> RUSSIAN PRISONERS OF WAR,
> MEMORIAL OF THEIR COUNTRYMEN
> AND FELLOW PRISONERS WHO DIED
> DURING THEIR CAPTIVITY IN
> LEWES WAR PRISON"

The three men had removed their hats. The wind was blowing from the east again, the old Baltic weather, and a few stray snow-flakes fell on Alexandra's crimson cloak. Brand, watching, saw her lips move. Falk and the doctor thought she was praying. Brand, who loved her, knew better when he saw her thin hands clench. In this ancient land beneath Mount Caburn, where the Roman camp and the tower of the Norman conqueror, de Warrenne, trailed invisible banners of old warfare high above the Saxon Downs, Alexandra Gyllenlöve was thinking of the war as yet so far from being won.

"The end of the road from Bomarsund," she said strangely. And then, "Even on their gravestone—'*Russian* prisoners of war'! Finland will avenge that insult—some day."

"Where are you taking me? To London?" she said, when she was in the hired cab waiting beside the prison, and they were driving slowly towards the High Street.

"I've engaged rooms at the White Hart Hotel," said Falk. "You'll find fresh clothing there, and we'll discuss the future in comfort, over an early dinner."

"This is Kristina's cloak, isn't it? I know the scent she wears."

"Yes, I borrowed some things of Kristina's for you. She doesn't need them at present."

"Why not? She isn't ill?"

Falk took refuge in "happy event" and "interesting situation" and Alix smiled.

"You mean she's having another baby, so very soon? Oh, don't look so shocked, Gunnar! We learned not to mince our words in Lewes War Prison."

At the famous old coaching inn the Christmas decorations were still bright, for there remained one day to Twelfth Night, and in an upstairs sitting-room reserved by Falk there were more sprays of holly in polished brass jugs, and the blaze of a log fire reflected on oak panelled walls. A discreet elderly maid hovered at the door of a connecting room.

"This good woman will look after you," said Falk to Alix. "You'll find port wine and biscuits in the bedroom. I want you to drink some wine before you change your clothes—it will do you good."

"You're very thoughtful, brother-in-law." Alix gave Brand a long wistful look and let the maid lead her away. To the American it seemed as if she had scarcely realized his presence.

"Well?" he said to Falk, when the door was closed. "What do you think of her?"

"Think? I think Alexandra's quixotic impulses have cost her dear, this time—not to mention what they have cost me."

"I don't give a damn what they cost you. I mean, what do you think of her state of health? It's my opinion she's worn out and famished, and not in any condition to travel to France tonight."

"I'm afraid there's no option about that. The Anna Larsson farce went well enough with those fools at the prison, but the Home Secretary knows her real name; and if it were to leak out that the daughter of Count Gyllenlöve, the Russian Rail Commissioner, had been released privately from prison, there would be a regular scandal in the public prints. My undertaking was to get her out of England without delay."

"One night's rest!" said Brand.

"My dear Endicott, it is the greatest piece of good luck to have found a Swedish freighter at Newhaven, to get us away without formalities; and Captain Ericsson must sail with the tide."

"Then let me explain the plan to her."

"I am legally the person to do that."

"Legality be damned," said Brand. "For the past hour you've done nothing but treat her like a criminal! She's shocked and exhausted, and not fit for that sort of thing—"

"Did you hear her in the churchyard?" Falk interrupted. "'Finland will avenge this insult', and so on? I don't think you fully realize that young lady's recuperative powers. Just wait until she is refreshed, and has a slice of roast beef and a glass of burgundy—and then, mark my words, Alix will be entirely capable of setting out to blow up the Winter Palace!"

... Eventually Brand got rid of the Swede by reminding him of the need to hire a carriage for the night drive to Newhaven. Then he stood for a while at the window, looking out at the handsome façade of the County Buildings, in the High Street where dusk had fallen. Down in the valley he heard a locomotive whistle. It reminded him of an item in the London halfpenny papers about Amateur Night at the Canterbury Music Hall and the Third Prize awarded to "a charming comedienne, Miss Amelia Chester, who sang 'Jolly Jane in the Railway Train' with verve and spirit". He remembered the passing trains which regularly shook the walls of the Canterbury, and thought little Milly had made a smart choice there. Amelia Chester, on her way to the top of the bill! Milly—it was odd she should make him think of Mary Ryan, who also meant to shine as a singer. They both knew where they were going. But— did Alix?

It was half an hour before Alix came out to him, after sounds in the next room as if the hotel servants were bringing cans of water or moving the heavy leather portmanteau he and Falk had brought from London. Then she was there, in a merino dress which matched the crimson cloak and hung loosely enough to show how thin Alix had grown, with her hair seemingly darker than usual and plastered close to her head. It was not until he had her in his arms on the big chintz-covered sofa beside the fire, that Brand realized the maid had washed her hair and rubbed it half-dry with a rough towel.

"Alix, dearest Alix, I thought I'd lost you forever!"

"I *was* lost, Brand. But oh! I lost myself!"

He held her close then, the runaway girl, the lost and found, cradled in his arms like a big child in the firelight, in an embrace which held no fever of desire. She seemed to take his presence quite for granted, asking nothing about his ship nor the departure from the Baltic, but simply resting there, kissing him and murmuring, until suddenly, as if her mind had begun to work again, she lifted her head from his shoulder.

"Brand, were you ill after Bomarsund? Did you have that terrible cholera?"

"I came down with it that very night. Darling, don't mind; they took me to the hospital ship, and I wasn't very bad. Only it tormented me to think that if I could only have stayed with you, I might have stopped you from going . . . Alix, tell me this. What did you really say to Mary Ryan that morning? That you were going back to Degerby—or what?"

Alix raised her head from his shoulder. "To Mary Ryan? I know I asked her to tell you something . . . Perhaps I said I was going to the Degerby men?"

"She insisted you meant you were going to Degerby island. Or Joe thought it could have been, back to the boat that brought you up from Degerby."

Puzzled: "Does it matter? I really don't remember. So much has happened since! The hulks, and the pneumonia time, and everything."

"They took you to the *hulks*! I didn't know that."

"We were in the *Devonshire*, off Sheerness, for six weeks."

"My—God!"

"You went to prison too, because of me."

"For ten days," he said, horrified. "Ten days in a open prison, and only because I was a fool! You've had *four months* of it, because you wouldn't desert your own people in their trouble—"

"That's not the whole truth," said Alix. "Of all the Finlanders in Lewes jail, I was probably the only one who really deserved a prison sentence."

"Alix!" Brand believed, for one shocking moment, that privation and fanaticism had turned her head. But she moved away from him on the sofa, and the firelight showed her expression perfectly calm and rational.

"That day at Bomarsund, I stabbed Erik Kruse."

"Kruse was *there*?"

"He was on duty with his General. Apparently he knew the Ryans were going to the islands, and he was hanging about the boat looking for the girl. But he came after me, and it all began over again as it had been in Sweden ... So I lost my head, and drew my *puuko*, and then I slashed him in the face."

Brand gave a deep breath. "My God, I thought you meant you'd killed him!"

"Oh no. He bled very much, but it was only a flesh wound." And as Brand sat speechless, staring at her, Alix rose and took up a taper, held it to the fire, and lit the candles on the mantel.

"Gunnar will be shocked if he finds us in the dark," she said.

Brand rose too, and pulled the curtains across the window with a jerk. He looked at Alix. In the warm room her hair was drying quickly: the bell of pale gold had begun to swing out round her face and neck.

"Well, good," he said. "I'm glad you didn't kill him. I've a personal account to settle with Captain Kruse. But I wonder if this had anything to do with the Home Secretary's decision?"

"What decision?"

"That could account for some of Falk's anxiety. After all, Kruse was a Swedish officer at Bomarsund on an official mission; if he was found wounded, and gave them any inkling of what happened back in Sweden—"

"Brand, *what* decision?"

"Darling, the British would only release you on one condition. You must leave England at once. Tonight."

He hadn't done it any better than Falk would, Brand thought miserably, watching her stricken face. For Alix looked round the pleasant room as if it would vanish like a stage backdrop and leave her back in her prison cell.

"Where am I to go to now?"

"Alix, Madame Karamsin is in Paris. She wants you to go to her again, at her sister-in-law's house—they both want you, dear."

"Gunnar doesn't want me to see Kristina, then?"

"I believe she really isn't well—"

"Aurora is very forgiving. And Princess Mathilde is known to be—hospitable."

"Alix, don't look like that! Can't you put up with them for a matter of three weeks or so?"

"Why three weeks?"

"We could be married in three weeks by a British special licence."

"But—I'm a Lutheran!"

"I know. And I'm a Presbyterian, but Gunnar says Doctors' Commons will issue a licence just the same. And it doesn't have to take three weeks either, but I don't believe I'll have my new ship much before then."

"Brand, what are you talking about? Aren't you still in the Navy?"

"Oh no. We were paid off, every jack of us, when the Baltic Fleet came back to England. Of all the wasteful, silly systems, training men to fight and then dismissing them! Alix, the British want to win this war, but they're doing their level best to lose it. Even with this ship of mine, there's been endless delays; nobody, not even my grandmother, can make their mind up to anything. But the Letters of Marque will be granted next week—"

"A privateer?" she said incredulously. "And you'll be the captain?"

"Will you sail with me, and be the captain's lady, Alexandra?"

She put her hands up to her hot face.

"Brand, you mustn't hurry me! Think, only two hours ago I was in Lewes War Prison, believing you were hundreds of miles away, and now I'm here in your arms, and you talk of marriage and special licences—of vows we must take to each other for a lifetime . . ."

Brand took her by the shoulders and looked into her brilliant eyes.

"I only ask for one promise," he said, "that you'll never run away from me again."

"Oh Brand!"

She leaned towards him, her lips were very close to his. Brand said insistently:

"Did you mean what you said in the churchyard, about Finland's vengeance?"

"You know I did!"

"Do you blame the British for the death of those Finnish boys?"

"I blame only Russia for the war and all its consequences."

300

"Then will you marry me and sail against the Russians, Alix?"

Her face lit up, she pressed her mouth to his and said:
"I will!"

Princess Mathilde Bonaparte, the sister-in-law of Aurora Karamsin, ocupied a most unusual position among the leaders of the war between the West and Russia. She was the first-cousin of Napoleon III, who as President of the French Republic seized autocratic power in December 1851, and became Emperor by a plebiscite vote twelve months later, and she had acted as his official hostess until his marriage to the beautiful Spaniard, Eugéne de Montijo. On the other side she was closely related to the Russian Imperial family, since her mother, born Princess Catherine of Württemberg, was a first-cousin of the Czar Nicholas I. At the same time she was the wife, judicially separated, of Prince Anatole Demidov, Duke of San Donato, whose brother Paul had been Aurora Karamsin's first husband; and it was a measure of Princess Mathilde's tact and political talent that when so many persons with Russian associations were obliged to leave Paris for a time she was able without censure to entertain the bereaved Madame Karamsin at her house in the rue de Courcelles.

At thirty-four Princess Mathilde, whose profile as a girl had had some of the stern beauty of the young Bonaparte's, had become stout and, with her blotched complexion, rather dissolute in appearance. Lord Clarendon, the British Foreign Secretary, had nicknamed her "The Cook" and her brother Prince Napoleon "The Assassin", but in this he was a good deal less than fair to the princess. Mathilde, with her lover and her pug dogs and her salon for raffish literary men, might be laughed at by the British, but she was one of the most talented persons at the court of Napoleon III, and next to the Emperor—always her superior in subtlety and in the ability to see France as an extension of his own monstrous ego—she was by far the cleverest of their generation of Bonapartes.

Such was the lady who was painting in her studio, and humming a little tune past the mahlstick held between her teeth, when Alexandra Gyllenlöve was announced on a morning when the light was excellent, and one of the beloved pugs was sitting for his portrait.

"Why, bless my heart, child, you're a beauty!" exclaimed Princess Mathilde, as Alix dropped a curtsy and advanced respectfully to kiss her hand. "Aurora never told me (down, dogs!) how ravishing you were. Crimson dress and blonde hair; h'm, I like that, very paintable. Where's your guardian?"

"He asked for Madame Karamsin, *Madame la Princesse.*"

"'Princess' will do until we know each other better. Well! Glad he didn't deposit you on my doorstep like a foundling. Who exactly is he? Your brother-in-law? He's kept the Swedish Legation busy decoding telegraphic despatches about you for the past few days. What have you been doing—trying to elope with the footman, hey? There! Don't mind my fun. Just untie my pinafore, there's a good child. Pouf! I can't reach the back of my own waist any more."

"If you please, Madame," said Alix, folding the tent-like Holland apron, "is my godmother very angry with me?"

Princess Mathilde became serious. "Not angry. Sweetly sorrowful—you know her style? She says you deserted her in her hour of need."

"Oh! she had half a dozen other people to dance attendance on her when her husband died!"

"Well, she hasn't half a dozen here; 24 rue de Courcelles isn't run on Russian lines. She hasn't even got her precious Paul at present; he quarrelled with the Karamsins, and was packed off to my former husband at Florence after the funeral. Which of course," said Princess Mathilde, removing a smudge of paint from her cheek with a rag soaked in turpentine, "is as short a cut to hell as any boy could take. Come, are you ready to face *la belle Aurore?*"

On the way to Paris Alix had reached a better understanding of her brother-in-law. Gunnar Falk's anxious formality hid a kindly heart, and once he had put the Channel between them and the Home Secretary, he gallantly set aside his anxiety over his wife's health and halted their journey to let Alix rest for a whole day and night in an hotel at Dieppe before proceeding by coach to Paris. Either his diplomatic persuasions had worked upon Aurora, or she was disarmed by her first sight of Alix in the too-large dress, for she had not one word of reproach to give the runaway. "Darling child, I am so glad you are come back," was all she said, with both hands for Alix and her sweet, head-tilted smile for Gunnar Falk. The girl kissed her with spontaneous affection, and was grateful for Aurora's pardon.

In Princess Mathilde's jovial presence there was no opportunity for heart-searching, but Mathilde was often from home, and then Alix and her godmother spent long hours together while the girl recovered from her experience of prison. Madame Karamsin was more preoccupied with her own health and beauty than she had been before her husband's death, and did not harrow Alix by probing into the story of the hulks and the prison cell. She had put on a little weight since the previous summer, and there was a faint sagging beneath her chin, so masseusses and corsetières now took up a good deal of her time. The mirror which Aurora had seldom glanced at in the days when she took her beauty for granted was never far from her hand. It was as if the petals of the full-blown rose had begun to crumple at the edges and prepare for the inevitable fall.

Nevertheless Aurora was quietly cheerful, and often said how much she was looking forward to going to Princess Mathilde's country house at St. Gratien, and the summer parties and picnics they would all enjoy there.

"Darling Paul's visit to San Donato will end in May," she told Alix one afternoon when they were in her boudoir. "He will be so happy to be with you at St. Gratien, my dear. He needs young company."

"But I shan't be here in summertime, Aurora."

"Why not?" The blue eyes opened wide.

Blushing: "I shall be married to Brand long before then."

"Darling, is that quite wise?"

"I *must* do what Brand wants, Aurora," said the girl with a flash of the old desperation. "I mean so well, and everything I try to do goes wrong! I disappointed *you*, and I wasn't allowed to see my own sister . . . but I can't disappoint Brand—"

Aurora put her arm round Alexandra's shoulders.

"I was sad when you left me, dear," she said, "but I forgave you long ago; and Kristina is far too self-centred to worry about you—just like your poor mamma. And her baby boy is a week old now and both of them doing splendidly, so dear Gunnar says; Kristina must be perfectly content."

"But the others, Aurora! Aunt Kitty still angry, and poor old Carl with no hope of getting work at Karinlund again, and dear Miss Agneta—"

"Quite safe with the Mannerheims, and with Josabeth and your own maid to look after her."

"And poor Tora Kivi and little Henry left behind."

"Darling, you know Gunnar Falk got all the Finnish women released on parole, and I've made the boy and Mrs. Kivi's new baby my personal charge—"

"You're very generous, Aurora."

"I'm very rich. Do riches mean nothing to you, Alexandra?"

"Not compared with Brand. I love him, Aurora! Tell me, for all the riches, did you really love Paul's father?"

It was the first time Alix had felt adult enough to ask Aurora such a question. Her godmother hesitated before answering:

"The Demidovs are really an impossible family. And Paul's father was a very difficult man. He drank, you know—well, to excess, and then he was quite violent. But he died very soon," said Aurora, brightening, "and of course I had my baby, and then there was darling André. So everything came right in the end."

"As it always will for you, Aurora."

"And not for you, dear child?"

"The drum said 'Only so far'."

Life at 24 rue de Courcelles became very gay on the evenings when the princess received, although Madame Karamsin, observing a full year of mourning, seldom appeared at the brilliant literary and artistic gatherings, at which she only allowed Alix to be present on one or two occasions. It amused the girl to think that a former prisoner of H.M.S. *Devonshire* should be considered too much of a *jeune fille* to meet some literary lion in the company of his mistress, or some pair of epicene young men in the plush breeches and lace ruffles affected by their kind, but at the same time she was thankful to be spared the salon. Princess Mathilde and her own *cher ami*, Count Nieuwerkerke of the Beaux Arts, set far too high a standard of conversation for the brightest student in Miss Harring's school at Helsingfors.

As for the musical improvisations, the epigrams, the sonnets and the *avant-garde* searchings of the soul which Princess Mathilde's guests offered as a matter of course at each soirée, these had a paralysing effect upon Alix. One of her nightmares at that time was that she was standing up in her prison dress and reciting "Döbeln at Juutas" before that mocking company—either "Döbeln" or the Sveaborg inscription; both, in the dream, were greeted by a rising tide of laughter.

In Princess Mathilde's salon literature and art came first, and public affairs were only lightly commented on. There was a cabinet crisis in Britain, where Lord Aberdeen's administration seemed likely to be brought down by a private Member's Bill—that, of course, was a good subject for derision. The Kingdom of Sardinia had declared war on Russia, and intended to send an army to the Crimea—this was considered richly comic; and the terrible sufferings of the troops before Sevastopol were almost never mentioned. France had thrown herself naked at the feet of her seducer, and in the despotism of Napoleon III there was no parliamentary opposition to his personal rule, no place for a William Howard Russell to write such articles from the Crimea as had aroused the wrath of Britain; above all there was no Florence Nightingale. Alix understood little of the Emperor's influence. She had lived all her life between Finland and St. Petersburg, and knew nothing of the realities of Western politics. Inevitably, and in spite of her brave words to Brand, she felt some subconscious resentment against Britain, where no distinction had been made between Finlanders and Russians, and where the prisoners of war had been subjected to the horrors of the hulks. In that frame of mind, and in the lively company of Mathilde Bonaparte, Alix began to think more and more of Napoleon III as the true champion of the West against Russia, the liberator who might one day set Finland free.

The princess was drawing Alexandra. Oil paint had been given up as too heavy for the subject, but line drawings and charcoal were more successful, and while Aurora devoted the mornings to beauty treatments Alix spent hours on the model's throne with the pugs curled up on her skirt. Alix enjoyed the studio, with its frowsy clutter of stacked canvases, brass trays in which pastilles of incense burned, the great *salamandre* kept stoked and glowing red, the imitation Chardins, the fake Boucher, and all the examples of Princess Mathilde's genuine but erratic talent on the walls. It was a kind of world the girl had never known.

"There! I'm pleased with that," said Mathilde Bonaparte.

"Full profile, with your hair loose—that's the right pose for you. Shall I give you one of the rough sketches, to send to that sweetheart of yours?"

"He would be flattered to have anything from your hand, princess."

"Take care, Alix, you're becoming a courtier; you should keep such compliments for the Empress Eugénie."

"I have never even seen Her Imperial Majesty."

"That's true. She hasn't been outside the Tuileries since Christmas. Sickly miscarrying Spanish fool, she spends most of her time on the sofa with her feet up, as if that were likely to promote conception! She told my cousin it was his duty to go to war for the Holy Places, but she hasn't done her own duty by giving him an heir for the dynasty. Bah! I've no patience with her."

"The Holy Places, Madame?"

"Yes," said Mathilde dryly, "don't you remember? Who should keep the keys of the Holy Sepulchre was what started the Russian War. As poor Princess Lieven wrote to me after her flight from Paris, 'all this for a few Greek priests!' Even you, I see, have forgotten the Greek priests now."

"I should have said the Czar's desire to push the Russian frontier further into Europe started the war, Madame."

"If it was, he is paying dearly for it. I know he is now the enemy of France, but still," sighing, "I can't forget how fond Nicholas was of my mother, and how kind to me. I hate to think of him alone at Gatchina, with all those memories of his crazy father and his own unhappy childhood; and very unwell too, they tell me."

"Is the Czar at Gatchina again?"

"He says he can't endure St. Petersburg this winter. The sufferings of his troops in the Crimea have told upon Nicholas fearfully. He can't forget the slaughter in the November battles. Your father is a very clever man, Alix, but even he couldn't lay several hundred miles of rail across the steppes to Sevastopol in six months' time! The return of the Inkerman troops to Moscow must have been as frightful as my Uncle's retreat through Russia with the Grande Armée."

"May I get down and stretch now, princess?"

The hard months had so disciplined Alix that she no longer blazed out against the Czar, but as she jumped off the model throne she exulted at the thought of Nikita, nursing regrets and black memories at Gatchina, with the ghost of the mad Czar Paul for company. May his health endure until our victory, she prayed as she helped Princess Mathilde to put away her crayons. May he live long enough for all the suffering to come back on his own head.

"See if you can find some Bristol board, dear," said the princess, groping in the disorder of her desk, "and then you can prepare the sketch for Captain Endicott. He deserves some reward for all the letters he sends you! One a day, isn't it? What does he do—write poetry?"

"He has a great deal to say about his new ship," said Alix demurely. "Her tonnage—breadth—draught of water—crew —and things like that."

"But he tells you that he loves you?"

"Yes. Over and over again!"

"And do you really love him?"

"Oh, princess, *yes*!"

Mathilde grunted. "H'm! I see you do. Then stick to your guns, my child, and don't let Aurora talk you out of marrying him as soon as you like."

"She couldn't do that!"

"No, but she could withhold her consent to your marriage, while you are under age. She is your godmother, standing in your father's place while he is out of reach, and she might make it difficult for Captain Endicott to obtain a special licence."

"Could she really? I don't know anything about English law."

"I don't say she will. I only say—watch out! Aurora is very feminine, you know, and I think she wants to pay you back, just a little, for running away from her last June."

"I never thought of that."

"I know you didn't. You're not that sort of girl. In fact you're not a modern girl at all. You should have lived seventy years ago, in the Revolution; or there may be girls like you in your beloved Finland seventy years from now. But you don't belong to the Europe of our time, and that's why I think you should marry your American and even go back with him to his own land some day."

"I shall never leave Finland until the war is won!" said

Alexandra sorely. It was not pleasant to be called a misfit in her own times.

Mathilde shrugged. "We shall see. I would put the man before the country if I were young and beautiful like you. Oh heavens! how sad it is to be middle-aged and fat! But when I was sixteen, child, and as slender as you are now, I had my chance to be a happy wife. I had my first love, and when he —failed in a task he set himself, my father ordered me to give him up. So then I married Anatole Demidov, and how vile the Demidovs were to their women is something Aurora and I try to forget . . . If I had followed my Star as Louis followed his— ah, well, that's an old story now," said Princess Mathilde, recollecting herself. "But you have your life before you, Alexandra. Don't fight only for your country! Fight for your own happiness!"

One day at the end of January Princess Mathilde lunched alone with her brother, Prince Napoleon, who though unpopular stood high in the councils of the Imperial family. Since Napoleon III and Eugénie had as yet no child, he was the heir presumptive to the throne.

After he went away Mathilde appeared in Aurora's boudoir, in high good humour and with her blotched face redder than ever after the lunch-time brandy.

"Well, Alexandra," she said boisterously, "one of your dearest wishes is about to come true. My brother tells me that His Majesty— and the Empress—will honour us with a visit tonight."

"Good heavens, Mathilde! A State dinner at such short notice?" said Aurora.

"Nothing of the kind. Just a quiet family visit, such as my cousin so often paid me in the evenings, after dinner, in the days when he was President and living at the Elysée. He wants to ask my advice on one or two matters of importance."

"But isn't this one of your evenings for receiving?"

"I shall send notes to some of my regulars, and the footmen must turn away the others. I only want you, my dear sister-in-law, and of course our little Alix, to be present when I receive Their Majesties."

"Mathilde, you must forgive me, but I shall not appear," said Aurora with decision. "It's far too soon after poor André's

308

death ... Yes, I know what you're thinking, that André died fighting the Turks; but the campaign would have been over, and my husband spared, if the Allies hadn't gone in on the side of Turkey ... I am Russian by marriage, and at present I ought not to meet the Emperor of the French."

"As you please." Mathilde did not contest the point. "But I insist that Alix must be there. Count Gyllenlöve's daughter can hardly be presented at the Tuileries, but surely there is nothing to prevent Mademoiselle Alexandra, my guest, from meeting my cousin quietly at my own fireside?"

Aurora bent her head in gentle agreement. As evening approached, indeed, she became almost as excited as Alix over what the girl should wear for the occasion, and produced a diamond brooch to pin in the low neckline of the plain white dress. Then the straight fair hair had to be dressed fashionably by Madame Karamsin's new French maid : the hated Blenheim Spaniel ringlets were out in Paris, and the "Eugénie" style of a middle parting with the hair brushed up and back was just as definitely in. Alix had not been so grand, nor so perfectly groomed, since the last festive evening in the Demidov palace.

At ten o'clock, when she was sitting in the large salon with Princess Mathilde (resplendent in purple satin and a tiara) they heard a two-horse carriage draw up at 24 rue de Courcelles, and in a few moments Alix was curtsying low to the Emperor and Empress of the French.

"We are glad to know you, mademoiselle. Princess Mathilde has told us something of your devotion to the Allied cause."

"You are gracious, Sire."

Alix looked up at her hero, the enemy of the Czar. When she rose from her curtsy, she saw that he was very little taller than herself, grey-haired at forty-six, with nicotine stains on his heavy moustachios, and a small grey imperial. Napoleon III was wearing ordinary evening clothes with no decorations and affably requested the ladies to be seated before he took his place on a velvet sofa near the fire.

It was all completely different from the style of the Czar Nicholas, just as the grey, twitching Czarina was not to be compared with the radiant creature who had entered on Napoleon's arm. The Empress Eugénie was twenty-eight years old and at the height of her extraordinary beauty. She wore a grey silk dress trimmed with little pink bows from the low neck down to the hem, and entirely covered with rose-point lace; and with her own audacity in fashion she had set a pink camellia in the thick wave of her red-gold hair. She made every Grand Duchess in Russia look like a person hired to do a good day's washing.

"Are you enjoying your visit to Paris, mademoiselle? Shall you remain for the Exhibition?"

Eugénie's voice was as delightful as her appearance, her manner to Alexandra perfect. It was a perfection extended to the footman, whom she permitted to remove her tiny shoulder cape of ermine, and even to the little "Cuba dog", as she described it, which she carried on her arm. The dog's name was Linda. Did Alix like dogs? What did she think of Princess Mathilde's pugs?

Conversation on that level, and the service of champagne and sugared fruits, occupied the first ten minutes of the quiet family visit. Alix, with eyes and ears alert for the Emperor, observed that he talked to his cousin steadily and almost inaudibly, and that Mathilde more than once shaded her face with a handscreen meant to keep off the heat of the fire. At last, when the footmen had gone and the Empress was silent, sipping her champagne, the princess spoke out clearly:

"Then, if those fifteen thousand Sardinians are ready to embark at Genoa, I advise, I entreat you to let them go! Such a force of fresh troops could lead a new assault upon Sevastopol and put an end to the sufferings of this terrible winter."

"But, as I've just told you, I can't possibly go out to the Crimea before March. The Sardinians ought to be held in reserve until the time of my arrival."

"And I repeat, you should not go to the Crimea, Louis. Whatever happens, you must remain in Paris."

Eugénie said: "But don't you think it would do wonders for the morale of our brave men, to see and hear their Emperor before Sevastopol?"

"It's open to doubt, my dear Eugénie. Louis would find conditions in the Crimea different from one of his state visits to Troyes or Chaumont, with the school-children and their teachers ordered out to wave the Tricolore and cheer his speeches—"

"You are pleased to be sarcastic, *chère* Mathilde," said

Napoleon while the Empress looked affronted, and Princess Mathilde agitated the handscreen. Alix looked uncertainly from one to the other. She was not sure that she had heard aright. Could the Emperor really want to hold back the troops of his new ally, Sardinia, and prolong the war until he himself could travel to the Crimea and reap all the glory of a victory? He looked quite imperturbable, lighting a cigarette; removing it from the mouth where all expression was hidden by the huge moustache. There was a curious opacity in his cold eyes.

"For just one reason your—very emphatic advice is not ill-timed," he told his cousin. "The King of Sardinia himself is anxious to commit his troops to action. So is Signor Cavour. And—I have great plans for the future of them both.

"The Russians think Sardinia an insignificant ally. I do not. In this terrible struggle France needs loyal allies, and loyal to me Britain is not, and never will be. Never, until their pitiful notions of democracy give way to the rule of the Individual, the responsible, self-sacrificing Guide. But I have known what their parliament is ever since my Carlton Terrace days—a hotbed of socialism and worse! Consider the present crisis in the House of Commons! Can you imagine, in France, a Deputy, a private Member, carrying a motion for a parliamentary enquiry into the conduct of the Russian War?"

"I can't imagine your allowing it," said Princess Mathilde shortly. "Do you intend to air these views when you're the Queen's guest at Windsor?"

"Much may happen between now and April, cousin."

"If Louis goes to the Crimea, Sevastopol will yield," said Eugénie positively. "And then— my dream is, that he will press on to Jerusalem. Imagine what it would mean to the Christian world to see a French Emperor delivering the Holy Places from both the infidel and the superstitions of the Greek Church!"

Napoleon turned towards his wife, and there was the shadow of a grin on his expressionless face.

"Thank you, chère amie," he said. "You are a constant inspiration . . . Mathilde, your charming guest is looking at me with great eyes. You are the daughter of Count Gyllenlöve, are you not, mademoiselle? Your father has made his name as famous, in the past few months, as those of Menschikov and Gortschakov."

"I don't share my father's views, Your Majesty," said Alix. The Emperor made a deprecating gesture, and a shower of grey ash fell on his dress coat.

In that salon, where every available inch of wall space was covered with mementoes and pictures of the Family, his nephew was an odd contrast to the great Napoleon. There was Bonaparte at Arcola, gaunt and triumphant, there was Bonaparte with the crown in his own hands, heavy with majesty—the man who sat beneath these portraits was by comparison mean and common, with his big nose and his protruding stomach, and the thick workman's fingers spread upon his knee. Alix looked at her hero with a sinking heart.

"When the war is over, I hope Count Gyllenlöve will visit Paris," Napoleon said. "There will be room for a good technician in the reconstruction of my country."

"You are too kind, Sire. My father will no doubt wish first to repair the damage to his estate in Finland, which has been cruelly used by his Russian friends."

"Where is the estate?"

"At Ekenäs, Sire."

"Ah, Ekenäs! The scene of an abortive exploit by the British, I believe."

"Before the French arrived in the Baltic," Alix said.

"It really has been most regrettable," said the Emperor dreamily, "that the British campaign in the Baltic should have been so completely null and void. They have lost all their old prestige as the masters of the sea. Nobody has any fear of the British Navy now."

"I think the Russians have, Your Majesty," said Alix, and the Empress laughed a light disbelieving laugh.

"Forgive me, Sire," said Alix desperately, "but I have seen the Navy in action! I was at Bomarsund, and I know how many, how terribly many French soldiers gave their lives there for you. But it was the British who kept the Russian fleet and the Russian troops locked up in the Baltic from one winter to another, and they will be there again, I know, as soon as the ice goes out. The Royal Navy, Sire, is your best shield in France!"

"I'm glad you said all that about the Navy," said Princess Mathilde an hour later, when the Imperial guests had been

312

curtsied from the house. "There are far too many people round my cousin now who dare not disagree with anything he says."

"I was terrified," confessed Alix, "the Czar would have sent me to Siberia for half of that."

"Oh come, you're too hard on poor Nicholas. But now I'm going to ask you to forget that conversation, Alix. Don't pass on any of the details to Aurora."

"Of course I won't."

"We can only hope," said Mathilde Bonaparte, and her large red face was very sad, "that the British themselves will prevent him from doing anything so—dangerous—as going out to the Crimea. *She* has no influence over him at all."

"She is very lovely."

"Yes, she is. But he has changed, changed, since he became Emperor. I dread his new philosophy of the Leader, the mystic destiny . . . Oh Louis!" Mathilde's eyes were full of tears. "That wasn't how you talked by the lake at Arenenberg, when you and I were young!"

At Alexandra's sudden look of understanding, she achieved a smile.

"You didn't know whom I meant the other day, did you, when I told you to fight for your happiness and marry your true love? Yes, Louis Napoleon Bonaparte was once my promised husband. If I had been as true to him as he has been true to himself, then I, and not that beautiful doll, would have been Empress of the French."

313

CHAPTER SEVENTEEN

THE DUCHESS OF FINLAND

I

ALIX spent a restless night after her meeting with the French
Emperor. For the first time she had to face the knowledge that
Napoleon III was prosecuting the war with Russia, not as a
crusade of righteousness, but for his own selfish ends, and that
men and women like herself, single-hearted about the future
of their own countries, were being manipulated to excellent
effect by the plotter of the Tuileries. She answered Aurora's
eager questions briefly. Eugénie's dress, and Eugénie's Cuba
dog, were described by Alix in far greater detail than Napoleon's plans for the Crimea.

Happily a new topic at once engrossed the ladies in the
rue de Courcelles. In Britain, the parliamentary enquiry into
the mismanagement of the war had caused the fall of Lord
Aberdeen's government, and on February 6 Lord Palmerston
kissed hands as Queen Victoria's new Prime Minister.

Lord Palmerston was the darling of the British public. At
seventy he was as youthful and exuberant in spirit as when he
had been Secretary at War against Napoleon Bonaparte at
the age of twenty-five. He had held office in many Cabinets
(being at the time of his new appointment none other than the
terrible Home Secretary who had struck awe into Gunnar
Falk) and had made any number of enemies during his long
career, but to the average citizen his was the authentic voice
of Britain. Lord Aberdeen had twittered, Lord Aberdeen had
appeased: Lord Aberdeen, as recently as last June, had made
a speech in parliament which was almost an apology for Russia.
Lord Palmerston, who never minced his words, was just the
man to give the Bear a bloody snout.

The new Prime Minister had long expected the worst of
Russia and now was proved to be right. He actively loathed
the Germans, and predicted future trouble with Prussia, but a

romantic streak in his nature had given him some degree of blindness where France was concerned. He had known Louis Napoleon Bonaparte when the Adventurer of Carlton Terrace was a refugee in London, and he was willing to take him, as the Emperor Napoleon III, for an honest ally of Great Britain. This was well known in Paris, where the advent of "Lord Firebrand" to power was greeted with delight.

Certainly it meant an immediate shake-up in the corridors of Whitehall, where the fusty old jacks-in-office, fighting Russia with the weapons of the eighteenth century, were tumbled out to make way for new men. Admiral Napier, who had been a crony of Palmerston, felt himself secure enough to attack the Admiralty and his old enemy Sir James Graham in a speech at the Mansion House on the very night that "Pam" took office, but even the Prime Minister could not protect the admiral who had let the Russian ships pass Sveaborg. Graham was replaced at the Admiralty by Sir Charles Wood, but Napier, for all his blustering, was not reappointed to the Baltic command.

The immediate result of all this for Alix was the hurrying on of her marriage to Brand Endicott.

Brand arrived in Paris within a week of the appointment of Admiral Sir Richard Saunders Dundas as Commander-in-Chief of the Baltic Fleet of 1855. He had Letters of Marque for the American snow brig in one pocket and a special marriage licence in the other. He was madly in love, wildly exuberant, and literally lifted Alix off her feet in his first embrace.

"We've done it, darling, we've done it!" he exulted. "My grandmother put down the purchase price of the snow brig as soon as she heard the new Chief was to be Dundas!"

"But how? Why? I don't understand," begged Alix, clinging to him. Princess Mathilde had left them alone in the salon of the Bonaparte portraits, and the victor of Arcola waving his plumed hat above the cannon smoke seemed to be cheering Brand's dash and spirit.

"Oh yes, you do. Grandmother doesn't approve of an official from the Admiralty taking over a sea command! She says even with Palmerston in charge it'll take months to get the gunboats and the mortar ships they'll need to bombard Sveaborg. Also she's mad at the Navigation Act and says British shippers will be beaten by foreigners in their own front yard under the new laws, so she's happy to invest in goods carried under the American flag. Darling, are you glad?"

"Darling, are you sure?" she echoed him.

"Sure I want to sail this soon? If it's another early spring—"

"Sure you want to marry me?"

Of course Brand was sure. He was in love with Alix. He had never been in love before. The Milly Chesters of his life (counting one night with Milly, and numerous other nights, in other ports, of the same sort) were not to be compared, even in thought, with the girl who had entered his heart when she entered his ship from the icy quay at Marstrand. If he was not quite so much in awe of her at the rue de Courcelles as he had been at the Villa Hagasund it was entirely due to the nine months in the Royal Navy, which had taught him among many other things that not passionate feelings but superior weapons were needed to beat the Czar. *Posterity! stand here upon your own foundation*—it sounded fine, especially when spoken in Alexandra's lovely voice, but to the Yankee a snow brig mounted with a carronade was a great deal more practical when it came to dealing with the Russians.

"Sure enough to bring you this," he said, taking a plain gold ring from his pocket. "Gunnar said I mustn't give you jewels yet, just two gold rings. Will you wear the first one for me now, my darling, and let me put the second on in church?"

Alix kissed him solemnly as the betrothal ring slid on her finger.

"Gunnar sent you a present from Kristina and himself, and a letter. Would you like to read the letter now?"

"'My dear sister-in-law,' [Alix read aloud] 'One of the advantages of being a neutral is that one can communicate with both sides. Through Stockholm, I informed your father of Kristina's safe confinement, and in congratulating us he said, "Tell Alix I consent to her intended marriage. Nadine and I hope she will be as happy as she deserves to be." This removes any difficulty connected with the marriage licence...'"

Alix folded up the note and shrugged her shoulders.

"The paternal blessing!" she said flippantly. "Gunnar will be delighted. I think he was afraid Lord Palmerston would forbid the banns. Come, let us show this backhanded compliment to Aurora."

Aurora, as usual, was tactful and soothing, and Brand was most deferential to her when they met at luncheon, although firm about making arrangements for an immediate marriage, and the limit to what her godmother might give his bride. The wedding dress, yes; very well then, the whole wedding outfit provided they didn't waste time at the dressmakers, but no other falderals. Brand was comfortably aware of money in his pockets, for Mr. Tarras had been very generous to his American nephew. He intended to buy Alix everything she needed as soon as she was his wife.

When he stood at the altar, and declared that he John Brand took this woman Alexandra Aurora Paulina to be his wife, Brand felt not that he was marrying a stranger with a stately name, but all his dreams of Alix merged in one. By his side stood the girl from Marstrand, in a cloud of white veiling like the mist that had hung that first night over St. Erik's Bay, in a white watered silk dress that reminded him of the snow glittering beneath the evergreens in Brunnsparken, and Alexandra's hand was no colder, as he placed the second gold ring above the first, than it had been when he first touched it in the cabin of the *Girdleness*. She stood in the empty church, where a handful of Princess Mathilde's friends were lost in the space constructed to hold seven hundred, not so much a beautiful bride as a vision of light. While nothing could have been plainer than her dress, or the Swedish Bible which according to custom Alix carried instead of a bouquet, she was literally hung with jewels such as the British Embassy church had never seen. Lamenting that the bridal crown of the Gyllenlöves was under lock and key in Helsingfors, where it had been deposited after Kristina's wedding, Aurora Karamsin had insisted on Alexandra's wearing one of her own diamond tiaras to hold her veil in place. The effect was so lovely that a diamond necklace was added, then the diamond spray which was the Falks' wedding present, then earrings and diamond bracelets lent by Princess Mathilde; and after that Aurora had produced the great Sancy diamond itself, her morning-gift from Demidov.

"But I don't want to wear Aurora's jewels!" Alix protested, while her grandmother was out of the room. "What will Brand think? I want to marry him just as I am!"

"Do it to please her, dear," the princess soothed, "and don't

317

worry about that young man of yours. He'll buy you diamonds as fine as any of these, long before you reach your silver wedding!"

"Twenty-five years from today—I can't imagine it!"

"You don't need to look a minute beyond tonight," said Mathilde with a nudge and the ribald laugh which always chilled Alix's feelings. She hardly dared to look at Brand, unfamiliar in his black coat and white camellia, when Gunnar gave him her hand in marriage. She was frozen, like her borrowed diamonds, pale as a princess of the snows, when the ceremony ended and Brand led her from the church.

But there was sunshine in the narrow rue d'Aguesseau, sunshine touching the flaking stucco of the old houses in the Faubourg to a deeper cream, and late sunshine mingling with gaslight and firelight in Princess Mathilde's salons, into which all her literary friends— scenting a party from afar—had crowded to drink the bride's health and wring the hand of an American whom they had never seen before nor would again. The newly married pair did not stay long. Alix went upstairs and took off all the jewels except the diamond spray while the second relay of hungry artists was still arriving from the Left Bank. Then she put on her new mantle, the colour of imperial violets, and went shyly down to kiss her friends and thank them for her wedding day.

Brand had reserved an apartment at the Hotel Meurice. It was still daylight when they were shown into the salon; light enough for Alix to ask for the drawn curtains to be opened, and to stand admiring the view of the Tuileries gardens just across the way. Brand took a quick glance through the rooms and nodded approval to the hotel servants. They had remembered white flowers, good, and champagne in a cooler with glasses, right, and everything else seemed in order, *merci beaucoup*. He was alone with his newly married wife.

Alone at five o'clock in the afternoon, and Brand Endicott was in the quandary known to so many bridegrooms of his day and generation. He had made no plans at all beyond the wedding breakfast, reserved no *loge* at the opera nor table at one of the famous restaurants, and no theatre or restaurant would in any case open before nine. Should he start making love to her, as he wanted to do? And if so, how should he

318

approach that slim figure, somehow still unapproachable in the bridal gown, looking down into the rue de Rivoli? Could he open a bottle of champagne and ask her to have a drink with him? Or should he—

"There is still light in the sky," said Alix in a constrained voice, "what a beautiful day this has been."

"Yes it has." He crossed to the window and put his arm around his bride.

"The Parisians call this 'the false spring'. In Finland it is still high-winter."

"There was nothing false about our wedding-day, was there?"

"No." Alix turned her head towards him and took his light kiss on her cheek.

"Darling . . . I couldn't find words to tell you before . . . in the carriage, or in all that racket at the rue de Courcelles— how beautiful you were today. I'll never forget it. Never! All those diamonds sparkling, and your eyes so dark when you said 'I will' . . . I never dreamed that anything so lovely . . . could be mine."

"Then I'm glad Aurora made me wear them. And my new spray from London, isn't it pretty? . . . I love my gold rings best."

Then Brand was able to kiss the hand that wore them, and her lips, and take her closer, but still gently, into his embrace. And Alix murmured:

"There's just one thing of my own I should have liked to wear today."

"What, sweetheart?"

"A white fox cloak I got in Petersburg."

"Did you leave it there?"

"No, it's at Helsingfors. I left it at the Villa on my way to Degerby."

Petersburg, Helsingfors, Degerby. The war names fell like stones into the quiet room.

"We'll get it back for you some day," he said.

"When we sail to Finland in the *Snow Queen*?"

"The—?"

"Your grandmother's ship."

Brand smiled as he kissed her hair. If she had confused snow brig and *Snow Queen* so much the better; he had a surprise, in that line, waiting for her at the London Docks.

"My grandmother sent you a wedding gift," he said.

"Brand! Why didn't you give it to me before?"

"Because it was addressed to Mrs. John Endicott. I couldn't very well give it to Miss Gyllenlöve."

In the last daylight of the false spring he saw her blush.

"I *am* Mrs. Endicott now—"

"Are you? Or should I keep this for a morning-gift?" With pretended reluctance he put his hand inside his coat.

"Brand, don't tease!"

He gave her the small packet, and without letting Alix leave the circle of his arm, turned up the lamp which stood on a console table.

"Oh, Brand, *more* diamonds!"

There was a ring inside Isabella Tarras' letter, a thick band of gold set with three stones, slightly yellowish in tinge but newly cleaned and sparkling.

'My dear Alice' [Alexandra read aloud]

'My best wishes and blessings to John and you upon your wedding day. I send you the ring which John's grandfather gave me to commemorate the victory of Waterloo. I hope it will send you victorious in your war with Russia.'

"Is that all?" said Brand.

"Just her signature. Isn't it enough?"

"By God it is." He watched Alix fit the Waterloo jewels on her bare right hand.

" 'Send you victorious', " said Alix softly. "Is that good English?"

"Good English or not," said Brand, "it's their national anthem.

" '*Send her victorious*
  Happy and glorious—' "

The lovely cold face so close to his own came alive suddenly with warmth and laughter, and he caught Alix to him, he knew it was all right and he could love her now, tonight, all night, all their lives—

"Happy and glorious!" she repeated as he caught her off the ground. "Oh Brand! I am! I am!"

Happy and glorious were the days which followed, when the

false spring continued, and all Paris was a playground for Brand and Alix. He took her everywhere; to supper at the Café Anglais; to see the foundations of the Great Exhibition, which was the circus planned by Napoleon III for France in 1855; to return the ceremonious wedding call made upon them at the Meurice by "*Madame la Princesse Impériale and Madame la Princesse Demidova*" (so the hotel servants impressively announced the visitors) and to shop in the rue de Rivoli. In one of the fascinating boutiques under the arcades Brand bought his wife a hat, the first article of dress he had ever bought for a woman, and a momentous purchase in a season when, as the lovely Empress began to set the fashion, the bonnet was going out and the hat coming in. Alexandra's hat was white, of course, with a veil of *point d'esprit* and a posy of February snowdrops attached to one side. Her husband said she "looked a dream in it", and every time they were in their rooms preparing for a fresh outing he begged her, "Don't you want to wear your hat?"

They were as extravagant and gay as two happy fools could possibly be on a Paris honeymoon. Brand was even surprised at his bride's wild gaiety, and put it down to reaction from the terrible months behind her, but it went deeper than that. Alix was enjoying for the first time in more than a year the freedom to come and go, walk, drive, admire, without deferring to the wishes of an older woman, and for the first time in her life the companionship, as well as the admiration, of a man of her own age. She thought Brand very handsome, as indeed he was, for his rather slouching walk had straightened under Navy discipline and his fixed purpose gave new strength to his face; and he, of course, thought she was beautiful. When he took her to the opera on their last night in Paris, many glasses were levelled at the fair beauty in the white bridal gown, and more men than Brand found their attention distracted by Alix from the performance of *L'Etoile du Nord*. It had been playing to packed houses since the spring of 1854, when the Baltic was first discussed in the French press, and Meyerbeer, the composer, cleverly rearranged some numbers from his own *Camp in Silesia* into a new show with a Northern interest. Brand was mildly bored by the music but charmed with the evening, and why not? He had his own North Star, more exquisite than ever, safely by his side.

His pride and possession became stronger still in London, where they went on the fourth day after their marriage. The small hotel in Jermyn Street to which he took her was hardly in the style of the Meurice, and Brand felt obliged to apologize for the low-ceiled rooms and somewhat thread-bare carpets. It was on their first morning: they had slept late after the Channel crossing, and Brand, hunting for his razor-case found Alix in her wrapper, completely baffled by an English chimney and the sulky English coal.

"Darling, ring for the maid and make her fix the fire," he commanded, "and have her bring breakfast right away. I'm going to be infernally late in London Wall."

"Can't I come with you?"

"To the office? Not likely! I mean, not today, anyway."

"But shan't you be going to see the *Snow Queen*?"

"Maybe." He let her persist in the mistake, it was his private joke, but he said:

"You'll have plenty to do this morning unpacking, won't you? There doesn't seem to be a lot of wardrobe space. Darling, will these rooms really do?"

"Of course! If we haven't much space, it's a good preparation for shipboard. And I'd rather be here than staying with our relatives, wouldn't you?"

Brand fervently agreed. But their relatives, naturally, could not be ignored. There was a grand luncheon party in South Street, at which Brand found his sister-in-law to be a pale copy of Alix, with dark hair, and a gentle but complete absorption in her own health and the well-being of small Karen and the infant Carl Gustaf. Kristina Falk, so well sheltered from the winds of the world, had been told little about Alexandra's previous life in England, except that she had been "very foolish and headstrong", and was now anxious to avoid any painful topics and rejoice in her sister's marriage to a thoroughly presentable man. The festivities at Camberwell Green were more prolonged, as owing to the distance from St. James' the bridal couple had to be invited to dine and sleep, and also more complex. Mr. Tarras, a typical British merchant, bluff and middle-aged at forty-one, was frankly delighted with his new niece by marriage, and said so. Mrs. Arthur Tarras, who had social ambitions, was secretly overawed by Alexandra. She wished to extract full prestige from a bride who had been married from the house of the French Emperor's cousin, and was a god-daughter of one of the richest women in the world; but at the same time she hardly knew how to explain to her Camberwell acquaintance that the young couple were not setting up house and shopping for carpets and curtains, but actually planning to sail together on a snow brig to the Baltic! She begged "Mrs. Brand" not to mention these plans to the friends and neighbours, some thirty in number, invited to the musical soirée which followed a dinner for twelve.

Brand had never so thoroughly realized the completeness of Alexandra's social training as when he watched her grave admiration and polite applause as one inferior performance followed another. The star turn of the evening, which was the star turn in every English parlour at that time, was a recitation of "The Charge of the Light Brigade", on this occasion performed by Miss Flora Tarras. There was something very funny about plump Flora in her plaid silk dress, with her round Scottish face flushed with excitement, declaiming:

> "Cannon to right of them,
> Cannon to left of them,
> Cannon in front of them
>   Volleyed and thunder'd;
> Stormed at with shot and shell,
> Boldly they rode and well,
> Into the jaws of Death,
> Into the mouth of Hell
>   Rode the six hundred."

—at least, it was funny to Brand, but Alexandra's composure never wavered through the six long stanzas of the poem. Later, when they were alone in the icy guest room, Brand remarked:

"What a ridiculous thing to let a kid like Flora recite the 'Light Brigade'!"

"Why?"

"She's got no idea what it's all about. It's a man's poem, anyway."

"Are there special poems for men and women? I thought Flora spoke it very well. As if she meant it—that's what counts."

After this defence, it was exasperating to find the same Flora, in charge of the tea urn when Brand came down early to breakfast, in a faintly critical mood.

"How's cousin Alix this morning, Brand?"

"Very well, thank you, Flo. She'll be coming downstairs presently."

"Cook is making coffee for her. Mamma says Finns drink a lot of coffee. Is that true?"

"Perfectly true."

"Brand . . . Cousin Alix isn't really a Finn, is she?"

"Better not let her hear you say that!"

"Bell thinks she's a Russian princess, *incognito*."

"Bell and you are a romantic pair." Brand tweaked his young cousin's ringlets as he passed her chair on the way to the sideboard to help himself to eggs and bacon.

"Oh, we think Alexandra's lovely," Flora assured him, as he returned to the table. "*Absolutely* lovely, and so stylish in that white watered silk. But . . . Brand, does she always look that way, as if she was seeing something over a person's shoulder?"

"Don't be ridiculous, Flora! Alix looks you as straight in the eye as anyone on earth."

"Oh dear, I didn't mean to make you angry! Of course, she looks at you when you're talking, it's when you're *not* . . . I can't explain. But we both think she's beautiful — we really do."

It was only schoolgirl nonsense, of course, and yet Brand found himself watching for that look. He thought he caught it once or twice in their own rooms that evening, when the east wind rattled the chimney-pots of Jermyn Street; but when he spoke her name the grey eyes met his own with love and brilliance, and that night in their bed beneath the eaves she had never been more completely his own, more wild in her abandon to his passion. The next morning he judged the time was ripe to ask her:

"Like to see the brig today?"

"Oh Brand, at last! How wonderful!"

It was still windy, for the false spring of Paris had become a wintry London February, and there were occasional rain showers as their cab drove slowly down to London Docks. But Alix was in high spirits, eager to hear all the details of the "*Snow Queen*" and the signing on of her new crew.

"She's Greenock built, you know," her captain said, "American registry but Greenock built, 238 tons, and she's square-rigged with a trysail mast abaft the main. Her regular complement allows for two apprentices, but I don't want boys along on this trip, so there'll be six men in the forecastle—Gordon and Webster out of the Tarras Line *Balgownie*, and four old Navy hands paid off from H.M.S. *Tribune*. Then there's Joe Ryan . . ." he paused interrogatively.

"He's to be mate?"

"Yes. And I've had word that he'll be here tomorrow, Alix, coming in on the mail boat from Copenhagen. Is that all right with you?"

Wide-eyed: "Why shouldn't it be?"

"I don't know why not. Only there *was* that mix-up at Bomarsund, remember? I've never really made out how Mary came to give me that message about you and Degerby."

"Does it matter now? I'm quite sure Mary meant no harm." Alix spoke with such indifference that Brand was faintly irritated. But they were nearly at the docks, and after walking some distance along the wharves came upon the snow brig at her moorings, with the Stars and Stripes drooping from its staff.

"There she is!" Brand looked at Alix in triumph. "What d'you think of her? Why—what's the matter?"

"I thought she was called the *Snow Queen*!"

"You made that up yourself, darling. Don't you like her real name?"

Brand had had the brig's old name, *Hertiginnan av Finland*, painted out, and the translation, *Duchess of Finland*, painted in. The figure-head, a woman with her hands clasped on her breasts, had also been repainted in the white bodice and black skirt of a Finnish country girl, and the painter in a valiant attempt at the blond hair described by Brand had given her a chignon of brassy gold.

"Brand, I think it might be an unlucky name."

"Will you please tell me why?"

"You see . . . it's the title of a book, a true story . . . about a Finnish woman who betrayed her country."

"Good God!"

"Her name was Eva Merthen. They called her the Duchess of Finland because she fell in love with a Russian officer during the occupation—"

325

"Which occupation?"

"In the Lesser Wrath—about 1741."

"That's going pretty far back, even for you," said Brand. It was the first time he had ever spoken to Alix sarcastically, but he was "riled", as the Yankees said: he had been so proud of his new command, and so eager to show Alix the fresh paint jobs and carpentry work in the captain's quarters that it was exasperating to have her go off on the old tack of Finland's historic sufferings. And since she said nothing, but looked dismayed, he was moved to speak more sharply still.

"Come on, let's go aboard. And look here, Alix, if I were you I wouldn't bother about books or all that superstitious stuff you got from Anna. The brig's been registered as the *Duchess of Finland*, and that's all there is to it. As far as luck goes it's up to you and me."

* * *

"Cheer, boys, cheer! Our Queen shall hear our story,
Courage, brave hearts, shall bear us on our way—"

It was a new song, a music hall song; a song for Your Very Own Sam Cowell to introduce at the Canterbury, and—unexpectedly—it was being sung by a crowd in Piccadilly, watching the troops go by.

"Good Lord," said Joe Ryan to Brand. "Just look at them! What are they—a Line regiment?"

"They're Guardsmen, the newspaper said. On their way to the Palace to be decorated by the Queen."

"If they can get that far, poor devils." The red-coated ranks limped painfully by. The men were walking wounded from the first contingent invalided home from the Crimea, and showing in their faces no less than in their bandaged limbs the ravages of the dreadful winter.

"The crowd are crazy about them, aren't they?"

"Bastards." Brand dispassionately surveyed the London throng. "They've followed the troops all the way from the Strand, and that's as near as *they'll* ever get to the Black Sea. Every second man you see in London wears a Crimea beard and smokes a long cigarette with a straw mouthpiece, but that doesn't make him a war hero. We turn off here, Joe."

They left behind the dying strains of "Cheer, boys, cheer"! and made for Jermyn Street. It was Joe Ryan's first visit to London, and he looked at the West End shops eagerly, already

326

thinking of buying a present for Mary. It was also the first time Brand had seen him without his peaked cap and seaman's jersey, for Joe had made himself smart for the occasion in a new blue serge coat and a tall beaver hat. His usually merry face was grave.

"Here's our hotel," said Brand. "I wish you'd brought your bag along. I told you I'd reserved a room for you."

"I wouldn't intrude on a newly married couple! Besides, I think I ought to sleep aboard the *Duchess* and keep an eye on that carronade."

"Well, don't feel you're intruding and sling your hook as soon as dinner's over. Alix has been looking forward to having you spend the evening—Alix!"

The sitting-room, which Alix had brightened with some early spring flowers, was empty, but the fire had been made up, and was cheerful.

"She must be in the bedroom. Take your coat off, Joe."

But Alix was not in the bedroom. The Paris hat was on its little stand before the dressing-table mirror, and everything else was in fresh, neat order. Brand returned to Joe Ryan.

"I thought she would be back by now," he said. "It's getting dark."

"You said she was spending the day at her sister's, didn't you? Depend upon it, they started chattering and lost all count of time."

"Sure," said Brand. "What'll you drink, Joe? I've everything but brännvin."

He poured the Scotch and water, listening for her footstep on the stairs. It was the first time in the two weeks since their marriage that Alix had gone anywhere without him, and Brand caught himself in the fear that she had run away again, never to return. Absurd! He said to Joe determinedly:

"I think we should be able to put to sea on Monday. Up to Hull for the textile cargo, deliver it to Copenhagen, run across to Malmö for the flax, and out again. With a look in at Skagen and Frederickshavn coming and going, just to let them get accustomed to us, and then, the next run, try our luck between Lübeck and Stockholm."

Joe nodded. "That's the run if you're looking for trouble, Brand."

"That's what I'm cruising for. And you'd better make up your mind to it before you ship with me."

"I have already, you know that. It's been a cruel winter for a man in a small way of business, and I was beginning to wonder how to stay afloat. Mary's a wonderful manager at home, but she does like pretty clothes—all girls do—and her singing lessons cost a bit of money."

"Is she still aiming to sing like Jenny Lind?"

"She might, at that," said Mary's father. "She's improved a lot since she started with this new teacher; maybe he'll give her a chance to sing in public next season."

Like Milly Chester, Brand thought. Another girl on her way to the top of the bill!

"You left her with her aunt in Queen Street?"

"I had to," said Joe. "Couldn't leave her all alone in Bollhus Alley. Did you hear something?"

"It's Alix," said Brand thankfully. He sprang up and opened the door on to the dark landing.

"Darling, you're late! Joe's here."

"I'm sorry," she said, pausing in the doorway. "Captain Ryan, I'm sorry I was detained. My brother-in-law came back unexpectedly from the Legation—with some news—"

"Alix, what on earth has happened? Come and sit down!"

But she stood still, leaning her weight on the door knob, with a ghastly look of triumph on her face.

"Their Minister at The Hague telegraphed to London," she said. "The Czar died at one o'clock this morning."

Nikita had been ailing for a while, although of course it was kept secret—Alix told the two men breathlessly, when they had made her take off her cloak, and drink a little wine, and sit down at the table which held the papers relating to the *Duchess of Finland*. He—Nikita—had been stunned by news of a battle at Eupatoria, where the Russians tried to recapture the Allied beachhead and were beaten off with heavy losses by the Turks. This Turkish victory, which threw back at the Czar his old gibe at Turkey as the sick man of Europe, had so added to his burden of guilt for the Crimean dead, and the sick and wounded trailing back to Moscow, that he could no longer sleep. He walked, by night, miles through the empty rooms, the chilly corridors of Gatchina, where his mad father had walked before him in pursuit of sleep. Weakened, he fell a victim to influenza. Further imprudence brought on an apoplexy, and in the first hour of March 2, 1885, death claimed the Emperor Nicholas I.

"But it's still February in Russia, Old Style!" Alix interrupted her own recital. "Oh, Brand, that's what I heard him say the day we watched the flying squadron off Cronstadt, and I know he said the same thing to other people, too! General January and General February will win the victory for Russia! Now General February has struck Nikita to the heart!"

"So," said Joe Ryan after a silence, "will the killing stop?"

"What do you mean?" said Alix.

"I'm thinking of the Crimea veterans we saw in the street this afternoon. Just an advance guard, you might say, of the lucky ones who'll get back alive to England. Or France. Or Moscow. I've always heard the Grand Duke Alexander was a different sort from his father. Humane and progressive. They even say he means to free the serfs. And . . . he's a good friend to Finland, Mrs. Endicott!"

"A Romanov, and humane?" said Alix scornfully. "He has a better manner than his father, that I admit. But as for his humanity—well, let the Czar Alexander II sue for peace, and make reparations to Turkey, and withdraw his ships from the Black Sea, and I'll believe in him. Until then, we fight on!"

Brand nodded. It was exactly what he had expected Alix to say. She sat looking at them both, and yet—as Flora Tarras had noticed—at something just beyond them, something that belonged to the night and the wind and Finland. His bride, that shy and gracious changeling, had departed, and in her stead he had the old Alix, wholly dedicated to her hatred of Russia. With Gothenburg and Lewes jail behind us we are still prisoners, he thought. Prisoners of war, as truly as if we were behind iron bars, and only peace can ever set us free.

When the meal was served and they filled their glasses, they were no longer three friends round a dinner table: they were a council of war.

II

When the *Duchess of Finland* put to sea on March 25, the Norway-Sweden coast as far south as Gothenburg was still under snow, and the nor'-wester was blowing as hard as it had blown when *Arrogant* was on her way to Portsmouth.

Alix was prostrated with seasickness on the North Sea crossing, but revived as soon as the brig passed The Skaw and reached the more sheltered waters between Danish Jutland and western Sweden, although even in the Kattegat there was floating ice to be seen in that bitter end of winter. She was well enough to stand in the bow, wearing sou'-wester and oilskins, when Brand mustered his crew of six and with Joe at his side read aloud the Letters of Marque which commissioned him to "cruise against the commerce or war vessels of the enemy". Such letters belonged to a bygone age, and privateering was still lawful only because no naval reformer had as yet succeeded in erasing it from the statute book, so Brand threw in a few excerpts from the Articles of War for good measure, in case the legality of his proceedings were ever called in question. He did his best to model his reading on a well-remembered performance by Capain Yelverton, after the war communiqué was brought to Køge Bay.

Brand was determined that the *Duchess* should be run shipshape and Bristol fashion, and by the judicious use of routine and the Navy discipline which had been drilled into himself he soon had her on the way to being a taut ship. The four ex-Navy men responded remarkably well to the handling of a skipper who three months before had been a Seaman Gunner in H.M.S. *Arrogant*, and the two Scotsmen were orderly fellows who quickly came up to standards rather higher than those of the Tarras Line. Alexandra's manner with the crew was perfect, neither too aloof not too familiar. She very seldom went for'ard but remained aft with the two officers, and in the first week, of course, she was busy arranging their living quarters. In a brig 26 feet broad by 126 feet long it had not been possible to do much for her comfort, but she was living under the same conditions as many skippers' wives in time of peace and quickly made the best of them. All the food eaten aboard was prepared in the forecastle galley by Gordon, one of the Aberdonians, who was an excellent hand at frying fish; but at London Docks Brand had installed a miniature galley for Alix, which she used chiefly for brewing countless pots of coffee. Most of her Paris finery had been left, stored in two massive trunks, at the Jermyn Street hotel, and she wore a fisherman's jersey over a short skirt beneath her oilskins, and was happy.

Following staunchly in the path of the Baltic Fleet in 1854, Brand anchored for gunnery practice not far from Vingäsand, and had the tarpaulins off the little carronade. As a weapon, the carronade's heyday belonged to Nelson's time, but it was effective enough at point blank range to be known as the "devil gun", and with an elevation of 4° could hit a target at 1000 yards. The 32–pr. on the *Duchess'* deck was four feet long, flinging balls of 5 lb. weight, and being mounted on a sliding wooden carriage was light and fairly easy to handle by a crew of four men. The ex-Navy men, who all had some gunnery experience, formed this crew, with Goode as captain of the gun, while Brand, Joe, and the two Aberdonians went through the drill as auxiliaries. Like all carronades, their weapon was not without some danger to their own ship, barely clearing the port sill when run out, and Alexandra's part in the exercise was to bring up four buckets of water in case of fire.

Brand's first cruise, to Copenhagen and Malmö and back to London, was entirely peaceful. That, at least, he owed to his grandmother, and by proving that neither the enemy nor his "infernals" (as the Infernal Machines were now called) were anywhere west of Bornholm he opened up the way for a return of the Tarras Line freighters to those waters, with a new agent and clearing house in the Jutland port of Frederickshavn. Brand was inclined to fret at the delay. Still, he was weeks ahead of the Navy in the Baltic, for in spite of Lord Palmerston's energy and inspiring speeches, in spite of the new men at the Admiralty, the shipyard workers were making a slow job of constructing the gunboats and mortar vessels which experience had proved would be indispensable to an attack on the Russian fortresses. And in spite of Brand Endicott's eagerness to engage the enemy, the gun-runners, like the warships, had not yet emerged from their home ports.

Policing by Napier's squadrons had already reduced their number. The Danish contraband carriers were the most daring and at the same time the most foolhardy : on a memorable day in the previous June, when Napier was on his way to Cronstadt, H.M.S. *Archer* had captured no fewer than three vessels carrying war materials under the Danish flag, as they all ran together for the Russian port of Riga. *Archer*, of course, had performed this feat under steam power, and Brand Endicott, who had no auxiliary screw in *Duchess*, knew that he could hardly hope to challenge either the gang calling itself the British Steam Navigation Company, which operated out of Dunkirk, or—at least on the high seas—either the *Lorelei* or the *Wotan* belonging to Müller and Sons of Lübeck. That left the *Sealark*, the notorious barque seen off Kiel and again off Bornholm since Brand came into the Kattegat, but which on her summer runs between Antwerp and Memel had never permitted so much as a sight of her cross-trees to the patrolling British ships of war.

On their second trip, Brand set Joe ashore at Gothenburg to make certain enquiries among his old trading acquaintances, and moored at the Stigberg quay, a mile from the old Tarras berth at the Stone Pier.

"And you're not going ashore here, Mrs. Endicott!" he told Alix. "I've had quite enough of setting you down at Gothenburg! Some one or other is sure to recognize you, and I'll finish up in the hands of the Watch again! Nothing's changed much here in twelve months, has it?"

"They say more people than ever mean to emigrate this spring. I don't see much sign of it so far."

The Stigberg quay was almost deserted, and the snow lay as thick as on the February afternoon when Brand and Alix walked down the Stone Pier and into their own future. It was easy to see Joe coming a great way off, laden with packages and parcels; soon he was with them in the cabin, warming his hands at the stove.

"Well, Joe, what's the news?"

"We missed *Sealark* by exactly twenty-four hours."

"What! You mean she actually put in to Gothenburg?"

"To pick up her owner, or one of her owners. Mr. Svensson."

"He's aboard *Sealark* now? Bound for Memel?"

"The word around the docks," said Joe, "was that *Sealark's* bound for Copenhagen. Maybe Svensson means to go ashore there. As you've described him, I hardly see him on a trip to Memel in this weather."

"Why not? He probably wants to do some business with his Russian friends. What's *Sealark* carrying?"

"Liége cartridges, shipped at her home port, Antwerp."

"Damnation," said Brand, "we could have had her in the

North Sea. But it'll be worth the delay, if Svensson's still aboard when we catch her up. What do you think, Alix?"

"I think he will be," Alix said, not understanding the question. "What if he has decided to go to Russia for good?"

"And leave his establishment in Gothenburg?"

"It's not what it was," said Joe. "I hear Mrs. Tarras has been very active since you showed up his connection with the Prussians. She's got him black-listed by every British firm that employed him as an agent, and he couldn't afford that. He's been living above his means for years."

"Well, he can go to Russia and stay there for me," said Brand, "just so I have a word with him en route. Was *Sealark* heading for the Belts or for the Sound?"

"The Belts."

"All right, she has the wind against her; if we take the Sound we may catch up with her at Copenhagen. Call all hands, Joe, and we'll weigh anchor."

"Skipper!" said Joe as the American stood up, "wait five minutes! Can I say something, not as your lieutenant, but as your friend?"

"For God's sake!" said Brand impatiently, "when we're here together you can say what you like, Joe, you know that."

"Well then, look here! Are you going after *Sealark* to capture a Russian cargo, or settle your own score with that man Svensson?"

"Both."

"Brand, Svensson himself isn't worth powder and shot. He's an old man who wanted to keep you out of his own backyard, and that's about it. Knocking him out of the war with the *Duchess of Finland* behind you is on the same level as Napier at Bomarsund—using a big force to capture a little fort."

"I know what it took to capture Bomarsund better than you do," said Brand in a rage. "Call all hands, Mister! And you put on your warm coat, Alix and come on deck to see the last of Gothenburg."

He missed the *Sealark* at Copenhagen but only by two hours; picked her up again at Bornholm on a foggy morning, and saw the gun-runner turn north between the isle of Oland and the east coast of Sweden.

"Where's he bound for, up the Kalmar Sound?"

"Stockholm?" suggested Joe.

"Not very likely. Maybe one of your hidey-holes near Mönsteras, or maybe Farö Sound. Anyway he's giving us an easy trip so far. Last time I was off Kalmar I was leadsman in the *Lightning*, calling the depths for Captain Sulivan. I wonder where old Sulivan is now?"

Where were they all now, his shipmates of less than a year ago? Slowly, inevitably, as they came into the Baltic proper, Brand began to remember the men who would never sail these seas again. Lauri, the first of them to fall; foul-mouthed Morgan, who had called Lauri Brand's fancy boy; Campbell, the swimmer always half-frozen with cold but who never had any thought of giving up, and all the others who struggled with him to drag the guns that shelled Fort Nottich and died raving in the grim wards of the hospital ship *Belleisle*. They were coming into waters which the men who had sailed in H.M.S. *Tribune* knew as well as he did, if not better; the long stretch of open sea between Älvsnabben, where Napier had tried too often and too long, and Gotska Sandön, where Campbell and he had first – and so many times later – carried out the exercise with the Bickford fuse. And the *Sealark* was skulking along the east coast of Gotland, the principal cruising ground of the Swedish Navy; hanging in the wind at the entrance to the Sound, and finally anchoring in Farö harbour, still half invisible in the fog.

"We'll drop anchor in the roads," said Brand, "and make fast to a mooring buoy; and Joe, you can go in to Farö in the jolly-boat."

"I'm going too," said Alix. "Two people speaking Swedish will bring back more news than one."

"You'll do better speaking English," Brand told her. "There's a little shop at Farö owned by an Englishman called Grubb. Matter of fact I told my grandmother she ought to buy him out and open a shipyard there, and a ship's chandler's store, when the war's over. He's got two daughters, girls about your own age. You go up and make friends with the Miss Grubbs and find out what they know about *Sealark*, but don't whatever you do, go near the barque yourself or be seen by anybody belonging to her. Wait at the store for Joe until he's ready to bring you back aboard."

It was the first time she had ever gone ashore without him, and Brand was half-wild with impatience before the boat came up to the mooring buoy and Joe helped Alix up the ship's side.

"What the hell have you been doing all this time?" he burst out when he got them in the cabin, and Alix was unwinding a fog-drenched woollen scarf from her damp hair. "You had me badly scared."

"I couldn't get the young ladies to let Alix go," said Joe. "They were having a coffee party no mere man could break up."

"Well, between the pair of you, what did you find out?"

"*Sealark* has a Prussian skipper and a Belgian mate," said Joe. "She's carrying six hands, the same as us, and it's confirmed about the cargo. Cartridges for the Minié rifles she's been running in to Russia since last year."

"Two officers, six hands—and one passenger," said Alix with sparkling eyes. "The Grubb girls know Svensson by sight, and they saw him in the store this morning. He's going all the way to Hapsal."

"*Hapsal*? Not Memel?"

"On the west coast of Esthonia," said Joe.

"I know where Hapsal is. East of Dagö," said Brand irritably. "I spent November between Hangö Head and Dager Ort, if you remember. But Hapsal! There's a small Russian garrison there, but what about facilities for landing contraband?"

"Hapsal used to be a holiday resort," said Alix. "There's a good carriage road as far as Reval. If anyone wanted to get into Russia quietly, that way is as good as any."

"I'm not worrying about Mr. Svensson. It's how to get at those Belgian cartridges once she comes out of Farö—"

"You'll follow the *Sealark*, then?"

"Certainly."

"She has two sixteen-pounder guns on deck, I heard today. If we order her to heave to she'll put a shot into us, as like as not."

"The carronade being idle at the time, eh?"

"For God's sake, Brand!"

"You're not weakening, are you, Joe?" said Brand coolly. "After all the good work you did round the Stockholm docks, ferreting out who owned the *Sealark*, and the Minié rifles she ran in to Memel, don't tell me you want to give up on the chase now!"

Joe looked from the American to Alix. She was sitting with

her chin in her hands, watching Brand and smiling; there was no doing anything with *him*, of course, with that lovely hallucinated face beside him.

"Remember that fine letter you wrote me last summer, before Ekenäs?" Brand went on. "You said it made you mad to think of gun-runners sheltering behind the Stars and Stripes. Do you still feel the same about Old Glory now the chips are down?"

"Yes, damn you," said Joe Ryan. "You know I do."

The gun-runners' barque slipped out of Farö Sound at midnight and set a course nor'-east. Brand followed her masthead light at a discreet distance, making a long tack south to keep the pursued from suspicion of the pursuit, and making north again when the livid daylight came. *Sealark* was setting a spanking pace. During the forenoon Brand had to crowd on every inch of canvas, and Joe listened uneasily to the creaking rigging.

" 'A stern chase is a long chase', skipper!" he ventured to quote at last.

"I'm not fighting Trafalgar, Mister. I'm keeping the enemy in sight."

"Aye, aye, sir."

It began to snow as they approached the Gulf of Finland, where the great ice barrier stretched from shore to shore, and Alix came to stand near Brand when he took a trick at the wheel, balancing gracefully as the brig plunged ahead. The keen wind whipped carnation to her cheeks. Brand looked at her adoringly. Seen thus, gazing through the snow at *Sealark* hull down on the horizon, looking beyond *Sealark* towards Finland, she reminded him of the Duchess beneath the bowsprit with the gold paint hair and the carved hands clasped upon the sea-wet breast.

Hours later, when Alix had long since been sent back to the warm cabin, and the face of every man on deck was glazed and stiff with salt spray and blown snow, they saw their quarry alter course slightly, and begin a complicated tacking movement.

"Stand by to go about!" Brand shouted above the whistle of the wind, and then to Joe:

"Now where the devil is he making for? He can't be heading south for Siele Sound?"

"Not he. He daren't risk running aground on Palmer Ort in this weather. He'll wait to go into Hapsal in daylight, and then take the passage by Worms Island."

"Land ho!" the man on look-out yelled.

"Dager Ort," said Brand, and snapped his glass shut. "You're right, Joe. He's going to wear out the night off Dagö, and if he goes in to Dagö harbour, I think we've got him. Heave to, and send the hands to dinner."

It was not a comfortable dinner, either in the forecastle or the cabin, as the cross-currents raced in the darkness off Dagö Head, the Dager Ort of *Arrogant*'s long patrolling, but a double ration of rum put heart into the crew, and Blythe, bo'sun by virtue of having been an Able Seaman in H.M.S. *Tribune*, was grinning at the prospect of action when Brand explained the plan to him.

The worst of it was the long wait between the fall of darkness and ten o'clock, which Brand judged the earliest possible hour for a surprise attack on the barque. He said frankly that if her cargo had been rifles instead of cartridges, and if any of his crew had been as good a swimmer as his old partner Campbell, he would have been tempted to use a Bickford fuse, of which he carried several in the hold, and try to explode the *Sealark*. Such an attempt would however be suicidal, and even if it "came off", he coolly said, the death of neutrals aboard *Sealark* might "lead to trouble". So he proposed to board and scuttle the barque, leaving her people with a fair chance to apply for help to the unfriendly fishermen of the village, and continue their trip to Hapsal over the rough tracks of an island which boasted neither horse nor carriage.

"Tell me again how they were berthed at Farö, Joe."

"They'd only the anchor watchman on deck when we pulled round them. Berthed right up at the main quay, snug as you please, with all hatches battened down and lights out; no sign of life aboard."

"They've gotten careless. Eight of them, and eight of us; not bad; only I must leave Gordon aboard with Alix, and Webster stays in the boat. Come on and let's go through it with the hands."

With a quick kiss for Alix, Brand pulled his pea jacket over

337

his thick jersey, and led the way to the forecastle, where the men were waiting. He went through the plan again, behind the shut door, for on a windy night voices might carry over Dagö Bay, and he was nearly sure that *Sealark* knew nothing of the pursuit. The men were issued with Colt revolvers, spikes, chisels and crowbars. The jollyboat was lowered with muffled oars, and with a word of reassurance to Alix, Brand followed Joe and the four ex-Navy men over the side.

It was a longer row than he had reckoned on to cross the bay, *Sealark* had gone right in to Dagö, where the fishermen's stone cottages were dark and silent, and her dim anchor light showed the watchman, rolled in a blanket, sitting on an upturned mess kid with his back against the mast and facing in the direction of the village. The *Sealark's* ropes, and the moorings of the fishing boats further down the quay, creaked in the wind and helped to muffle the jollyboat's approach.

Brand caught at the battens on the ship's side, levered himself out of the boat and was over the rail like a cat. Jenkins, the youngest and most agile of the crew, came after him in the very instant when the watchman shouted and went down headlong on the deck with Brand on top of him. Joe and the three other seamen were scrambling aboard, and Blythe, as planned, led his mates in a rush to the forecastle.

The operation nearly foundered on the watchman. He was a powerfully built fellow, quite a match for Brand Endicott in height and weight, and he gave the American more of a fight than Brand expected. He heard the yells of *Sealark's* crew from the forecastle through the blood drumming in his head as the watchman's gouging fingers reached his eyes and throat. Then he was on top again, and had the man's head in his two hands, knocking him senseless against the wooden mast, and as he rose breathless to his feet he heard the sound of shots and a cry from Joe.

The Prussian captain and his mate had had time to load their pistols while Brand fought, and Joe had hesitated too long before shooting his way into the cabin. He was not down, but staggering against the rail with his hand clutching his left arm, and he kept his wits about him—when Brand tackled the young mate round the knees and brought him crashing to the deck, it was Joe who kicked the pistol from his open hand into the scuppers. But it was Blythe, the bo'sun, who settled the captain as he came charging out of the cabin, with a shot over Brand's head into his shoulder.

"Bring a rope, Blythe! How about the forecastle?"

"All serene, sir. We gunned 'em into the galley and fixed the bar. You want this lot tied up, sir?"

"And that watchman too. Jenkins! The hold?"

"Full of cartridges, sir, and a lot of metal stuff, glass tubes too."

"Good enough. Now get busy, but post a man at the galley hatch. Those lads will try a break-out any minute—Joe! Are you all right?"

"Sure!"

"Then keep your gun on those three beauties. I'll have a word with Mr. Svensson."

With the Colt, now drawn for the first time, in his hand, Brand kicked open the swinging cabin door. There was no one inside. The door of the double berth, presumably shared by the officers, stood wide open. A second door was discreetly closed.

"Drop your gun, Mr. Svensson," Brand called, "and come on out."

"I am not armed," said a muffled voice from inside the berth.

"I am," said Brand. "Come out unless you want me to shoot my way in."

A bolt was reluctantly drawn back. Sven Svensson, the Good Samaritan of Gothenburg, appeared in shirt and trousers, with the handsome furred cloak which Brand remembered slung round his stooping shoulders.

"Who spoke my name?" he said.

"I did," said Brand. "Have you forgotten me?"

With a kind of humiliation he realized that Svensson had indeed forgotten the simple-minded American who had been so easily persuaded to send himself to prison, just over a year ago. He made no allowance for his own changed appearance and rough clothing; he only realized that Joe was right, and this faltering, elderly man, half-speechless with fear, was not worth the hatred he had nourished for a year.

"Brand Endicott," he said.

"Not—Mrs. Tarras'—not the American?"

"That's me. The American you thought you'd railroaded out

339

of the Baltic when you saw me safely off to jail at Gothenburg. Where's your accomplice?"

"I—don't understand you."

"Your partner, then. Captain Erik Kruse."

For the first time a gleam of his old self-assurance crossed Svensson's livid face.

"Ah!" he said. "Gone where you will never find him!"

"Then he's in Russia or in hell. Alive—or dead?"

"Alive. As you may find out to your cost some day—you dog! What are you doing aboard my ship?"

"Listen!" said Brand. "You can almost feel her go, can't you?" For the blows of his own men on spikes and chisels, the decided list to the cabin floor, betrayed the operation under way.

"In the Queen's name!" said Brand. "We've scuttled the *Sealark*. Her crew's lives depend on you, Mr. Svensson! Unbind your officers and release the crew, and you all have a chance to see tomorrow morning. Good luck to you in the Russian Empire!"

He ran out on deck. Joe was there, holding his gun steady on the three prisoners, ghastly pale and with blood soaking through a rough bandage on his arm.

"Blythe!" Brand shouted. "All of you! Over the side at once!" There was a rush to obey him. The *Sealark* was sinking fast, and Webster was moving further away in the boat to get clear of the down-drag. There was a splintering of glass and wood at the galley hatch. Up in the village one or two candles had been lit at last.

"'Ow about Mr. Ryan, sir?" panted Blythe.

"I'll look after him. Joe! Hold on!"

Brand thrust his Colt into his belt and raced for the bow, pulling his knife from its sheath as he ran. He leaned out far over the bowsprit, and hacked away, intact from its staff, what had been impudently hung there.

"Here, Joe," he gasped, pushing the flag into Joe's sound hand. "Old Glory—yours by the right of conquest!"

CHAPTER EIGHTEEN

UNDER A FLAG OF TRUCE

IN the darkness and the snow it was easy for the *Duchess of Finland* to escape unseen from Dagö Bay. Through the anxious night, while Alix used all her limited knowledge of first aid to stanch the bleeding from Joe's arm, Brand ran south to Ösel island, and in the early morning he went ashore himself at the fishing port of Arensburg and brought a doctor off to the wounded man.

Joe had lost a good deal of blood, although his wound was ragged and shallow rather than deep. He spent all of that day in his bunk. When he got up he was quiet and thoughtful, but so he had been since he arrived in London; the difference now was that he was quietly burning for a new attack by the privateer against the enemy who had drawn his Irish blood. This exactly suited Captain Endicott. Brand was in a restless mood, already dissatisfied with the scuttling of the *Sealark*, and regretting he had not had enough hands to put a prize crew in the barque and take her back to England. Or —when commonsense reminded him that from the Gulf of Riga to the Port of London was too long a way for a snow brig, under sail, to bring in a prize singlehanded—if the Navy had been in the Baltic instead of at Spithead, he might have been able to hand over his prize, the notorious gun-runner *Sealark*, to one of the ships of war or frigates. He liked to picture Captain Yelverton's face if he had turned her over to *Arrogant*.

While Joe was recovering he tacked back across the Baltic to Slite, the principal naval port of Gotland, where he had arranged with Mr. Arthur Tarras to call regularly for mail. Then he went south and east towards Karlskrona, and was lucky enough to fall in with a Danish two-master about to enter the Kalmar Sound with a cargo of gunpowder consigned to Russia via Haparanda, and with such a cargo aboard, her captain struck his flag when the first shot from the little carronade hurtled across her bow. The Kalmar Sound was a favourite northbound corridor for contrabanders with a low draught of water, and thus a happy hunting-ground for the privateer. Joe, as he had once boasted, did indeed know every creek and cove in Blekinge and Småland, and at Mönsterås and Figeholm they smoked out in quick succession two Dutchmen and a Belgian with Minié rifles and bags of grapeshot, a Hamburg barque with more of the zinc and glass seen in the *Sealark's* hold and used for the manufacture of "infernals", and—further north at Västervik—a Norwegian laden with timber for the new Russian works at Bomarsund. After that capture the cabin stove and the forecastle galley had fragrant pine logs to burn for a long time, for with Alix at his elbow Brand took everything that came his way. In the old days "my captain" and other high-minded British sea officers had disdained to take prizes from "poor fishermen", or "poor farming fellows" who might be ruined for life by the loss of their boats, but Brand had no such scruples. He might not be able to take the contrabanders in as prizes; he seized or destroyed anything which could benefit the Russians.

Although nothing was heard of the disappearance of the *Sealark* in the snows off Dager Ort, the capture of so many contrabanders off a populated coast could not be kept a secret, and the American privateer who sailed under British Letters of Marque soon became a legend in the Baltic. There was no British ship to share the limelight with the *Duchess of Finland*, for whereas Admiral Napier had put to sea too soon, Sir Richard Dundas, Vice-Admiral of the Blue, seemed likely to put to sea too late, and the snow brig's appearances in Slite harbour were always watched with interest by the huge Swedish garrison, which now declared itself "heart and soul for England". Alix, Brand and Joe were stared at when they went ashore together. The beautiful fair girl in the fisherman's jersey, the tall American who always held her by the hand, and the wiry fellow with black curly hair were the most discussed trio in the whole of Gotland.

The *Duchess* was becalmed off Slite when the first division of Dundas' fleet came through the Baltic, and Brand lowered his topsails in the merchantman's conventional salute to a man-of-war, a dozen times, as half the twenty-five steam line of battle ships went by. He identified Admiral Dundas' flag in Napier's old three-decker, H.M.S. *Duke of Wellington*, and

Admiral Seymour's square blue flag at the mizzen topgallant mast of H.M.S. *Exmouth*, 90; he looked in vain for *Arrogant* and *Imperieuse.*

"I wonder if they aim to reconnoitre Sveaborg or Cronstadt first?" he said, when the stately convoy had gone by.

"The Gulf of Finland must be open now," said Alix eagerly. "Let's go up after them and find out !"

"I'll do that, darling, as soon as I've fitted a sweeper for the 'infernals'."

"I'd admire to see your face," said Joe, "if we come up with *Arrogant* in the Gulf, and Yelverton threatened to come aboard you and see if *you* were carrying contraband !"

"Captain Yelverton wouldn't challenge the Gridiron, not after President Pierce's speech on the right of search. 'Nemesis' Hall would, like a shot."

"Hall of the *Hecla*?"

"*Hecla*'s been sent to the Crimea. 'Old Nemesis' has the *Blenheim*, with sixty guns, and Captain Sulivan has *Merlin*, with six. Big promotions in the Fleet these days."

"Would you be missing the lower deck, by any chance?" said Joe dryly, and Brand laughed. He liked the Irishman's occasional sarcasms; they reminded him of the salty speech of Maine.

"Homesick for the Navy !" he said. "Homesick for the hospital ship *Belleisle* ! There's a breeze springing up, Joe. Let's go on in to Slite for the mail."

"Hands aloft to set topgallants and courses !" Joe had seized the speaking trumpet from the beckets in the wheel, and the *Duchess* shook out her canvas and made her graceful way to port through seas which the first fine weather of May had given a surface like dark blue glass. Brand whistled "Nancy Dawson" as he changed his coat to go ashore.

"We'll leave for Kökar in the morning, Joe. Will you keep the last dog watch with Jenkins, Smith and Webster?"

"Aye, aye, sir."

"You coming ashore, Alix?"

"I don't think so, dear. I'm rather tired, and I want to look out lighter clothing for tomorrow. It's been warm today. Only six weeks to Midsummer !"

"Well, don't wear yourself out, you do look tired tonight. I'll be back in a couple of hours."

Alix, with a kiss for him and a smile, remained alone in the cabin, and there was a sound of locker lids opening and closing as she got out Brand's thin shirts and her own white cotton bodices. Then Joe heard her moving in the tiny galley, and presently she came out on deck and said:

"Coffee, Joe?"

"Thank you, ma'am!"

The captain's cabin in the *Duchess* had none of the bright feminine decorations which Mary Ryan had added to the cabin in the *Molly-O*. It was neat and shipshape, but no more. The doors of both berths were open, and the ports above the bunks, so that the warm May breeze blew through and through.

"Your stove's nearly out," said Joe. "Want some more wood?"

"No, thank you; it's going to be hot tonight."

Joe watched her, leaning back with closed eyes in Brand's heavy desk chair, which was not meant for relaxation; and saw that underneath the warm suntan Alexandra's face was subtly weary, with the curve of her high cheekbones more clearly defined than before.

"Tired?"

She sat up at once. "No—why should I be?"

"Well, I don't know why not! You've had two months of a pretty rough life up and down the Baltic, different from anything you've ever known before."

"And if you knew how I love it!" she said, glowing. "If you knew how miserable I was a year ago in that great house in Petersburg!"

"Do you think you'll be happy as a skipper's wife aboard a trading brig once the war's over, and Brand's running freight for Tarras and Company again?"

"I never think of that," she said, wide-eyed. "I never think of anything beyond the war!"

"Well, I didn't mean to get you all upset! Brand is mighty happy now, he enjoys being free to come and go as he pleases —Kökar tomorrow, and then across to Eckerö and back to the Kalmar Sound—and he won't be a trading skipper like me when *he's* pushing forty. No fear of that! It's you I'm thinking of. After all, you won't be able to stand up to this sort of life longer than a few months more."

344

In the evening light pouring in through the open ports and the door of the cabin, Joe saw Alexandra's sudden burning blush.

"What—on earth do you—mean?"

"I mean *no* woman can stand the Baltic after the end of September! Mary can't, and none of the Stockholm captains' wives stay at sea after the first ice shows in the Gulfs. And they've been bred to it all their lives—not like you."

He watched the blush fade, not all at once, but leaving an ugly mark on her white neck.

"Alix . . ."

"What?"

"Nothing . . . Is there any more of this good coffee?"

"In the galley."

Joe refilled his cup thoughtfully and came back to the cabin. Alix had not moved. She was leaning on Brand's desk in a favourite position, with her chin cupped in her hands.

"You're down in the dumps tonight, aren't you, Alix? Pity Mary isn't here with her guitar! She's the one to sing the songs that would cheer you up!"

"Irish songs?"

"Irish, Swedish, sailor ballads—anything you like! She's learning to sing songs in Italian now."

With relief at the change of topic: "You miss her, Joe."

"Sure I miss her. My little Sea Peddler! This'll be the first summer I haven't had Mary for a shipmate since she was ten years old."

"But she wanted to stay in Stockholm for her singing lessons, didn't she?"

"Sure she did. But I don't know . . . she's not too happy at her aunt's, this time."

Alix took her courage in both hands. She and Joe Ryan had become good friends, but there was a certain reserve between them, and she had hesitated, in breaking it, to seem to criticize the girl her father adored.

"Are you . . . worried about Mary? Really worried?"

"I—it's just that a girl as pretty and smart as Mary gets a lot of admiration, don't you see? And sometimes the wrong sort of people . . ."

"People like Captain Kruse?"

Joe looked at her quickly. "Did Brand tell you? She was

345

quite frank about it, that day he volunteered for the Navy, when he took us to the Golden Peace. Explained how she met him at her aunt's, and everything . . ."

"And that's why you're worried about Mary staying with her aunt now?"

"Oh God!" the man said, "where else could I leave her? Not in our own apartment . . . sitting watching by that mirror . . . for the officers to come off duty . . ."

"Joe!" Alix got to her feet, shocked and troubled beyond words. "Joe, what can I do to help?"

"Would you be a friend to her, Alix? Would you ask Brand to go to Stockholm some time soon? If Mary could have a talk with a girl like you . . ."

Alix wrested her hand from Joe's sudden clasp. "Hush," she said "I hear the jolly-boat coming back."

Brand came into the cabin with his sandy hair ruffled and fresh colour in his windbeaten face.

"It's blowing up a bit," he said, after kissing Alix. ". . . The British are off to the Gulf of Courland, Joe. Cooper Key in *Amphion*, Rundle Watson in *Imperieuse*, and all the old hands. The blockade officially begins tomorrow."

"Only in the Gulf of Courland? Not the Gulf of Finland?"

"Not yet. And here's mail—a letter for you, darling, and one for Joe."

Joe Ryan glanced at his daughter's handwriting and stuffed the letter in his pocket. "Thanks," he said. "I'll go my rounds now and see the lights out, and then I think I'll turn in and read what Miss Molly has to say. Goodnight to you both."

"Goodnight, Joe." Brand lit the oil lamp and flung a bundle of Tarras Line letters on his desk before sitting down on the arm of Alexandra's chair.

"Falk's safely back in London? How is Kristina?" he enquired.

"Much, much better. Oh, but Brand, listen to this:

" 'Gunnar and I had a letter from father' [Alix read aloud] 'sent through the Russian Embassy at Stockholm. He has been able to get the Russian troops withdrawn from Ekenäs manor, and Anna, our Lapp maid of the olden days, has been installed there to clean up the mess. One of the Mannerheims, who drove A. over from Åbo, says it was left in fair condition, but mamma's nicest furniture, of course, is missing. Father adds that the Russian garrison has been withdrawn from Ekenäs. He thinks that after last year's fiasco at Gamla Karleby, *the British will not dare* to attack a Finnish town again ! Gunnar says . . .' The rest is all about her husband," finished Alix.

"Ekenäs evacuated ! That means the Russians are massing their troops in Helsingfors."

"They are preparing to defend the fortress," Alix said.

"Darling, I'm worried about Joe."

Brand and Alix were lying side by side among the wild flowers in a meadow where no cattle had ever grazed, on one of the myriad islands in the Finnish archipelago. Faintly, from one of the distant coves, they could hear the shouts of the crew, come ashore for a freshwater bath and a swim after one of the hardest weeks of their long cruise.

Rear-Admiral Dundas, the former Second Naval Lord, appeared to have learned procrastination at the Admiralty. After a lengthy reconnaissance of Sveaborg he spent much time in waiting for the French, who on this occasion took thirty-seven days to reach the Gulf from Cherbourg. Rear-Admiral Pénaud, as soon as he arrived from France, threatened fire and slaughter to the citizens of Helsingfors, for his Imperial master, Napoleon III, had been dissuaded by the British from making speeches in the Crimea, and was in a blood-thirsty mood. The French Emperor had a new project; a weapon of his own invention to be called the Incendiary Fuse, which self-propelled from one site should explode on another at a certain distance; and while he developed his Fuses for the glory (he said) of France the British in the Baltic went on doggedly "creeping and sweeping" for the Russian mines.

Lying off the Kökar Rocks, the *Duchess of Finland* had intercepted a Prussian schooner bound for Åbo with a large consignment of the zinc and glass tubes used in manufacturing the Russian mines, and after a hard chase and ranging shots fired from the carronade, Brand had been able to hand her over to a ship of the Baltic Fleet. Not to H.M.S. *Arrogant*, which would have been his ultimate satisfaction, but to H.M.S. *Cossack*, 20, a vessel actually in course of building at North-fleet to the late Czar's orders, and confiscated by the British when the war began. Captain Fanshawe had shown the young privateer captain every courtesy, and invited him to take wine in the saloon hung with the double eagle and other fittings ordered to suit Nikita's taste, and when Brand took his departure the *Cossack's* sideboys were mustered, the bo'suns' whistles shrilled as for a Navy officer, and the American returned to his *Duchess* flushed with pride and pleasure. Now he was exhausted, half asleep; Alix was not sure that he had even heard what she said about Joe Ryan.

"Brand, are you listening?"

"M-mm." She saw his grey eyes smiling at her between long sandy lashes. "Alix, you do look lovely. I used to dream of you like this when I was in the hospital ship. In your white bodice with your arms bare . . ." He laid his warm hand on her breast.

Alix stirred in drowsy contentment. They had been swimming and diving for an hour, and to Alix it was always a joy when Brand praised her power as a swimmer and her grace in the water. Now a certain lassitude, which more and more often invaded Alexandra's body, prompted her to turn to Brand and sleep the afternoon away in his embrace. A forbidden thought—impalpable, surely no more than a fancy—moved like a mouse in the corridors of her brain.

She sat up reluctantly. "Brand, *please*! I told you I was worried about Joe."

"Sure, I heard you. Joe's all right. There's nothing the matter with his arm now. Fact is, that was a lucky shot, it did Joe Ryan a power of good. When he joined at first, I had a feeling he only came in with us for double pay, so he could buy sheet music and dancing slippers for young Mary. But ever since his blood was shed Joe's been as crazy to chase the gunrunners as you or me."

"Oh, but I wasn't talking about his arm! Poor Joe is so upset about Mary—"

"What's Mary been doing now?"

"She isn't happy with the relatives in Stockholm." Not even to Brand would Alix repeat all Joe's confidences about his daughter, for it was not in her nature to betray another girl. But Brand merely looked bored, and giving up the hope of sleep, sat up himself, and lit one of the new cigarettes whose popularity had spread even as far as Gotland.

"Well, that's Joe's problem," he said reasonably. "Why should he bother you about it?"

"Perhaps it's our problem too, dear, in a way. If you hadn't met the Ryans at Gothenburg, Joe wouldn't be sailing with you now; and if I hadn't lost my head at Bomarsund I might have been able to help Mary over Erik Kruse instead of antagonizing her—"

"Does Kruse come into this?"

"I hope he doesn't, Brand. But I keep remembering what he said, that horrible day, about Mary being a garrison toast, or something of that kind, and that her aunt's house was notorious—"

"Oh, nonsense! The Engströms are perfectly respectable people. There may be a bit of flirting, with so many girls, but that's all. Joe must have been trying on a bit of Irish blarney; you mustn't let him upset you, dear."

"I can't help it."

He hated to see her looking sad, with her fair head hanging. Perhaps he had been taking Alix too much for granted lately. She was such a wonderful shipmate, he hadn't been coaxing or caressing enough, maybe? It was sheer fatigue— nothing more! Even without the chase, the strain of conning *Duchess* through those unfamiliar reefs and islands had begun to take its toll of him. He was getting sharp and irritable, and as for making love to Alix—for nights past in spite of the splendid vitality of his twenty-four years, Brand had been too tired to do more than fall spreadeagled on his bunk and spend in sleep every blessed minute of his watch below.

He twined one of her long fair locks round his finger and said:

"Well, what do you think we ought to do about it?"

"Couldn't we go south, when it's time to go back to Slite, by way of Stockholm? So that Joe can spend a day or two with Mary, and make sure that she's quite well and happy? It would mean so much to him—"

"No doubt," said Brand. "And if Mary isn't well or happy, are we to take her back to sea with us?"

She jumped at that. "I don't see why we shouldn't."

"Good God," said Brand. "Two girls on board! The hands will think I'm running a hen frigate."

349

"Is that Navy slang? It sounds disgusting."

"Look, Alix, having the captain's wife aboard is a time-honoured custom; but a single girl, that's different. Especially a girl like Mary, simpering and fluttering her eyelashes at all the men!"

He would have been pleased if Alix had asked provocatively, "Did she ever flutter her eyelashes at *you*?" but she only smiled and shook her head. Brand said conclusively:

"Besides, where would she sleep?"

"She could have Joe's berth, and Joe could bunk for'ard in the apprentice's berth, where they keep the logs for the galley fire."

"I see you've got it all figured out, Mrs. Endicott! But it needs some thinking over before we get to Stockholm. If Joe is going to pine away without his daughter—and mind! I don't think she was very straight with *you*—then maybe he'd rather go back to peddling oranges in the *Molly-O*, and I'll promote Blythe to be mate in the *Duchess of Finland*. This is war, you know, Alix—not a pleasure cruise."

"I know it." Her eyes slid fractionally past Brand's with the intent look he was coming to recognize. "But you *will* go to Stockholm . . . won't you?"

"If it means all that to you." Brand stubbed out his cigarette carefully in the young heather and pulled Alix down into his arms. "I believe you just want me to buy you another hat!"

"I believe *you're* really going off to sleep."

"It smells good here under the firs," he said drowsily. "Makes me think I'm back on Jewell Island . . ."

"Where you picked the arbutus to carry to Aunt Betsy?"

"M–m."

"Did you often go to sleep with a girl in your arms on Jewell Island? And did she kiss you like this?"

"No!"

"Well then, like this . . . ?"

*   *   *

Of course Mary Ryan was with them when the *Duchess* sailed from Stockholm. It would have taken a harder heart than Brand's to resist the hope in Joe's eyes, or Mary's gratitude at being delivered from her uncle's house and what she called the boredom of Stockholm now her singing lessons had come to an end.

She did not embarrass them with thankfulness. Mary Ryan had changed a good deal in the past year. She was actually taller, and even prettier, with the childish roundness gone from her face and the black curls subdued by combs and a snood into a very creditable version of the "Eugénie" coiffure. She had also acquired a sophisticated manner which rather surprised Alix, keeping the conversation very much in her own hands while all four were at the evening meal. But when the two girls were alone at bedtime she said with diffidence:

"Mrs. Endicott, you're very generous to let me sail with you. I want to apologize for all the hateful things I said to you at Bomarsund."

"Please," said Alix, "that's all past and done with. Brand and I are glad to have you with us now."

"You see, I was very jealous of you at that time."

"Because of Brand?"

"Yes, a little. I couldn't help it, I liked him so much, but I always knew he was in love with a girl at Helsingfors. But really it was because of Erik Kruse."

"Did you see him again that day?" said Alix with an effort. It was the question which had long gnawed at her sense of guilt; she was already prepared for the answer.

"Of course I did, what do you suppose? I ran back along the path I met you on, and there he was—bleeding and faint—"

"He wasn't badly hurt!"

"It left a mark. In Stockholm he passed it off as a duelling scar."

"But then?"

"Then I took him right back to the Molly-O. I knew it was safe enough, that papa would stay talking and drinking at the jetty for an hour. I bathed his face, and dressed it, and gave him brandy, and that was how it all began."

"What all began?"

"Our love affair."

"You don't mean—"

"Yes I do," said Mary defiantly. "Look here! Up to that time it was only a flirtation between Erik and me. Letters in bouquets and stolen dances at Gröna Lund—that sort of thing. But after I took care of him that afternoon it seemed to make him more—more mine, and he was gentler, and so grateful; and not long after that, when we went back to Stockholm—" She made a little helpless gesture.

"Mary!"

"What of it? I'd seen Brand and you together. I wanted *my* lover too. And it was just my bad luck that it had to be Erik Kruse."

"Mary, you don't mean—"

"That I'm going to have his child? Of course not, I'm not such a fool. I knew it couldn't last—at least I knew after the first few weeks—and it was over even before he went off to join the Russian Army—"

"Erik has joined the Russian Army—?"

"Yes, as a military advisor on the Baltic. Didn't you know? He got into trouble with his Swedish General and was asked to send in his papers. They'd heard about the gun-running, and were furious."

"No wonder!" said Alix indignantly. "He will never be allowed to set foot in Sweden again."

"Oh, do you think so?" said Mary indifferently. "The West and Russia won't be at war for ever, you know, and then he can go where he likes. But I hope you and Brand will never have to see him again, because he hates you both. I don't know what might happen if you three were to meet—"

"And don't you hate him, you poor child?"

"Oh please don't stand on your two gold rings and your dignity, Mrs. Endicott, and poor-child me! I'm all right! Pretty soon I shall get a good theatre engagement in Stockholm, and after that I'll go to Paris. I'm sick of the *Molly-O*, and being papa's grand little first mate, and all that sentimental nonsense! And if ever I meet Erik Kruse again—"

"Yes, Mary?"

The pretty defiant face broke into tears.

"If I could only hope he would come back to me!"

Alix went unhappily to bed. To her single heart, Mary Ryan's view of Russia was horrible, and those sad words "I wanted my lover too!" roused all her old revulsion against Erik Kruse. But next day the younger girl made no reference to their brief talk. She was gay and cheerful, giving most of her attention to her delighted father, and amusing them all— not least young Jenkins at the wheel—by naming every rock and reef in the channel of the Stockholm archipelago down which the *Duchess* was moving between the Bogskaren rocks and the Kopparsten out to sea. It was the second day of June, and only the faintest breath of wind was in the snow brig's sails. After the midday dinner she and Alix sat in the nest of rugs in the bow, and chattered about Paris and the new fashions, and the prospects for the Great Exhibition—silly talk, which Brand enjoyed hearing at a distance. He thought having another girl for company was a pleasant change for Alix, and Mary, so far, had hardly glanced in the direction of the crew. To be fair, the crew—except for Jenkins—had hardly looked at Mary; but that was probably because they were all suffering from the after-effects of the inevitable debauch in Stockholm.

Brand himself had much on his mind. He had received a letter from Mrs. Tarras at her Stockholm bankers—a letter she had thought important enough to send in duplicate to Stockholm and to Slite. It began by complimenting him on his three months under Letters of Marque, which the astute old lady was pleased to call "a good investment". It went on to say that with an enormous naval force in the Baltic (doing no better, alas, this year than last) she felt that the "armed vessel" purchased by Tarras and Company would be better employed in convoying the Tarras ships to Baltic ports than in chasing gun-runners, which was a task for the Navy's new gun-boats. So Brand was accordingly to rendezvous with all four ships of the Tarras Aberdeen fleet at Frederikshavn in Jutland on or about June 21 and from there convoy them to all ports between Frederikshavn and Sundsvall in Sweden and intermediate destinations.

Brand, pacing the deck of the *Duchess*, knew Mrs. Tarras was quite right. She had to look to the future—her commercial future—because what future could the British people now expect in the Baltic theatre of war except the reduction of the fortress, Sveaborg? Even Sveaborg was of no importance, in the public mind, compared with Sevastopol, which wore around it all the halo of suffering, chivalry, romance. And yet Brand knew that he would go on convoy duty unwillingly—while *Arrogant* and the frigates went up the Gulf to Helsingfors.

In the evening Mary sang for them. It was again the season of the white nights, and the sunlight lingered on the deck of the *Duchess* until ten o'clock and later, touching Mary's head with a nimbus of gold as she stood up to sing with her back against the mast. It was of course the "Italian songs" she had just learned that Mary gave them, beginning with an aria from a new opera, La Traviata, which showed off all the power and flexibility of her half-trained voice. Mary was not a coloratura, like her idol Jenny Lind, but she had a high soprano which was heard to great advantage in "Home, Sweet Home", (requested by Joe as "something we can all understand") and which not one of her unmusical audience was qualified to appreciate.

"I'll sing again tomorrow night, if you like," she said when they asked her to continue, "but I think Mrs. Endicott is tired now, and so am I."

"If you call Brand, Brand, you must call me Alix, Mary dear." It was almost all Alexandra said by way of goodnight. She was tired, and her head aching, but she forgot fatigue when Brand came in and said Mary's singing had made him think of the Paris Opera when they heard L'Etoile du Nord, and how beautiful Alix looked then in her white bridal gown; and how beautiful she was now, how much more his, in this narrow bed in the Duchess of Finland . . .

She slept, after love, so close to Brand, so cramped against the wooden edge of the bunk that she woke after he left her to go on deck when the middle watch ended, and for some time lay quietly relaxed with her cheek on her hand. The milky morning light was filling the berth and the Duchess was moving quickly through the water. Alix felt wide awake and rested; physically much better than she had felt for days. She was sure that her recent misgivings were all nonsense.

In the silence she heard a sound from Mary's berth on the far side of the cabin. It might have been a sigh or a sob, and was followed by the creak of woodwork as the girl turned restlessly in bed. Alix felt her heart contract. She had never been aware of Joe's presence when he occupied the mate's berth. She was always, in Brand's arms, shut away from all the world, but now she was painfully aware of the nearness of another young woman, restless and unhappy, longing perhaps for love. It seemed a trespass on their own privacy. She got up, and pulling on her skirt and jersey, went on deck.

Everything was quiet. There was a pleasant smell from the forecastle galley, and Brand, watching the compass, held a mug of steaming coffee in his hand. Blythe, the bo'sun, was at the wheel. Above, seagulls were hovering above the white spread of canvas, and the scent of pinewoods came out across the water to greet the ship.

Brand, with a smile, took Alix by the shoulder and turned her gently to the east. Ahead she saw evergreens against the sky, smooth red rocks sloping to a cove, and a scatter of white houses round a clover meadow.

"There's Finland," he said. "You're home again!"

"This has been a wonderful day," said Mary Ryan.

"Charming for you two, perhaps, but not for us!" said Brand.

It had been a long day of tacking as the *Duchess* came into Finnish waters; half-way to Hangö Head and back again, up the channel between Korpö and Nagö in the direction of Åbo, where a Finn fisherman told them the whole British fleet had gone up the Gulf from the rendezvous in Nelson's old anchorage at Nargen to reconnoitre Sveaborg, and that a French squadron was following to join them there. On this Brand had dropped anchor in nine fathoms of clear water, in a steep-shelved, sheltered bay off one of the thousand islands, and the two girls had gone ashore with Joe and the bo'sun to buy provisions at a friendly farm.

"Maybe we can swim tomorrow," Alix said.

"Tomorrow I'm going to weigh anchor at first light and run back to Hangö Head, my dear."

"This was too good to last," said Mary. She had turned her hand to a hundred things that day; mending her father's clothes, helping Alix to rearrange the cabin, cooking chickens bought on the islands with parsley butter and wild onions— even discovering a lean ratting cat, whose presence in the hold Alix had never suspected. To the animal's dazed gratitude Mary had promoted it to the status of deck cat, with a personal bowl of milk and a ribbon bow.

"We're south of Korpö, aren't we?" she said now, leaning on the rail.

"Due south," her father said.

"Then this is where Queen Blanka flung away her crown," the girl said lightly, and Alix said, "I don't think I know that story."

"Oh—it's not a true story, Alix, it's a legend, about the Swedish queen, Blanka, who came from her own country to Finland over the water, and when she came among these islands, and had her first sight of Finland, she said 'I must do homage to so much beauty!' She took her crown off—so the legend goes—and cast it away from her into the sea. And ever since Queen Blanka's voyage, all this stretch of water has been called The Golden Crown."

"How lovely!" Alix said. "Mary, isn't there a poem about it?"

"Not that I know of." Mary looked suddenly quenched and indifferent. But she sparkled again when the bo'sun came aft, and touching his forehead to Brand, begged to know if "the young lady would kindly favour with another song. Jenkins, 'e had 'is clari'net, e'd be proud to come in with the 'armony."

"Tell Jenkins we know his clarionet too well," said Brand. "Miss Ryan has her guitar, maybe we can persuade her to play her own accompaniment."

"Thank 'ee, sir."

The men gathered round the forecastle. Mary fetched her guitar. Adjusting the broad ribbon round her neck, she began to play songs the sailors loved, old ballads and sea chanteys, while Brand and her father lounged at the rail to listen, and Alix sat among the rugs in the bow, entranced by the beauty of the scene. It seemed to her this was a night to remember for ever, here in The Golden Crown, with the blue dusk falling and the stars coming out over Finland, and Mary's pure thrilling voice holding the rough seamen spellbound.

"One more," said Brand, when the last applause from the forecastle died away.

"Oh—I don't know any more songs." Mary Ryan swept her hand over the guitar strings as she spoke and played a few broken chords.

"Hey," said Brand, "isn't that a song? Seems to me I've heard that tune before."

"This?"

"Sure I've heard it. I had a messmate once, a kid called Lauri, used to play it all the time."

"Oh," said Mary, "it's a Finnish tune. It's called 'The Lapp Boy's Song'. I used to sing it often at the summer fairs."

"Do sing it now," said Alix. "Please."

356

"I must stand up to sing it, then." Mary rose smiling from her folding stool, and shook out the skirt of her yellow cotton dress. The seamen were only a blur now in the shadow of the forecastle.

"This is a song for the end of the day," she said. Her voice, hardly raised at all, travelled clearly over the deck and the silent sea. Alix, listening, was struck with the charm and power of the little figure standing beneath the mast. Mary Ryan might never be a prima donna; she already had some of the qualities of a star.

"This one I used to sing when our stall was nearly empty and the women and children were hot and tired," she said, and played a ripple of cool notes. "Then they were quiet, and afterwards they'd almost always buy . .

"Father, do you remember Halmstad?"

"Sure I remember Halmstad, baby," said Joe, clearing his throat.

"Remember the creek where we tied up the *Molly-O*, beside the little square with the lime trees, near the church? That's where we were, the last time I sang 'The Lapp Boy's Song'."

Music, gentle as the water on the snow brig's side.

"Run, my sweet reindeer,
Over mountains and field,
With my girl's tent.

Scratch up the snow
Moss lies beneath the fell
Let us quickly go,
Here only wolves dwell.

The day is so short,
The way is so long,
Run with my song."

"That was wonderful, Mary," said Alix, when the two girls were alone together in the cabin. "You really do sing beautifully."

Mary put the guitar inside her berth and turned round.

"Alix," she said, "does Brand know you're going to have a baby?"

357

"What—what makes you think I am?" Alexandra's eyes were wide and dark.

"Well—aren't you?"

"I don't know."

"Oh, Alix! I was sure of it as soon as I saw you, just by the way you looked—"

"I don't see how it could be."

With a dry laugh: "I see how it could be, very well. Then you haven't told Brand. I was afraid of that, this evening."

"Afraid?" said Alix, with a touch of hauteur in her voice.

"Alix, you called me a fool at Bomarsund, and I know now I was a fool to go on believing in a man like Erik Kruse. But you're a much bigger fool if you don't tell your husband now about the baby, and let him take proper care of you, and be glad about it—"

"I'm not going to say anything to Brand yet, Mary. I'm going to wait another month until I'm absolutely sure. I want to stay at sea until September anyhow—"

"September!" Mary said. "This is the beginning of June! What made you fix upon September?"

"Because the campaign in the Baltic *must* be over before then."

"Oh, good heavens," said Mary, "do you think babies wait for battles to be won? Let the men do the fighting with Russia, they're enjoying it, they can go on this way for years yet, but *you* tell Brand he's going to be a father and get yourself to some place on solid ground and stay there. Supposing you were taken ill at sea? Brand would never forgive himself if anything went wrong—"

"Mary, please, this is my own affair—"

"—and what's more, he might never forgive *you*."

Alexandra kept out of Mary's way next morning, as far as the cramped quarters of the ship allowed. She was angry with the girl, and angrier with herself for being led into such an intimate discussion, all the more because she knew that some of Mary's arguments were right. Brand, too, was irritable: he had spent days now, looking in vain for a quarry, and he was hardly likely to find one in daylight in the vicinity of Hangö Head.

"I wonder if it's worth while running across to Dagö?" he

said to Joe. "We did pretty well off Dager Ort with the *Sea-lark*."

"Seventy-five miles of solid tacking in weather like this."

"I guess so."

"Sail ho!" the man on look-out shouted.

Brand had his glass to his eye at once. "Looks like a Navy ship," he said. ". . . It is."

"I thought they'd all gone up to Nargen."

"Maybe he's bringing sick men out. Remember, there's a smallpox outbreak in the *Duke of Wellington*."

"He's not going out of the Gulf, though. He's making for Hangö, or I'm a Dutchman."

"And it's *Cossack*," said Brand, shutting up his glass. "I think we'll lie off Hangö Roads for a bit, and see what Captain Fanshawe has in mind."

Hangö Head, the southerly extremity of Finland, presented a grim appearance as it came more closely into view. A British attack in May, 1854, about the time *Arrogant* and *Hecla* were engaged at Ekenäs, had partly destroyed two of the small forts in the harbour, and other, more recent fortifications had been destroyed by the Russians themselves rather than let them share the fate of Bomarsund. The lighthouse on Hangö Head had, of course, been dismantled by the Russians at the outbreak of war, and the Russian garrison had later been withdrawn from the little town. As the *Duchess* moved inshore, there was no sign of life on the Hangö shore.

"Leadsman, call the depth!" cried Brand.

"By the mark, nine!"

"*Cossack* heaving to, sir!" from the masthead. "Lowering a boat!"

"She must be going for provisions," said Joe.

"Under a flag of truce?" Brand handed the telescope to Joe.

"You're right, that's a white flag in the cutter!"

"It might be a return of prisoners. *Cossack* took several in the fight ten days ago. Joe!"

"Sir?"

"I don't like the look of this. Why isn't *Cossack* herself flying a white flag? Why aren't the Russkies somewhere they can be seen from the boat? I'm going in closer to have a look. Leadsman!"

"By the mark, seven fathoms, sir."

"Right!" said Brand in answer to Joe's look. "Sulivan charted the harbour at five fathoms, and we're nowhere near the harbour yet." But he kept an eye on the line of broken water, where the sea bubbled over the hidden reefs of Hangö Head.

"Brand, are we going in to land?" said Alix at his back. She was wrapped in a boat-cloak and looked pale and depressed.

"No. Come and watch this. Where's Mary?"

Mary joined them quietly. No glass was needed now to watch the *Cossack's* cutter, rowed purposefully towards the beach with the flag of truce waving high.

"Fanshawe had an odd idea of what constitutes a truce," said Brand. "Some of those damned fools are holding muskets."

In another minute he added, "They've sent the surgeon in— that may be smart! His name's Easton—one of the officers I met . . ."

"There are six—no, seven Finlanders in the cutter," Alexandra said.

"Leadsman!"

"By the mark, five!"

"The wheel to Mr. Ryan, Webster." The Aberdeen seaman stepped back thankfully. "Try the channel between Gustafsvärn and the old fort, Mister. That cutter is covered by Rysön island now. Fanshawe has no idea what's happening to his people."

The three vessels now formed a triangle: *Cossack* lying out in the Gulf, her cutter about to enter the dismantled harbour, the *Duchess* moving very slowly in to the old fort on Hangö Head. The men in the cutter, commanded by a young lieutenant, rowed steadily on.

"Muster the gun crew, bo'sun! Run out the carronade! Gordon, fill the water buckets! You two girls, get into the cabin!"

They obeyed him so far as to huddle inside the little galley, clutching each other in a sudden fright.

The *Cossack's* boat pulled in to Hangö beach and was dragged up on the shingle, the men wading in through the shallow water to the shore. The young lieutenant shook out the white flag and held it high above his head.

"My God!" the girls heard Joe exclaim.

Out of the abandoned buildings on the shore had burst a

score of Russians, with an officer wearing the familiar green epaulettes waving his sword and pointing at the British.

"Under a flag of truce!" the *Cossack's* lieutenant called.

"To hell with your truce!" the Russian yelled in English. "Riflemen, fire!"

"Prime!" Brand shouted to his gun crew. "Point!"

It was impossible to give the final word of command, for on Hangö beach friend and foe were now struggling in a solid mass. The British, flinging away the white flag, had hurled themselves on the Russians, swinging their clubbed muskets, while two of the Finlanders were frantically trying to push out the boat. The sound of shots crackled across the water.

"Enemy on the port bow, sir!" shouted the man at the masthead.

Brand swung round. Joe had taken the *Duchess* very close inshore, close enough to bring them well within the range of four men in the familiar Russian uniforms who had emerged from the ruins of the old fort on the point. They were all armed with Minié rifles. A single shot sang over the snow brig's deck.

Brand shouted an order. The panting, swearing gunners struggled with the traverse of the little carronade.

Boom! at last came the sound of a British gun across the water.

"That's *Cossack*, coming to the rescue!"* gasped Alexandra. "It's all right now, Mary! It's all right!"

But Mary had crept out of the shelter of the galley door to stare at the four men in Russian uniform.

"Alix, it's Erik Kruse!"

Cold with sudden panic, Alix recognized her old enemy. She knew Brand recognized him too, for she saw him jerk out his pistol. In that look from one man to the other she relaxed her grasp of Mary's waist.

The young girl ran forward to the rail. From the rocks two rifles cracked.

"Erik! Oh, Erik, don't fire! It's *me*!"

It was doubtful if Erik Kruse heard the words. But he saw the yellow dress fluttering in the wind, and fired as callously

* In fact it was 4.30 p.m. before Captain Fanshawe sent H.M.S. *Cossack's* gig in to Hangö with a second flag of truce.

on the woman as his Russian friends had fired on the flag of truce.

The bullet only grazed Mary Ryan's temple. But the glancing blow and the shock caused her to fall against the rail. While her father clung helplessly to the spokes of the wheel she toppled forward, and fell headlong into the churning sea.

Alix threw aside her cloak, kicked off her shoes, and dived after Mary into three fathoms of water, as the *Duchess* rasped on the sand, and Brand yelled "Fire!" and the devil gun scored a point-blank hit against the enemy on Hangö Head.

Alix was aware, first, of a jarring of her whole body and a dull, stunned sensation in the right side of her head. She was well under water, in a maze of barnacle-encrusted rocks on which her hands struck as she fought her way back to the surface against the under-surge which battered her upon those rocks for a second time.

Two yards away, when she came up and shook the water from her eyes and nostrils, she saw Mary's yellow dress. With strong strokes she had the skirt in one hand, and grasped Mary floundering helplessly in the water she had never learned to master—but still alive.

As soon as the girl felt Alix touch her, she rolled with the dragging wave and turned her white face to her rescuer. The sea had washed the blood from the flesh wound on her brow, but a bubble of bright red formed and reformed where the black hair trailed dankly over her skull, and Mary's mouth was open, gurgling words which the salt water choked, as she flung her arms round Alexandra's neck and dragged them both beneath the surface of the sea.

"Mary, Mary, let go!"

Alix had them back to daylight again, a strange daylight shot through with red bars and heavy with the smell of gunpowder. She pulled the girl's clutching hands away with all her strength. They struggled together until Mary's head fell back and once more the water filled her mouth, and Alix in despair got one arm beneath her shoulders and trod water, looking vainly round for help.

They had already drifted some distance away from the *Duchess*. Only the cliff of Hangö Head rose up above them, shutting from Alix's view the fearful scene of carnage on the headland, and offering in the fringe of red rocks which extended far into the bay some handholds and footholds for strong swimmers. Alix, with her one free arm, struck out in their direction.

"Brand!"

She shrieked his name once only, and as the water filled her mouth, making her choke and spit, she shut her lips firmly, to save every breath for the task that lay ahead. But Mary lay helpless on her arm, and Mary's wide yellow skirt, belling in the water, was a dead weight, while her own much shorter garment clung to her thighs and checked the free movement of her legs. And the undertow off Hangö Head was her enemy, thrusting her back every time her bleeding fingers almost closed upon a spur of rock, dragging her burden out of her weakening hold.

"Mary, oh Mary ! Try to keep your head up !"

The face against her shoulder was an unconscious face, blue and bruised, with only the spurt of bright red blood, washed and welling like the movement of the tides, to tell of the life which a moment ago had been so vivid and so hopeful. Alexandra was fighting for her own life now as the yellow dress, opening like a great flower, drifted away from her on the currents of Hangö Bay.

Alix had no idea if an hour or a minute passed—for the sea had become the sky and the sky the sea as the waves broke over her head and enclosed her in a shuddering world of greyness where time ceased to be—until she was seized from behind by two strong hands, and Brand's voice said :

"Just—be still. Don't try to swim. You're all right. Jenkins, here !"

She tried to tell Jenkins that Mary was "not far away", but the words came out in a meaningless gurgle, and the young seaman was sharing her weight with Brand and swimming with her out of the undertow, back to the brig and safety.

"All right, Jenkins, I can take her in. Look for—" and then the voice became a roaring in her ears, and she knew nothing more but climbing hand over hand up the ship's side where Blythe waited to take her from Brand; and the world ended with the sight, fifty times magnified, of Joe Ryan's anguished face.

When she came to her senses, Alix was lying on the cabin

floor, where they had laid her in her dripping clothes, with the smell and taste of brandy everywhere. She had coughed up salt water, it lay revoltingly on her chin and the wet neck of her dress, but someone put a clean towel in her hand, and she sat up on her elbow, choking and scrubbing at her lips.

"Alix, you must get out of those wet clothes at once. Do you hear me? Do you want me to help you?"

She guessed at the torment under Brand's peremptory voice. "I'm all—right," she said. "All right. Just—help me up."

He lifted her to her feet and steadied her with one arm round her waist. "Take off your clothes here and get into bed," he said. "Jenkins brought Mary in—there may be just a chance—"

"Oh, *hurry*!" Brand took her at her word. There were voices outside the cabin door, and the tread of men carrying a burden carefully across the deck.

Alix stripped off her dripping clothes. All her movements were slow and heavy. There were rough towels on a chair: she dried herself as best she could, and passing into the berth, found and pulled on a thin wool dress. She was standing up barefoot, trying to rub her hair, when someone knocked heavily at the cabin door.

"Mistress Endicott!" It was Gordon, one of the Aberdeen seamen, who had been on the deck when Mary fell.

"Here's a drop o' broth to ye. Ye sud drink it hot."

"Will you put it in my galley, Gordon, thank you very much?"

Alix was surprised at the sound of her own voice. It was much as usual, a little rougher maybe, and she felt no inclination to tears. In her trance of deep shock she opened the door, reached into the little galley for the broth, and saw her cloak and buckled shoes lying where she had cast them off—how short a time ago.

The soup was very hot and very salty, like everything the Scots boy prepared, and her throat closed against it even while the strong liquid spread its warmth through her numbed body. She drank a few mouthfuls, pressed a towel to her lips again, and went back to the berth.

Perhaps it was the stealing cold, numbing her thoughts, which made her limbs so heavy and so weak. Alix lay down on top of her bunk, pulling the heavy boat cloak over her shoulders, winding her bare feet in the folds. The pillow felt cool and fresh beneath her cheek. She began to drift away upon a tide of sleep.

Suddenly Alexandra's eyes opened and she caught her breath.

Deep within herself she felt the onset of a cramp.

CHAPTER NINETEEN

L·A·P·P M·A·G·I·C II

IT MIGHT have been ten minutes, it might have been two
hours before Alix roused to awareness of a jarring and grinding
through the whole ship, accompanied by shouting from the
deck and the reverberation of a screw engine not far away. As
she sat up carefully and looked through the open port she
saw the empty Hangö shore at a different angle and realized
the *Duchess* was afloat.

Still very cautiously she put her feet over the edge of the
bunk and stood up. Her bruises smarted and there was dried
blood all over her hands where she had clawed at the rocks,
but there was no faintest twinge of the pain which had as-
sailed her before she lay down. It was a strain, she told herself,
some little twist or sprain from the struggle in the water; that
was all. She poured out fresh water and cleaned her hands.
Then, with the first drag of the comb through her disordered
hair, it came—not a cramp but the premonition of a cramp—
again.

Alix became aware of the sound of weeping.

She crossed the little cabin and gently opened the door of
the other berth. Joe Ryan was on his knees beside the bunk
where Mary lay, and his shoulders were shaking with great
sobs.

There had never been any hope for Mary Ryan, although
Joe and Blythe had tried, one after the other for over an hour,
to restore her breathing. She was dead when Jenkins brought
her aboard, and now they had wrapped her in a long dark
blanket through which the sea water soaked in strange salt
rings and whorls. Her face was bare, and though the shallow
wound in her temple had stopped bleeding, the force of the
bullet had raised ugly black swellings beneath her closed eyes.
The one unchanged beauty was Mary's hair, and some gentle
hand—no doubt her father's—had arranged the black locks
gracefully on her brow and neck. In a strange semblance of

life, the hair as it dried was fluffing and spraying into the familiar curls.

This much Alix saw before Brand's hand interposed to shut the door and turn her gently away from the presence of death.

"Not now, darling," he whispered. "Let him be alone with her for an hour. Poor devil, he's beside himself—"

"Brand"—reproachfully—"you didn't change *your* clothes—"

"I won't come to any harm. *Cossack* came in and warped us off the sandbank, and I had my hands full . . . Thank God we didn't strike a reef!"

"Is *Cossack* towing us now?"

"Only into Hangö Roads. Fanshawe is sending a landing party in—Marines and seamen, to hunt out the Russians. I've two British officers aboard, Alix, will you come and speak to them?"

The two officers of the Royal Navy on the *Duchess'* deck bowed very low when Brand presented them to Mrs. Endicott. Such cool beauty and such a manner were unexpected aboard an American privateer. Mr. Thurston, the senior lieutenant— one of the grizzled veterans who had waited too long for a step up the overcrowded Navy ladder—begged leave to hope that Mrs. Endicott had taken no harm from her very—ah!— courageous attempt to save the life of an unfortunate young lady.

"I only wish it had been successful, sir," said Alix.

"May I respectfully enquire if she was still alive when you reached her, madam?"

"Yes, she was. She—she flung her arms round my neck and clung to me."

"Extremely distressing—and of course extremely dangerous. Then, in your opinion, was death due to the bullet wound or due to drowning?"

Alix clasped her hands to still their trembling. "Only a doctor could tell you that, I think. The wound was bleeding very much."

"And by all that's unfortunate our surgeon was one of the victims of Russian treachery," admitted the lieutenant. "You may not know, madam, that the enemy has disappeared in-land with all our people in the boat? The best we can hope for Mr. Easton is that the Russians have made him a prisoner-of-war . . . However, Captain Endicott, the surgeon's mates will take good care of your wounded seaman—"

"Was one of the men hurt?" exclaimed Alix.

"Webster was shot in the thigh . . . you see, sir," said Brand, "Mrs. Endicott didn't know the full extent of our casualties. She was attempting to save life when Webster was hit—the only person so engaged aboard the *Duchess of Finland*."

"My husband saved *my* life," said Alix.

The younger lieutenant looked at Brand sympathetically. Both their ships were in trouble together, *Cossack* and the *Duchess* too, and there would be an almighty row at the Admiralty, but trouble was the Navy's portion, and this privateer fellow (come up from the lower deck apparently) though a tough-looking customer, seemed a bit too highly strung to pull quickly out of the mess he'd got himself into. Not pleasant, thought Lieutenant Cheadle—engaged to be married to a post-captain's daughter at Chatham—to be a skipper with your crew under fire, your carronade ready to run loose and your ship going aground, while your wife stages a Grace Darling performance in the swimming line! The ship aground was now a standard sight in the Baltic; Captain Sulivan was for ever warping off some unwary frigate or other—even the acting flagship once; the Yankee had no need to be ashamed of that. But the girl! To know a girl who looked like that, spoke like that, might have been as cold as the other poor creature, if you'd put your ship's welfare first for five minutes longer!

"I trust you will forgive my questions, madam," said Lieutenant Thurston. "They are painful but not irrelevant. When the Court of Enquiry on this unfortunate affair takes place, it will certainly be a matter of consideration whether the deceased young person, who according to her father was an American citizen, was in fact slain by a Russian bullet. It is a fact, because it was seen from H.M.S. *Cossack*, that Russian fire was opened on a ship flying the American flag, and that the American ship fired on the Russians—excellent shooting too, if I may say so, a direct hit at three hundred yards; none of *them* left alive to tell the tale, ha-ha!—and that, taken in conjunction with Miss Ryan's death, may well have international consequences."

"Is Erik Kruse killed, Brand?"

"Yes, he's dead."

"Thank God!"

"Did you *know* one of the Russians, Mrs. Endicott?"

"Never mind that," said Brand roughly. "That'll come out at the Court of Enquiry, if and when it's held; though I don't see why the United States Government should be dragged into this. I reckon a British Court of Enquiry will be more interested to know why a boat's crew carrying a flag of truce were also carrying firearms!"

Those damned muskets, commented Lieutenant Cheadle inwardly, and Lieutenant Thurston's grave look turned to one of active disapproval. Trust a Yankee privateer to upset the applecart, he thought. Goes to sea with women aboard, gets one girl shot and the other half-drowned, and then he bandies words with an officer of the Royal Navy! He said stiffly:

"As to that, you are, of course, a material witness, captain. You and your crew are the only persons who actually saw the Russian attack on our white flag. I am commanded by Captain Fanshawe to ask you not to leave this area until all the circumstances are established; and he suggests you withdraw at once to Tvärminne, where H.M.S. *Esk* has been signalled to rendezvous with two gunboats."

"Brand, I want you to put me ashore at Tvärminne."

Alix was lying on her bunk again, and Brand was at last changing into dry clothes. She had not yet talked with Joe Ryan, for Joe had mastered himself and gone on deck to pull the dislocated crew together and set a course for Tvärminne.

Brand stopped in the act of buckling his belt.

"Put you ashore? Yes, if you like, you can go ashore for an hour or two, but don't you think you should stay aboard until Joe decides—" He jerked his head in the direction of the silent berth on the far side of the cabin.

"I want to go ashore to stay, Brand. It isn't far, by road, to my own house at Ekenäs. I want to be at home tonight!"

He sat down on the edge of the bunk and took her hand.

"Darling," he said gently, "I know you've had a terrible shock, but you surely don't know what you're saying. You just want to run away from trouble, Alix, like you used to do; remember you promised me at Lewes you never would again? We won't be in any danger at Tvärminne, and you'll get a good night's rest at anchor and feel better in the morning—"

"I don't want to run away from anything. I only want to go home to Ekenäs."

"But you can't think I'd let you go off to that lonely place, that the Russians gutted not six months ago? Through woods that very likely are infested with Russians, like the treacherous brutes we saw today? Darling!" Brand took her in his arms. "You're trembling! Have you caught a chill?" He reached out and shut the glass portlid.

She tried to stop the chattering of her teeth, the shaking that ran in long waves across her body. She said with her face in his thick jersey:

"Brand, I'm going to have a child."

She felt him catch his breath. Then he held her away from him, looked down at her with a look of joy that transfigured his set face, and passionately kissed her.

"Oh, Alix! oh, my love! is it really true?"

She nodded without speaking. Yes, it was true, and had been true for weeks; it was only now, as the trembling became uncontrollable, that Alix acknowledged her body stronger than her will.

"So you see, Brand, that's why I must go ashore, just for a little while. I haven't been feeling very well, and then this morning—"

"Oh God, this morning," he said, and the happiness faded from his face. "You don't think it could have done you harm?"

"Oh no, no, no; but—please, Brand; I want to sleep for a few nights in my own room and have Anna look after me—"

"Oh yes, Anna. But who else is there?"

"The farmer and his family. It's not a lonely place, Brand dear, it's only two miles from Ekenäs, and not so very far from Tvärminne."

"Look here." Brand knew nothing about pregnant women except that they had "fancies", usually for food; he assumed this was a fancy, far more natural if Alix had had her mother to run to instead of that crazy Lapp. But he was so grateful, so anxious to please her, that against his better judgement he said :

"If I can send someone inland from Tvärminne, and make sure the Russians have really evacuated Ekenäs, I'll take you up myself tonight. But don't count on it, sweetheart. I won't go a step unless I'm sure. I've got to take proper care of both of you from here in on."

"Oh, Brand !"

"Don't cry, darling. It's going to be all right. Just lie back and have a good rest until we reach the rendezvous. I've got to go on deck now, Joe's at the end of his tether."

He got up and pulled his jacket on, looking down at her and smiling, touching her cheek with his hard hand.

"When will the baby come, Alix? Next February?"

"Have you been counting on your fingers, Brand?"

Brand grinned. "Like all the old pussycats back in Portland. My God, Alix ! I still can't believe it. You and a child ! I've got everything I want to live for, now."

Alix was able to smile until the door closed behind him. Then she lay back on her pillow, scared and shaking, as once more deep within her belly the finger of death tapped at the door of life.

The long sandy road ran between the pines, and afternoon sunshine lay in bars across the green woods floor where hart's-tongue fern and harebell gave delicate colour to the Finland June. It was a road which Alix had known all her life, and it was strange that now, as the *bondkärra* jolted on towards Ekenäs, it should sometimes seem to be the road from the Villa Hagasund to Traskända, where she had often driven with Aurora Karamsin on the spring mornings before the war began. It even turned into the dreary no-man's land between the Russian frontier and Terijoki which she had crossed on her flight from St. Petersburg, and once, alarmingly, it became a street in Lewes, and a stable-boy's arm was raised to fling a clod of mud at the red shawl. And then it was once more the Finland road through Nyland province, a sandy heath-lined cart track over which the *bondkärra* jolted fearfully, and her husband's strong arm was round her, and the Russians had gone miles away.

"Brand !"

"Yes, darling." He glanced at her; his gaze was for the woods, right and left, and Brand's Colt was as ready to his hand as if a regiment of Cossacks were charging down the road.

"When we get home. I'm going to the sauna, and have a steam bath, and then a swim. Have you ever had a Finnish sauna?"

"You're going to bed as soon as we get there. We'll try your sauna bath another day."

"All right." It was only a fancy, of course, that a long steam bath would stop the shaking and the sense of cold. Her father had built a new bath house above the lake, only two years ago; Alix could almost feel the steam rise as the water was dashed on the hot stones, and the bunch of birch leaves whipping the bruised feeling from her bones.

"Here's the post house, Alix. Will you talk to them about a change of horses?"

"There's less than three miles more to go."

"These poor nags aren't going to last out one."

There were friendly faces at the post house to smile on Mamsell Alix, and a tow-haired boy eager to mount a pony and ride to tell the people at the manor that their young lady and her husband were coming home. Alix accepted a cup of coffee offered in friendship; Brand, for the good of the house, bought brännvin and beer. While the horses were changed, Alix departed to a bedroom kept for the convenience of lady travellers, and when she came back to the log-walled room, adorned with cheap chromos of Queen Victoria and the King of Sweden, her face was very pale.

"Brand, the post wagon for Åbo stops here tomorrow. I think we should send a message to Mamsell Josabeth."

"Who's she?"

"Miss Agneta's housekeeper at Degerby. I believe the Mannerheims would spare her to come to Ekenäs for a little while."

"Just as you like, of course." Brand waited while Alix asked for paper and pen. He had forgotten the quiet Swedish woman in the clapboard house among the birches at Degerby. Degerby was a long way back.

Alix wrote a few lines quickly, sealed the page, addressed it to Fröken Josabeth Sandström, at Villnäs near Åbo, and stood up.

372

"You don't think you're going to be ill, do you?" Brand asked her anxiously, as he lifted her into the *bondkärra*.

"No, of course not," she said, white-lipped, "but it would be nice to have Mamsell Josabeth with me if you have to go to their wretched Court of Enquiry . . ."

That set him off about his ship, as Alix had intended, and speculations on the *Cossack's* landing party, and the gunboats going up to Sveaborg. Neither of them had yet dared to talk of Mary's death or the extermination of Erik Kruse. They were enclosed in a bell of shock as surely as any diver descending through coils of seaweed to the ocean bed.

For Alix that bell was breaking; perhaps, at the post house, it had already broken. What she felt now was more than a finger tapping, it was a hand opening and closing, that presently would be a fist. Her silent cry went up through the green tassels of the Finland larches; I have seen so much blood shed today without flinching; oh God, if You exist, stop, stop now, dry up and heal, this new, unobtrusive, streaking blood of mine.

Around the little manor which had belonged to the family of Alexandra's mother, the evergreen forests had been cleared, and a hundred acres of arable land stretched between the manor gates and Ekenäs town. When Brand came out on the weed-grown carriage drive in the evening light, he saw peaceful fields of waving green where the young rye was sprouting and black and white cattle standing in clover meadows.

That the cattle were there at all was a tribute to the Finnish crofters, who had hidden them in underground shelters during the Russian occupation; although it had not been possible to save the furnishings of the manor. The place looked well enough from the outside. It was built in a curious style, the upper storey having windows only at the back of the house, with the grey slates in front giving the manor a top-heavy look. The ground floor was well proportioned, with a white rough-cast front pierced on each side of the door by three windows, but here again a heavy and depressing appearance was given to the place by lilac bushes growing rank and wild, and several unpruned copper beeches which shaded the side windows. Brand concluded that Count Johan Gyllenlöve, the life tenant of the place, had not felt inclined to spend money on Alexandra's inheritance.

As a house it compared unfavourably with the old Brand house on State Street, now rented on a short lease to one of the leading ministers of Portland. The house Miss Betsy Brand had left to her great-nephew had well-proportioned halls and a graceful central stairway, far superior to the steep narrow stair to the right of the door at Ekenäs. Lapland Anna, after one look at Alix, and two sentences exchanged, led her into a bedroom on the ground floor, opening off the principal parlour of the house.

Brand knew there was a bed in that back room, for he had seen it through the half open door. Of the broken windows in the parlour, two had been reglazed and three covered with thick cloth, and the high white porcelain stoves—one at each end of the room—had been cracked and hammered by the Russians beyond all repair. Marks on the wallpaper showed where pictures, mirrors and girandoles had been removed. The only piece of furniture standing on the pine floor, to which Anna had restored a beautifully polished surface, was an inlaid mahogany spinet. Brand lifted the lid out of curiosity to know why such a thing had not been looted with the rest. The strings and hammers had been torn out, and a few straws sticking to the four corners showed that the spinet had been found of use. The Russians had used it as a manger for their horses.

Two hours now since Alix had gone away with Anna, and there hadn't been a sight or sound of either of them since. The farmer's wife had taken him into a small room with a stool and table, to eat the usual country supper of smoked fish and curds—the curds not of the freshest; and she had made him understand in her limited Swedish that he must send the *bondkärra* away. "The lady is sick," she said decidedly. "You stay tonight." It was then he went out to walk up and down the neglected carriage drive, lighting cigarette after cigarette to keep off the mosquitoes, conscious of the farmer's tow-headed children watching him over the meadow gate, and thinking of his ship in Joe's charge, and the drinking his crew was undoubtedly doing in the tavern at Tvärminne.

On one turn, which took him near the front windows, he heard Alix crying: not screaming in pain, but weeping loudly enough to be heard across the empty parlour, and he

374

dashed into the house and knocked imperatively on the bed-room door. The crying went on unheeding, but Anna came out at once, still in the black costume he remembered but without the beads and the scarlet cap, and tying a clean apron round her waist. He had always thought of her as "an old witch", an old woman; without the *hilkka* he saw how black and thick her hair was, and knew that in years Anna was still young.

"What's going on in there?" he said. "What's the matter with Mrs. Endicott?"

He had to change the name to "the Lady Alexandra" before the Laplander chose to understand.

"You don't go in," she said, "the child is lost."

Brand's eyes beheld a closed door; his brain refused to work. The image of a *lost child* meant only one thing to him: a child straying in a city street, perhaps asking help from a stranger . . . Then it came to him that what was lost was his own child, that future soul, that speck of immortality, and he struck his clenched hand against the broken porcelain until it bled.

It was nearly an hour before Anna came to him of her own accord in the little side room, where the farmer's wife had spread a chaff mattress and two knitted blankets on the floor. It was after sunset, but the long white night lay across the land and penetrated the thick scented lilac beyond Brand's open window, and it was light enough to see fear in the Lapp woman's face.

"She has much fever," Anna said. "Will you fetch ice?"

He would have fetched an iceberg from the Polar seas, and willingly; he took the small pick and pail she gave him and ran to the spring house beside the lake, hacking and hewing until the farmer's wife came after him to call enough, he was splintering all their summer store. Brand was not sure what they wanted the ice for; he knew fever patients were sometimes given ice to suck. But surely Alix had not a fever, a hospital fever, as well as—what had happened? He tried to interrogate the Finn woman. "The lady bleeds too much," she said. "The baby was—" she made an expressive gesture with her hands. "Three months growing."

Brand had thought it strange, sitting in his little prison,

how quickly the seed of fatherhood had sprung to green life in his own heart that day. "Less than twenty-four hours! Less than twenty-four hours!" he had said more than once aloud. In one summer day, already packed with war and death, he had thought of the *person* of his child; seen a creature with Alexandra's eyes become a boy, the boy become a man in his own image; and had said farewell to that hope before the sun had set. "My poor darling!" He had said that aloud too, for she had surely had very little longer to nurse her dream of motherhood—

Three months growing.

If he had known, if she had told him, she would be in Stockholm now, and Mary Ryan too. Mary alive, and his child still—growing.

It was after midnight, in the one dark hour of the Finnish June, when Brand heard a door creak somewhere in the house, and a quiet step crossing the backyard. He was on his feet in a moment, creeping out by the front door, listening. The thought of Russians lurking in the woods was still in the back of Brand Endicott's mind.

He saw Anna in the distance, walking swiftly along the side of the meadow.

Brand's first impulse was to turn back to the house. With that fierce guardian absent, he could enter Alexandra's room, and if she were awake tell how much he loved her, how she was the only creature who mattered to him. But it seemed so strange that Anna should desert her post that he was impelled to follow, and he did so, always at a distance, as she left the meadows and plunged deep into the forest path.

Anna, in the woods, was like a shadow moving, but Brand, too, could move as quietly as when he played Indians with his schoolmates at home in Deering woods. He followed the Lapp unseen for more than twenty minutes, and never once gave her cause to turn her head at a crackling twig, until they came to a clearing where thorns grew, and among the trees stood a crooked stone.

This stone stood higher than the Lapp woman's head. It was not solid, and a long gap in the middle gave a view of the paling sky. Since the night was warm and still, there was no sound from the dangling objects hung on every branch of the surrounding trees, but as Brand's eyes grew accustomed to the place he saw that these were copper and iron rings, offerings to the troll stone, and knew that he was looking at the *seite* of the Lapland woman.

Riveted to the ground he saw her kneel before the *seite* and heard her, three times, utter Alexandra's name. Then she called on Jubmel, who is Odin, the lord of all, and Frigga, the great mother, and on Tiermos the god of war, and on the Tonttu, the churchyard spirit, who had had his share of un-born flesh that night. While the cold sweat ran down Brand's face, he felt the unseen pass by him, and heard the old gods mutter in the Finland dark.

Then Anna stood up and took from beneath her apron a cockerel with its head tucked under its wing, and seized it by the legs so that its head swung loose and its squawks filled the thorn clearing. Anna drew her *puuko*. Above the cackle of the sacrifice Brand heard her calling on the god of the wind.

> "Biegg-Olmai, how long wilt thou fly?
> I bind thee under land, under strand!
> Thou shalt stand in God's hand!"

The knife descended. The young cock's blood spurted over the tree bole and over Anna's hands. Then the copper rings and iron shards on the trees before the *seite* rang together in a fearful dissonance as the wind rose, and in one great howling gust swept through the glade where Anna lay prostrate be-fore the troll stone. Brand was swept up like a leaf and driven into a wall of thorns. When he dragged himself clear, scratched and bleeding, he seized the Laplander and pulled her to her feet.

There was blood on his hands where they touched hers, and with a groan of revulsion he wrenched the knife from Anna and threw it on the ground. There was a violent clap of thunder and it seemed to Brand he heard the dead cock crow.

"In the name of Jesus Christ!" he gasped, "put an end to this—sorcery!"

"Jesus also commanded the winds and waves," the woman said. She stood in Brand's grasp motionless, while the great wind blew itself out in the branches overhead, and slowly, almost in shame, the American relaxed his grasp on her arms. Then Anna looked up at him, her slanting eyes full of hatred, and spat out:

"The Lady Alix burns with fever, stranger. Through your

fault—yours—yours! And I knew no way but the old way to cool her blood and ease her suffering! Think of that before you strike me dead!"

"You crazy bitch," said Brand, "don't talk to me of dying."

He let her go. Anna slid away from him through the silent forest, while the slain cock's feathers were ruffled by the faint breeze of dawn, and the heathen offerings were touched by the first sunlight. Brand staggered away from the glade of the *seite*. His knees gave way beneath him and he buried his face in the wet moss beneath the trees.

After an hour he returned to the manor. The cows were standing quietly in the meadow and the slate roof glinted under beech tree boughs. Anna stood waiting for him at the door.

"The Lady Alix is cool now, and refreshed," she said respectfully. "She waits to see her husband."

Brand went to his wife as he was, marked by the night and the forest, into a room from which all the physical signs of suffering had been removed. The raging wind raised by the Lapp had fallen to a fresh breeze which carried the scent of dew-drenched lilacs through the open window. Clean homespun sheets on the bed gave out a pleasant scent of myrtle.

The fever which had devoured Alix all night had broken. Only her hair, dark with sweat and matted on the pillow, and her voice hoarse with crying revealed what her agony had been.

"Do you remember what the drum said, Brand?" she whispered. "*Only so far?* It meant our—our—"

"Alix, my love, don't think of all that now!"

"Ah, but do you remember what I told you once?" she asked him cunningly. "How Anna read the future, and predicted that a child would be born to save Finland? Her *seite* told my fortune again this morning when the great wind blew. She said, 'There will be a music which shall sing the song of Finland, but you will never hear it play. And there will come a child who will save Finland, but he will not be your child—'"

"Oh, Alix, Alix!" Brand burst out. "Remember, it was my child too!"

His endurance broke, and he fell down beside her, with his head upon her aching breast.

CHAPTER TWENTY

THE FORTRESS

THERE was always a scent of lilac in Alexandra's room. The window was never closed, and the June smell which was part of Finland, the smell of wet grass and lilacs, poured in all day long.

There was not much to be seen through the window. Lying flat in bed, Alix saw only the living creatures who moved across her field of vision at fixed hours of the day; Mikko, the young farmer, going off to harness his horses, or his little sister bringing the cows home to be milked, and the cows themselves, who walked to the yard two by two, glossy in black and white and placidly chewing their cud. These were the constants in Alexandra's world, where all else changed and shifted from hour to hour.

Sometimes the big empty bedroom became as wide as the Gulf at Hangö Head, and she was alone in the water, endlessly reaching out to grasp the hem of a yellow dress that became seaweed when she touched it. Sometimes there were so many evil faces round her bed that she choked and gasped for breath; Paul Demidov, greedy and clutching, Napoleon III, clay-faced, and Nikita of the leaden eyes, and one with a knife-wound on his cheek, but most often she knew that these were visitations from another time, and that the one who was real and always present was her husband, Brand. If she could have laid down the burden of guilt she carried for the secret too long and too well kept, Alix might have asked Brand some of the questions she asked Anna, and to which the Lapp woman knew no answer.

When is a soul born? When a child comes forth at its due term; cries, sucks, sleeps, can be dressed and laid in its cradle? Or at the moment of conception, when the invisible joins with the invisible, and the some-day visible is made? If it was then, had my child a soul, which we are taught to believe immortal; and if immortal, shall I know my child again when I too have crossed the dark water where the Swan of Tuonela sings?

Mamsell Josabeth came with no delay from Åbo, and listened to those questions, and shook her head and put her handkerchief to her eyes. She brought with her the trunk of clothing Alix had left behind at Degerby, with a jewel case inside it, and Captain Sulivan's worn Bible, and Alix propped on pillows sought through its pages patiently for help. There were texts which she remembered learning as a child about the House of many mansions, and the One who cared even for the sparrows, which she thought might throw some light on the home and the importance of the departed soul. She found these in the New Testament, and put markers at the place, and read them often. But each time she took up Sulivan's Bible from her bedside table it fell open of its own accord at the great passage in Ecclesiastes which bade her do with all her might whatever her hand found to do.

Because Alix was young and strong her body healed very quickly. Brand brought a naval surgeon to her—the same doctor who had examined him when he first joined the Fleet at Stockholm—and Mr. Johnson, while admitting that cases of miscarriage seldom came his way at sea, declared that Alix was "in good shape" and that the women in charge had handled the "disappointment" well. To Brand, in private, he issued an immediate prohibition against taking his wife to sea for several weeks, and a general warning against allowing her to jolt in a *bondkärra* for miles over backwoods country roads next time a happy event was anticipated. Mr. Johnson did not pretend to understand "nerves", and there was no one close to Alix wise enough or experienced enough to understand the deep confusion of her spirit. Nature had recoiled on her with cruel force; having too long refused to admit that a child was on its way to her, she now desired that lost child with all the strength of her frustrated body.

Brand came nearest to understanding, because he loved her; but Brand too was struggling with a load of guilt. He ought to have prevented that crazy dive to save Mary, he ought—as he knew too late—to have forbidden the journey to Ekenäs; but then, he argued with himself, if he was kept in ignorance, how was he to know any better? He was revolted by the thought of Anna's mumbo-jumbo with the chicken and the troll stone, and could hardly look at the Lapp woman when he saw her in Alexandra's room. He told Mamsell Josabeth that Anna was to be taken back to the Mannerheims at Åbo and kept there. But in the meantime these withdrawals and revulsions helped to erect the intangible barrier building up between Alix and Brand.

At the first possible moment Brand had returned to Tvärminne, and brought the *Duchess of Finland* up the narrow channel to an anchorage in the Pojo vik near Ekenäs town. From then on two members of the crew slept every night at the manor, even though the most thorough investigation revealed no trace of Russian troops in the neighbourhood. It seemed as if the little force at Hangö had been the last detachment of the enemy in Nyland province.

Alix saw none of the crew until the first day she was able to be out of bed, and then it was Joe Ryan who first broke through her shell of misery and drew her back from the earthly Tuonela in which she was astray. She talked to him lying on a sofa in the parlour, which was not so forlorn now, for when word reached Ekenäs that the young lady at the manor had come home in delicate health, townsfolk who would not go near the place while the Lapland woman kept house alone hurried to offer food and the loan of furniture. In addition to the sofa the parlour now held a *rya* rug, a table and three assorted chairs.

Joe took one of the stiff wooden chairs when he came in, but before long he was on his knees on the rug beside Alexandra, holding her hands in an abandonment of grief as he told her how Mary's body, brought once from the water, had been returned for ever to the deep.

"I was all for taking her back to Stockholm, to lay her beside her poor mother," he said, "but the Navy captains persuaded me to bury her at sea. We took the *Duchess* out to the middle of the Gulf, near a place Brand thought was where his shipmate Lauri was buried, and the other poor lads who fell at Ekenäs, but the tide was running strongly, Alix, and I've doubted since that there's no rest for the dead there."

Alix was weeping for the first time for a grief outside her own; gripping Joe's hands as she pictured the body of the little Sea Peddler carried far from the Gulf of Finland, moving with Queen Blanka's diadem among the islands of The Golden Crown.

"The Captain of the Fleet himself read the burial service,"

Joe went on, "and Captain Sulivan was there, and the Captain of the *Esk*. The words were so grand, and the sun was shining, and I could never believe it was my Mary lying on the deck there, covered from my sight and wrapped in the American flag. 'Twas the same flag we brought back from the *Sealark*, and little I thought that night where I should see it laid. But my poor little girl cared nothing at all for flags and fighting. She only wanted to sing like Jenny Lind."

"Joe, can you ever forgive us—Brand and me?"

"For what?"

"For coming into your life and . . . destroying what was so precious to you."

Joe shook his head. "That won't do. I shipped with Brand of my own free will, and poor Mary carried on her—her flirtation with that man in spite of all the warnings . . . Of course I wasn't firm enough. I spoiled her, Alix. Maybe I was too young to be a wise father, but first she was a darling toy, and then my grand little shipmate, and I couldn't realize that she had turned into a woman. No, Alix, if anyone was to blame for Mary's death it was her poor silly father, and neither Brand nor you . . . and now you must lie still and not distress yourself, or your Mamsell will put me to the door. We'll have another talk when I come back from Nargen."

"You're weighing anchor in the morning?"

"Yes, to be interrogated by the Commander-in-Chief, no less." Joe got to his feet. "If it wasn't for leaving you alone for a bit I'd be glad to be on the move. I couldn't get my hands on Erik Kruse and choke the life out of him, but there are plenty of Russians left to fight, and the war's a long way from being over."

With these words, which lingered in her mind long after the *Duchess* had sailed for the anchorage where the British ships of the line were lying, the first phase of Alexandra's grief came to an end. The war against Russia went on, and she had committed herself wholly to it; her task now was to fit herself again for the struggle, and to that end she forced herself to eat simple meals and drink the eggs beaten with port wine and the fresh milk which Mamsell Josabeth was always urging upon her, and to walk, for a longer time each day, on the sunny side of the tree-shadowed house. When Brand came back from the official enquiry into the affair at

Hangö she met him at the little landing stage on the Pojo *vik*, looking almost her old self in a soft green dress, and wearing the necklace he had once thought of as beads, with the diamond ring which his grandmother had sent her.

"Alix! Darling! You look wonderful!" Brand kissed her and held her in a close embrace. It was the first time since that fatal sixth of June that he had touched her without feeling she might break.

"Oh, I'm quite well now," she told him. "Brand, what happened at Nargen? Did you see the Commander-in-Chief?"

"Yes, I did, for a few minutes. His flag lieutenant did most of the interrogating—Joe and me first, and then they sent for Blythe too. Poor Captain Fanshawe's in trouble, Alix. He said himself—and, of course, we all knew it—that he omitted to hoist a white flag on *Cossack herself* before he sent the cutter in to Hangö. Now the Russians claim they didn't see the cutter's flag of truce and thought they were being attacked. We all gave evidence that that flag, at least, was perfectly visible, but the fact that his men were carrying muskets will tell against old Fanshawe, I'm afraid."

"Have they been in communication with the Russians?"

"Captain Sulivan arranged an exchange of letters about the prisoners, up at Sveaborg. He's still running the war single-handed, as far as I can see."

"Aren't they active then, at Nargen?" Alix said uneasily. "Did you see Captain Yelverton?"

"Yelverton is with the squadron off Cronstadt, making sure the Russians don't come out—not that they're likely to. Cooper Key had a skirmish with the enemy, though, at Sveaborg."

"You mean he actually fired on the fortress from his ship—I've forgotten her name—"

"*Amphion*."

"From *Amphion*, as Captain Hall fired last year on Bomarsund?"

"Not on the fortress proper, but he did fire on the Sandhamn batteries, and he went in close enough to do a thorough reconnaissance of Sveaborg. And listen, Alix, this *was* clever: Cooper Key had two of *Amphion's* boats painted white, and ordered the crews to wear all white—white shirts with their white duck trousers—so they were practically invisible at midnight, when it was hardly dark at all. How's that for an idea?"

"Very good." They were in the house now, entering the cool half-empty parlour where the lilacs filled the air with scent. "Brand—didn't anybody congratulate you on—on what you did at Hangö Head?"

"Admiral Dundas did," Brand said briefly. He had no intention of repeating the praises for his costly victory, and went on to say quickly:

"The British newspapers made a good deal of the affair, with most of the facts wrong, of course. 'The Massacre at Hangö Head' they're calling it now! Fanshawe comes in for a good deal of blame . . . and oddly enough so do I."

"You, Brand?"

"Oh, decidedly me. 'Yankee freebooter' is only one of the names they pinned on me. Damned Grub Street hacks, who've never been nearer the Baltic than the public-houses round St. Paul's! Joe is bringing the papers along for you to see."

"Well, really!" said Alix indignantly. "You don't mean the government newspapers printed stuff like that?"

"Not likely! But all the Peace Party rags did. They're very vocal these days, the negotiated-peace fellows, and the public knows the war in the Crimea isn't going well."

"But at Sevastopol, the French took the Mamelon, didn't they?"

"Yes, early in June; but there was a big setback on the 18th. The news reached Nargen while we were there. It seems the French general, Pélissier, planned an attack on Sevastopol on two fronts, the British at the Redan and the French at the Malakoff tower, and both operations failed. So the newspaper fellows will have plenty to weep about now."

"Oh, Brand, how terrible!"

"Well, there's nothing we can do about it." Brand hesitated. "Alix, you were all right while I was away, weren't you? Not nervous, or lonely, or anything?"

"I missed you, darling; why?"

"Because I ought to set sail for Frederikshavn now. I'll be late at the rendezvous, but that doesn't matter; I got a telegraphic message to my grandmother about—about going to Nargen, and she understands all about the delay. But I ought to get her ships into convoy now."

"Of course, Brand, we discussed it before poor Mary was drowned. I know you have to go."

She smiled at him with her beautiful grey eyes, yet fixed, in the way Flora Tarras had observed, on something just a fraction beyond him. He said, half jokingly:

"What are you thinking of, Alix, turning the Waterloo ring round and round on your finger like that?"

"Sveaborg."

He ought to have been thankful that her sorrow was no longer uppermost in her mind. Instead, he felt a pang of jealousy at her obsession.

"Sveaborg, of course," he said. "'Posterity! stand here upon your own foundation'—that sort of thing?"

"I have no personal interest in posterity."

"By God!" said Brand, "you've given me ample proof of that."

She stared at him, pale and proud, and something in that disdainful look enraged Brand so much that he burst out:

"There's something you and I have got to get straight between us, Alix, and maybe now is as good a time as any. I had a long talk with Joe the night we were at Nargen, and he told me something I didn't know before. He said that last morning before we weighed anchor at The Golden Crown, Mary was alone with him in the cabin and she whispered to him that you were going to have a baby and she'd advised you to go ashore. Did you tell Mary about it of your own free will?"

"Mary guessed."

"Oh, Mary guessed, did she? Well, Joe guessed too, even before we went to the Kökar Rocks. One night at Slite, he says it was, and he thought you weren't looking well and came to the right conclusion. I asked him why the hell he didn't mention it to me, and he said he thought, of course, I knew."

"That was very proper of Joe Ryan. It was no business of his or of Mary's either."

"By God, it was *my* business, though!" Brand got up and walked impatiently up and down the room before turning on her again. "Alix, you can't imagine, you'll never know, what a helpless fool you've made me feel. Why didn't you tell me there was a child coming? I'd have been wild with joy, I'd have done everything a man can do to keep you safe. Tell me why you hid it from me! And tell me the truth!"

"I wasn't really sure for a long time," she said white-lipped. "And I wanted to stay aboard the *Duchess* as long as I was able."

"Exactly. Now that is the truth at last! And more still, you *married* me to be aboard the *Duchess*, or any other ship that would bring you back to Finland, and give you the wonderful feeling that you were helping to win the war against Russia! You didn't marry as any normal woman might, to have a home and children—"

"I married you because I loved you, Brand."

If she had burst into tears, or hurried from the room, or shown any sign of weakness, Brand would have gone on his knees to her and begged her to forgive him. But the sight of her set face and squared shoulders drove him on to relieve his own hurt by hurting her.

"I think you did love me when we were married, in your own way. But you loved what I could give you, too. Going off in the *Duchess* with me was the best runaway of them all, wasn't it, Alix? And you didn't have to forge anybody's name to get your freedom!"

"This is monstrous!" Alix was on her feet now with her eyes blazing. But Brand had gone too far to stop. He seized her by the shoulders, not caring if he hurt her physically, and blurted out:

"You've always managed to get the best of both worlds, haven't you—until now? You took all Aurora Karamsin's kindness and repaid her by deception and flight, and she forgave you because darling Alix is a noble-hearted patriot who can't be judged by ordinary standards! You urged me to get into the Navy and then complained because the Navy started a fight with Finns, Finns not Russians, at Gamla Karleby! You've told me how brave the Finns were in the war of 1808, but I'm damned if I've seen them lifting a finger to help our side in this war! They're not going to rise against Russia, and all the poetry you care to quote won't alter that fact. But you go ahead and lament the glorious past as much as you like. You're right here in Finland, where you wanted to be; and at the same time if a regiment of Cossacks surrounded this house tonight you'd still be safe enough. You'd only have to say, 'I am Alyssa Ivanovna, daughter of your Railway Commissioner, Count Gyllenlöve', and you'd get as much deference from the Russians as if you were the Czar Alexander's wife!'"

It was their first quarrel, and they made it up, of course, in each other's arms. Long before the sun of that June day could go down upon their wrath they had asked each other's pardon; Alix for keeping the knowledge of the coming child from Brand, and Brand for all he said when nerves and temper had reached breaking point; and Alix wept, and Brand kissed her tears away and swore he loved her even better than before. The next day she went aboard the *Duchess of Finland*, at anchor off Ekenäs, and talked to Joe and the five remaining seamen, a visit which held distressing memories of Mary Ryan, but had to be paid; and she was at the manor landing-stage to wave when the *Duchess* started down the creek on the long sail to Jutland.

Alix was waiting still, in the classic waiting of the sailor's wife, when Brand came back from his mission. The oak woods round Ekenäs were thick with the foliage of a wet July and rain dripped from the eaves of the manor as she said goodbye to Mamsell Josabeth and Anna, and to all the people of the farm. The whole southern coast of Finland seemed to be hushed in anticipation of the coming storm. For Admiral Dundas, weary of waiting for the mortar shells, and the remainder of the floating batteries which never came, had decided at last to move in full strength up the Gulf of Finland, and when Brand weighed anchor for the last time at Ekenäs it was still not known if the Admiral's objective was the city of Helsingfors or the fortress, Sveaborg. They could get no positive information at Nargen, but there at least Brand picked up a cargo, for provisions came in so slowly from England that sacks of food were being dumped on the island long after the Fleet had left. A friendly neutral vessel was a godsend to the storekeepers, and Brand with a full hold and loaded decks followed the fleet to Sibbo fjord.

By comparison with Napier, Admiral Dundas now had an enormous fleet at his command. The total Allied strength amounted to twenty-five line of battle ships, thirty-one frigates and corvettes, twenty smaller steamers and gunboats, and eighteen other craft, and Brand saw a good many of each class on the long tack across the Gulf from Nargen to the Finland side. The mortar boats rolled fearfully, their masts were nearly flat on the water in the heavy seas, and among them were several brigs of a type unknown to Brand and Joe, which Blythe identified as fireships, or in the lingo of the lower deck, "the coffin traps". Among the gunboats which overhauled the *Duchess*, steaming ahead for the rendezvous, were the *Snapper*, the *Biter*, the *Boxer*, the *Clinker*, the *Cracker* and the *Grinder*, and others with the more poetic names of *Jackdaw*, *Magpie*, *Redwing* and *Skylark*. Alix in her streaming oilskins remained on deck till darkness came down at ten o'clock, identifying the British ships through Brand's glass.

He had not the heart to send her to her bunk earlier, especially as he didn't mean to share the berth with her, but bunk opposite in what had been Mary Ryan's place. Brand knew next to nothing about women and their ailments, but the naval surgeon had uttered a gruff word of advice, precise enough to warn him that he must not make love to Alix until a few more weeks had elapsed, and he knew—after a whole day of having Alix aboard, beautiful and excited and her old self again—that he was not strong enough to heed that warning if he and she were alone together in the little berth where their passion had so often marked its rhythm to the pounding of the waves. It was two o'clock in the morning when Brand went to lie down, after the gale had blown itself out. Then he did open the door gently, and look at his wife asleep in the pale light of the coming dawn. He saw the Waterloo diamonds on her finger above the two gold rings and knew she had slipped them on, after she undressed, as some sort of luck-bringer for a British victory.

If Alix was excited when they began to follow the fleet, first to Barö Sound and then to Sibbo, it was nothing to her excitement when the cargo was delivered and Brand weighed anchor. For in Sibbo fjord they were a bare ten miles from Helsingfors, and the Navy ships, now properly provided with Russian money, had opened a trade for meat and poultry which the island fishermen brought from the city itself; and with the food, of course, a load of rumours about the immense concentration of Russian troops in Helsingfors and the general exodus of the civilians. In no time, as it seemed, the *Duchess* was within sight of the town. Only the rain and fog had prevented them from seeing the blue cupola of the Nicholas Kirk on the previous day, for that great landmark was visible over twenty miles out at sea. Now in the sunshine, Alix could see the gold stars sparkling on the blue, repeated on that other, lesser cupola of the Greek Orthodox Church on Great East Svertö, and the three towers of the city Observatory on Ulrikasborg.

It was by the church and the towers that seamen took their bearings for the approach to Helsingfors. The Gråhara channel, of course, was closed by the old three-decker which Alix had seen moving into place in the previous year, and now, as they came within four thousand yards of the guns of Gustafssvärd, Brand could see that the other main channel, that between Langörn and West Svartö leading to the Kronborg fjord, had been blocked by another Russian ship of obsolete design.

"They've done it, just as my father said they would!" cried Alix.

"Done what?"

"Blocked the Langörn channel. Now the Allies can't get into Helsingfors unless they blow both the blockships up."

"Doesn't worry me at the moment," said Brand.

"Where will you berth then?" Alix said.

Only the eye of love could have discerned, at that distance, the beautiful façades of Engel's waterfront, still less the words of the great inscription on the King's Gate of Sveaborg, but Alix in her heart was home again and frantic to go ashore. Brand answered reasonably:

"Not at Sandvik anyway. My God, just look at the new batteries! The Russkies must have fortified every island in the bay since last year, and if their gunners get excited they may loose off a shot or two at a strange ship, even if it is flying the Stars and Stripes. Joe, you've been in to Helsingfors—"

Joe's opinion was that one of the northerly creeks would be a safe berth—Lappvik or Edesvik, or even as far off as Munkesnäs; Alix when the chart was spread out, begged Brand to decide on Edesvik.

"Look," she said, "it's due west of the Villa Haga-

389

sund, and I know there's a road of sorts to the Tölö side. We can easily walk across, and if Senator Walleen is at home he'll tell us what is going on—"

"Provided we get there," said Brand drily. "Alix, nobody goes ashore until I'm sure it's safe. I don't want another interrogation by the Third Bureau or whatever their damned special police are called."

"I'll risk it," said Joe Ryan shortly. Joe spoke seldom and to the point these days, as if Mary's death had dried up all his store of Irish fun and chatter, and he had proved to Brand on their trip to Jutland that personal danger had no terrors for him now. It was Joe who took the wheel when they left Sveaborg to starboard and began the long tacking to round the southerly end of the populated peninsulas into which Helsingfors town was divided, anchoring just before dark in the bay called Edesviken. There was no light or sign of life on that green shore.

Next day Brand yielded to Alexandra's persuasions to go to Hagasund. It seemed as if with their arrival in the vicinity of the fortress, so near the place where his infatuation had driven him to seek her out, and her obsession had sent him away to join the Navy, she had completely reasserted her spell over him. She didn't need the magic drum, he thought, as he helped her ashore and started off down what was no more than a cart track. She didn't need the *arpa* moving round the little red figures, or Biegg-Olmai, god of the wind, to make him follow her like a blown leaf. He took her hand as they walked east, and held it closely until they came to the crossing of the main Åbo road.

"Look at the people!" exclaimed Alix, "they *are* going away!"

There was indeed a movement out of Helsingfors. In this part of the land beyond the town there were no houses, excepting two or three turf-roofed farmsteads, and the procession of refugees was conspicuous, as in *bondkärras* and sleighs mounted on wheels, on foot and pushing handcarts, the people of Helsingfors escaped from the threat of the Allied invasion.

"We may find Mr. Walleen has gone off too," said Brand.

There were no signs of life at the Villa as they walked up the drive where thyme, aubretias and violas now filled the rockeries and bushes of delphinium and phlox were growing on either side of the open door. There was no one, not even a caretaker, in the servants' wing, and neither carriage nor horses in the stables.

"Yes, they've all gone," said Alix blankly. "Come, Brand, let's go into Helsingfors."

"It could be dangerous."

"I don't think we'll be stopped," said Alix, and in fact they went down the Åbo road, up which the refugees were pressing, without let or hindrance from the Russian troops. In seafaring clothes, tall and blond enough to be taken for a native of Finland Proper, Brand was not conspicuous in the streets of the Finnish capital, while Alix with a kerchief tied round her head and the high boots of a Finnish woman looked like any peasant on her way to the stalls of the Market Square. They bought eggs and butter there, and an osier basket to carry them in, though Brand said warningly :

"We can't do this often, Alix; if somebody speaks to me I'd give myself away, and I'm responsible for the ship and the crew. We'll have to buy food up at Edesvik or send Joe into town if we need extras."

"Oh, but don't let us go back yet!" She wanted to see it all, her capital, in all its miniature perfection and harmony of line and colour. Cream and terra cotta, blue and gold, Helsingfors lay under paling skies in which the opal clouds of late summer floated above the band of turquoise which always marked the meeting of the horizon and the sea. Brand walked by her side through the Senate Square, now a bivouac for Russian troops, and back up the Esplanade gardens to where the Finnish Life Guards in their summer uniforms of rough grey linen stood unwillingly on sentry duty outside Engel's beautiful theatre, where a Russian council of war was going on.

"The people are all going towards the Well Park," Alix said. "Can't we go too and see the British ships?"

"It's too far for you today, darling; remember, we've got to go all the way back to Edesvik. We'll try to get to the park tomorrow, as long as we don't have to go through the town."

"Perhaps Dundas will attack tomorrow," Alix said.

But all too clearly Dundas was not prepared for any dramatic dash for Helsingfors. He had a bombardment *en règle* of the great fortress in view, and as the Allied ships slowly took up their stations before Sveaborg, it was plain that the British had prevailed over Napoleon III, and that Helsingfors would not be destroyed. As the tension slackened, it became almost a pastime for the citizens to climb the Observatory hill or walk in the Well Park to watch the disposition of the British ships.

Joe, whose fluent Swedish was quite as good a cover as Brand's appearance, went freely about the taverns and brought back whatever news he heard. They could not, of course, go ashore together. Either the captain or the mate had to be aboard the *Duchess of Finland* in case of a swoop by the Russians, for the four Englishmen and one Scotsman who made up the crew were liable to arrest and seizure as prisoners of war, and Brand began to fear as the days passed that this might eventually happen. His five seamen were unruffled and reasonably patient. They had spent all their pay and enjoyed drink and women to their hearts' content while convoying the Tarras ships through the Baltic, but Brand's New England conscience began to tell him that he ought either to be working for the Navy or for Tarras and Company.

The inaction at Sveaborg became all the more difficult to endure as reports continued to arrive in Helsingfors of the exploits of Captain Yelverton, the officer whom Brand had at first detested and then come to admire above all others. The British squadrons in the Gulfs of Bothnia and Riga had done well in maintaining the blockade, but for dash and initiative Yelverton now ranked with Cooper Key as the best fighting captain in the Baltic fleet. He had been in combat with the Russians at Lovisa and Viborg early in July. On July 21, with *Arrogant* at the head of a squadron which included H.M.S *Cossack*, *Magicienne* and *Ruby*, he engaged the new Russian batteries at Frederikshavn, east of Helsingfors, and caused the enemy to abandon his guns; and on July 26, with four mortar-vessels, four gunboats, and a detachment of Royal Marines, Yelverton captured the Russian-held island of Kotka.

These achievements gave H.M.S. *Arrogant* pride of place as the vessel having seen most action in the Baltic campaigns.

"And I wish to God I'd been aboard her," said Brand, when the news of Kotka reached the town. ". . . Now, Alix, don't look like that! You know what I said has nothing to do with you; we're together, and that's what matters most. But the odds and ends we did in *Duchess* earlier in the summer seem mighty small compared with Yelverton's pitched battles at Frederikshavn and Kotka. I bet they had a double rum ration in the lower deck that night."

"Then do you feel taking command of the *Duchess of Finland* was a waste of time?" said Alix.

"Not a waste of time; don't be silly! It seemed the right thing to do when the Fleet was paid off last December, and I don't regret it. But Alix, my dear, sweet, determined Alix, do you realize that since we first walked in the Well Park, and you persuaded me that fighting Russia was the duty of every decent man, I've given nearly eighteen months of my life, while you suffered imprisonment and I fell sick of cholera, and —and the rest, just to carry on that fight? Do you wonder I'd like to be doing something more than watching Captain Sulivan putting down buoys in front of Sveaborg, as if it was this time a year ago and we were still before Bomarsund?"

"And don't you think I'd like to be doing something more than strolling in the Well Park watching the British ships doing nothing?" Alix flared. "I'm tired of being a spectator at the war."

"It seems to me," said her husband drily, "that you've taken pretty drastic action on more than one occasion, but would you kindly tell me what more I can do than I'm doing already? I spent all last week going out with the fishermen, to see what I could find out about Joe's story that the Russians have laid down 'infernals' controlled by wires from the town. I've got four Bickford fuses in the hold, and powder to fire them. I thought if I could get near enough the wires I could swim out and use a fuse with a light charge to explode them. You know what I found, that every one of the bay islands is a miniature Sveaborg; I'd have had my head blown off if I'd rowed within five hundred yards of them. Alix, I am so sick of this war, and all Russia has done to ruin our lives, that I'd risk my own willingly, if it weren't for leaving you alone here—"

"You mean you don't care what you do, you'd do *anything*, to strike a blow at Russia?"

"Anything!" said Brand recklessly.

"Some day soon I may keep you to your word."

On Monday, August 6, Admiral Dundas arrived on the

393

scene at Sveaborg, leading his tremendous fleet from the flagship, *Duke of Wellington*, and between that night and the
following morning he was joined by an equally impressive
French squadron under Admiral Pénaud. The whole of the
next two days was occupied in mounting a French battery of
four 10-in. mortars on the little island of Abrahamsholm,
south-west of Sveaborg, and in stationing twenty-one mortar-
vessels 3900 yards from the Russian batteries. Every separate
move was watched through glasses or with the naked eye, by
crowds of the inhabitants of Helsingfors assembled on the
slopes of Brunnsparken and the high ground of Ulrikasborg.

Upon the mortar vessels a great part of the anticipated
victory depended. They were drawn up in a semi-circular line
behind the Abrahamsholm battery and there remained in
station, while the gunboats, operating in four separate groups
to port and starboard of the mortars, were to engage the Russian
batteries and troops on the islands lying beyond the fortress
proper. These two arms of the fleet, by reason of their shallow
draught of water, were intended to bear the burden of the
fighting. The old ships of the line in all their useless splendour
remained at anchor behind the line of frigates and protected
by the Skogsholm and Skogskär islands.

But the mortar vessels, by reason of bad planning at the
Admiralty and shoddy work from the contractors to whom
much of the misery of the Russian War in both theatres was
due, carried within them the certainty of incomplete success.
The iron of which the Baltic mortars had been made was defec-
tive when it left England. Mortars expected to stand up to 350
rounds of firing, the fire power of those used in the Napoleonic
Wars, were either totally unfit for use or burst after 200
rounds, endangering the men who worked them and also the
vessel's crew. No replacements for guns put out of action for
any reason, including enemy fire, had been sent from England,
and worst of all there was no reserve supply of the great 200-
pr. shells, each with a descending force of 60 tons, which were
intended to reduce the fortress, Sveaborg.

This terrible deficiency was concealed from the watchers on
the hill by the dense smoke which rose soon after the bombardment started early in the morning of August 9. It was hardly
possible to see what went on aboard the mortar vessels, although their projectiles were clearly seen as they hurtled across

394

the water and burst on the two most heavily defended islands of the fortress, Vargön and Gustafsvärd. When Brand and Alix arrived on the scene, shortly after nine o'clock, the frigates operating to the westward were clearly in view, and Brand had the satisfaction of seeing *Arrogant*, with *Cossack* and *Cruiser*, moving to engage the Russian garrison on Drumsiö island. By this time fires were raging on Sveaborg, and at ten o'clock a tremendous explosion on Gustafssvärd suggested to the watchers that the main magazine of the fortress had been blown up.

The Russian fire, by contrast, was far from successful. Although their big guns had a range extending far beyond the mortar vessels, they failed to destroy any of the twenty-one, and the Russian gunners were not able to keep pace with the Allied gunboats which, as in some lethal ballet, slipped in and out of the battle line unscathed. The worst damage sustained by the British during the first day's bombardment occurred in the little squadrons, including the redoubtable Captain Cooper Key in *Amphion*, which engaged the enemy's turf batteries on Sandhamn.

"They're towing away the old three-decker!" exclaimed Alix, when a wind rising in the afternoon blew away the smoke screen and showed the blockship between Gustafssvärd and Bakholm being hauled further up the channel. It had been under fire all morning from H.M.S. *Stork* and H.M.S. *Snapper*, which were mounted with the new Lancaster guns.

"I wonder why they don't go for the other," said Brand. "Too near the Långörn batteries, maybe?"

The second blockship, a great high-pooped Russian 74, lay north-west of Svartö in the fairway guarded by Långörn island and the great St. Nicholas battery on Stora Räntan, and carried her own long-range guns.

"She's the *Ezekiel*," said a knowledgeable bystander, who heard Brand's remark. "Her last engagement was the battle of Navarino, twenty-eight years ago. She'll do a bit of damage yet, unfortunately!"

Brand said something in agreement, and lowered his glass. He remembered that the Russians at Navarino fought on the side of the British and French. And all the old impatience with Europe and the grim set-to-partners of the European powers filled his mind as he thought of the allies of 1827 become the enemies of today, and the possibility that after all the bloodshed of 1855 they might be allies again against some other enemy in a future war. He looked round at the Finnish people on the slope of the hill. Many of them were desperately tense, like Alix, as if fully aware that the future of the Grand Duchy hung on this day's work. For others the occasion had become a tremendous spectacle to be watched without great danger. The lime trees were still flowering, after the wet summer, in the Brunnspark avenues, and under the smell of gunpowder the delicate scent of their blossoms persisted.

It was late at night before Alix could be persuaded to leave the scene. At half past ten in the evening the boats of the British fleet, some thirty in number, moved into place in front of the mortar vessels and began an attack by rockets on the fortress. The effect of this bombardment, in which each explosion showed through the darkness as a perfect circle of flame followed by a mushroom-shaped cloud, was particularly awe-inspiring. The *Duchess'* crew were all on deck when they returned to Edesvik, watching the red light in the sky.

Next morning Joe Ryan walked into Helsingfors, and reported a steady stream of Russian boats carrying wounded from the fortress into the town. The human losses of the enemy had been tremendous; the material damage no less great. Powder magazines, barracks, hospitals, stores on all the westward islands of Sveaborg had been hit indiscriminately, apparently without any successful reprisals on the Russian side; and when Brand and Alix returned to the park in the afternoon they saw the whole of the fortress, from north to south, as one great sheet of flame.

But the Gibraltar of the North was still impregnable. By the morning of August 11, when nearly all the batteries of Sveaborg had been put out of action, and no shots at all were being fired from the fortress, the British mortars had either burst under pressure or ceased firing from lack of ammunition. The Allied bombardment had lasted two full days and nights, the British alone expending one hundred tons of projectiles. The Greek Church cupola, so long a landmark, lay in ruins, the Russian wounded filled the Helsingfors hospitals and public buildings, fires were raging in the island batteries, and on Vargön and Gustafssvärd nothing but blackened and skeleton buildings were to be seen. Yet the Allies were powerless to follow up their great success. They could not scale the granite walls of the fortress, Sveaborg. When all the Russian works were ruined, these remained; no British admiral would enter by the King's Gate, or read the great words of Ehrensvärd written on either side.

"'Posterity! *stand here upon your own foundation!'*" Brand quoted to Alix on that Saturday afternoon when the Allied Admirals announced that "operations were closed" and prepared to withdraw to Barö Sound.

"Confess, Alix, in your heart you're not sorry that the fortress was not carried and can never be?"

"I, not sorry?" she said indignantly. "Not sorry that the Russians still hold Sveaborg, and that the Allies have had to leave with the victory incomplete?"

"The Russians are claiming it as their victory already," said Joe.

"Was that what you heard in the market, Joe?"

"Tomorrow's Sunday. They're going to sing the Te Deum in the Russian church near the Nicholas Kirk, to give thanks for their victory—"

"Well," said Brand, "there's nothing we can do to prevent it. The British have done their damnedest, and Sveaborg still stands. Now I've got to think of my duty to the crew and to my owners. We've lain up here in Edesvik for over two weeks without seeing a Russian, but that can't go on; once the British move away they'll soon spread out from the city along the Åbo road again, and we'll be in trouble if we stay much longer. I'm going to weigh anchor in the morning and go down to Barö with the Fleet."

"Stop a bit," said Joe. "Tomorrow's Te Deum won't be the only celebration. There'll be one tonight which you might care to—interrupt."

Joe had not shaved that morning. Brand noticed inconsequentially that although the Irishman's curling hair was as black as ever, the light stubble on his chin was grey.

"What d'you mean, Joe?"

"This is what they're saying in the market. General Sorokin and his officers have been telegraphing all morning to St. Petersburg, claiming, of course, a Russian victory. Tonight they're going to celebrate it at a grand dinner, with vodka and champagne in streams; and as the Governor's house was

397

shattered like most of the army quarters, the feast will be held aboard the *Ezekiel*."

"Aboard the blockship in the fairway," said Brand slowly. "And you think . . . ?"

"That it's up to you."

"With a fuse," breathed Alix. "Brand, you said you would do anything!"

"It would be suicide," said Brand.

"It would be the end of the Russian high command on Sveaborg."

"If I could swim," said Joe, "I'd do it like a shot. But I can row the boat, and hold the gutta percha rope—"

"If I had Campbell, my old partner," said Brand, "I think it could be done, but it takes two strong swimmers, accustomed to swim underwater for yards at a time, and powerful enough to carry a load of powder—"

"Jenkins is a good swimmer."

"Jenkins isn't good enough. Joe, I hate to say this, but we nearly lost Jenkins that day too."

Both men had a searing recollection of the young seaman, gasping and choking at the *Duchess'* side, with Mary Ryan's drowned body in his grasp.

"I swim much better than Jenkins," said Alix, stating a fact.

"You, Alix? Are you crazy? You don't know in the least what all this means! Listen to me: I've done the fuse exercise, with a trained partner, exactly fifteen times. We did it in a reasonably calm sea, without enemy interference, and we exploded old hulls and derelict boats—just wood, you understand? Plain wood. The *Ezekiel* carries long-range guns, therefore she has a powder magazine. If we explode that, we haven't a hope in hell of getting out of range of the explosion, not if all the gutta percha in the hold were to be spliced together. I don't believe we could even pass the island batteries, before we reach the target; but if we did get there, it's a thousand chances to one we wouldn't come back alive."

"We could pass the batteries," said Alix, "if we dressed all in white, as Captain Cooper Key's crew did in June."

Joe ignored her. His eyes were fixed on Brand.

"Skipper," he said, "if that's your mind, then I'm through. I'm going to jump ship tonight, I warn you, and lie up in

Helsingfors until tomorrow morning. Then I'll try to shoot Sorokin as he goes to church for the Te Deum. I'm a fairly good shot and I'll shoot to kill. I owe the Russians a death, and by God! I'm going to pay it somehow, and what happens after doesn't matter. Since Mary died I haven't given a damn for my own life, one way or the other."

"And since what happened at Ekenäs," said Alix, "I haven't cared a damn for my life either."

Brand looked from her pale, determined face to Joe.

"One chance in a thousand," he repeated. "All right then, I'm prepared to take it. Mr. Ryan, pass the word for Blythe."

At midnight, when the Allied fleet was a few miles west of Sveaborg, heading for Barö Sound, the *Duchess of Finland* slipped out of Edesvik and rounded Sand Head and Sundholm to make for the Porkkala fjord. The lights were out all over Helsingfors. The shuttered villas in Brunnsparken, round which the crowds had gathered earlier in the week, stood silent and emptied of their Russian tenants. A strong smell of charred wood and fires still burning came over the water from Sveaborg.

"Heave to," said Brand, "the celebration is going on, all right."

He had been thinking all the way that the rumour of a dinner aboard the *Ezekiel* might well be false. But the old two-decker showed rims of light round her closed portlids, and there was bright light in the window of the great stern cabin, from which the sound of music came.

"Now, Blythe," said Brand quietly to the bo'sun, "you know exactly what to do. Take up your station west of Ronnskär and wait for the boat to come back. If we don't join you in an hour, then go after the frigates; *Arrogant* was one of the last to leave and can't be far away. Ask for a lieutenant to be put aboard you, if one can be spared, to act as master until you reach London. If not, then you take command, Blythe; I've written out your orders, and entered them fully in the ship's log."

"Aye, aye, sir." Blythe knuckled a worried brow. "Sir?"

"Yes?"

"Jenkins 'as asked leave *again*, sir, to do the swim instead of madam."

399

"Thank Jenkins," said Alix with a smile. "Tell him I do this of my own free will."

She was shivering a little in her white dress, for the night was cold, and she had cut the sleeves out of the bodice and looped the skirt to knee length for greater freedom in the water. The two men wore white shirts and white duck trousers, and the boat, when they took their places in it, smelled strongly of fresh white paint. Brand had the Bickford's water fuse in his arms. He had attached it to its wooden plug and shell in the hold of the *Duchess*, where he had measured out the powder into two tin boxes: twenty pounds weight for himself and ten for Alix. It was scanty enough measure to blast off a Russian 74, but he reflected grimly that the *Ezekiel*'s hull powder magazine would take care of that.

They had tried the weight round her neck in the cabin, and Alix had sworn it was not too much for her. But when they slid over the boat's side into the water, Brand heard her suppressed gasp as the load of powder dragged her down. Although he knew how well she swam he dreaded the unaccustomed load, and watched anxiously to see her come up from the long slow glide under water with which the exercise began. Then she appeared on the surface, only a little way behind him, and almost immediately put her head under water again, forging ahead with a soundless powerful stroke that matched his own. They arrived with their burden of death at the black side of the *Ezekiel*.

The Russians, in their vanity, had left no sentry posted; the carouse was going on for'ard as well as aft. The great danger—Brand didn't know if Alix realized it—was that some reveller might throw open the window of the stern cabin and hear the sound of boxes being placed beneath the chains. But the singing went on above their heads uninterrupted; he relieved Alix of her burden first and fixed it in place with steady hands. She trod water beside him, clinging to the chain with one hand, while Brand put his own load of powder underneath the first and the armed shell beneath them both. Then, although every second counted, he yielded to an impulse he could not control, the impulse to kiss Alix; and he took her into his arms in the water, feeling her wet limbs coiling and folding round his, and her cold wet face, and then the burning lips pressing and questing against his own. In a rush of feeling which left his limbs weak Brand released her and pointed back towards the boat.

In a few moments Joe was helping them aboard. He held the end of the gutta percha rope connected with the Bickford fuse and had the match ready in his hand. At Brand's nod the little flicker caught the rope, and began its course under water towards the ship.

"How long?" whispered Joe as Brand unshipped his oars.

"Quarter of an hour—less. Row, man, for our lives!"

They pulled at the muffled oars, Brand setting a powerful stroke, while Alix at his order crouched in the bottom of the boat. She lay at his feet like a drowned girl, with her white kerchief untied and her wet hair unbound, and he looked from her to the *Ezekiel* and counted the minutes off, as he knew Joe Ryan must be counting too.

". . . Thirteen!" gasped Joe. "We're going to do it, Brand!"

An enormous yellow flame leaped to the skies. With a single tremendous explosion the powder magazine of the *Ezekiel* splintered the old two-decker, and made of it a burning tomb for every man aboard. The great guns, blown high and falling heavily into the water—the masts shattered like young trees by lightning—the hull riven in two—all, from the glass of the stern window to the double eagle flag of Russia, rose in the tremendous blast heard across the bay and in every house in Helsingfors.

"Row!"

In one more minute Brand realized they were too late. The boat was rocking from side to side in the tremendous wash set up by the explosion, and on the islands the Russian gunners were running to their batteries.

"Can they see us, Brand?" Alix raised her head.

"Keep down!"

Yes, they could be seen: the white clothes and the white boat were useless now, as the flames from the *Ezekiel's* hull lit up the fjord. And the first gun of the Nicholas battery on Stora Räntan had fired a shot that hurtled just above their heads.

"Row!"

Then it came, the thunder-clap, and the blow in the side from flying metal that knocked Brand across the seat, and made him loose his hold on both oars, and turned the world into a spinning chaos of light. From far away he heard Joe Ryan's voice.

"Alix! Brand, help her, for God's sake!"

He realized that Joe, alone, was rowing like a man possessed to get them out of range of the Russian battery. And Alix was still lying in the bottom of the boat, but now her face was upturned to the night sky, and her neck and shoulder were dabbled with dark blood.

Brand managed to get to his knees beside her. There was something in his ribs which kept him from breathing, and brought a trickle of blood to his lips when he painfully achieved a gasp, but he got the soaked kerchief off the floor of the boat and held it to Alexandra's throat.

"She's . . . alive . . . Joe. Row!"

"I'm off course," gasped Joe, "drifting down on Skogsholm."

He struggled to make westing, to reach the *Duchess* at her station off Ronnskär. And Brand kept the hand he could still use heavily pressed above the wound in Alexandra's neck.

"There's a frigate ahead!"

Brand lifted his head painfully. Slowly, with all sails set and the Blue Ensign flying, the last and best of the frigates to leave Sveaborg was gliding like the Swan of Tuonela towards the Porkkala fjord.

"*Arrogant!*" he said, and Joe, catching the faint whisper, shipped his oars and cupped his hands to his mouth to send a shout ringing over the water:

"*Arrogant* ahoy! Ahoy!"

CHAPTER TWENTY-ONE

SURF BREAKING ON BOTH SHORES

THIRTY-THREE days after the destruction of the *Ezekiel*, Brand Endicott stepped ashore from a Danish fishing smack at the little Jutland port of Skagen and made his way to a cottage on the outskirts of the town.

"Good-day, sir captain!" cried the red-cheeked woman who opened the door to his knock. "Your good lady didn't expect you here until tomorrow!"

"The Christiansens brought me up from Frederikshavn," said Brand. "Where's Mrs. Endicott?"

"Gone walking, sir, about an hour before the great news came."

"She hasn't heard it then?"

"Not unless they had it at the lighthouse first, and that's not very likely. She has gone towards the Point, sir; it's her favourite walk."

"I know. I'll have a wash and follow her right away."

The woman stood aside and let him pass. Brand went up a steep stair, little better than a ladder, to the room he had shared with Alix for the past two weeks. It had a sloping roof, with a big bed beneath the eaves spread with a billowy white Danish eiderdown, a painted wooden wash-stand and a small mirror in a seashell frame hung above the dressing-table. Captain Sulivan's Bible lay underneath the mirror.

Brand laid down a bundle of newspapers, letters and packages, poured water and washed the salt spray from his face and hair. As he changed his coat he looked round the little white room affectionately. He had told Alix more than once that it reminded him of his boyhood's room on Jewell Island, in the brown "linter" which stood like this fisherman's dwelling within sound of the sea; and better than that, it was the place where Alix and he had been one again.

He sat for a moment's rest on the bed where they had lain together in a renewal of their first passion for hour after happy hour in the days following their release from hospital in

403

Copenhagen. There, under the little skylight in the slanting roof, he had seen her grey eyes focused on his face alone, as if her old vision of the enemy had vanished for ever under the guns of Stora Räntan. In the crash and conflagration of the Russian blockship, which had brought death to every soul aboard, Alix had won freedom from the long obsession of her hate. The bars across her spirit had fallen already; the news which Brand had brought to Skagen might be the order of release for two weary and wounded prisoners of war.

Then the thought of what he had to tell her, and the dread of how she would receive it, sent Brand limping out of the house and along the road to Grenen Point. When he was tired, as now, he still walked slowly and clumsily, for his broken ribs were tightly bandaged, although mending well. The flesh wounds had healed by first intention after H.M.S. *Arrogant's* surgeon (complaining of the presumption of a promoted Seaman Gunner in taking on a Russian two-decker) had removed the splinters of metal from the Stora Räntan gun. Slowly, but steadily, Brand went on, stopping once or twice for breath as the road grew rougher and became a mere track across the sands. There was no hurrying now. He knew exactly where he would find Alexandra in the dunes at the extremity of the Point.

There, at the tip of The Skaw, as British sailors called Skagen, was to be seen a sight which fascinated Alix, as the waters of the North Sea, breaking on the western shore of the peninsula, mingled with the waters of the Kattegat, the gateway of the Baltic, on the east. Even on the calmest day there was always a boiling, a miniature fury where the two seas met, always a murmur on the last spit of sand; Alix, Brand knew, could watch and listen to it all for hours.

She was sitting where he expected to find her, with her back against an upturned boat dragged up to the shelter of the dunes, and all the pale hues of sand and the couch-grass and the old boat's faded paint blending with the cream coloured cloak she wore and the thin veil which covered her hair and neck. She was hugging her knees and gazing seaward to where, beyond the millrace of the Kattegat and the North Sea, a British frigate had appeared on the horizon.

"Alix!"

He called her name from a long way away, so as not to

scare her on that lonely shore. He had the joy of seeing her scramble to her feet and run to meet him over the sand and the tough green plants which held the track firm beneath their feet. He caught her laughing into his embrace, while the north wind whipped at her cloak and blew the veiling back from her fair hair. He saw the red welted wound which ran from beneath her ear under the collar of her dress. He saw no trace of the old withdrawn look in her eyes.

"My darling!" said Alix, with her cheek against his, "back so soon? I would have stayed in Skagen—I would have been down at the harbour, if I'd known."

"You didn't walk too far?"

"Oh no, I love it here, but you?"

"I'm all right. So is Joe, he sent his love, and the hands their best respects, you may be sure. They'll pick us up on Thursday on the way to Aberdeen."

"So I shall really meet your formidable grandmother?"

"There was a letter from her. She says she's 'thinking long to see Alice'. She seems to have made up her mind to call you Alice."

"I like it," Alexandra smiled. "Much, much better than Alyssa Ivanovna. What was the rest of the news?"

"Well, that's just it, Alix. There's—some tremendous news. That's why I came back with Mats Christiansen a day ahead of time. I wanted you to hear it from me first."

"Oh—what is it?"

"Sevastopol is down."

"You mean—surrendered to the Allies? When?"

"On the tenth. The British attacked at the Redan without much success two days before. Then on the ninth the French carried the Malakoff tower, and Sevastopol fell the next day. The Allies entered the fortress just a year after the beginning of the siege."

"The Allies in Sevastopol," said Alix strangely. "What a triumph! What rejoicings there will be in the West!"

"It's a tremendous defeat for Russia."

"I only wish Nikita had lived to see it. The one victory the Allies longed for, the only fortress in the war that mattered! What was Bomarsund, what was Sveaborg, compared with the great Sevastopol!"

"By God!" said Brand, "you and I did our fair share at

Sveaborg! Remember the day we landed from *Arrogant* at Copenhagen, and Captain Yelverton had you piped over the side with bo'suns' whistles and sideboys, and the hands cheering as if you were Queen Victoria?"

"Yes"–unsmiling–"it was like the text in Captain Sulivan's Bible, 'time and chance cometh to every man'. We took our chance at Sveaborg, darling. We did it with our might ... Can you recognize that ship out there?"

"*Imperieuse*," said Brand. "Outward bound from England with letters for the Fleet."

"It will be letters of recall soon, won't it?"

"After Sevastopol? I guess it will."

They were silent, watching the frigate in full sail coming up with all the majesty of a disappearing world.

"Let them shout themselves hoarse for Sevastopol," said Brand. "We know that if it hadn't been for Sulivan and Yelverton and Cooper Key and Hall and all the good men in the lower deck, there might have been a very different ending to the Russian War. There would have been Russian ships of the line off Newcastle and Gravesend and cruising out into the Atlantic; there would have been Russian troops landing on the beaches at Cherbourg. When we kept the Russians bottled up in the Gulf of Finland, it was the British Baltic Fleet that saved the West."

"You say 'a different ending'," said Alix in a whisper. "Do you really think the Russian War is ending now?"

"I think the Russians will have to go before a peace congress, very soon. They've lost their one great battle; they'll have to accept peace terms and get out of the Black Sea and the Danube Principalities. Then I suppose the Allies will be satisfied."

"And Finland will still be a Russian Grand Duchy," Alix said.

He had known this would come, of course. This was why he had hurried back from Frederikshavn as soon as he heard the news, why he had her hands tight in both of his and was kissing them, while the wind blew the veil further from the wound she carried from the fortress, Sveaborg.

> " 'O Finland, who can now thy fate foretoken?
>   Thy future lot as yet remains unspoken
>   Thy fortune good or ill none can portray—'

"I used to recite that to the prisoners in Lewes jail," she said. "They will be free to go home soon now—poor fellows! Shall we walk a little way across the sands?"

Brand put his arm about her and they began to walk slowly towards the spit of land where the two seas met.

"I was thinking, back there in the dunes," said Alix sombrely, "that it would end like this. I know now that what the drum said at Degerby had nothing to do with you and me. *Only so far*—the message was for Finland, not for us. This war with Russia will not set Finland free."

"Then do you think that all we tried to do, and what you did at Sveaborg, was done in vain?"

"What we did at Sveaborg was well done," she said proudly. "Only—this too is in Sulivan's text—the race is not to the swift, nor the battle to the strong! Maybe the *words*, the words Nikita used to fear so much, will conquer in the end. Some of the Finnish boys at Lewes will remember 'Döbeln at Juutas', I think little Henry Kivi will; and those are the boys who will try again for Finland's independence, and will win!"

"You still believe that, don't you?"

"With all my heart," said Alexandra, "but I know, I am sure now, that it will not come in my lifetime."

Brand was silent. They were near the tip of The Skaw, and the sands were wet beneath their feet.

"What did you decide about the future, Brand? What has Joe made up his mind to do?"

"Joe's going back to Boston, dear."

"I thought he would."

"He says he can't bear the thought of living alone in Stockholm or sailing without Mary in the *Molly-O*. And he has his family to go to in Boston. Brothers, sisters—a whole clan. They all seem anxious to have him back again."

"And Joe's not thirty-eight yet," said Alix. "He may marry now. He may have another child, or children; life goes on."

"Yes," said Brand. "For you and me too, Alix."

"Have you—thought any more about London?"

"My uncle repeats his offer of a partnership. Working ashore, of course."

"You wouldn't like that, Brand!"

"It might do very well, you know. You would be near your

407

sister, and make new friends, and—darling, when all this is over, you could surely visit Finland quietly—"

"No!"

Never again the dripping woods of Ekenäs, the empty room filling with pain, the scent of lilacs . . .

"I will never go back," said Alix, "and you, my darling—haven't you sacrificed enough for me?"

Brand said, "I have only loved you."

"I have been a very selfish woman, Brand. I dragged you after me into sickness and danger, prison and pain, for the cause that I believed in. Now the time has come to think of you. You're an American and you're a sailor. You don't want to wear out your life in an office in London Wall."

"But if I thought you—"

Over the bar the waters raced and surged.

"Here we can see surf breaking on both shores," said Alix. "Your shore and mine! One sea running back to the Gulf of Finland, where Russia will still rule for a time. The other flowing west to the new world. I think I chose that shore, my darling, on the night I met you first at Marstrand, when you promised to see me safely on my way—"

Brand bent his head and kissed her.

"Where are you going to now, Alexandra?"

"Tell me again about your islands," she said humbly. "Tell me about our American home."